CW00502274

Also by Pony Louder

The Memory of Blood

'Unforgettable'

★ ★ ★ ★ ★

'So good I want to scream'

★ ★ ★ ★ ★

'Luminous'

★ ★ ★ ★ ★

'My book of the year'

★ ★ ★ ★ ★

First published 2023 by Louder Books

This book is based on the experiences and recollections of the author. Names and some locations and dates have been changed to protect the privacy of others.

A catalogue record for this book is available from the British Library.

Book design and typesetting by Victoria Heath Silk
Internal images © Harshil Gudka

ISBN 978-1-7396336-5-3 – Paperback
ISBN 978-1-7396336-2-2 – Ebook

www.ponylouder.com

OCTOPUS

PONY LOUDER

LOUDER BOOKS

For Doy
Who taught me to read and gave me the world

And for Margot and Michael
Who showed me the world, and gave me a few other things besides

With a host of furious fancies
Whereof I am commander,
With a burning spear and a horse of air,
To the wilderness I wander.
By a knight of ghosts and shadows
I summoned am to tourney
Ten leagues beyond the wide world's end:
Methinks it is no journey.
– *Anonymous*

'We were all going to hold hands, take LSD, find God – and what happened? We ended up at the drug dealer's door, carrying guns and in total madness.'
– *Dennis Hopper, the Guardian*

Prologue

A note about the weather

Go deep. Be real, they say. Write the truth.

Good grief.

I've tried to. As far as I can tell, the real story's the most interesting one.

Problem is, truth is slippery as water. It's not easy to cup in your hands. Sometimes there are scars: anchors on your skin you can follow. Pulling yourself, hand-over-hand, back down through murky depths to the events. Mostly though, truth relies on the wet work of memory. And memory is weird. Things aren't always in the places we left them. Sometimes memory and imagination feel like the same thing.

When we were kids, the truth was simple. It was what we couldn't talk about. And maybe this isn't my story to tell.

I was there.

This is what I saw.

That doesn't mean a dozen other people might have seen something else. Or that any of them would be wrong.

Memory tells lies. None of us remember easy. But I've done my best. I've gone deep.

Oh, and I know about the weather. I know you're not supposed to open with swirling snow and black canals frozen solid. Fuck that. I say the weather is truth too.

Also, I changed the names. Trust me, you would have too.

Amsterdam, 1983

A little after 1am

It's snowing outside.

Beautiful twirling flakes, fat and fluttery as ripped paper. They're piling up on the balcony and collecting in heaps along the edges of the canal below.

This is the first city we've lived in where it's snowed while we've been in it. Not just a shake of grey in the air and wet spots on the footpath. This is proper white. We're living in a fairy tale. It's like walking around inside a giant snow globe that's being ever-so-gently shaken.

The apartment we're staying in is on the Prinsengracht, close to the Westerkerk church, right in the centre of Amsterdam. Across the canal is the Anne Frank house, where Anne's family sheltered from the concentration camps. Most afternoons there's a line of people over there, slow-shuffling up the street, waiting to go inside and take a stickybeak around the annex.

I've not been over myself, but I can picture the tight coil of stairs, the wooden rail worn shiny from too many hands. It's not hard to imagine the claustrophobia of being sealed shut behind a wall for two years.

Maybe it's respectful. Something about the long queue feels ghoulish. Like gawping at a car crash. It reminds me of how people slow down on the motorway to look at tyre burns and windscreen fragments. People want to see blood. Whoever owns the house now must be raking it in.

So it's beautiful, but also sad. When there's no queue, the Anne Frank house looks like a normal home. From the outside at least. Same as ours. I try to pretend no one was ever dragged down those stairs to their deaths, and just soak in how lovely the tall Dutch houses look across the frozen canal.

I can't get enough of the view. The crazy-thin, six-storied buildings, the looping black bridges, the twirling snowflakes. I could stare at it for hours, but we have to keep the curtains drawn. Even in Amsterdam, where everyone seems so easy-going and nice, it would be pretty bad if anyone saw what we're doing.

What we're doing is tablespooning extremely high-grade cocaine into the hollow legs of camera tripods.

It's kind of snowing inside too.

It's a little after 1am and the air is cloudy with powder. It's all hands on deck. Besides Mum and Dad, there's Nils and Baz and myself.

In their day jobs, Nils and Baz are freelance graphic designers. They specialise in album covers that look like photographs but are really airbrushed paintings. Photoshop doesn't exist yet, so Nils and Baz are in big demand. Skinny and generously haired, they look more like rockstars than some of the rockstars they work for. You could picture them strutting around an arena somewhere. Hogging up front of stage, doing all those extended guitar solos. Baz with one boot on the footlights, Nils sliding to his knees. Both of them with their heads thrown back, eyes closed, lost in their own strumming and the crowd's rapturous applause. They are best friends, but you know they'd fight over who played lead.

Right now, they're dusted in cocaine. I look down and see it's all over me too. It's settled on my arms and t-shirt and around the hip pockets of my jeans. It's the colour of slightly off-white icing sugar.

There's a small window of time in which this needs to be done. The mood in the room is bright and industrious. Think Snow White's seven dwarves marching home. Which is kind of appropriate, if you know your eighties drug slang.

It's fairly dull, repetitive work that anyone could do. But, as usual, I'm keen to show how helpful I can be and stuffing it down extra hard into my tripod. *Heigh-ho. Heigh-ho. Scoop, scoop, down the metal leg we go.*

Rather than whistling, everyone is humming along with Fleetwood Mac. Via the stereo near the bookshelf, Stevie Nicks is singing about going your own way. Which is maybe also appropriate, if you believe all the rumours about how much blow Stevie got through making this record.

This is the purest cocaine anyone in the room has ever seen or snorted.

People tend to lie about drugs. It's one of the associated problems, certainly in the procurement stages. When it comes to drugs there's a lot of exaggeration over quality. Everyone swears theirs will be the best gear ever. Then they go and deliver something that's been stepped on more times than Tiananmen Square. The chances of getting the purity you've ordered is so desperately optimistic that no one really expects to.

Except tonight, when the consignment arrived and the tests were done, it turned out to actually be 99.2 percent pure, uncut cocaine. Turns out, it pays to buy in bulk.

Bulk. No one in the room is actually saying this out loud, but I get the feeling that ordering up a bunch of 1kg bricks of Bolivian cocaine is not the same as seeing them stacked neatly in front of you on the dining table.

Luckily the dining table is a big one. It and everything else in this apartment belongs to Nico, a friend of Nils' who is living elsewhere at the moment. From the outside, her flat looks like a traditional Dutch house. Inside it's all chrome, butter-soft black leather and two large banana trees. It's weird to see tropical plants growing somewhere so cold, but I guess if the bananas stay indoors, bunched up near the radiators, they'll be OK.

Nico is great. Most people don't like it if you tell them you don't know how long you'll be living somewhere. It's a lot to expect someone with a regular life to understand, but Nico didn't blink twice. Maybe because her boyfriend is in a band and always travelling too. Nico has a decent bookshelf and she was really nice about that as well. 'Eh? You like *my* books? Of course! Read, read!'

Probably she was surprised because she knows I can't speak Dutch or French, but there are a few English paperbacks, and half her shelves are art books, so you can still look at the pictures. There's a whole shelf taken up by those extra-glossy sexy-type books, but you can't have everything.

From this point onwards, the cocaine will be divided up. Some of it will be travelling in wine bottles, so the first job was to weigh out the portion that needed to be converted to liquid. Nico's glass-topped dining table was given a quick polish and the bundles of coke were razored open.

Once it was freed from its tight bundles, the amount of cocaine *was* impressive. Even to me. It's a table that comfortably sits eight chairs, and it's now heaped with powder. Like someone went outside, raked up a couple of wheelbarrows of snow and dumped it here, all over the glass. Hence the chipper mood around the table.

I imagined it was a pile of Ferrero Rocher chocolate balls to get the vibe.

The wine bottles were specially blown. Just like Nico and Anne Frank's houses, they look normal from the outside, but like Anne's, each bottle has a secret compartment. Below the cork there's a small section that will be filled with wine, leaving three-quarters of the bottle hollow. Baz and Nils designed a wine label to hide the seam that separates the coke from the wine. With its embossed gold printing, their label looks super-authentic. You don't even notice that it goes right around each bottle.

Behind the green glass, the two liquids look the same. Even if you pick up a bottle and shake it. Anyone curious enough to actually uncork it will find shiraz. Everyone's pretty pleased with this bit of sneakiness. Hopefully that curious person won't want more than a few sips.

Along with the tripods, we'll take half the wine bottles. Travelling separately, Nils and Baz will take the other half. If anyone asks, this is my grandparents' favourite wine. Our story is that Nanny and Poppa have a big anniversary dinner party coming up. We're helping them celebrate their years of wedded bliss by bringing the red to be served with mains.

That's the story, but all goes well, no grandparents anywhere will ever know anything about this wine.

The bottles have been boxed in special carry cases, then wrapped in Happy Anniversary gift paper. Now we need to concentrate on getting the rest of this cocaine into the tripod legs.

It's hot in the apartment, the central heating's on and we obviously can't open the windows. Nils has stripped to a vest. Baz has rolled the sleeves of his fully unbuttoned denim shirt about as high up his arms as they'll go. I'm in my baggy *Hungry Like The Wolf* t-shirt. Mum and Dad are both still in warm long sleeves, but they don't own any short-sleeved clothes anymore. Anything that didn't hide the inside of their arms had to go a while back. Even the pretty dresses Mum had made for her.

Mum has tied back her long red hair. Her beautiful face is glowing. She's happily moving in time to the music. I imagine she's wishing I wasn't so uptight. I keep spooning, packing it down as hard as I can.

In addition to the spooning, there's a lot of furious sniffing going on around the table. Also running fingers over the front of teeth, licking the insides of the bundle wrappings and laughing about just how superb the sight of a massive pile of almost entirely pure Bolivian cocaine really is. There's jokes and general hilarity about how much a sneeze could cost us right now: 'Anyone feel one coming on, Chrissakes step away from the table! Mwahaha,' etc etc.

Earlier, getting the cocaine into the perfect wine-like consistency was precision work that involved extensive product sampling, so everyone's pretty happy right now.

Everyone but me.

Instead of 'living in the moment', I'm thinking about what would happen, exactly, if the police barged in now. Even in Amsterdam where everyone seems so nice, there are laws about this amount of class A drug. I can't see how the adults wouldn't go to jail for a long time. None of them are Dutch, so most likely they'd be extradited, which could mean life sentences.

That's nothing new. Mum and Dad being carted off to spend the rest of their lives in gruesomely unhygienic jail cells has been a nagging strain for a while. Right now, there's also the worry of how we're going to get all this cocaine into the tripods: I don't see how it can possibly fit. I'm spooning like mad, stuffing the metal tube solid, really cramming it in, and the mountain in front of me doesn't seem to be getting any smaller. There is just so much stupid cocaine.

I keep looking up at the clock on the kitchen wall. We have a deadline and it's coming up very soon. If we miss this deadline, the supply chain tumbles like a domino chain all the way down to Sydney, Australia. My understanding is that this would be *very* bad.

As usual, I'm the only one who seems the least bit concerned. 'Dad, we're not going to make it.'

'Course we will,' says my father, a light dusting of white over his goateed chin. 'Just pack it properly.'

'We ordered too much,' I say, mostly under my breath.

'What on *earth* will we do with a spare pile of pure cocaine?' says Nils in mock horror. Everyone chortles.

Switching to my third tripod leg, I start going faster. Jamming the coke down with the back of my spoon. Standing on tiptoes to put my weight into it.

I'm not a fan of drugs. They make things very stressful.

There's a building rush in my head, a roar in my ears.

I look down at my feet. They look small and far away. Down there, under the snowy glass tabletop, they seem entirely disconnected from the rest of me.

I'm pretty sure I'm standing still. My feet aren't moving, but my chest is tight and loud, like I've been running up stairs. My eyes feel extra wide-open and fluttery. Faster and faster I pack. My hand's moving so fast now, it looks fuzzy around the edges.

What I don't realise is that I'm coked off my head. High as a kite, just like the adults. You could peel me off the ceiling.

I'm so anti-drugtaking that it never occurs to me, or anyone else in the room, that some of the stuff clouding up the air and coating my clothes could have floated up my nose or into my mouth. No one's thinking about face masks or gloves. The air is so thick with cocaine, we could probably be getting high just from the particles hitting the membrane on our eyeballs.

I look up at the clock again. The more freaked I feel, the more relaxed everyone else seems. No one looks the least bit worried, about anything. Dad's not even trying, he's loosened up his silk cravat and is leaning down to leisurely snort up another bump from the edge of the pile, one arm behind his back like a posh waiter about to pour from a bottle of Chateau Margaux. Baz is fiddling with the stereo.

My heart's now pounding so fast, I think I might go blind.

Then, suddenly, the tightness in my chest surges up and pops like a bubble.

In its place deep blue sadness. Fizzing with sharp feelings. All the feelings, about all the things: that life is swerving precariously, evermore out of control. That I haven't been to school for years. That my father just spent the night in jail. No one can understand how he could possibly have been released with the drugs and passports that he had on him. It's great, obviously, that he got out, but *how*? Is my Dad an escaped convict now? On top of everything else?

None of this can be a healthy home environment for my little brother and sisters.

Fantastically emotional now – oblivious to the fact I'm enjoying a quality of high that most users can only dream of – I get to the worse bit. I'm twelve. In just four months I'll be thirteen: three whole years into my second decade and I've done *nothing* with my life. When she was my age, poor doomed Anne Frank was writing a book that's been read by half the planet. I can barely make myself commit to writing a shopping list.

I'm so old. I've achieved zilch. And I don't fit in. Not with normal people. Not with the people in this room. We've been to a lot of countries: I'm on my third passport and most of its pages are stamped. It feels safe to assume that if I haven't fitted in anywhere yet, that place probably doesn't exist. I'm obviously weird as hell.

The whole thing is unbearable. Excruciating. All I want is a normal life with normal parents and normal friends, and there's nowhere in the world I'll ever belong.

I feel so old and tired I could collapse on the carpet right here.

Finally, the tripods are packed solid.

As the adults are scraping up the glass table, I slump over to the balcony. Drowning in self-wallow, but still very careful not to ruffle the curtains as I open the door, I step out into the night.

Outside everything feels muted and still.

It's late on a Tuesday night in January and there's no one out. Snowflakes are all that's moving. They're falling soft, but thoroughly. It's very cold. There's a blue wash to the light and everything is ridiculously pretty. I know I should be thankful to be here, alive. Especially with poor dead Anne Frank just across the canal. My life's a sunshine picnic compared to hers. Hundred percent I should be grateful. Can't be arsed. How much I don't want to be me right now is too consuming.

To add to the misery, I've just realised my face is crying. There's a salt-sticky trail that's freezing down each cheek. It is *very* cold out here in my t-shirt. Instead of going back into the warmth, I stay put, melodramatically freezing. Maybe catching pneumonia, I think.

Raucous peals of laughter come from inside. Grace Jones's *Pull Up To The Bumper* is now thumping out of the stereo. It sounds like everyone's singing along. Possibly dancing. There's a chorus of woohoos. Tucked snug in their beds upstairs, my siblings are used to noise. Hopefully Nico's neighbours are also good sleepers.

I'm so tired. I brush some of the snow off the ledge so I can sit with my back against the balcony door. Really, when you give it proper consideration, our whole situation is hopeless. My presence is definitely not improving it.

As I sit down, the single-edged razorblade I've got in my jeans jabs my leg. This happens a lot. I'm always forgetting to take them out of my pockets. I don't even need to carry one around, there's plenty of them scattered throughout the apartment. The blades are designed for old-school shaving razors, the ones you pop and screw in, but the sharpness of the blade, coupled with the blunt finger guard down the other side make them super-handy to do lots of other things. Whisk the brown bits off apples, snip threads of cotton. I use them all the time. They cut so neat, you feel really powerful and precise.

Mum and Dad use them for chopping up lines. More fun than using a credit card. Tougher on mirrors though. Most places we stay, any mirror that can be pulled down from a wall and laid flat gets scratched to hell. After a week or two, you have to squint to see your face past the webs of lines cut into the glass.

The razor in my pocket I'd last used when I was helping slice open the bricks of coke. I'm fiddling with it now, feeling the fine edge of the blade with my fingertips.

In the dim light, I can just make out the thin line of blue under my skin, the vein running vertically up my arm from my upturned wrist. Everyone knows horizontal cuts are for losers and show ponies. Anyone who means it, would cut vertically. Even I know that.

The blade slices softly through my skin. It's so sharp, it glides almost tenderly along the vein. There's almost no resistance. Like cutting jelly. It doesn't even hurt much.

There's a moment of nothing. Like everything is frozen blue. Me and the canal and the beautiful Dutch houses all holding our breath, waiting for what I've done to actually happen.

Then it does.

A line of dark red appears and bubbles up. It drips off my arm, down to the snowy ledge beside me. Warm enough that it melts deep into the snow. I peer down at it, thinking of Snow White again and her mother's ruby red blood in the beginning of the fairy tale. My blood looks quite atmospheric.

Then the cut starts to sting. It stings like a bugger. Suddenly there's a lot of blood. It's pouring through the fingers of my other hand, which is now gripped in horror over where I've sliced myself.

The blood's coming out like a tap. Soaking the snow.

Panicked, I start kicking all the red snow off the balcony onto the street below.

One hand clamped to the other wrist, I'm now doing this weird little kicking dance, like some demented Riverdancer, trying to get rid of all the red snow. But the more red snow I kick away, the more red snow there is.

My blood's gushing out like it's super-excited to be leaving me behind.

I'm also *really* cold now. I'm shivering so hard, I'm kind of juddering.

This is not going well.

Whatever this is, it's not going well.

I've made a right cock of things.

Typical.

Part 1:
The Seventies

In the beginning.

Auckland, New Zealand

Ten years earlier

'Absolutely not. It's dangerous. We are not having that shit in the house.'

It's 1973 and Martin T. Starling, my dad, was glaring at the box I'd just carried in like it might end us all.

'Maybe if we let her keep this one... We'll tell your parents not to buy any more,' offered my mother, Vivienne Starling, not really wanting to get involved.

I rested the box gently on the rug and took a small, hopeful step backwards. Imagining it might seem less treacherous out of my hands.

The three of us looked down at the set of Lego I'd just been given. My birthday present from my grandparents for turning three.

Dad was a bit ahead of the curve on this one. In 1973 everyone loved plastic. As far as I knew, everyone thought it was superb. Or at least when they looked at children's toys, no one was thinking of whales washing up dead on beaches with 100kg plastic balls lodged in their stomachs.

I certainly wasn't. I'd never wanted anything more.

My chubby little paws were shaking to hold the box again. Just carrying it around from Nanny and Poppa's had been intoxicating. So bright. So shiny! The rattle and shuffle of the pieces inside pure joy.

Even the sticky cellophane smell of it called to me. It was the smell of what normal kids had. I already had an inkling we weren't quite like everyone else, but I was young enough to think this could be fixed with a 350-piece set of building blocks.

'You can't destroy it. Lasts forever. *Forever*! Something man-made lasting forever, can you even *imagine* how seriously ridiculous that is?! And they're churning out *more* of it,' yelled Dad. 'We are *not* having that petroleum, man-made bullshit in our house.'

Our house wasn't really ours. Strictly speaking, it wasn't even a house. We were living in a small cottage behind Dad's parents' home. Their place wasn't really a house either, it was a three-levelled mansion on the side of a 470ft volcanic mountain.

The address was number 231 Remuera Road, and everyone called it Two-three-one.

My whole family lived at 231. A colony of Starlings (and for a glorious but brief time, one Conway-Smith, my other grandmother). Like Miss Havisham's place in *Great Expectations*, there was a general feel of expired glamour at 231. Built at the top of a private driveway, the house had been fitted in the very finest style. But that had been some time previous and no one had done much since.

Rooms were still lit with crystal chandeliers. The carpet still richly patterned, but puddles of threadbare beige had started to creep around doorways and down the middle of some of the hallways. If you pressed the wallpaper with your fingers, sometimes you could feel air bubbling behind the gold filigree swirls.

The laundry dated back to another time altogether. It was called the washhouse and consisted of an open tub that hissed and gurgled grey water like a witch's cauldron. It had a mangle to wring out wet clothes and a wooden board for particularly stubborn stains. This being the seventies rather than the 1870s, it was a fairly antique operation, but it was used daily without discussion or complaint. By the women at least. I never saw a man venture into the washhouse, I don't know what they did with their dirty clothes.

The nearest neighbour down the mountain was a nose and ear specialist who lived behind a dense trellis of kiwifruit vines. Five more minutes down the driveway was inner-city Auckland, New Zealand's biggest city, but living on Mount Hobson felt rural. Cows stomped freely over the parklands next door. If our side gate was left open, the herd would come barrelling into the front garden. They were not friendly and left behind hauntingly large pats. Anyone of my size unfortunate enough to fall over near one could find themselves coated head-to-toe in slimy horror.

The house rambled, an unidentified shape. No one could say for sure how many rooms there were. I'd tried to count them, but there was never a time I could access every room. At some point in its history, the mansion had been divided up into self-contained flats. The flats had different combinations of bedrooms, lounge, kitchen and bathroom. Two of them were just large rooms with locks on their doors and a shared bathroom down one of the long dark corridors.

My grandparents had six children, but there was always space for everyone. At one point, when there wasn't, and Uncle Lance had to move back home with his pregnant girlfriend, he and Dad got the hammers out. Everyone helped bring down the walls in the front basement. Narrowly escaping total structural collapse and turning it into a hilariously oversized open-plan living space. Once the beanbags were in and some macramèd pot plants were hanging from the ceiling, it looked pretty cool.

Always, throughout 231, the key aroma was toast. You could smell it as soon as you walked into the hallway. Toast was the breakfast, snack or light meal of preference. Specifically well-buttered wholegrain; usually topped with thin-sliced tomato and a shake of salt. In this, unlike many things, the Starlings were united. Whatever time of day, it was pretty reliable that someone, somewhere in the house, would be toasting bread or slicing up a tomato.

As well as Starlings, there were four tenants at 231. Whether by design or chance, all of them unmarried men. The bachelor tenants came and went, mysterious and largely unseen by me. I'd occasionally glimpse one of them hurrying across the grand hall or lightly jogging from their mailbox. Reversing at speed out of the carpark.

They paid for their flats in brown envelopes that would be slipped under the glass doors of Nanny and Poppa's flat. Sometimes, if you were lucky, you'd see a dark shadow approaching the frosted glass, then one of Nanny's pre-labelled little envelopes would slide under the door. Always, my dream was to fling open the doors and make friends, but I had strict instructions not to disturb the tenants. No running or singing past their doorways. Definitely no talking to them.

One tenant drove a pale green Citron DS. A highly exotic car for New Zealand in 1973, when everyone else was tootling about in brown and white Fords. It looked like its bum was hanging down in the road, but this was the design. The Citron-driving tenant worked for an unnamed government organisation and was mostly away overseas. It was generally understood that he was a spy.

Another tenant wore Old Spice aftershave. You could smell it wafting down the corridors long after he'd scurried past. When he moved out, years later, to live with his boyfriend, I got to see his flat (five rooms if you counted a walk-in closet). Weeks after his departure, the flat still smelt of Old Spice and Benson & Hedges; a faint undertone of grilled bacon.

I worried for them. The idea of living alone in family-less, bacon-y bachelorhood seemed lonely to me. Nanny said the tenants preferred it that way, 'If they didn't, they'd just pop up and go, wouldn't they?' It was true the tenants stayed for years, two of them had been in their flats long before I was even born.

The Starlings themselves were less settled. Within the family, tensions felt tight and watery, always ready to crack open like a watermelon. Mostly they sloshed over my head. I didn't understand why Mum and Dad so disliked living in such a great home.

Every so often there'd be a sharp moment for me to puzzle over. Once Mum and I accidentally brought death flowers for Nanny. We'd picked the creamy white calla lilies before we knew that they were cursed harbingers of doom. They just looked like flowers. But when Nanny saw us standing in her kitchen with them in our hands, she let out a bloodcurdling scream.

Even as we backed away out the kitchen door, Mum hiding the lilies behind her, Nanny was still screaming. 'Get out! Get *out!*' over and over again, in the worst voice.

On the steps outside Mum and I looked at each other. We'd done something really bad. Hurrying back to the car, our hands sticky from the lilies, Mum promised me we hadn't brought death into the house. It was just that 'no one would ever be good enough for that woman's precious son'.

Mum was right. No one ever died at 231. There are photographs of family members out on the lawn, and that's how I remember the house: wrapped in warm sepia tones, like some kind of sun-faded, daisy-freckled sanctuary.

I loved coming back to 231, even if it was just to visit. Wherever we travelled to, whatever else changed, it was a lovely feeling to know that 231 would be waiting, ready to catch us safe. The red brick walls would stand fixed. Forever losing their battle to the creeping fig, but constant nonetheless.

★

Back at the gardener's cottage in 1973, a decision had been reached. I would play with the Lego for half an hour. As I ripped the cellophane away (Dad: 'More plastic! *Seriously* unnecessary!') and ecstatically tipped the bumpy rectangles out onto the rug, this seemed like joyous news.

I don't remember what I built, how many little red and blue and yellow and green towers I stacked. But each one of the blocks clicked together like a dream. As I sorted the blocks into neat piles of colours, I had an electrifying rush of being normal. Lego was where all the other kids were. The place where things fit together with a reliable snap.

There was a lot of wailing when I had to put the pieces back in the box. It was pretty disappointing for Mum and Dad too. They'd assumed I'd spend five minutes with the plastic menace and come to my senses. Instead, there was such an upsetting amount of fuss, I had to be sent to my bed for an afternoon nap. I kept weeping there. Even after I fell asleep.

When I woke up, the pillow under my cheek was grainy from salt and Dad had gone out. Mum gave me some sliced apple and a coconut-and-date ball. You could tell there'd been talk. Poor Mum and Dad. With all the advantages of free-thinking they'd given me, was I really going to be so pedestrian? Hundred percent I was. I had no time for Mum's pity smiles and stalked outside in a sulk to talk to Emma, our dog.

★

Dad was interesting from the start.

He says his first memory is lying in a cot, watching a swaying cobra rear up over the edge of his wicker basinet. Its tiny shiny eyes watching him back, its flickering tongue tasting the air near his cheek. Nanny Starling says this is unlikely because she watched him like a hawk when he was napping outside in his basket: she would have noticed a lethal snake peering at her first-born child.

But Dad swears it's true. He says he remembers its hood flared out above him: he was fascinated and not the least bit scared.

All we know is that there are five types of cobras living in fairly plentiful supply in Zimbabwe, formerly Southern Rhodesia, where he was born. And their hooded necks *are* quite distinctive.

One of my first memories is looking up at something swaying above me too. It's a tree. A beautiful old willow. I'm under it, watching the tendrils gently rippling in the breeze. The branches and leaves take up the whole picture-frame of my memory, but what I'm thinking about is the song I can hear playing from inside the house. *Summer Breeze* by Seals & Crofts. I'm listening to the lyrics and I'm worried. I'm super-concerned about how you got jasmine blowing inside your head, and if pulling it out would hurt.

And so it went.

I'm not saying this comparison is all you need to form a clear picture of either of us. But I wouldn't rule it out.

★

Most of the Starlings moved around 231. Swapping flats with each other across the house as we came and went over the years. But

Nanny and Poppa's flat was theirs alone and no one but them ever lived in it.

By the time I was born, Poppa and Nanny had been married twenty-one years. I don't know how happy those years were. If there had been a time of lingering looks and close laughter. I never saw it. I don't remember seeing them smile at each other. I only vaguely remember them being in the same room together. It didn't happen often. If Nanny and Poppa were both at home, they would be in different ends of the house. They looked at each other like it hurt their eyes.

It wasn't that they were rude. There wasn't any yelling. If there had once been a bargain struck dividing the tasks, they both kept to it with the honour of samurai warriors. Poppa had the bills, repairs and garden. Nanny took care of the housework and did the cooking. Poppa loved mushrooms, Nanny thought them repulsive, but she would be browning them up in a buttered pan with finely chopped parsley, the way he liked, once a week.

Nanny's queendom was the kitchen and adjacent sunroom. Poppa had his study. They took turns in the lounge. Their flat had a lot of glass. Down the side of it that overlooked the mountain, windows stretched from kneecap to ceiling. In the lounge, glass cabinets filled with Nanny's porcelain Meissens (couples in full skirts and breeches dancing on tiptoes with lambs, mostly) competed with Poppa's tall ships (one in full sail inside a large bottle, another two framed on the wall, eternally on the brink of watery ruin, pinioned by rocks and thundering waves).

Everything rattled and clinked. You had to tread softly. Anyone in a huff – and people were often in a huff – travelled through Nanny and Poppa's flat in a symphony of tinkling. The bronze fireguard and tools, hanging by the fireplace that no one used anymore, would chime in with reverberating clatters.

When I was very little, Poppa sometimes took me out for forbidden ice-cream cones. He always bought us both orange choc chip. We'd sit together, licking our ice creams in the car or on a bench outside the shop. He'd tell me about how his kids were ungrateful ratbags (probably true) and that my mother would kill us both if she found out we'd been eating ice cream (definitely true). I don't know why he stopped taking me out. I never told anyone about the ice cream, but I got the feeling I'd become another family member who had disappointed him. None of his children turned out the way he'd hoped, and I'd somehow let him down too.

Built precariously off the edge of the lounge on the second floor, Poppa's study was almost entirely glass (like Cinderella's slipper or Wonder Woman's plane, except that it was a rectangle that didn't go anywhere). Mostly how I remember my grandfather is seeing the back of his head in his glass slipper study. He'd be sitting there with his papers and his scotch, looking deeply out the windows or into the dark seas of one of his floundering ships. He'd be playing classical music on his record player, loud enough that the glass walls would be shaking. No one was allowed in his study if he wasn't there, and if he was there, he was not to be bothered. The music always sounded scary: sawing strings and crashing cymbals. And you could tell, just from the back of his head that Poppa was furious too. You'd tiptoe past, but he'd be too far away to know anyone was there.

I liked to imagine it was different in the beginning. I picture it all a bit *Casablanca*. Popa in his uniform, Nanny with pinned-back curls and bright-red wartime lipstick, but maybe that's just rewriting history. There was a Bogart connection, loosely speaking, but that came later.

Sheila was a pretty, dark-haired girl from a poor catholic village in Ireland. At sixteen, she'd had to leave home to find work. Robert grew up very differently in south east England. In photos he's dashing, fearless. He looks ready for anything as he smiles, squinting into the sun.

They met in London on a night of bombing. I like to think it was a romantic meeting. Coming together from different backgrounds in a time and place when life and death must have seemed like fleeting chance. How could those moments they stole together not have felt epic?

What I know is that he was on leave from the war. She had been ill. Too ill to leave her bed. Alone in the city and dangerously sick, she had spent weeks lying in her rented room, feverish, starving and listening to bombs drop around her. One afternoon, someone slid a chocolate bar under her door. I never saw Nanny eat any chocolate, but she told me once that a Mars bar saved her life.

Years later there was talk of an earlier, better-loved woman. But what makes me hope Nanny and Poppa liked each other a lot in the early days was that, soon as they could, they set off for deepest Africa together. Leaving the UK for good. Just the two of them. Nanny always spoke fondly of Ireland, but neither grandparent ever saw their families or where they grew up again.

Rhodesia was hot and strange. Robert got a job working on RAAF engines, Sheila got pregnant. Dad was born, then Lance. By the time Uncle Lance was toddling around, Sheila wanted out of Africa. She looked at her kitchen shelves: the label on the tins of powdered milk they ordered in for the boys featured a scene of well-fed dairy cows grazing serenely in cool, green meadows. It must have reminded her of Ireland. The tin said 'Made in New Zealand'.

Batting flies from her face, standing on her dirt-floored kitchen in 45-degree heat, Nanny decided that's where they should live.

A few months later the family set sail for one of the furthest habitable points of the globe. On the ship out Nanny realised she'd have to change her name. Sheila being Antipodean slang for woman. Mid-voyage she became Sylvia.

The long sea journey with two young boys couldn't have been easy. They arrived in Auckland during a cold winter and, until Poppa secured a steady income, the family lived in a catering tent. Poppa had bought the tent from a film crew just back from shooting scenes in the Congo for *The African Queen*.

As he stood there under the beating African sun, bargaining a fair price for the leaky old tent, all the rain and mud that would be waiting for them in New Zealand must have seemed very distant. Did the knowledge Humphrey Bogart and Katherine Hepburn had once eaten their lunches inside the tent make it any easier to live in? Nanny always said she was more of a Clark Gable fan.

Theirs is a classic immigrant story of entrepreneurship and hard work. Arriving with no more than the clothes on their backs and what they could fit into one large packing trunk, Sylvia and Robert worked days and nights. Within a couple of years, they had a small fruit farm. A few years later, a bigger farm. Within fifteen years, they had expanded and saved enough to move off the land and buy an old mansion on the side of a mountain in the leafy suburbs of Auckland.

By the time I came along, the first grandchild of at least a dozen, they'd lived enough for several lifetimes. They'd gambled on sailing across the seas to a new world. They'd had six children and started various businesses. At one stage there was a textiles factory in Queensland. A kaftan-importing enterprise, the duty-free emporium on Norfolk Island. Some investments worked, some didn't.

I've always liked backstories and theirs must be a good one, but I don't really know it, or what went wrong. No one talked about the past.

When I think of what they experienced together, all the trail-blazing adventure that was theirs alone, it's sad to think they didn't live some of it as friends.

1970

Sweet air

For some reason, Mum and Dad took over the running of a care home. With no qualifications, or the slightest puff of nursing/hospitality experience between them, it seems like a bold plan. But the elderly residents liked them and, for a while, they made a go of it. It must have been 1970, because there are pictures of baby me there. Chilling out with the old dears in my matching cardigans.

Sometime around my fourth or fifth month, one of the grannies bought me a walker: those chairs on wheels with leg holes that let babies power themselves around on tippy-toes. Apparently, no baby has loved independence more. As soon as they slid me into it, I was whizzing about. Speeding into walls and ricocheting off table legs, chortling with gleeful abandon. Drunk on milk, high on life.

At some point, someone left the kitchen backdoor open. Beyond the door was a steep flight of concrete stairs. I went spinning off the top step, *Thelma-&-Louise*-style into wide, blue sky.

There was a moment when everyone thought I was dead, all the sweet old dears crowding around in horror, but I'd just knocked myself out. Mum said my whole head was covered in blood, bright red as a candy apple. I don't remember any of this, but it sounds like a signature move.

1971 and 1972

These years are a bit of a blur

Mum and Dad gave up the retirement home. For a while the three of us lived in a house with a big weeping willow out front. Then we moved back into 231. This was the time we got the gardener's cottage. There might have been other places in between, but no one remembers those.

1973

Fairies

Being the only kid at 231, the big project was getting someone to play with me. Adults always had their own thing going on, so mostly it was me and Emma hanging out together. You couldn't fault Emma, she was ace, but I was keen to get some non-canines involved too.

Then I found out about the fairies.

My four aunties were often tasked with babysitting. Minding me was a total buzzkill: there was no money in it and no one was particularly wowed by my conversational skills. Not as bad as having to vacuum the hallways. But best avoided all the same.

My sticky-pawed desperation to spend time with them wouldn't have helped. Bridget, the youngest, was only ten years older than me. But at three, thirteen seemed a world away. The 'girls' were so cool and grown-up. All long straight hair and corduroy miniskirts. Smoking and chatting and tweezing their eyebrows and flicking through magazines with their legs propped up against the wall. I *really* wanted to be part of the gang.

I'd be outside, banging on their door with my pudgy fists. I'd hear them laughing inside and know they were never going to let me in, but most days I'd come back to try my luck, just in case.

Then one afternoon, they asked if I wanted to look at a book with them.

The book was about fairies. Fairies were real! There was proof. Actual photographs of the tiny creatures flitting about on gossamer wings, dancing to miniature panpipes in front of two English girls. My aunties explained that these fairies could be my friends too. I could play with *them*.

'Really? Fairies here, at 231?'

'Oh yes, absolutely. Out the back, just past the washhouse.'

Fairies were tricky though. They wouldn't play with just anyone. For them to even *consider* showing themselves, there were three tests that must be passed.

Firstly, you had to believe in fairies. Really, truly believe in fairies. Fairies could tell if you were just saying it. Second, you had to be good. Fairies could lose their magic around the wrong people and they didn't like taking chances.

Third, and most importantly, you had to be very quiet and patient to earn their trust (or so my aunties assured me, shooing me back out into the garden).

I spent hours and hours sitting very quietly in the garden waiting to play. Imploding with hope at the sight of any butterfly or dragonfly that fluttered past. My face crinkled like a raisin with the effort to be good.

I tried to keep upbeat about it, as time wore on. But, given that fairies could see into your actual heart, it was upsetting to be failing their test. Seeing a fairy was irrefutable proof you were a good, pure-hearted child. I'd seen zero fairies. Was I secretly a bit shit?

Or was it that they were sensing my niggling, impure-hearted doubts?

I hadn't read the book yet, but as I sat there waiting, for hours, days, months, I understood the *Catch-22* of my situation. The longer I waited, still as a pebble, not seeing a single shimmering fairy wing, the bigger my doubts grew... My chances of ethereal buddies becoming incrementally smaller and smaller.

I never saw a fairy.

Then, a year or so later, we did.

According to Uncle Lance, Dad's younger brother, my name was Little Miss Fat Product. He called me this up until I was about seven because I had a chubby round head, and because he'd always get an amusing reaction out of me. I did *not* like this nickname, not at all. In my family the word 'fat' seemed interchangeable with lazy. It was pretty clear he was deeply insulting me.

As much as my aunties swore fairies were true, Uncle Lance laughed at me waiting around to play with the little people. But that was just his way, Uncle Lance teased me about most of the things I did. Everything was a hilarious joke to him. It was very annoying.

One afternoon, Emma and I were leafing through one of my Little Golden Books together, when Lance came running up.

'Saylor! Saylor! They do exist! They do!'

The fact he hadn't called me Little Miss Fat Product should have been a clue.

'What does Uggie Ouce?' To be fair, I didn't use his proper name for the first few years either. But that was because of some trouble I was having with my Ls.

'FAIRIES! There's one in the garden. Come quick!'

Emma and I scrambled up and ran after him to the back garden.

I saw nothing.

'Where? Where!?' *Please let it still be there. Please let me be good-hearted.*

'There! Up in the tree…' He sighed, 'Oh it's so beautiful. You were right. All this time you were right. I should never have doubted you.'

I squinted up into the tree. The fairy was perched high in the branches. It was difficult for me to see properly from my height perspective, but it didn't look quite what I was expecting. For starters, the fairy was neon pink.

I looked back at Uncle Ouce, 'Is it really real?'

'Course it is, can't you see?' he whispered, his face bright with awe.

'Lift me up?'

He lifted me up so I could get a better view. The fairy was very still. Not dancing or skipping at all. She had no panpipes or flowers in her hand. Her dress was ruffling in the breeze, but instead of the pale art deco stylings I'd seen in the photographs, it was kind of poufy and princessy. She looked suspiciously shiny.

'It doesn't look real.'

'Ssh, she'll hear you.'

I peered back at the tiny figure in the branches hopefully. I so wanted her to be real. Maybe this was how fairies looked in New Zealand. The ones in the Cottingley book were all from England.

Lance started to snicker.

I knew then. It wasn't real. Somehow he had done this. Whatever this was. My uncle had done this terrible thing. I wriggled out of his arms so I could stand on my own two feet, to better convey my fury. He was now laughing so hard, he was doubled over clutching himself.

The disappointment was overwhelming, I burst into tears and ran off, past Mum hanging clothes on the line.

'What's the matter?'

'Uggie Ouce!' I wailed as I bolted past, face wet.

Probably I should have been touched by my uncle's effort. It wouldn't have been easy to get Ballroom Beauty Barbie 20ft up a tree. He'd needed to climb a ladder, then scale several more branches to best position his little person. Having carried her home a few miles from where he'd spotted her on one of his nights out – head-down, legs-up in someone's rubbish bin.

1974

Tobias

The big thing that happened in 1974 was my sister.

She rocked up from the hospital like a hurricane hitting shore. Even at three-and-a-half, I could see this baby meant business. Tobias Starling had magically vertical, bright red hair and impressively strident opinions. She did not like sleeping at night. She wasn't keen on napping during the day. Being put down or left alone for more than a minute made her angry. She was angry about a lot of things.

When she cried, she put her head back so far that you could see right down her neck. Even her insides looked angry. Some days she cried so loudly, it felt like the cottage walls would crack.

It had been pretty quiet with just me and Emma. Neither of us were big criers and you could leave either of us unsupervised for hours. Tobias was not at all happy to just chill, placidly looking at things. She was never going to be bothering with sitting around in the garden, waiting for fairies to turn up.

From her first appearance at the cottage in 231, it was clear who was going to be the fun, naughty one. I looked at her in her crib, her tiny red hands all fisted up in fury, her midget feet fighting against the blankets, and couldn't have been prouder. We had a sister!

Dad sat me down on the cottage step. Tobias was going to be my best friend. No one would ever understand you or stick by you like a sister. I nodded my head, taking it in. This was the greatest news I'd ever heard.

'You're a big sister now. You have to be responsible. Look after her.'

I took this seriously. Mostly it involved trying to make her laugh. Or even smile. Tobey didn't like to waste these gifts. Sometimes you'd have to hop around doing silly dances and pulling faces for hours. It was worth it though: getting one of her gummy little grins was like the sun coming out.

Once she was crawling around, it was more about making sure that she didn't tumble backwards or fall down a hole or slice her own head off with a kitchen knife. Tobey was fearless and very attracted to anything sharp. She'd want to jam it into her soft pink mouth as fast as she could, just to see how danger tasted.

About two months after Tobey arrived, Mum and Dad took a trip overseas. Mum's mother, Grannie May, was going to look after us. Mum and Dad needed some time off.

Gran took extended leave from the hospital where she was head nurse and moved into the cottage with me, baby Tobey and Emma the Doberman. Apart from Tobias' round-the-clock shrieking, it was a really relaxing time.

Grannie May was the best. There was no time I didn't love spending with Gran. She was just so great. She had a little silver clock on a chain that she wore upside down over her heart. I asked one day why she didn't just have a wristwatch like everyone else.

'Watches aren't practical for nurses. We wash our hands too often. And we're always needing both hands. Or we might scratch a patient.'

'Why is it the wrong way up though?'

'Think about it, Saylor. Why would *you* wear it upside down?'

'I don't know! Tell me!'

She smiled and carried on chopping carrots for dinner.

Later it came to me, 'Ah! So you can tell the time just looking down, no hands!'

Things that seemed strange made sense once Grannie explained them. She didn't mind stupid questions. She would listen to you witter on. She didn't care how long it took for you to button your cardigan by yourself. She had a way of making you feel that you could be interesting and helpful.

In the cottage, we read stories and chilled out together listening to the radio. She baked cookies and didn't get mad when she had to wash the floor after I'd helped. If baby Tobey was up for it, we'd take the pram out for a walk. Life was pretty magic with Grannie. Nothing was a rush and everything she promised always came true.

★

When Mum and Dad got back a few months later, they needed to leave 231 more than ever.

About the time Tobey started walking, we moved out of the cottage and into a van. Mum said the cottage had gotten too small. We'd be needing the whole of New Zealand. Dad traded in the MG for a beat-up Volkswagen Kombi and we hit the road.

Up and down the length of New Zealand the Kombi tootled along, criss-crossing mountains and deep gorges; through wilderness and countryside dotted with sheep and canary-yellow gorse. Dozens of times we caught the ferry across the Cook Strait to the South Island, and back again to the North.

We'd often cross at night, the ferry lurching side to side through the infamously moody Strait, foamy waves swishing up over salt-blurred windows. You'd be pitched high into the sky. Then down so low that all you could see through the windows was dark water. In 1968, fifty-three people died after a ferry capsized. But it never occurred to me that we wouldn't be bobbing back up again, so crossing was just fun and exciting.

We had the Kombi for years. Its lovely old V-shaped face and big round headlight eyes were home for much longer than any of the houses we rented. The front seat was exclusively for parents. Tobey and I would be squabbling over the real estate of the backseat. Mum and Dad smoking and laughing with each other up front. Mostly Dad drove, though Mum was the better driver. If we felt carsick in the back, and I did several times a day, we'd point our chins to the horizon and open the windows wide until the petrol fumes had blown away.

There'd be long, hazy hot afternoons and dark, starry nights driving through the landscape. Mum usually had a cosy nest of crochet blankets made up for us. We'd fall asleep to the hum of the Kombi motor. Wake up in the bright arch of headlights from the occasional oncoming motorist, then snuggle back under again.

We stopped at rivers to wash. Sometimes Dad would pan for gold, keeping the little pieces he found in glass jars next to the roadmaps in the glovebox. Lunch and dinner on the road were most often cheese and garlic sandwiches: assembled out of brown paper bags with a buck knife on Mum's lap, and passed back. We'd snack on green apples, nuts and raisins. There was always music. A handful of cassettes on tight repeat. We knew all the words to Carol King's *Tapestry*, both of Pavlov's Dogs, Tim Buckley's *Greetings From LA*… anything by Leonard Cohen.

We'd often pick up hitchhikers. If Mum and Dad saw someone with their thumb out, they'd usually pull over. The door would slide back with a creak. There'd be a strange grinning face and a 'thanks man' and suddenly Tobey and I would have someone sitting beside us in the backseat. There'd be a smell: clothes that hadn't been washed for a while, musky patchouli undertones, but mostly everyone was nice. Sometimes they became our friends, sometimes it was just for an hour or so up the road until we reached their turn-off.

Everyone was united against 'The Man', a murky amalgamation of war, government and personal liberty infringement laws. 'Rich men wanting to get richer by controlling everyone else,' said Dad.

Proof of The Man's ruthlessness was the war in Vietnam. There were always copies of *TIME* and *LIFE* magazines around, and the big cover story was Vietnam. The photographs showed scenes from the jungle. A soldier crouched in the mud, cowering against gunfire, another soldier bloodstained with a background of blazing fire. Crying, barely dressed children running down a road from napalm. It looked awful.

Unlike America and Australia, there was no conscription in New Zealand. If you were a Kiwi going over to get involved in all that death, you actually wanted to.

'What kind of mucus-ball would sign up for *that* reality?' Dad wanted to know. '*Seriously* embarrassing.'

There was an army base along the highway we regularly passed. We always gave them the TP salute. Rolls of toilet paper flapping from each window. It felt a bit embarrassing, but everyone did it. Any hitchhikers with us would automatically reach for their rolls too. We'd all reel our paper up again once we were down the road, so no trees were wasted.

Dad was a pacifist. Entirely against war: '*Criminal* waste of life! Just corrupt old men making money from young men's lives.' But it wasn't unheard of for Dad to come home a little blood-splattered from some unofficial conflict.

Where he'd been, or what he'd done, wasn't talked about. Dad didn't work often, but when he did, it could involve a certain amount of night-time activity. There were the antiques, but also other, more unclear things he worked with. And everyone knew how short Dad's fuse was. How quickly his anger could turn a run-of-the-mill situation into something very different.

One night, Dad came home with a knife sticking out of his leg. A ten-inch hunting knife wedged deep into the calf of his artificial leg. Bobbing there for anyone to see. You couldn't miss it. Luckily it was so late in the night, it was early morning, and no one was around on our street to see.

Each time Dad took a step, the knife bounced. It made you think of those joke knives on headbands that people wear to pretend they've been stabbed in their head. This wasn't a plastic knife though, and it really had gone right through.

Whoever had tried to stab Dad must have been pretty determined. His leg was made out of thick fibreglass. I tried pulling the knife out, hard as I could. But it just twanged there cheerfully, bar-ding, bar-ding, up and down.

'It's lucky they got this leg, isn't it Dad?'

'I swung my right leg in front.'

'Oh.'

I couldn't understand why they'd aimed so low. Had the man been a dwarf?

'No,' said Dad. 'He was on the floor.'

Dad was splashed with blood. Enough to make his clothes stiff and earthy smelling, but he said it wasn't his, and when he took the clothes off, his skin was bruised but unbroken. The only red was the knuckles on his right hand.

1975

Murchison

Formed during the gold rush, Murchison was a clump of houses bunched together in the middle of nowhere. More of an abruptly colonised stretch of road than a town.

Take a two-hour drive over the mountains from Nelson, a hairpin turn off Highway 6 where the Buller and Matakitaki rivers meet, and there it is. Deep, deep country. The kind of place with one general store, no traffic lights and a thriving pub.

This was where we were going to settle down.

Besides the gold, 'Murch' was known for being the epicentre of the 1929 earthquake, one of the deadliest earthquakes in New Zealand's history. When we arrived in early 1975, the town's population wouldn't have stretched beyond a couple of hundred people, and none of them seemed keen on expanding their number. Certainly not with the likes of us.

We rented the long-abandoned vicarage. How Mum found the house or the town, or why either of my parents thought we should live in it, was never clear, but certainly the cheap rent would have been a factor. And the house was beautiful. A wisteria-twined, Edwardian-era bungalow with an old, overgrown garden.

Tucked away behind the church, we were set back from the road and out of kilter from the neat row of our neighbours' houses. To the front were matching white-painted fences on both sides, but our back garden rambled out into untamed New Zealand wilderness.

Past the rusty clothesline and a tumbledown woodshed were miles of grasslands and distributary creeks. In the distance, a mountain range flared up out of the plains. My bedroom was the sunroom out back where all the buddleia trees grew. Some of the windowpanes were a bit cracked, so when the purple flowers bloomed, their powdery honey scent curled through my room.

We were poor. Neither parent had an income at this point and there was just no money. That didn't matter at Murchison. There was a pumpkin patch: already teeming with implausibly large orange spheres when we got there. There were bunches of peppery green watercress to pick from the rivers. There were eels – and always a plan to go eeling. Although the eels were too smart and slippery for us and we all knew it.

Mum dragged a sack of flour home and we lived off watercress soup and pumpkin scones. Our grocery shop was basically dog food, toilet paper, tobacco and a chunky yellow bar of Sunlight multipurpose soap. This was A-OK with five-year-old me. Mum's scones were delicious and I was loving life: spending my days out the back, exploring the creeks and grasslands with Emma. There were tadpoles to be found, dams to be built.

I'm not sure if Mum and Dad were looking for a quieter life. I don't know if they got it. There was a steady stream of friends and Dad's siblings (and *their* friends) who had made the long trip down from Auckland or somewhere overseas. We usually had someone staying with us. At night there were people sprawled out smoking and laughing around the fireplace. The furry, tomato-plant smell of hash thick in the air.

One misty blue morning, I woke up and under the crotchet blankets with me was a sleeping person – all the other beds and couches must have been full. I watched the bobbing cones of the buddleia flowers outside the window for a while, wondering who this person was, and how I was going to climb over them without waking them up.

No one who stayed with us looked like the people who lived in Murchison. And the people who lived in Murchison did not like the look of us. This was six years after Woodstock. In many of the places we'd lived, the counterculture vibe seemed positively mainstream. But none of that free-living colour had made it to Murchison. Or maybe it had taken one look at the town's two tight rows of picket-fenced houses and carried on down the highway, not even stopping for gas.

Any time I walked with Mum to the store, it felt like all eyes were on us. Not in a welcoming way. We kept to ourselves. Mum was polite. Back at the house there was always music playing, but it'd be coming from a tape deck or someone thumbing a guitar or blues harp. There were no amps or even decent speakers, so nothing was ever loud enough to be heard past our garden. Any other behaviour that could be termed 'antisocial' was similarly under wraps. No one wanted trouble. Everyone smoked dope, but everyone also had a friend or a cousin or a friend of a cousin who'd been locked away for a chunk of their youth because of marijuana. It only took one anonymous call to bring down the tombstone heft of the NZ Narcotics Act.

The hippy thing feels pretty innocent now – young people with flowers in their hair, sitting around getting stoned and not putting on their shoes. It's easy to forget the scary undercurrent that was also happening back then. Hippies might have been all about peace and love, but they inspired a lot of aggression. People really went out of their way to dislike them, and the good folks of Murchison thought we were hippies.

Whatever we were, it wasn't that. We were never really part of that scene. Mum and Dad weren't against it, just always separate, not quite involved. Perhaps because we moved around so much, or maybe we just weren't any good at joining in. And Dad always wore shoes, even at the beach. He wouldn't even entertain a sandal. He said he didn't like them, but maybe it was because of his moulded plastic right foot.

We'd visited a few places called communes. One of them was actually a house we'd lived in before Tobey was born. A sweet federation-style bungalow with a beautiful old willow tree out the front. When we went back to visit, there were a lot of people there, like it was a party, but it was in the middle of the day. *They* were hippies. You could tell because they had no proper furniture. There had been a table, armchairs and a sofa in the lounge when we were there, but they'd taken it all out. Now it was just blankets and beanbags.

Everyone was stretched out, lying on the floor and propped up together on the beanbags. There were ashtrays, and empty wine bottles rolling about. The air was a penetrating smog of hash, burning incense and patchouli. No one had shoes on.

The people had drawn flowers on their faces. The walls were covered in similar drawings – a lot of these same, casually-inaccurate blue-petaled flowers. To my judgemental little eyes it was amateur work. Especially for a bunch of grown-ups. I'd only been drawing for a year or so myself at the time. Already my flowers were neater.

We must have been back at our old house to score some gear. My parents went through to the kitchen to talk to whoever was dealing and I was left frowning at the walls. The people on the floor might have been on something trippy. Everyone shrieked and gathered around me like they'd never seen an averagely-heighted three-and-a-half-year-old kid before.

'What is it? A pixie? A fairy?'

'It's a magic little person!'

'I'm not a fairy,' I said grumpily. I knew all about fairies, and these people were *way* off.

They were delighted: 'It speaks. Look at it. It's adorable!'

'Why so serious, little pixie person?'

I asked them about the walls.

'It's cool isn't it, it's the power of the flower.'

Someone offered me a blue crayon, but I wanted no part of this. What a bunch of outrageous unfairness. When we lived here, I'd been in trouble for drawing a stickperson. A small, neat stickperson, waving hello on the wall by my bed. Now the walls were *covered* with messy drawings and Mum and Dad weren't saying a thing.

I could see my parents laughing and talking in the kitchen with these bad drawers like nothing was even wrong.

I stomped outside to wait under the willow tree. The same tree I'd once laid under worrying about mind-invading jasmine. The tree looked different, there were wind chimes in the branches now and someone had dragged the sofa from the living room out here. The sofa was just sitting there in the tall grass. What if it rained?

On the drive home Mum and Dad talked about the house. 'They've totally wrecked the garden. All those sweet peas I planted. Dead, all of them. Such a waste.'

The garden? What about the *walls*?

★

At Murchison, there were kids next door. Other children who could be friends. Almost as good as fairies. Maybe better, because they appeared straightaway. Flitting about on the other side of the hedge. Flashes of bright red and yellow-striped t-shirt; calling to each other in loud voices.

Their house was one of the newer, squarer ones. I could see these were proper, normal kids whose mother kept peas in a freezer and made sandwiches out of white bread and cut those sandwiches in half, then half again. These kids went to school and everything.

By all accounts, our moving in next door had horrified their mother. I wasn't allowed in their house and she definitely didn't want them coming into ours. She was reluctant to let her children associate with me on any level, but eventually she said we could play in the space between our houses, where she could watch us from her kitchen window. I was vibrating with excitement.

The kids were cool. After a day or so, more kids came over from down the road. The games normal children played were repetitive and pointless, but mind-blowingly fun. We basically just ran around, taking turns to chase each other, hiding behind bushes a lot.

Things were going well.

Once, when their mother drove to Nelson for the day, the kids from next door showed me inside their house. It smelt like fried food and looked like *The Brady Bunch*'s lounge. Their decor was heavily brown, nothing like our place at all. No pieces of art, no Persian rugs or anything hanging on the walls. It was thrilling.

A few weeks into this charmed period, we were playing hide and seek. Tobey was still learning how to walk, so a bit young to join in. But Emma was with us, playing too. All of us running about as usual, shrieking and laughing. Emma barking along, as giddy as me to be involved.

Emma wasn't a small dog, but she was too sweet and waggy-tailed to worry anyone. She didn't have a docked tail or the angry-looking clipped ears that some people do to their Dobermans. She definitely hadn't been trained to be fierce. She just looked smiley and cute with her soft, floppy Dumbo ears.

The next-door family had a dog too, a long-suffering German shepherd about the same size as Emma, who was well-accustomed to being pinched and yanked around. But Emma wasn't used to that at all. When four-year-old Scott swung his weight off one of her super-sensitive ears, she snapped at him in shock. Only a play snap, but enough to leave two tell-tale red indents on his hand.

Scott ran off wailing to his mother. The game came to a panicked halt. The kids from down the road bolted, leaving the rest of us standing there looking at each other. I could see my neighbours were scared, but I hadn't quite grasped the horror of our situation until their mother came out. She came out yelling.

'Get away from my children.'

'Sorry Mrs Leonard. She didn't mean anything. She's a good dog.'

As if to agree, Emma came to sit neatly beside me.

The woman towered over us, jabbing the air with her finger, 'If I see that animal again and it's not chained up, I'll have it shot.'

Hiding in the bushes around the back of our house with Emma later, I cried and cried. The two oldest kids braved their mother's wrath and came to find me. Putting their arms around me, they told me not to cry, that was just how their mother was. But her look of disgust had been unmistakeable.

As she'd walked off, she had shaken her head, revolted, 'Filthy dirty hippies.'

Her children weren't allowed to play with me after that. None of the kids from down the road came back either. I was very careful to keep Emma away from their side of the property.

It's funny what gets in. What sticks. How big a small event can seem when you're a kid. I don't think Mum and Dad noticed my adventures with the neighbours and I never told them what happened, but the woman's disgust stayed with me, twisting for years. The look she gave me lasted a long time.

When she said I was dirty, I knew she didn't just mean I needed a bath: I had one every night. She meant something deeper and far worse. I smelt wrong, but not in a way you could wash off. I'd always understood that we didn't live like everyone else. Now I knew for sure that not being normal meant we were something less.

I moped around for a bit. Did some half-hearted drawings and made a few higgledy-piggledy attempts at the alphabet. I'd been reliably informed alphabets were the first step to reading. I really wished I could skip that step.

Then, a month later, the best thing happened.

Emma had her puppies. Her tummy had been getting bigger, and one morning they were finally here. Dad had been up helping Emma through the night. He woke me just after dawn to come meet them. I tiptoed into the woodshed and there in the hay were tiny squirming bundles of almost unbearable cuteness. Where it had just been Emma, now all these brand-new lives existed in the world, right in front of us.

It was a cold morning. Our breath little clouds, but inside the shed was warm and soft-smelling: fresh hay and milk-sweet puppies. Emma was sitting up, cosy with pride, looking over all her babies.

After about two weeks their eyes were open and they were clambering around, and so much fun to play with. If you sat down anywhere near them, they'd barrel over and climb on top of you. Licking and sniffing. Their little tails wagging, their scratchy little paws all over you. It was the best. They were just the cutest. They were so happy about everything. Watching them made your whole body smile. The only problem was remembering to concentrate on making sure everyone got their fair share of pats and love.

★

However low funds got, Mum and Dad always made sure there was gas in the Kombi. Being trapped was unthinkable. Whatever we were doing, wherever we were, we needed to be able to leave with a turn of the ignition key.

Also, Mum and Dad didn't want us going stale, like slimy water caught in a rock pool. We'd go for drives, out for the day exploring a different bit of countryside. Mum and Dad, me and baby Tobey, and whoever was staying with us at the time. Emma had always jumped in the backseat with us, and now the puppies came too.

It took them a while to get the hang of riding in a Kombi. They'd try to keep walking around, wobbling unsteadily on their chubby little legs, tumbling into each other as we turned a corner. They'd do their best to stay awake, but the purr of the engine was too strong. Within minutes they'd all be conked out. Collapsed in our laps, snuggled up and fast asleep.

One morning, we pulled up at the Buller River. The river's Māori name was Kawatiri, meaning deep and swift, and at this part, it really lived up to its name. The water narrowed and deepened, thundering past. None of us had a clue how deep it was, somewhere between 20ft and really, really deep.

We rarely came here, even at the shallowest edges there was no watercress to pick. No vegetable had a hope of gripping on in that furious current. But what was cool about the spot was a long finger of rock that reached out from the shore to halfway into the river, a yard or two above the waterline. You could step out along the middle of the rock and watch the dark green water rush past with safe, dry feet.

There were three other adults staying with us that day. We all spilled out of the Kombi and carefully shuffled along the finger of rock, out into the river. The puppies sniffing everything and wagging their tails.

We were in the heart of winter. It was a bright, shining morning: cold enough that the edges of the river had frozen white. I was looking at this. Fascinated by how the cold could turn such fast, dark water into something so still and pale. Not really listening to what anyone was saying, when Dad started throwing us in.

It happened fast. One moment I was peering into the swirling waters. Then suddenly Dad was flinging the puppies into the river. Two at a time, one in each hand. He was systematically picking them up and swinging them high into the air and then splat into the water.

It was so shocking it took me a second to understand what I was actually seeing. Everyone was just standing there, watching him. Like it was fine to throw little puppies into a deep icy river. I was about to start yelling, when, in horrible slow motion, I was being lifted high and swung out into the air.

Apparently it was for their own good. This was how you taught dogs to swim. Assuming they survived, the cold would also make them stronger. I must not have been able to swim at this point either, because Dad – I hope spontaneously – had decided it was time to teach me too.

Hitting the water was like being charged with an electric current. A complete, pure sense of cold. I don't remember going under, just the gasping, dark green cold. Then seeing all the little front paws in the water with me, frantically paddling towards the rock. I'd started doing the same, before I'd realised I even knew what to do. The surface of the water around me now churned white with tiny splashes. All of us desperately paddling away from the cold. Back towards the line of shoes and cheers of encouragement coming from above our heads.

Sitting in the Kombi minutes later, teeth clattering, someone rubbing a blanket over me to bring back the feeling in my arms and legs, I still couldn't believe what had happened. Yes, I was fine now, and actually starting to feel nice and glowingly clean. All the puppies seemed fine too, apart from a few miniature sneezes. But that Dad could toss us into the river, like we were rubbish! In front of everyone! So humiliating.

Luckily he had thrown us against the current, so it swept us back against the rock. None of us would have made it otherwise. Dad was laughing about it all being perfectly safe and a great demonstration of how the natural instinct always kicks in. Babies are born with the ability, blah, blah. But instinct or not, I'd been in thick corduroy trousers and two woollen jumpers. It was luckier still that Tobey had been safely out of arm's length in the Kombi, uncharacteristically napping.

Over the following months the puppies were given away, each one a terrible loss. I kept asking, how did we know they were going to good places? Growing up on a farm, Dad was matter-of-fact about this. We didn't. When dogs had puppies, you had to give most of the litter away. That was just life. Emma would have other puppies.

But what about *these* puppies? Dad just shook his head.

I couldn't stop thinking about it. I'd lie awake for hours. Their whole life had been the backyard, the Kombi and the shed. They loved each other so much. All they wanted to do was to play together. You never saw any of them playing alone. I was so worried about how lonely they'd be.

Most of the puppies went to strangers, but two went to people we knew. Collected just half an hour apart, they couldn't have gone to more different homes. There might be many ways of understanding what is fair, but I could not make sense of their lives. There *was* no fair reason I could see.

Both puppies were perfect. As keen to learn and explore as each other. One was spoilt and had a superb life. The other treated very badly. The man who had chosen the second puppy – taking him from the safety and snuggles of his mother and siblings – was cruel. He said he couldn't be bothered thinking of a name. When he got sick of people telling him he couldn't just call his dog 'Puppy', he named him Guppy to spite them. Poor Guppy grew up scared and quivery. He flinched if you moved too quickly, his eyes always expecting pain. You could sometimes see his ribs. I begged Dad to take Guppy back, but Dad said you couldn't interfere with how a man treated his dog.

Not long after that I learned you couldn't do much about a man killing your goats either.

I'd be given two kid goats to take care of after their mother died on a farm nearby. They were delightful. Super-cute to look at, and really affectionate and fun to be around. Jumping up and climbing over everything with their sweet little hooves. Bouncy as popcorn. One was a soft brick-red and the other black and white. I named them Ginger and Mary-Ann after my two favourite characters on *Gilligan's Island*.

Ginger and Mary-Ann would follow you about, butting their hard little heads literally into everything you were doing. Sometimes they'd creep up behind you and headbutt your hands for pats. Not that you'd ever get tired of patting their velvet-soft necks. Feeding them was a wonderful feeling: you held their bottle high up, standing on tiptoe, as they gulped down the milk.

In the mornings if I didn't get up early enough, they'd clip-clop around to the outside of my bedroom window and bleat cutely until I put my head out and said hello.

In the afternoons, Emma and I would lie in the clover looking at books and they'd nibble an outline around us on the grass. They were just beautiful, smart little animals. The loves of my five-year-old life. I was so lucky to have them. I couldn't imagine sweeter, more loyal friends.

I'd just started thinking about what sort of tricks I could teach them when we had to make a trip up to Auckland. I didn't feel good about leaving them, but Frank, one of Dad's friends who was staying with us, would be looking after the dogs and goats while we were gone. Ginger and Mary-Ann were self-feeding by this stage, so all he'd need to do was make sure they had fresh water and give them a few pats: just to reassure them everything was OK.

When we got back to Murchison two weeks later, I couldn't wait to see them. See if they'd grown, what they were up to. As soon as we pulled into the driveway, I raced around to say hi. Ginger and Mary-Ann were nowhere to be seen. I ran out to the creek; looked in all the bushes. I even crawled under the house.

It turned out that Frank had a hangover on the third morning and couldn't be bothered getting out of bed to give anyone a few pats. Ginger and Mary-Ann cried and cried, waiting for me outside my window. Apparently, they had cried for me during the first two days too.

Eventually Frank got out of bed, took a knife from the kitchen drawer and cut their soft little throats. To him this was the best solution to the crying.

I didn't understand how people could be so mean to animals. They were our friends, they trusted us. It was around this time I decided to be a vegetarian. Eating them was out of the question.

What made the decision more obvious were the butchers. Every country town had one: if you weren't getting your meat from the local butcher, you were killing it yourself.

Butchers' windows would be painted like children's picture books: all frolicking lambs and laughing baby cows, gambolling in their pastures. Then, on the other side of the glass, were their bodies, neatly piled up in pooling blood on aluminium trays.

You'd be skipping along, looking at the shop windows, minding your own business. The bookshop with interesting books on display, *skip, skip,* the clothes shop, the baker. Then suddenly… Bam! Blood, death, horror. It looked like the scene of a massacre.

I couldn't see how different my 'rump' or 'flank' would have looked if it had been me who was chopped up on the trays. And the smell. Argh. It was the smell of refrigerated death. The whole thing was horrific.

Mum and Dad understood, they never made us eat meat. They were always pretty cool about that sort of thing.

★

Mum and Dad connected at a party. I don't know if it was destined. Fate, etc. I'm not sure how many decent nightclubs there were in the metropolis of late-sixties Auckland. Back then, house parties featured heavily in the local nightlife.

The scene wasn't quite Laurel Canyon, but the cool kids all knew each other, at least to say hey. Dad had a reputation. There were rumours he worked undercover for a clandestine government department. Liaised with dangerous underground types. Came from British aristocracy. Only had one leg… Dad didn't bother denying any of it. He'd roll in late and drunk. He'd whisk away your girlfriend. Somehow people still kept wanting him at their parties.

Mum had just moved to Auckland. With her high boots and long auburn hair, she caught attention. She was doing a bit of modelling, meeting new people and having fun.

She'd been warned off him. Her friends told her that he was a bad guy and a womaniser. There were plenty of nice, attentive men for her to choose from, but Mum saw something she liked the look of in Dad. Probably, her friends' warnings just made him seem more interesting.

On their first date, Dad said he had to drop something off on the way. He popped the boot outside a dark house. Two men were waiting. Stubbing their cigarettes and moving out of the shadows as Dad pulled up.

'Sorry about this,' Dad smiled brightly to Mum. 'Won't be a minute.'

Mum said it was the clear implication that she should stay put, like a good girl, that did it. She waited a beat, then hopped out to see what was being unloaded from the back of the car.

Dad's boot was filled with guns. Dozens of them glinting up in the dark. In a variety of sizes.

Dad looked at Mum from the other side of the car. Between them, the two men were swiftly unloading the guns into a series of duffle bags.

Dad raised one eyebrow cockily. 'Should I take you home?'

The challenge was implicit, could she handle the drama? Would she be cool?

Mum looked back at him, her eyebrow raised in return. 'Not necessarily.'

Maybe it was inevitable they'd hit it off. Any sensible woman would have run for the hills.

If I was there: in the back of Dad's car, or standing at that party, watching them flirt with each other from across the room, I'd probably have been screaming, 'Noooooo'.

I don't think I'd have been able to help myself.

They could have done anything; been anyone, but they liked each other and that was that. Maybe no one could have stopped them. I've often wondered how different Mum's life would have been without Dad. How much longer her life might have been. I never wondered this about Dad. It felt like his die had been cast way earlier than this. But maybe different people bring out different stories in each other.

Mum liked the sense of danger. At least in the beginning. Dad was the first person she'd met who believed *everything* was possible. The rules didn't matter, to him they weren't even relevant.

Up to this point her life had felt small, too safe. She wanted out. Here was a man she could have adventures with. He wasn't like anyone she'd ever met. It was 1968, suddenly nowhere was out of reach.

I guess this was an interesting time. Freedom must have felt real back then. The great wars were distant history. No one knew yet that you could die from sex, not since penicillin anyway. It was decades before anyone would be talking about climate crisis and the end of the world, at least publicly. The fifties had been stuffy, but now young people could make brand-new decisions. They'd be the first generation to dress differently from their parents. To want different things. To live the way they wanted.

Within the year, Mum and Dad were married and speeding through the Australian outback together in Dad's cherry-red MG convertible. A hilariously unsuitable car for the often-unsealed roads of one of the world's most scorched landscapes. They were in Australia to do some work for Poppa, who had just bought a textiles factory in Queensland. But first they were taking a roadtrip across the desert, a cloud of dust in their wake. They were sleeping in the car, surviving on not much more than cigarettes, and having a whale of a time.

Arriving in Brisbane and getting to grips with a fully operational factory was a bit of a bummer, but nothing to the news that came later. Mum wasn't feeling too flash. A visit to the doctors revealed she was precariously anaemic, and also pregnant. Not just pregnant, but verging-on-actual-motherhood, far-too-late-to-do-anything-about-it pregnant. Her period had never been regular and they were both thin as matchsticks, so this last bit of news was especially shocking.

Dad wired Nanny and Poppa that they were going to be grandparents, and could they send some money please. Mum says all she felt like eating was grapes.

The roadside hotel where they were staying was hot and airless. The next few months were spent staring at the TV and adjusting to the idea of parenthood. They didn't have long to think about things. Three weeks ahead of the due date, I arrived. Boringly early, 7.05am on a Friday morning.

Having me must have been a colossal bummer. Mum was still feeling weak. The hospital experience had been violent; she'd lost a dangerous amount of blood during the delivery. Her poor, already stressed body was exhausted, and I'd rocked up with a lot of noisy, smelly demands. Baby me expected constant attention. There were bottles, nappies. None of it would have looked like fun.

It would have been so much easier to have left me behind with the nurses. They were in a faraway city. It was just the two of them. They could have walked out and never looked back on the whole traumatic episode, like two action heroes striding away from an explosion.

Mum's own birth mother had left her as a newborn in a hospital, so the thought would have been present, drifting down the corridors like antiseptic. But I don't think my parents ever considered it. A baby wouldn't have to dent their style. They were going to keep me and we were going to be a family. The kind of family they'd wanted to be part of when they were growing up.

With me bundled in a few hurriedly bought blankets, they caught the first flight they could back to Auckland.

The wild Australian adventure was over.

Mum was nineteen years old. Dad twenty.

1976

School

No one remembers how long we lived in Murchison, but when we couldn't afford petrol, it was time to go. Mum and Dad were sick of watercress soup. We'd run out of sacks of flour, too. We needed to move to the city to make some money.

In 1976, we were back in Auckland. Renting a gorgeous old rambling house not far from 231, on a street called Ladies Mile. A year later the house would be declared derelict and pulled down to make way for a block of flats, but to us it was perfect. Stained-glass windows that let the sun shine in like rainbows and a wide, wraparound veranda. Mum hammered down its loose floorboards so Tobey and I could play outside even when it was pouring.

For reasons that are lost in history, when we were living at Ladies Mile, I went to live with Dad's mother, Nanny, and her eldest daughter, my auntie, Erin, on Norfolk Island.

I don't know if I was in trouble, but I remember being chuffed to bits. The whole thing was adventure. First of all, flying there felt magnificent. It was a crisp, sunny day. Blue skies with just the right puff of cloud. The plane was small: two seats wide on the inside. At five-and-a-half, I felt extremely grown-up sitting in my big seat, cruising through the clouds all by myself, watching the back of the pilot's head through a gap in the pleated curtain.

Like the plane, my destination was compact. A pine-dotted, fifteen-square-mile of basalt lava rock, rising up from the Pacific Ocean, halfway between Australia and New Zealand. Norfolk Island is where the majestic Norfolk pine trees come from. It's possibly better known as a former penal colony for 'the worst description of convicts' and later for being resettled by descendants of the HMS Bounty mutineers.

In 1976, everyone seemed really nice. Nanny and Poppa had bought a shop, and Nanny and Erin were living there, running it. We must have presented as a strange trio: three generations of women living in a small flat next to a grove of avocado trees on a windy lump of rock, but life felt superb. Nanny and Erin were ace. There was a daily routine. Mealtimes were regular. Nights were quiet. Even the decor looked normal.

The island's chief income was tourism, and Transworld Duty-Free Emporium was doing a roaring trade. After breakfast and a refreshingly uninterrupted sleep, I'd ride with Nanny in the pick-up to spend the day helping with unpacking, stocktaking and other bits and pieces. I'd spend hours artfully arranging the windows and store displays. Feeling blissfully helpful as I repositioned every leather wallet and carton of Camel Lights precisely back into place after each tour bus had stomped through.

Some evenings, once the shop was closed, we'd drive five minutes over to the west side of the island to watch the sun sink into the sea from the cliffs. In the centre of the island was an overgrown peach orchard. Acres of old peach trees that no one seemed to care about. Actual paradise.

Erin would park the truck and I'd scramble out to fill Nanny's fruit bowl. The best-tasting peaches I'd ever eaten. Not even James' giant one could taste better. I'd scoff peaches all the way home. Erin didn't get involved. She encouraged me, but didn't really eat food herself, consisting almost entirely on a diet of cigarettes, sunflower seeds and raw carrots.

Only two bad things happened on Norfolk Island, and both of them were a hundred percent my fault.

Nanny kept biscuits in the flat as gifts and for guests. The biscuits came in big round blue tins. You'd wedge open the lid and there they were, winking beguilingly up at you in their plastic trays. The overly processed, sweet taste of white-flour normal. *Ridiculously* delicious. I couldn't get enough of them. I was allowed one after dinner.

Its residents may have been the direct descendants of convicts and murderous sailors, but Norfolk Island felt pretty safe in the 1970s. Tourists were mostly daytrippers in from an ocean liner, everyone else knew everyone else. Nanny and Erin could comfortably leave me in the flat on my own.

I was happy. My merchandising wages had been paid in the shape of my first and only stuffed toy, a canary-yellow Tweety Bird from the store, so I didn't really feel alone. The two of us would dance around the rug listening to Val Doonican's *Paddy McGinty's Goat*. Both of us big fans of the song's storyline about an Irishman of note, who fell in for the kind of fortune that involved buying yourself an exploding goat.

Anyway.

Nanny kept the biscuit tins safely out of reach on a floating shelf, high above the kitchen bench. One afternoon, by not-entirely-sheer-coincidence, I discovered I was just tall enough to edge out one of the tins. If I stood on an upturned saucepan that happened to be on a stack of photo albums. Providing the pan and photo albums were balanced on the foamy seat of one of the barstools. And I was on tiptoes.

Prying off the lid, the sight of the biscuits – adorable in their neat trays – made me giddy. I took a bite. Then another.

Sugar-rushing off my head like a little maniac a few mouthfuls later, I decided the best, least noticeable, way forward would be to take a bite out of every single biscuit. Then they'd all look the same.

Once I'd put a carefully uniform-sized bite (or two smaller, joined-up bites) into the side of each biscuit, I re-taped the tin and edged it back on the shelf.

When Nanny got home, the first thing she noticed was the tin, half hanging off the shelf, the tape sealing it all wonky. Me lying on the rug, sick as Paddy's goat might have been another clue.

'Saylor, do you know what happened to these biscuits?'

‘No Nanny,’ I said, peering deeply into the rug. What choice did I have but lies? I wasn’t ready to leave convict island.

After a thorough questioning, it was deduced that if I hadn’t eaten them, and no one else apart from Nanny and Erin had been in the flat, Erin must have been the thief. Erin protested her innocence, but Nanny insisted that I would never lie. Such was the gravity of the crime, the fuzz were called.

It wasn’t until the police officer (a friend of Nanny’s bizarrely up for popping around in his old uniform for a spot of amateur dramatics and police intimidation) got his handcuffs on Erin’s wrists that I tearfully fessed up.

The other bad thing I did was sail out to sea.

The second (and last) merchandising paycheque from Transworld Duty-Free Emporium was also Tweety-Bird yellow. An inflatable canoe with blue rope printed down the sides that smelt intoxicatingly good – similar to felt-tip pens but even better – and came with a superb pair of oversized, matching yellow goggles. Once Erin had blown it up for me, the canoe was perfect: just big enough to sit in, feet squished against the end. Small enough that I could propel it along, paddling my hands at each side. The moment you sat crooked, weight even slightly off balance, the canoe capsized, but once I got the hang of that, I was off.

The beach was packed. The water pond-smooth. Both were deemed, quite reasonably, safe. Nanny and her friend Margaret were chatting and sunbathing up on the dry sand. My instructions were to stay at the waters’ edge and not go anywhere near the big kids – one nudge from a reckless eight-year-old and I’d be sunk.

It was a beautiful day: wide blue skies overhead, crystal clear water below. Norfolk pines lined the bay and the sand was ablaze with brightly coloured towels and swimsuits. Out in the far distance, a few white yachts dotted the horizon.

Everyone was having the loveliest time. I was having the loveliest time. Only slight problem was that floating in the shallows meant my view of the pebbles and tiny fish darting about was distorted by the ripples of the water hitting the sand.

A few yards out I encountered new obstructions – other kids, messing up the pebbles, kicking up the sand and frightening the fish. I saw a gap and paddled fast.

A bit further out, the big kids looked worse. I didn't want any trouble. Especially as I wasn't sure I could reach the bottom now. More paddling took me past the danger, and out past a few stray adults.

Sanctuary and the perfect view. I did notice that the pebbles had disappeared and that the sand seemed quite a bit further down, but I didn't really analyse the situation.

The goggles had to be kept under the water's surface to see anything properly, so I wasn't looking anywhere but down. There were interesting coral reef bits now appearing and lots of fish, some of them quite big. It was much quieter out here, so I could really concentrate on the excellent views and keeping my balance, as I leaned into the water.

I don't know how long I floated along. Merrily peering downwards. But I got quite a fright when the coral reef ran out, and I looked up to check on Nanny. Instead of seeing her blue-striped umbrella, I could only just make out the distant shoreline of land.

It was then that I noticed the yachts weren't tiny white triangles, they were now massive big boats and they were very, very close. They looked very sharp. Sharp enough to pop my canoe like an overstretched balloon.

I hadn't seen the bottom for a long time. A scared feeling gripped my stomach.

I started paddling back towards the thin line of sand and coloured specks. Frantically as I could, without tipping myself out into the dark blue water. But it was *so* far. My arms were tired and sore. I didn't seem to be making any progress. If anything, the yachts were now even closer. Looking up at the nearest one was like looking up a tall building. My whole view on one side was curved and white. There were little waves now and my canoe was wobbling precariously. Water was splashing in. I started to cry.

What almost definitely saved my life was that someone on the yacht happened to glance down and see a freaked-out kid in a massive pair of yellow goggles bobbling along beside them in a pocket-sized inflatable canoe. They stared in amazement.

A complicated rescue mission was set in motion. The yacht crew threw down a lifebuoy and someone had to jump into the sea with me – at a safe enough distance that the splash wouldn't upturn me. Thanks to this hero, who managed to balance me in one hand and grip the buoy in the other, without losing either of us, the yacht was able to drag me and my canoe close enough to land that two lifeguards could swim out and bring me back to safety. Back to the coral and then the sand.

Then the pebbles, the big kids, the little kids… and my emotional grandmother.

Poor Nanny Starling, she must have aged ten years during my stay.

Not long after that, I was flying back to Auckland. Tweety under my arm.

★

There was magnificent news at Ladies Mile.

I was going to school.

Neither of my parents were keen on the idea. Mum and Dad had both been expensively educated, and they didn't want that kind of 'bullshit institutionalisation' for their children. But, argued all three grandparents, she needs to learn to read and write. No one disputed that getting through life without these abilities might prove challenging. But Dad being a certified genius, and me being his first-born, my parents had assumed I would teach myself. I'd proved most disappointing.

'Dad, school's for mucus-balls,' I overheard my Dad tell Poppa. 'They make robots out of those kids.'

'Martin, she can't even write her own name,' said his Dad.

Thank cripes the grandparents pushed, because otherwise Dad might still be waiting for me to harness enough paternally-inherited intelligence to autodidact myself some alphabet. That was never going to happen. No matter how many stories they told me about the clever children who had taught themselves to read with twigs and bits of tree bark or those kids who could play Bach concertos after scratching a keyboard in the dirt, I just wouldn't apply myself.

All my blue-lined exercise books, purchased expressively for writing practice, were covered with drawings. Back at Murchison, Mum had pinned a poster of the alphabet in my room for me to copy out. I'd given it a couple of half-hearted whirls, but after getting half the letters backwards, twice, I drew flowers and stick-figure people instead. I'd also been bought plenty of storybooks. Instead of trying to understand the words like an intelligent, responsible child, I just cracked on drawing flowers and making up my own fake stories to go with the pictures.

Personally, school sounded tremendous. I was pumped. Mainly because FRIENDS!!! I was keen to meet other kids and play more of those bizarrely fun, running-around games. I also liked looking at books. I *really* liked the idea of being able to understand them. This all happened at school.

Mum had gone to a boarding school not far from our house. She'd loathed it while she was there, but now its day school for primary pupils seemed like a nice family tradition. Plus, it was only fifteen minutes' drive away.

I hardly slept for a week. Finally, I could be with my people. The ones who had neat hair and names like Jo and Jane, which they didn't have to repeat a bunch of times before anyone believed that yes, that *really* was what they were called.

Mum and I went into town to buy my uniform. A crisp white shirt and dark blue tunic. A special hat called a beret. There was even a specific type of sock and shoe that had to be worn. Every detail was prescribed. It was exquisite. There was no way I wasn't going to fit in. Poor Mum was having traumatic flashbacks. I was dancing in the change room. *Hello* normal. Whoohoo. All my dreams coming true.

On the morning of my first day, Mum popped a necklace of bright tribal beads around my neck.

'Mum, no!'

'Sssh, you need something to jazz up all that navy. Besides, who will notice?'

Like Mum's boarding school, the primary school was run by Catholic nuns. They looked like a flock of grumpy penguins. Difficult to tell apart at a distance, but close-up you could see the frowns had individual characteristics. The nun in the enrolment office was frowning extra hard. No jewellery was allowed at St Joseph of Cluny. Only a small gold cross, to be worn *under* the uniform.

'Oh, that isn't jewellery,' breezed Mum. 'It's an excavated artefact from Jaipur. My daughter must wear it for religious reasons.'

Religious reasons? WTF? Once Mum established it was a fixed aspect of our catholic faith – as adopted by the faraway residents of Rajasthan, north western India – I had to wear that stupid, clunky necklace every single day I was at that school. The only girl with any visible jewellery in the whole school. Thanks Mum. And *everybody* noticed. Even the cleaner gave me side-eye.

Mum sashayed out and I was taken to my new classroom. It wasn't just the necklace that wasn't right. We'd arrived late. Late in the morning, and late in the school year. Class had started two hours and five months earlier. The other children sat neatly at their desks. Their heads turned like sunflowers to look at me. The nun at the blackboard was also interested in why I was late. Thinking yourself above the rules wouldn't be wise here, she said.

There were a lot of rules. Official rules and the secret ones that took longer to work out. From the front gate (don't go anywhere near it. Unless it's home time, then go *through* it) to the last toilet cubicle (looked fine but had cooties: like germs, but worse), everything in the school had some sort of rule.

There were rules about how to sit on the classroom floor (cross-legged, arms folded, taking up as small a space as possible. NO FIDGETING!). There were books, and you could look at them (but only Tuesday and Thursday after Big Lunch). No touching the class pencils unless the teacher said (but also, only losers used the class pencils). There were times you could speak (mostly you couldn't). If you needed to pee (or worse), you couldn't just quietly slip off, you had to put your hand up and tell the whole class (better to just hold it).

There were no shades of grey at St Cluny. You were either good (following the rules) or damned (getting the ruler/destined to twist forever in the burning pits of hell). The other girls knew the rules inside out: I could see being normal meant following rules, so I watched what they did closely as I could.

At the end of playtime, the bell would ring, telling you to get back to class. But you couldn't go in. You had to wait outside for Sister Mary to open the door. You couldn't just stand there waiting. You had to wait in a neat line, positioning yourself exactly behind the girl in front of you. Sister Mary said to imagine there was a thread running from the shoulders of the girl in front to yours, and make the thread absolutely straight. If you were out even a fraction, the whole class would be blighted. There were two places to wait. Under the awning if it was raining. Against the wall if it wasn't.

The first time I got the ruler was on a day that was rainy *and* sunny. Sister Mary was late opening the class door. First, we queued in the sunny area. All the other classes had been let into their rooms by the time it started to drizzle. Panicked to be caught in the wrong place, we ran to the rainy area.

A minute later the rain stopped. We bolted back to the sunny side. The rain started again. Then it stopped.

The running back and forth had begun in fear, but dissolved in giggles as things got ridiculous. Then someone looked up at the classroom windows and saw Sister Mary standing there, scowling down at us.

We were a disgrace. Running around laughing like that, we'd made fools of ourselves. The entire class would be getting the ruler. In our neat line, one by one, we were to climb the stairs to the classroom and put our hand out for Sister Mary to deliver the punishment.

Coming to the top of the stairs, I saw the girl in front of me struggle to put her hand out. Three times Sister Mary had to yell at her. There was the whistle of the ruler coming down, the crack on her small outstretched palm. She cried, then it was my turn.

Sister Mary looked down, her eyes flat with distain, 'Hand!'

I could see why everyone was terrified of the ruler. It stung like a wasp. Inside the classroom most of the girls were sobbing. All of us hugging our red hands.

★

Being in a room full of other kids was weird. I'd hoped being dressed the same (stupid necklace aside), would mean no one could tell I wasn't one of them. Somehow, wearing a uniform made me stand out even more.

Sister Mary had seen my lacking that very first morning. We were each given a piece of paper with a giraffe printed on it to colour in. With the stubby, unsharpened class pencils that no one else was using, I worked hard. Doing extras like giving the grass some flowers and a small snail. I'd kept my colours as realistic as possible, but when I couldn't find a nice mid-brown for the giraffe's patches, I'd taken hint from the fact the animal was wearing a bowler hat, and assumed we could detour slightly from nature, with respectful artistic licence.

Sister Mary wasn't having any of it.

'Giraffes aren't purple! And you've gone outside the lines.' She pointed to the top of the page. 'Where is your name?' She had a very loud voice.

I had to admit I didn't know how to write this. I'd drawn one of my best butterflies in the corner instead.

'You don't know how to write your *own* name?' she boomed. 'Oh dear. *How* old are you?'

Everyone spun around to stare at the hideous new girl.

Being six-and-a-half made me more than a year older than everyone else in my class. That was embarrassing. Worse, I was the only girl in the entire school who couldn't read and write. Out of hundreds of pupils.

There was something called kindergarten and everyone had gone to that. Cat, dog, apple… They were trotting out all sorts of words. I couldn't write the first letter of my name without getting it backwards. Usually, I just drew a smiling stickperson on a boat.

I came home that day and flopped down on the Gujarat rug next to Grannie May who was over at our house, doing some ironing in the sunroom. I described the situation woefully. My homework was to read a Little Golden Book, but I didn't know any of the words.

Gran listened sympathetically as she ironed Dad's shirt.

'It's not hard. Go get your book and we'll have a look together.'

Grannie May, best human in the world, showed me how to sound out the words. How the little squiggles worked together. She totally saved my life. Each afternoon that week we spent a couple of hours going over my homework before dinner. Turned out reading was brilliant. Having stories on my own, whenever I wanted, without having to wait for anyone to sit down and read them to me was glorious. It felt so free. I could even read them to Emma and Tobey. And Grannie was right, it wasn't hard. Within the month, thanks to Grannie, I was the fastest reader in class. Writing was harder, but it wasn't long before I could do handwriting that didn't make you wince to look at. My colouring-in was neat as a pin.

But being good at school wasn't just about doing the work. Getting there was a struggle in itself. Previously we'd all just woken up when we felt like it. Now, at least two Starlings had to be dressed and outside the house, at the same early time, five days a week. A particularly harsh adjustment for Mum and Dad.

One morning I forgot my beret. I didn't realise how haunting an error this was until I was made to stand on stage in front of the school assembly, and asked to explain why I imagined myself above the rules. I looked out on a hall of snickering faces, my mind a screaming blank, and completely understood why there are people who fear public speaking more than death.

Pick-up after school wasn't terrific either. Pupils would stand out on the footpath by the front gates and parents would swoop down like devoted seagulls. After a few minutes there'd just be ten or so uncollected girls. By the fifteen-minute mark, this had thinned to one or two pupils. Never the popular girls. Rarely the ones with the nicest plaits or best lunches.

After twenty minutes, the nuns would roll the gates shut. They'd look sadly at whoever was left. Clearly too disappointing for their parents to bother collecting on time. Then the tall gate you couldn't see through would clank shut. You'd hear the bolt slide into place on the other side and know that now you were just a kid standing on the side of the road.

Day after day, I'd be there, always one of the last to be picked up. Me and one or two other loser girls. Desperately avoiding eye contact with each other.

One afternoon I stood there for over an hour. Scuffing my shoes and watching for our car with a dark swallowing feeling, maybe Mum and Dad weren't coming for me. Most likely they'd forgotten.

It dawned on me that I could just *leave*. Probably it was the most helpful thing I could do. Definitely I didn't want to stay here, waiting pathetically, everyone seeing what a massive, unwanted loser I was.

I tightened my schoolbag strap and set off up the hill. I'd only ever travelled home by car, but I figured I'd remember the way as I went. It was through half a suburb and some busy roads but I wasn't frightened. Or at least not as much as I didn't want to stand outside the gates anymore.

No one was home when I got back to Ladies Mile. I sat on the back steps in the setting sun. The honey-coloured light shining into my eyes. I felt pretty good. It *had* been a bit scary, but I'd got myself home without being stolen or squashed like a grape in the traffic.

After about half an hour Dad came rushing past. He'd been to the school and couldn't find me. No one had opened the gates when he'd banged. He'd just lost all sense of time as usual. I was in big trouble, but I could tell he was also a bit relieved to see me still alive. In my mind, the whole episode was a win.

There's a picture of me around this time getting out of a light green minivan that no one remembers ever having. No one has any clue who drove the van or when the photograph might have been taken, but it's definitely me. I'm in my uniform, beret and all. I don't look concerned. My hand's resting on the mystery door handle with the nonchalant satisfaction of a great ride home from school. Cripes knows who drove me that day.

★

Always, always. The best fun was the stuff Mum and I did together. Just the two of us. Mother and eldest daughter. It didn't happen often, and it always felt like a secret mission. It was usually after dark, and always on the sly.

Mum woke me up one night when we were living in Ladies Mile. Moments later we were tiptoeing out of the sleeping house with the specific aim of liberating the lemons from a distant neighbour's tree. To Mum, the fact that good, healthy lemons were falling and rotting on these people's lawn was a crime of intolerable proportions.

We crept along the suburban roads in the post-midnight gloom. Mum hoisted me up and we climbed over the fence. The lemons glinted in the dark garden like golden treasure. Full and round, they came away easily from the branches with a quick twist. The heady scent of stolen citrus filling the night air. We filled our cloth bag, then our pockets. I jammed a couple down my top.

Suddenly the house's backdoor light popped on. We froze, abruptly illuminated. Eyes round as possums on a tin roof.

'Quick. Let's go.'

Mum boosted me back over the fence. I had just enough time to look up and catch the bag of loot before Mum landed cat-like next to me. We both ran down the road, laughing.

Mum loved me best when I wasn't really myself. Being a goody-two-shoes might have won me points with the grandparents, but the opinion that mattered most was Mum's. And she knew square behaviour was dull as dishwater. She was loose and free. I was wound so tight, fun had a hard time getting in.

★

Mum had been adopted as a newborn. Her parents were a couple who couldn't have children of their own. John owned and ran a busy country pub. May was a nurse at the district hospital. They were good, hardworking people, well liked in their community. When an unwanted baby was born at the hospital, May was asked if she wanted to look after her, and Vivienne came home with the Conway-Smiths.

Little Vivienne had a good childhood. But, like a lot of childhoods, it might not have been the right one for the child. Vivienne longed for danger and excitement, and got the calm of doting parents and a domestic routine. She wanted a horse, but got a bicycle. When she begged for a Great Dane, they bought her a dachshund puppy.

Mum always told the story of her early years as a long, lonely wanting of ponies and siblings. Apart from being the only redhead in a small country town, and having parents who were usually working, to me it didn't sound a million miles from idyllic. We never got to meet her father. He died suddenly when Mum was fourteen, but by all reports he was terrific. Her mother, my Grannie May, was obviously, indisputably perfect. John and May wanted to give Vivienne the best, so they saved up to send their daughter to a posh boarding school in the city.

Mum had glided out of five years of strict catholic education cool as a cucumber; her shine undented. Not a scratch of boring on her. I'd been totalled in it after two months.

And so it went.

I'm not saying this comparison is all you need to form a clear picture of either of us. But I wouldn't rule it out.

★

It never occurred to me that it was weird Dad didn't go to work every morning like other dads. I don't remember thinking it odd that some days he wouldn't leave the house until night-time. When you're a kid, you accept a lot of things as just the way it is. And, to be honest, the nine-to-five wasn't working out for me either. The whole school thing was a bit of a disappointment. The girls at St Cluny weren't fun like the kids at Murchison. I tried to be good, to follow all the rules, keep everything neat as possible. I always offered to share my pencils. But, whatever I tried, I could *not* get the hang of things. No one wanted to play with me.

Probably the need to be liked was coming off me like bog stink. All I knew was that it was going to take a lot more than a uniform to make me seem normal. And Dad was right about the mucus-ball regime. There was a *lot* of wasted time. It was very soothing to know what you'd be doing each day. But mostly what you'd be doing was sitting inside. Going over the same things you did yesterday, and the day before.

I liked the colouring-in. The reading was great. But I could do that anywhere, without having to sit by myself in the playground every lunchtime. Being by myself was fine at home. But at school, when everyone else was in tight clusters of friends, playing and laughing together, being alone made my stomach hurt.

Anyway, none of that mattered. We were moving to India.

1977

The new world

I couldn't understand what the men were shouting. They swarmed over us. Yelling and clamouring, pulling at our clothes.

I looked to Dad. He was fumbling with the rupees he'd just exchanged, focused on jamming the notes into his pockets. More men were sprinting towards us. Dozens of them, coming from both sides, with wild-looking eyes.

Mum had always wanted to see the Taj Mahal. She'd seen a postcard of a beautiful, ivory-white palace shimmering against sunset clouds. Its filigree arches and soaring domes reflected in tranquil symmetry down a long rectangle of water. The whole structure a testament to passionate love. We had to go.

You don't really think of your parents as young. Not when you're little. There's a photograph of Mum gingerly holding baby me: she looks about thirteen. It's surprising anyone let them walk off with a pack of cigarettes. Neither of them could've had the faintest clue what they were doing. They had no savings, no contacts and two chubby pink midgets in tow.

I never saw either of them flick so much as a sideward glance at a travel guide. Even now, such a trip would be bold. This was back when you made phone calls in public booths, waited weeks for money transfers and felt pretty flash about getting a telegram.

It never worried either of them that everyone else was finding jobs and homes. It wasn't so much that they wanted to be different, it simply didn't occur to them to be the same. As far as Dad was concerned, going off to work in an office each morning would have been about as realistic for him as strapping on a pair of disco rollerskates to go gliding around Saturn's rings.

They wanted to see places. They were crazy in love. And really, what else mattered? They'd stay up all night, talking and laughing and wrapping each other in a love that excluded all the boring stuff like where the next lot of money might be coming from.

'Your father's a hero,' Mum would explain. 'And, obviously, a genius.'

'There's no one like your mother,' said Dad. 'She's so beautiful. You kids be good for her.'

They'd always be murmuring in each other's ears. One of them then smiling and nodding in agreement. They looked great together. Even Tobey and I could see that: tall, glamorously hip. Thin in the way that everyone seemed to be thin in the seventies. No one got them like they got each other. They didn't need anyone else. This was their life, and the world was an adventure waiting for them.

Tobey and I got to go along for the ride.

The vaccinations were no joke: hepatitis A, hepatitis B, typhoid, cholera, yellow fever, rabies, meningitis, polio, measles, tetanus, Japanese encephalitis, diphtheria… Did these diseases even exist anymore? It felt like they'd just dusted off the exotic ailments box and given us one of everything. We had to keep going back to the clinic for the nurse to jab us with various-sized needles. The typhoid hypodermic was fatter than a Crayola crayon and stung like lemon juice going under your skin. Some of the inoculations made us woozy enough to willingly slump off to bed when we got home, even though it was still daytime outside.

Tobey cried on the second appointment. By the third we were both weeping. The nurse said we could have the empty syringes to play with afterwards, if we cheered up a bit. Immediately we both plastered on fake grins. The rest of the time we had at Ladies Mile was spent chasing each other around the backyard, squirting water from our needleless hypodermics. They were plastic, but Dad was getting used to plastic.

The flights were booked.

We were off.

Seventeen hours after departing Auckland, we stepped through sliding glass doors into a new world.

It's called Mumbai now. But when we arrived 3.55am one morning, overtired and ashy-faced, it was Bombay.

Back then you could smoke on planes. The smoking section was always in the back and we always sat in the thick of it. Mum and Dad and everyone else around them nonchalantly chain-smoking through the skies.

By the time we'd staggered, reeking of cigarettes, through immigration and baggage claim, it was dawn, the sky vivid pink and gold. Tobey and I were pretty used to odd hours and new places. I'd already lived in somewhere like a dozen homes. But this place was *really* different. You could smell it. The air weighed something here. It pushed up against you, spicy and fat with heat.

There wasn't much time to dwell on exotic aromas. Even before the airport doors had slid shut behind us, we were overwhelmed by arms and eyes and loud yelling. It wasn't until we were completely surrounded that I realised the men weren't trying to hurt us. It turned out they just *really* wanted us to stay at their cousin's, their brother's or their mother's special-quality, 'best-price-for-you' hostel.

'You two. Hold your bags,' Mum shouted back, meaning me and Tobey. 'Do *not* let them go.'

Bundled into a black-and-yellow Padmini taxi, we leaned back into the plastic-covered seats and breathed a sigh of relief. Tobey and I let go of each other's sweaty little hand.

The taxi peeled out into the highway and the land opened out. Soon we were driving through a sea of strange piles of rubbish. City towers rose up ahead in the far horizon. But to the left and right, on either side of the highway, as far as I could see, were miles of these odd little piles of junk. Plastic sheets and ripped tarpaulin stretched over sticks. Cardboard boxes roped together with corrugated-iron lids. Old car tyres. I wondered if they were some kind of huts.

Then I saw the people.

There were rows of feet lying in the makeshift doorways. Whole families sleeping together on bare dirt. Women stirring pots over fires. Little children everywhere. Along the edge of the road we were driving down were people casually squatting on the tarmac. I realised in horror what they were doing: how people were living here. They had so little, the public highway was their toilet. One man was pooping. I could actually see it coming out as he simultaneously brushed his teeth with a stick and chatted to his neighbour.

We kept driving and the huts didn't stop. Those poor, poor people. There were just so many of them. How could they survive in the rubbish? How could there be so many children?

I'd never really thought about money before: where we were in the scale of economics. I knew there had been times when we'd had no money to buy food, but it's not like we'd ever had *nothing*. We'd had clean rivers to find watercress in. Sometimes there had been fruit we could pick. Tobey and I didn't have toys or new clothes, but there had always been somewhere outside to play.

Driving through these slums, I knew we were rich. Suddenly we were ridiculously, uncomfortably rich.

After a week or so in Bombay, we took a night train out. Turns out the Taj Mahal in Bombay was just a hotel, a very nice hotel, but still, just a hotel. The real Taj Mahal was in Agra in the north. Also, it was a mausoleum, which seemed less fun.

Mum had heard from some people at the hostel that Bangalore, the garden city of India, was worth seeing, so we boarded a train five-hundred miles southward.

In Bangalore Mum and Dad rented out a room in a mustard-coloured house on the outskirts of town. We were still awkwardly loaded. The four of us shared two single beds in a room with a sink. We all slept and lived under the same wobbling ceiling fan, but we had real walls and a roof. There were cool brown tiles under our feet. We had plenty of food and didn't have to beg for any of it. Our white-country dollars converted to enough rupees that we could even eat in restaurants.

In our other life, if you saw someone lying on the ground or asking for money, you helped them. But you couldn't help everyone here. There were just too many.

Children our age were begging on the streets. It made you feel weird, and really sad they were doing that just so they could eat. You could see the difference between those kids and us was just chance. Like the puppies at Murchison. Tobey and I had been born in a fortunate country. We were the lucky puppies who had gone to the nice couple.

Mum and Dad loved India. Straightaway they were in their element. The architecture, the heat. How exotic everything was. We were so far from suburban Auckland, it was like being on a different planet. The colours were so intense here, they almost burnt your mouth.

Tobey and I liked how bright and spicy everything was too. We liked the food a lot. Our favourite place to eat was a canteen crowded with local office workers. Each of the Formica tables had a condiment holder with little pots of chilli sauces, ranging from hot to volcanic lava.

After we'd been to the canteen a few times, Tobey and I were allowed to sit on our own table. We'd look at each other with gleaming eyes.

'Bet you can't do a whole spoon of that green one.'

'Ha. Level or heaped?'

We'd keep ladling chilli onto our plates, daring each other to increase the burn. Even at four, Tobey was a dangerous opponent. We'd sit opposite each other, eyes streaming, noses running, until Mum would have to come over and tell us to stop causing a scene with all the coughing and choking and laughing.

Wherever you went in India, the place was packed.

It was like falling into one of our Richard Scarry's *Busy, Busy Town* storybooks. Every nook, cranny and patch of dirt had at least one person being industrious and hustling up some rupees on it.

There were so many people. And most of them were staring at you.

Waiting at the bank, walking along the road, sat in the backseat of a taxi parked down the alley behind a rug shop. Whatever we were doing, there'd be a bunch of people watching us do it. Basically, unless you were home, inside your room, with the door shut, there'd be someone staring at you. Mouth open, eyes bogged wide so they could stare extra hard. It was annoying, but you could sort of understand it: white children were rare. If we ever saw another white kid, we stared too.

If people were close enough, they'd want to twist our cheeks. It was meant to be friendly, but after Tobey got pinch-mark bruises on either side of her mouth, she'd flick her head away from their hands like a neighing horse.

Keeping Tobey safe was a bigger job now we were in India. There were so many more things she couldn't touch here. The dirt alone could kill you. Dad was always yelling at us not to touch our faces. Sounds easy, but maybe harder than you think. Especially if you're always a bit sweaty and you've got wispy, kid hair.

Where we lived in Bangalore, at the front of the mustard-coloured house was a small garden: a neat curve of lawn with oleander and Chandni bushes growing in the red dirt. It would have been a nice spot to play but as soon as we'd go outside, there'd be a raggle-taggle line of men standing on the other side of the gates, watching and chanting the begging-for-rupees song. 'Mar-mar, pisa, pisa.'

We played a lot in the bathroom. Getting clean took on a whole new allure. Dad was always sending us in. We'd groan at having to wash our face and hands *yet again*, then get distracted flicking water at each other until Mum would have to call us back out.

One day Mum let us stay in there all day. We went in to wash our hands after breakfast and didn't come out until dinnertime. We'd not been to a waterpark, but this was the level of excitement we were experiencing, slipping around on the white, soapy tiles. Not believing our good luck at still being in there.

Mainly though, you tried to avoid the bathrooms in India. The toilets were *bad*. It was hard to believe you could smell something so foul and still live. When Tobey needed to pee, you had to take her NOW. She didn't care who was watching, she had to go. One time we were in a hotel lobby, waiting for Dad to finish his meeting with someone in one of the rooms upstairs. I looked over to see Tobey pulling her skirt up and hoisting her little buttcheeks over the edge of a large potted palm.

Sunday morning was when the Magic Man came to the mustard house. He'd arrive with a grey monkey on his shoulder and a large, round wicker basket balanced on his turbaned head. One by one, he'd pull smaller baskets from its depths. He told us to be calm: it was *very* important to breathe slowly and never move suddenly.

Each basket contained a different snake, some we could hold, some we couldn't. This generally depended on whether he'd milked their poison recently. They all had fangs, but we never once got bitten. His piece de résistance – always brought out last in a flourishing finale – were the King Cobras. He would play his flute and the cobras would sway gently, rising up from the baskets. So elegant with their glittering eyes, their tongues flicking the air fast enough to blur. This was real, true magic.

Mum wasn't particularly interested in the snakes, but week after week Tobey and I sat cross-legged next to his baskets on the grass, in awe. Waiting for him to hand us the cool-skinned wonders that would wrap themselves around us. How heavy and strong they were was always thrilling. After an hour or so, Dad would pay the Magic Man the agreed rupees and he would promise to come again the following week.

One week he pulled out a fur pompom. He passed it to me and it sat easily in my palm, about the size of a small apple. It seemed entirely fluff, but then it opened its eyes and we saw the pompom was alive. It was hard to tell what kind of animal it was. He called it a baby pocket monkey, but any limbs or tail were obscured by ridiculously soft grey fur. We begged Dad to let us keep the pocket monkey, even after it had peed on my hand. We could not.

A few days later I found a sick baby rat. Back in New Zealand, I'd often carried home creatures in need of assistance. There'd be a faint cry or beep for help. Some poor little guy who'd faceplanted out of a nest or been dropkicked by their mother. It didn't always end well: you couldn't google specific care guidelines then, so I sort of guessed at what might help. My guesses generally involved keeping them warm and feeding them some kind of hideous, watered-down dog-food mix in an old eye-dropper.

Mum and Dad must have rolled their eyes to see me bringing home these ailing rescuees, tiny hearts fluttering in my hands, but they always let me stay up through the night, trying to save them.

I can't say there wasn't a vague awareness of the pestilence-potential this little sewer dweller might have: I'd read somewhere rats had been linked to more human death than all the wars combined. But *this* rat was just a baby, not very well (which should have been especially worrying) and really needed our help.

I carried the sick rat into the house in my cupped hands and asked if we could keep it in our room. Mum was appropriately horrified, but Dad overruled. Provided I washed my face and hands, thoroughly.

I put little Ratty in a shoebox with one of my socks and fed him some milk. He perked up overnight and looked like he was on the mend. By the second day he was up and running about in the box, taking naan bread with his milk. One more day and he'd be safe to set free. Whoohoo! Successful rescue.

That night we went out for dinner. We came home to complete darkness. While we'd been eating, a power cut had blown the bulb in our room. Mum went in first in case there was glass on the floor. Her Cuban-heeled boots clip-clopping confidently across the room towards her and Dad's bedside-lamp.

Halfway across the room there was a blood-curdling squeak.

We all stood there, frozen for a moment in the dark. Then Mum stepped forward and switched on the light, and we saw the horror of what lay on the tiles in front of us.

Poor, poor little Ratty had regained his health enough to want out. He'd chewed through the cardboard box and must have been on his triumphant escape back to the streets when we opened the door.

There was now a mash of pulverised meat where his tiny head had been: a long squirt of blood running from the top of his shoulders across the tiles. Mum had killed him. And it was a gruesome death. No milk and bread in the world would be bringing him back from this.

Tobey and I were put to bed sobbing while Mum got the Dettol and toilet paper out.

She felt bad. 'That rat should never have been in here.'

Dad chuckled, nodding at Mum's blood-splattered heel, 'Least it was a quick, stylish death.'

★

In 1977 parts of the world still felt wild and unchartered. Travel felt intrepid. You could arrive somewhere with literally no idea what you'd be finding. Often we'd be the only white people. We rarely saw other western children.

We'd make the necessary trips back to Auckland or London, but never for long. As far as our grandparents were concerned, we were based 'overseas'.

If anyone asked, Dad was an antique dealer. No one ever asked what Mum did for work.

Sometimes Dad told people he was a freelance photojournalist, on assignment from *National Geographic* or *TIME* magazine. That was OK for us to say too, and most people seemed to like it better as an explanation for all the travelling.

In another life, Dad working for those magazines might have been true. His pictures of us were consistently devastating. Dad was all about the arty angle or the gotcha-while-you-weren't-looking shot. He had a rare talent for making even Mum look awkward. But his landscapes were strong, and we went to places that commissioning editors would pay to see. The Hasselblad camera and all the fancy lenses were a hobby though, I don't think a single photograph was sent to a magazine. I don't think Dad even thought to send them.

Sometimes Dad told people he'd been a photographer in Vietnam, he'd pull up his trouser and show them his prosthetic leg as proof. They'd gasp at the shiny pink fiberglass and he'd shake his head regretfully, telling them how unimaginable it really was over there in the jungle.

We knew that wasn't how Dad lost his leg. But it wasn't always easy to keep track of what was right. Once a story had been repeated enough times, it could start to feel real for everyone.

There were things we accepted as kids. Parts of the family history that seemed reasonable, but might have been a version of the truth that didn't involve much truth. Some stories were farfetched, but then a lot of the things we saw happen around us were stranger. Mostly it all blurred together. Every so often, you'd have to stop yourself and ask, is that *really* true? What I'm telling myself. Did it *actually* happen?

One time I was talking to some people in an airport lounge, chatting away. They had lots of questions. Other white people in hotel lobbies and airports usually did. At one point the man said, 'Gosh, is that really true?' I remember nodding my head enthusiastically, but wondering myself.

You wanted to keep a picture in your head that was real. And to tell as few lies as possible. But mainly you wanted to give people the most normal-sounding explanation you could, so they didn't keep looking at you like you and your family were a bunch of weirdos.

★

The first time we went to Bali, our accommodation was about as basic as you could get without actually hiring out a jail cell. A damp-stained, musty-smelling room on the outskirts of Kuta. Two narrow cots in a windowless box. A single lightbulb, buzzing with bugs and mosquitos, dangled from the end of a chewed-up length of cable.

To add to the cell-like ambience, the toilet was a hole with two grimy feet spots, one either side; a large brown cockroach with its feet up, doing a slow dying dance on the left spot. The shower was a bucket of cold water and a hand scoop. Instead of toilet paper, you cleaned yourself with a second scoop and a smaller bucket of water.

Scoop washing turned out to be fine: it didn't take long to get used to this way of doing things, but I never got used to the cockroaches. Dad lifted up the thin foam mattress on our first night and there were hundreds of them. Scattering under the light. Big ones, little ones. All glossy brown: flicky antenna-ed and scuttle-ly. Dad got a few dozen with his shoe. Splat, splat. Tobey and I stood at the foot of the bed and watched in horror. Within seconds the base of the bed was evenly spattered with bodies. Dad flopped the mattress down over the still squirming legs, put our pillow back in place and told us to get into bed.

I wanted to cry. 'What about the cockroaches?'

'They don't bite. You'll be fine.'

We were so tired, we just clamoured into bed and fell asleep.

The next morning, I surveyed the sticky dead bodies we'd slept on with fresh horror.

Generally, I wasn't a big fan of killing things. There was plenty of death around already without me adding to it. And it felt mean to squish the life out of some little guy who was just trying to get by and be an insect in a tough world. Easier to carry them outside. But cockroaches. Argh. They are the worst.

Indonesia was terrific though. Straightaway we loved it. When we first started going, most of Bali was undeveloped. There were tarmacked roads in Denpasar city and a few stretching out across the island, but most of the roads around Kuta were still unsealed dirt tracks. Kuta, Legian and Seminyak were separate areas then, not a long sprawl of shops and hotels. There was one road threading them together: a much-potholed dirt track that people mainly travelled on moped. Whole families would cram on a single scooter – maybe with their pet dog, the odd squawking chicken and a whole branch of bananas. Everybody cheerfully tootling around the crater-sized potholes together.

There were westerners back then, but travellers rather than tourists. If you drove half an hour out of town, the whole village would stop and gather round, as if you and your little white face were something hilariously odd. They were friendly and laughed a lot though. I never got the feeling they didn't like us, they were just curious.

Food-wise, Tobey and I were in heaven. A lot of new fruit to try: salaks that looked like garlic-shaped brown snakes but tasted like lemony apples. Citrus called jeruk that were bigger than our heads. Spiky red rambutans that looked like creatures from space. Hundred-pound green and yellow jackfruit… All of it tasted superb. And dinner was served in banana leaves. No plates! Plates were for losers! Whoohoo. We were nasi goreng and gado-gado-chomping fiends.

As Dad's business increased, our accommodations improved. The next time we went back to Bali we were in a losmen guesthouse in Legian. Our room was a traditional hut made entirely from woven bamboo. The walls and door were bamboo, the ceiling an intricate masterclass of bamboo. Even the beds were bamboo. It was like sleeping in a beautiful basket.

At the time there was a spate of pencuri raids up and down the island. Gangs of thieves who would boat across from neighbouring Java island to rob the westerners. There were only a couple of fancy hotels back then, so these pencuries must have been really, *really* poor because any westerner they found would likely be a scrappy, twentysomething backpacker with a few dollars in their pocket. According to stories, these pencuries were tough. They didn't just rob their victims, they killed them. Quickly and mercilessly.

Tales of the murders spread like wildfire among the westerners. Attacks always happened at night. The pencuries were deadly and ninja-silent in their approach. We were told about a young couple found in bed with their throats cut. Their passports and a small camera missing. Apparently the pencuries hadn't even come through the door. They'd sliced open the bamboo wall of the couple's room using the kind of long curved parang machete that local men hacked open coconuts with. Someone said a woman was murdered ten minutes' walk from our losmen; she was found still pinned to a tree, skewered there by a knife through her neck. It was horrible.

There was camaraderie among travellers back then. The assumption that anyone staying in the same off-the-beaten-track losmen as yourself was probably likeminded enough to warrant staying up with. They'd come together around a few burning mosquito coils, talking and getting high, before everyone moved on to their next place. And Mum and Dad were all about the night-time; that's when they really came alive.

It had always been fine when they left us alone, but now I started to get scared. Obsessed with the terrible ninja pencuries. During the day I'd see the coconut-cracking machetes casually lying all over the place, so I knew the pencuries would have plenty of available weaponry. Even the sweet old guy who dropped off our fruit in the mornings wore a two-foot one looped through his sarong.

Tobey had become an outstanding sleeper. Sometime around her second birthday she woke up one day and decided sleep was cool. Bosch. Done. Instead of not wanting to sleep *ever*, now she was able to sleep anytime, anywhere, no matter what was going on. She made it look as easy as closing her eyes. I'd watch her amazed. One minute she'd be looking a bit bored, next she'd be out cold, entirely unconcerned by everything.

So Tobey would roll over and be half asleep before Mum and Dad had even got out the door. I'd lie awake on high alert. Watching the geckos scamper about on the basket ceiling and listening to the noises of the night.

All I could think about was how easily one of those machetes would slice through our wispy bamboo walls. And how dark and jungle-y the paths were outside. I knew Mum and Dad were only six huts away, but I also knew Tobey and I would be well dead, blood gushing from our severed necks by the time they made it back. Assuming I even got the chance to scream for help.

I kept imagining the dark machete blade glinting through the pale bamboo as it cut towards us.

The geckos were cute, but I had a feeling that when it came to the crunch, they wouldn't give a shit. I pictured the sprays of blood spurting out above our bed, splattering their little grey bodies.

Them slowly blinking their lizard eyes and tiptoeing away. They'd be no help.

Obviously, I had to protect Tobey. But what would that involve in this case? Should I run at the pencuries to give her a chance to escape? The trouble was, Tobey always took ages to wake up. Also, there'd probably be too many pencuries for her to dodge. Would it be best if she slept through the whole thing? But waking up dead would be upsetting. Worse than the time I was napping in the Kombi and got woken up by a wasp stinging my hand…

I never slept until Mum and Dad were safely back, giggling and drunk from their socialising.

But when the morning sun came up, it was another day. Epic, coconut-fringed blue skies. Black rice with sliced banana, roasted peanuts and palm sugar for breakfast. Then a single-file trek through rice paddies to the beach and swimming. The place was paradise.

At sunset we'd walk down the beach towards Kuta where all the warongs and places to eat were. As the sun dipped below the sea, the sky would be fiery reds and gold. The wet sand beneath our bare feet tattooed with intricate patterns made by countless tiny hermit crabs.

We'd walk back with our tummies full of spicy nasi goreng. There was minimal public lighting, so the nights were dark and full of sound. A constant call of frogs and geckos. We'd be sleepy, looking up at the deep, soft sky: darkest velvet blue twinkling with a million diamond stars.

The surf would be on our left, the line of coconut trees swaying on the right. The air sweet with frangipani flowers and open cooking fires. Every so often Mum and Dad would share a magic mushroom omelette, but you didn't need drugs to see it was so beautiful your heart could burst.

The third time we went to live in Bali, we rented out a whole bamboo cottage even further up the beach in Seminyak. The cottage was surrounded by fields of electric-green rice paddy fields. Instead of windows, we had bamboo shutters and you climbed a ladder to a little sleeping platform where we slept on mats. It was glorious.

The kitchen was a kerosene campfire, a small bench and a series of buckets. Instead of plumbing, we had our own well outside where you hand-pumped for water. At night we lit kerosene lamps for lighting, which made it really cosy. You'd look out of the bamboo shutters and feel like we were a ship sailing through a sea of rice paddies.

A woman from the closest village came by one afternoon to see if we'd like her to cook for us. Mum and Dad said yes and once a week Nyoman made us incredibly delicious yellow curries.

Nyoman spoke no English, and our Bahasa stretched to about fifty words, but you could tell straight off she was terrific. She taught me and Tobey some swear words and let us help make dinner, but her best trick was peeing standing up.

Tobey and I were talking to her outside one day when she widened her stance a little – not hugely, just enough to allow a little yellow stream to pour down between her legs. Tight and controlled, not getting a splash on her sarong. She kept talking and smiling, then laughing at our reaction.

When it came to peeing, Tobey was hard to impress, but even she bogged her eyes at what Nyoman was doing, right there in front of us on the grass. Nyoman couldn't believe we didn't do it that way ourselves. She had a point. I practiced in the bathroom later – a roofless little room with the traditional bucket and scoop situation that we'd got quite used to – but peed all down my leg like a clumsy westerner.

★

There was a story that Dad had been contacted by a special branch of the government. This was before we were born. His academic grades had triggered some sort of monitor. He'd skipped off to do all sorts of psychometric assessments with this government agency, proving himself to be both whip-smart and morally flexible. The exact combination they were looking for, as it turned out. They wanted to send him to the US for special training.

'You two could've had American accents', Dad would laugh. 'If working for the US government wasn't such a *seriously* mucus-ball consideration.'

I'd think about this story with biting regret. Not considering for a second what this work might have involved. I daydreamed about the gloriously ordinary life we could be having in a nice suburban house. Dad going off to work in a suit, Mum staying home, baking cookies like Mrs Brady. Tobey and I growing up speaking like Marcia and Jan, with lovely wisp-free hair.

Thank goodness this never happened. Obviously. When I was older, I dismissed the whole story as about as fictitious as Dad's Viet Cong landmine. Then, years later, something happened that made it seem considerably more plausible.

Either way, the story we told about Dad being an antique dealer *was* legit. That was how we paid for the travel.

Dad had a knack for antiques. When it came to seeing an artefact's age and how it might be valued, Dad had the instincts of a cat burglar. He could spot a replica at fifty yards. It was as if the pieces spoke to him. He liked to hold their history in his hands, imagining the lives of the people who had touched it through the centuries. In terms of age, BC (Before Christ) was usually best.

Antiques with stories that interested him he'd hold onto for a while. There was a large oliphant horn – possibly excavated mammoth tusk – whose previous owners included ancient warriors. You could hear the horn for miles when Dad blew it. It filled the air with an otherworldly vibration that might credibly wake the Gods. *Really* not the kind of sound anyone on the verge of battle would want to hear coming from their enemy's camp. We travelled around with that for years.

I don't know where Dad learned to be as good as he was. He had an outstanding memory for the things that interested him (old things mainly). He would read books and catalogues and inhale in the facts. But mostly his ability felt innate and largely unearned. Similar to how he was with animals. Some things were just inexplicably drawn to him. One time he was digging a vegetable plot in the garden. An hour later he walked back into the house with something his spade had hit. Once we washed the dirt off in the kitchen sink, we saw it was an art deco jewellery box, intricately carved gold and inlaid with sapphires. We wouldn't have believed it in a book.

Around the time I was born, Dad developed an interest in Chinese ceramics. It's lost in the sands of time what drew him to this specialism. I doubt he was calculating the value of becoming an expert, but that's pretty much what he did. By the time I was four, he was being described in newspapers as a foremost authority. He consulted at Auckland Museum, adding to their collection of Ming Dynasty ceramics. He advised interested private parties. In one newspaper clipping he's putting together what's described as the most important collection ever sold in Australia and New Zealand, including, 'most likely the largest celadon-glazed offering plate in existence'. The photo shows Dad lifting a three-foot Yuan Dynasty dragon jar out of a tea chest. The jar is mid-thirteenth century, he's twenty-four.

That was our life. We didn't have toys (Dad: 'Strictly for mucus-balls'), but we were often surrounded by very, very valuable artefacts. From ceramics, Dad expanded into wood: carved bowls and primitive art. Anything related to death and sex were in high demand. Hello blood-stained sacrificial bowls and fertility symbols. I wasn't sure about all the jutting penises, personally, but everyone else thought they looked tremendous.

At first it was about finding pieces at auctions, in pokey little shops, bringing them into the light and cleaning them up. Then, it was about sourcing artefacts in the countries they came from. One thing leads to another, but it would have started entirely legally.

Dad didn't see it as a particularly innovative business model. Since way BC Jesus, people had been traipsing things about. Find something readily available in one place: spices, tea leaves, potatoes ...disentombed tribal bowls. Trot it off to a different place, where they have none of that thing. Sell it for a price that covers your expenses: shipping, living costs, bribes and various sundry overheads (including, perhaps, a group of tribal villagers with machetes hired to assist your escape back out of the jungle), and you're in business.

★

Late July we flew into London. All the shops were playing Abba's *Knowing Me, Knowing You*. Tobey and I were singing along by the time we'd got halfway down Oxford Street. The counter displays at Selfridges had glittery blue and green eyeshadows like Agnetha and Anni-Frid wore. The second the sales assistants turned their backs to serve real customers Tobey and I would jam our fingers into the testers, smearing our eyelids quick as we could. Dad would look down at his child-daughters horrified, but Mum thought we looked nice.

Two weeks later Elvis died. We were walking through Leicester Square. Mum heard a newsman calling out, saw the headline and burst into tears. We couldn't understand why some old-fashioned singer in America was affecting our mother so much. She was talking about his hips and how he'd changed the world. We'd never even had an Elvis Presley cassette. To make us all feel better, Mum took Tobey and me to see *Sinbad and the Eye of the Tiger*, which was pretty good.

We spent a lot of that summer with Dad's friend Owl. His full name was Alistair so maybe he spelt it Al, but that way of writing it never occurred to me. He was Owl, and he was ace.

Imagine Sam Elliott crossed with some old-school Hollywood icon like Errol Flynn or Cary Grant. That was Owl. Even a seven-year-old could see the man had style. He dressed with the kind of easy charisma you can't even pretend to have. He'd wear a silk scarf and make it look breezy. There'd be tailored corduroys and band t-shirts under a leather jacket and it never looked underdressed. Wherever we were, he looked just right.

Tobey and I didn't care what he looked like. The man was all about having fun. He addressed Tobey and me as 'the Monkeys' and would swing us around like we actually were simians. Somehow this was delightful. Dad didn't pick us up unless we were asleep and needed carting in from the car, so this was novel *and* delightful. Nothing ruffled Owl, everything was amusing. He was always laughing. The whole family adored him.

We were living close to Hampstead. Owl had a flat above a shop at the top of the hill. In 1977 Hampstead village felt like a great place to be. The shops and cobblestoned lanes were cute as a button. There was a nice mix of artists and little old ladies living up there: the scents of sandalwood and incense mingling peaceably with teacakes and extra-hold Elnett hairspray.

Workwise, Owl had an art gallery and dabbled in a few different concerns: he and Dad had met at a fine art auction at Sotheby's. Owl's work was all above board and legal, but seemed to involve a lot of late-night socialising.

We'd run up to knock on his door and he'd come stumbling down, rubbing his eyes. We'd all eat lunch together in the Pippin vegetarian café, then wander up to the heath if it was a sunny day. Hampstead Heath was the dream: you'd thread your way down a narrow laneway and find yourself in a Narnia of wide-open fields of tall grass. There were glades of ancient trees to explore and ponds looped like a big beaded necklace. Dad and Owl would lounge like lions on a hill, propped up on their elbows. Looking out over their grassy savannah kingdoms to the city in the distance, while Tobey and I ran around like loons.

Owl's face attracted attention. Waitresses giggling as they took our order, then forgetting what we wanted. Women on the street going red and tripping, ladies in the bookshop peeking glances over their paperbacks. Everywhere we went you'd see women flashing their eyes like headlights on high beam at him.

Owl flirted politely, but his heart wasn't really in it. In the winter he had gone behind the Iron Curtain and fallen in love with a Czechoslovakian ballerina. Things were complicated with their love. Being part of the Soviet State, Czechoslovakia wasn't somewhere he could easily visit, and the only way she could come to see him was if he married her. Which had turned out to be an expensive and bureaucratic process.

Tobey and I were looking forward to impressive things. We'd seen Owl barely glance at some very beautiful women. We couldn't wait to meet the goddess who had captured his affections.

When she finally arrived, we were confused. Ireniska was not like Owl at all. He was a hoot. She was cranky. He was tall. She was tiny. Our key soviet references were communist propaganda posters at the art gallery and babushka dolls, so we'd been expecting dark hair, rosy cheeks and a hearty, marching-in-the-wheat-fields vibe. Ireniska was blonde and blue eyed. Her skin so pale, she was almost see-through. She seemed as robust as a paper butterfly.

But then. Her voice was piercing. In the way a small baby can take over a whole plane, her voice filled any room. She had a lot of complaints. Fair enough, where she came from didn't sound terrific, with all the food shortages and dictatorship. And we sympathised with her about the harshness of the immigration process – Owl was now having to go through more expensive paperwork so Ireniska's mother could also come and live in his cool, open-plan flat. But according to Niska, everything here in London was unbearable too. It was too rainy, too sunny. No one in London served proper food. She longed for a soup made from garlic and raw eggs. We couldn't understand why she wouldn't love a break from that. Maybe a nice jacket potato or toasted sandwich? But *ne*.

Mostly she puffed cigarettes, narrowed her eyes and sharply observed things.

Ireniska was a dancer, but she didn't like to walk. She teetered about in her cloud of smoke on needle-sharp stilettos. Cobblestones were difficult. Anywhere grassy was out of the question. Dad wasn't particularly interested in going to the heath without Owl, so now we couldn't go either. That was a bummer. But the worst, most baffling thing about Ireniska was that she didn't seem overly smitten with Owl. She was always complaining about *him*. Our dear, practically perfect Owl.

When we left London a few months later, we'd been seeing less and less of them. She couldn't face coming out in the weather; he couldn't leave her alone in the flat. Tobey and I couldn't understand any of it.

★

From London it was back to India. We were going to fly into Delhi in the north and make our way southwards overland. Traveling down to Mysore, or maybe Kerala at the far tip of the subcontinent, and stopping off wherever looked good along the way.

One night in Calcutta, sitting in a restaurant, happily chewing a piece of naan, something bit me. It hurt so much, I screamed, thinking I'd been stabbed with a dagger. We never found what it was. Dad was up on his feet in a second, racing around, pulling back my dress, but there was just a red bite mark between my shoulder blades. The waiters said it was probably a fire ant.

We saw a lot of temples. Mainly for the architecture. From what I could piece together, religion was like fairies. You had to believe with all of your heart. Any doubts and it just didn't take. Problem was, which one did you pick? Travelling had made this a bit tricky.

The nuns had been clear on there being just one God. At school we'd prayed to a semi-nude man, pinned like a poor butterfly to a bloody cross. He had died because of our sins. His dad had created everything in existence inside a week, but hadn't saved him. Earlier, a six-hundred-year-old man had built a boat large enough to float his family and two of every animal, bird and insect over a drowned world. They'd held off eating each other for more than a year, but then things got a bit Virginia Andrews' *Flowers in the Attic*.

Here in India, there were hundreds of gods. Maybe thousands. They were superheroes, and all the comics were about their adventures and reincarnations. I really got into them. Some gods were blue, some part-animal or multi-limbed. They all had useful areas of expertise and their stories didn't seem more magical than arks and talking snakes.

The people in Varanasi believed just as faithfully in their gods as the nuns in Auckland had in theirs. There was also Allah if you were brought up Muslim. Who was right? I read mythology. There were more gods in Greece; Celtic gods, Roman gods, Egyptian gods, Viking gods. Superb stories. People didn't necessarily pray to Thor, God of Thunder anymore, which seemed a shame. Did that mean our current gods would also pass out of time and eventually become folklore?

Maybe Mum and Dad were wrestling with similar complexities when we got to Bangalore. They'd heard about the teachings of Sathya Sai Baba. He was all about uniting religions and love and forgiveness. Also, going to an ashram was pretty chic. The Beatles had made that sort of pilgrimage groovy AF. And Sai Baba's ashram in the village of Puttaparthi in Anantapur was *the* place to be. All four of us would benefit from some enlightenment.

Puttaparthi was only three hours' drive from where we were staying, but high up in the mountains and chillier than we were used to. As we drove upwards, the sunshine disappeared and dark clouds closed in.

It had been raining heavily before we arrived. It continued to rain. Along some pathways the mud was shin-deep. For a brief respite one afternoon, the clouds parted and the rain paused. Mum, Tobey and I bolted outside to stretch our legs and ended up hiking further up the mountains. Above our heads, the sky was full of circling eagles who must have been making a break for it too, desperate to stretch their soggy wings. Two hours later the rain bucketed down again and we scrambled back to the ashram, wet and shivering.

The ashram was segregated, so we didn't see much of Dad. We'd just catch glimpses of him down the end of a corridor or up front in the hall. Barely recognisable, rocking his new tunic and loose dhoti pants.

It was traditional clothes only, so Mum learned to tie a sari (securing nine slippery yards of silk to yourself is not as easy as it looks). She'd bought a lovely green and gold one that was getting lots of frowns for being a bit bright, but she looked very pretty.

The three women in the shop who sold Mum the sari had been giggling at how tall she was. They looked like children, not much taller than me as they skipped cutely around her, showing her how to fold the silk and pull it down demurely over her long legs.

Tobey and I had already been wearing traditional clothes. Mum got them for us in a bazaar in Delhi. But at the ashram we had to wear extra scarves to cover our arms. We were only four and seven years old, but our arms were still immodestly female and had to be hidden at all times, even when we were sleeping.

The whole family got cool, matching Bodhi-seed prayer necklaces to wear.

Sai Baba's thing was Vibhuti (materialising ash from his hands). Apparently, he did this several times while we were there, but I couldn't see jack. All the people were like, 'OMG. He's a god, we're in a room with a living *god*'. It was exciting to be in the same room as a god, but the room was massive. A large hall really. And women had to sit in the back half of it. So when Sai Baba was in the room with us, he was just a distant figure up the front in a long orange dress. About four inches tall. At one point he walked down the length of the hall; we were sitting near the path he took and I got a little pat on the top of my head.

Everyone sat on the concrete floor. You weren't allowed to bring cushions in, not that we had any, but still. The vibe was very much about being uncomfortable and devoted. Which meant sitting head bowed, legs crossed on the cold concrete for a very long time. Sometimes we chanted.

Each time Vibhuti happened, cries of adoration rippled back from the front, everyone bowing their foreheads to the concrete with joy and wonder. The holy miracle was wasted on me. I knew I was an unworthy philistine, but ash felt a bit pointless. Sai Baba seemed like a nice man, but it wasn't exactly wine from water or feeding us all some nice fresh-baked baguettes.

Bread would have been welcome too, because food here was watery dahl and cold chapattis morning, noon and night. Occasionally there was a piece of fruit or some dates, but generally ashram life seemed to be about being bored, cold and a bit hungry.

Luckily, Mum and Dad weren't having a riot either. No smoking, no drinking and no drugs of any sort were permitted at the ashram. Men and women were almost entirely separated. I don't know what the men's situation was, but we were sleeping on thin cotton matts on the floor. Showers were icy cold. There were silent periods every day when you couldn't speak. At all. For *hours*.

The place just wasn't much fun. Tobey and I were hugely relieved when Mum and Dad decided to bunk off our enlightenment a week early. We squelched out into the mud, running down the hill with our hurriedly packed bags – arm scarves flapping to the winds – to hail a tuk-tuk to the train station. Mum and Dad puffing furiously on their cigarettes the whole way back to Bangalore.

★

Hotels were getting pretty familiar. By the end of 1977, we were spending more time in rooms rented by the night than by the month.

Mum made everywhere feel like home. Within a minute or two she could make a stark hotel room feel warm. We'd still be washing our hands (Dad: 'With hot water. *Hot* water! Plenty of soap'). She'd have scarves draped over the lamps throwing soft patterns across the walls. The furniture would be dragged into optimum arrangements. Grander designs occurred if we were staying more than a few days. Mum had a talent for creating atmosphere: in another life, she might have been a great set designer.

In New Zealand, we'd planted vegetables in our various backyards. We weren't always around long enough to eat them, so you tried not to get too attached. Sometimes we'd move into somewhere with something left behind from the last people: like a fruit tree or the big orange pumpkins we lived off in Murchison. So maybe it all worked out.

At one point Dad planted trees over 231. Partly to compensate for all the toilet paper we wasted.

(Poor Dad, if he knew how much we *actually* used he'd have passed out. He'd be at the bathroom door, yelling under the gap, 'One square. You only need *one* square.' I'd be in there, lavishly unravelling a minimum of four every time. Tobey was worse. At least I felt guilty.)

There was a sapling planted for each of the Starlings. Mine was the weedy-looking macadamia next to the washhouse. No matter how much water I gave it, the tree wouldn't grow an inch. Then I found out it would be twenty years at least before I'd get a single nut out of it. 'The mere blink of an eye for a tree,' said Dad happily.

The first thing Mum would always do at a new house was scrub the place from top to toe. Especially the bathroom and kitchen. If we were still there a few weeks later, the furniture would get moved around again. Some arrangements were more successful than others, but after Mum's tidy-ups everything looked fresh. You got a whole new perspective. The same chair could look surprisingly different in a new spot.

Dad was usually the one most surprised. Coming home at night in the dark, he'd walk straight into the table that had been under the kitchen window when he left, but was now sitting in the middle of the lounge. We'd hear a yelp of pain and snuggle back down in our beds, knowing Dad was home safe.

When it came to leaving, things happened fast. You'd overhear Mum and Dad talking about the next place and know tomorrow would be our last day in the current one. We had to move smoothly. Dad didn't like scenes: being back on the road should take no more than an hour. It must have been harder for Mum, rolling all those scarves and decorative furnishings into a tight bundle. But she was a ninja packer and took it all in her long, easy stride.

Tobey and I each had a Globite case, like the one Paddington Bear rocks up from Peru with. Tobey's was red, mine a dignified royal blue. Everything had to fit in our cases. There'd be gruelling choices each time we packed. Whittling our belongings down to a 16x12inch rectangle wasn't easy. Anything that couldn't be jammed, twisted and origamied in, didn't get to continue its journey with us. Nothing too heavy that you couldn't carry yourself.

It wasn't that we were preparing for a biblical exile across the desert of the world. Travelling light was healthy. Sentimentality wasn't cool. For Mum and Dad, it was always about forward movement. They never looked back. Tobey didn't seem bothered either. The only one of us even slightly troubled by such mucus-ball mentalities was me. I'd think about the things we left behind for years. I *still* miss *The Adventures of Ernest in Africa*, a square picture book too wide to fit in my case. There was something about the story of a brave photographer (Ernest) on a mission to photograph the notoriously publicity-shy sultan of Zanzibar that really spoke to me.

I started doing this thing, whenever we left somewhere, where I'd find an excuse to sneak back in and just stand there in the emptiness for a minute. I knew we'd never see it again. I liked to say bye, and wish the place well. Sometimes I'd run my hands over things, a kitchen bench, a chair, but mostly I just closed my eyes and thought about what had happened here.

I'd read somewhere that in the early days of photography, people believed that when a picture was taken of a person, a part of them was kept in the photograph. Like a shadow from that moment, locked forever into the glossy paper. Homes could feel like that.

Walking through the empty rooms, it was easy to imagine all the things we'd said and done swirling around me. Like tiny pieces of paper: the bits of us that we'd never see or be again.

Obviously, I kept *those* uncool ideas to myself.

If ever I felt too mopey about it all, I'd think about 231. Solid and sure on the side of the mountain back in Auckland. However far we travelled, there'd still be the bunchy blue-and-white hydrangeas growing outside the washhouse. Next to my weedy macadamia, that still wouldn't have budged an inch.

There'd be the overgrown rockery curving up to the old pear and grapefruit trees. The pothole at the top of the driveway that filled with hot-chocolate-coloured water every time it rained. Those reliably just-out-of-reach plums, dangling off the dark-leafed tree by Nanny and Poppa's backdoor.

It was soothing how 231 always stayed the same.

★

When we flew, Mum always asked for separate seats. Tobey and I would sit in a pair. Mum and Dad would be together in another row nearby. It was brilliant. Tobey and I always pretended we were flying solo, like two grown-up ladies.

We had our favourite airlines, and all variations were keenly anticipated and much discussed. Inflight entertainment was pretty universal back then: wherever in the world you were flying over, probably what you were craning your neck at was a blurry projection of *Storm Boy* or *The Towering Inferno.*

Mainly Tobey and I judged an airline on whether they had cologne and free toothbrushes in the toilets, and if a kids' pack was handed out. The best flights saw us disembarking down the airstairs smelling like guilty salesmen; clutching a mini colouring-in book and five-pack of crayons. Flashing our sparkling teeth.

Swiss Air gave you proper drawstring pouches with a wooden toy *and* a chocolate. If the attendant liked you, flying Qantas could mean a jetsetter pin or a tiny plane. Thai and Singapore Airlines were usually ace and had crazy-pretty flight attendants. Local airlines in India didn't give you anything, but on one of those internal flights, the passenger in the seat next to you could be a live rooster in a basket. So, there were upsides.

Whatever the airline, we always liked the food. Even if it was enigmatic mush, the little containers were so cute, like a doll's tea party. Packaged up like single-serve gifts. If Dad was seated near enough, you'd hear him narrating the arrival of all the unnecessary plastic used to wrap the, 'PRETEND, PLASTIC-TASTING FOOD!' but Mum usually let us eat it.

Tobey and I would hear people say all airports were the same. Amateurs. Dilettantes. *Tourists*. Sure, there were similarities: the lighting (universally harsh), the ambience (grumpy; air-con set to chill), the architectural stylings (see lighting). But beyond this was a spectrum to enjoy. Just for instance, Singapore's Changi International's delightful indoor carp ponds and potted orchids.

The best airports were either vast or very small. Miles to roam or basically a shed with an airstrip, so you could stalk across the tarmac and up the steps to your plane like a secret agent on a top-secret mission.

Hotel assessment was another area of much discussion. Once budget allowed, the pairs plan applied here too, with Tobey and me down the corridor in our own room. Again, there were single-serve gifts. The shrunken bars of soap, the mini cans of fizzy drink (foreboden to imbibe, but perfect to play shop with). Sometimes there would be shampoos and shower caps. Or an adorably petite sewing kit.

One of our favourite hotels was next to the Bombay international airport. A ten-or-so-floor building that was shaped in a hollow circle, like a seventies-era colosseum. Inside the landscaped centre was a pool and lots of tropical foliage. Running free within the tropical foliage were rabbits, turtles and a couple of peacocks. You could swim and then go find some bunnies. An actual dream. We'd stopover for the night here, then fly out first thing the next morning. Pretty hard to beat *that* hotel experience.

★

It never occurred to me to wonder why we didn't spend time together as a family, doing 'kid' things like playing ball games or jigsaw puzzles. In fact, it looked vaguely disquieting to see other Dads down the playground, pushing their children on the swing or teaching them some sport thing.

The way to spend time with *my* Dad was to help him with the antiques.

This was delicate, highly privileged work. All talking was reserved for intelligent, non-irritating questions, specific to the work at hand.

Me: 'Da—?'

Dad: 'Empty vessels make the loudest noise.'

Me:

Similarly forebode was nose sniffing or feet shuffling. Dad detested unnecessary noise. Something like a tap dripping in the bathroom upstairs could spiral him into a deep rage he couldn't come back from for days.

Wherever we lived, if Dad had an office, it would be a hallowed place, not somewhere under Mum's dominion. An untidied mishmash of things competing for his attention. In Dad's office, mugs of half-drunk coffee could hide from the sink for days.

There'd be newspapers, piles of magazines and catalogues from art exhibitions all over the world, overflowing ashtrays, maybe an interesting bit of driftwood. Some pinecones, seashells, a swirl of ammonites. And of course, the antiques.

They would be all over the room. Perched on magazines, balanced on tea chests, stacked up on any free bit of relatively flat surface. Like little islands of priceless artefacts. My dream would have been to collect them all together and arrange them in orderly displays. Like I'd done with the wallets and duty-free Benson & Hedges multipacks on Norfolk Island. But that wasn't cool with antiques.

There was nothing more important than antiques. Each one was unspeakably precious. Priceless was a word Dad used all the time. It meant that there was a *big* price, but also that the history contained within the antique told a story far beyond financial value.

I helped with the cataloguing. Dad would say something like, 'Small ceramic temple jug, Grecian BC', and I would shimmy around between the islands, counting up all the temple jugs as quickly as I could. It was *super* uncool to miss any, or confuse them with one of the non-Grecian, fired-a-year-ago-in-some-local-hippy's-kiln coffee mugs.

The BC or AD thing was pretty simple. BC stood for Before Christ. For ages I thought AD was an acronym of After the Death (poor Christ!), but it's Anno Domini, Latin for Year of our Lord. Unless it was something Jesus might have actually had in his hands, like say, a holy grail, BC was usually best.

For someone who could not go fifteen minutes without telling us to wash our hands, you'd think Dad might be suspicious of anything that had sat in dirt for a dozen lifetimes, but when something was really old, it was fine. Two thousand years of grime made everything clean again.

Generally, I was too busy feeling privileged and edging around the office to ask myself about my own views on antiques. But if I had, I'd have realised that I wasn't overly keen myself. Some dusty-looking jug that a centuries-dead Greek priest had once used to anoint their favourite statue's feet didn't hold much excitement for me. The other thing with antiques was that they were very fragile.

Part of the cataloguing job was to photograph every single antique. Dad had a camera set up on a tripod, pointing at a small table draped with calico. Two eye-wincingly bright lights shone down. Each antique would be carried – carefully navigating the islands of things, plus various tripod legs and electrical cables – to the table for its close-up. Every angle of each antique needed to be shot for the cataloguing. Dad would look through the lens and direct me to tilt it further, or show it from the bottom, or the other side, or whatever. He would take the picture, and we would keep going until all angles were done and we could move onto the next antique.

One afternoon we were doing plates from the Ming Dynasty. Shiny little blue and white ones. Smaller than a dinner plate, about the size of a teacup saucer. Quite pretty, if that was your bag.

I was putting them back on different surfaces, but I was running out of places. You couldn't stack them on top of each other like normal plates because they might chip or crack. A catastrophic thought. Especially since some of them already had cracks that Dad had been up all night painstakingly brushing with sheets of 24-karat gold leaf.

I didn't want to bother Dad with my storage problems: I was trying to be as efficient as possible. Something else Dad despised was careless work.

The next plate I picked up was thinner than the last dozen we'd just done. So thin and glossy it felt more like a brochure than a plate. Holding it under the hot lights, I concentrated on not leaving waxy little fingerprints on its delicate blue patterns.

Once we'd taken the plate through its different angles, I let out a breath, relieved to be getting it out of the bright lights and safely back to its home on a pile of *Christie's Fine Art Auctions* catalogues.

As I spun around, stepping backwards, towards the catalogues, the plate slipped.

I'd had it in both hands like I was meant to, but not properly. Not palms *and* fingers. Just fingers. And just the tips of them.

In terrible, heartbreakingly slow motion, the plate slid through my inadequate grip and down to the rug.

It hit the rug and flopped like a dying lotus, once, twice. Then lay still, jagged into pieces in front of our matching horrified faces.

I looked at Dad, my eyes wide. He looked at me with matching bogged-out eyes.

There would be no gold-leaf rescue for this little Chinese plate. It had made it through five hundred years: great wars and upheavals. But here, in this backroom in Auckland, New Zealand, was where its noble journey ended.

It was years before I was allowed to help again. Dad couldn't even bring himself to look at me. Not so much as a glance at the side of my head for weeks.

1978

Death and earrings

By early 1978 Dad was acquiring for The British Museum. These guys were the ultimate collectors. The rarer, the older, the more primitive and gruesome the better.

Things were getting a little blurry on the legalities side. You weren't really supposed to take artefacts from their country of origin. Tea-chesting them off to Bloomsbury, central London, was frowned on, even in the seventies. The museum were interested, but if there was any trouble, they'd be denying all knowledge.

We went to a lot of museums. In our regular life, not just for Dad's work. It was the one touristy thing we always did. Every city we visited, however small or old it was, you knew we'd be spending a chunk of our time at their museum. Dad studying the decrepit artefacts and fossils, explaining details to Mum. Both of them laughing and enjoying each other's fascinating company. Tobey and I trailing behind, scuffing our shoes, bored out of our tiny minds.

The best thing about museums was that they – along with art galleries, libraries and cinemas – were places Tobey and I could be dropped off at for a bit. Mum and Dad would pull up the car, Tobey and I would hop out and they'd come back for us a few hours later. Seeing a movie was the dream, but some of the museums were fun too.

Our favourite was in New Zealand. On the top floor of the Auckland Museum was an olde-worlde wing, coated in a thick layer of dust. We couldn't believe our luck when we discovered it one rainy afternoon. There were all these tiny houses, barely illuminated by yellowy flickering electric candles, populated by spooky waxwork people. They were frozen in time doing olde-worlde things, like hammering horseshoes or churning plastic butter. Busy, but *very* still. Their shiny faces locked in strange, doll-like grins.

Everything was slightly smaller than real life, but otherwise realistic, apart from all the dust. The place was laid out like a village, and you had to climb through ship-cabin-like doorways into each tiny dwelling.

No one else seemed to like the village. Tobey and I usually had the place to ourselves (apart from the little waxy people). Not even a museum guard. The whole village was dark and shadowy. Kind of like a horror film. We loved it. We'd climb up the stairs to the windowless top floor and creep around together, whispering about the lives these olde-worlde people would have had with their buckets of dusty butter and fussy-looking clothes; daring each other to touch them.

The other great thing about Auckland Museum was the large wharenui downstairs on the ground floor. An entire Māori meeting house that had been nicked from some poor tribe somewhere and reassembled inside the museum. The fake firepit glowing in the centre gave off its only light. A recording of traditional Māori war songs howled out of hidden speakers in the ceiling every so often. It always made you jump when it came on, but it was superbly atmospheric. You could totally picture the brave, ancient Māori warriors chanting themselves into a towering rage before leaping into their long canoes and paddling off to tear their enemies apart.

Probably the museum that Tobey and I spent the most hours wafting around was the one in London. Waiting for Dad to conclude his business downstairs, behind closed doors.

The British Museum's vast wings held many treasures. But left to our own devices, we'd always gravitate to the Egyptian galleries. Dad disapproved of this wing. According to him, Egyptian stuff was entry-level antique. Strictly for amateurs and the elderly. The Agatha Christie set. People who liked Egyptian antiques, he said witheringly, were the same people who collected Meissens (when he said this, I always thought of his mother, Nanny Starling, with all her porcelain figurines rattling in their glass cabinets back at 231).

Tobey and I were secret members of the Agatha Christie set. We thought Egyptian art looked nice, and the mummies were thrilling, lying there in their bandages with all their organs sucked out.

In Manila, Dad acquired a real-life, non-Egyptian mummy. She was curled up in a foetal position. Instead of bandages she'd been tattooed head to toe with blue tribal lines and swirls. Even her face was tattooed. Which felt pretty bold to me then. I don't know how old she was when she died, but when Dad shipped her out of the Philippines, she was hundreds of years old. Beautifully preserved, in smoke apparently. You could still see her eyelashes, and nails on her fingers and toes. Her eyes were all dried out like muscatel raisins. Her skin felt like soft old leather. Which I guess, it was. She looked sad and very tired, too tired to be travelling all the way to Bloomsbury in a wooden crate.

There wasn't much room in the flat we were staying in Manila, so I was sleeping on cushions in the living room. For a couple of nights before we flew out, the mummy and I were roomies. Sleeping next to each other on the floor. Me on my cushions, she in her wooden crate, nestled in packing straw. I ran my fingers over the raspy wood of her crate as I drifted off to sleep. It didn't occur to me to worry that she might wake up in the dead of night and curse us all. I doubt it crossed any of our minds.

It was good practice for sleeping under Charlie, my aunt Erin's skeleton a few years later. Erin had moved to Sydney at this point and was getting an osteopathy degree. All the serious students had their own skeleton.

When I stayed over at Erin's, I'd sleep on the sofa with Charlie the skeleton dangling over my head. When he was alive, Charlie had lived somewhere in India. I'd look up at his bony feet and wonder about his story and if I'd been to the place that he was from. Would he have been surprised to end up hanging on a metal stand in a one-bed flat in Potts Point, Australia? You had to hope that he'd agreed to his remains being used for medical science. And yes, he did have a lovely view out the window onto the harbour, but this was such a long way from his home.

I had a soft spot for skeletons. Despite all the death. Dad had come into possession of a string of tiny skeleton heads. They looked like ivory, but the mini skulls had actually been carved for a pirate king out of human bone, then polished up to a beautiful shine. Dad had the bone tested: it was legit human. Mostly femur. Did the pirate king wake up one morning and think, 'Lo, a necklace of human-bone skulls would really finish my look.' Or did he have a nemesis he hated so much, he had to make jewellery out of them? Either way, I don't suppose *that* person had had much say in what would be happening to their remains.

Mum threaded the tiny heads into earrings and necklaces with semi-precious stones like garnet and lapis lazuli. It wasn't like the poor sod wasn't already at least a century dead. The earrings looked so cool. I was desperate to have a pair, but Mum put the kibosh on that idea. The earrings were far too big for the structure of my face. Years later Mum did let me have a pair, which I loved, *loved*, but like almost all my earrings, eventually lost. A loss I mourned for years.

Mortality was a thing to ponder as we swished around the museums. Did it matter what happened to your body after you'd finished with it? Would I want to end up swinging from someone's ears? Probably I'd be more concerned with the harsh machete death I was about to experience.

There wasn't much existential musing for the Bloomsbury buyers. Death was big business there. Mostly Dad traded ceramics and wood. Mainly from independent local dealers. Sometimes more extensive fieldwork was required. Another of Dad's afterlife-themed acquisitions were the ceremonial grave doors from Sulawesi, an Indonesian island east of Borneo, where there was a village of living and a village of the dead.

Dad had heard about a funeral tradition in Sulawesi which involved wooden effigies carved in the likeness of their dearly departed. To be as realistic as possible, the effigies were finished with the deceased loved one's hair and dressed in their clothes. When the human bodies were buried, their effigies were taken to seats cut into a cliff where they could look out protectively over their still-living families.

The tribe also honoured their dead by keeping their bodies at home with them for years *before* burial. But that's a slightly different story.

In 1978 the remote highlands of Sulawesi weren't an especially easy place to get to. After an overnight boat from Bali, Dad and his local guides needed to canoe around the peninsula, then use their machetes to cut a path through thick jungle.

He'd hoped to get a family of effigies. But no matter what Dad offered to his contact from the village, not a single effigy was for sale. Even the very old ones were still distantly related to someone living. There was no way Dad's contact was taking on that sort of bad juju. The grave doors covering the bodies of the human, non-effigy, relatives would have to do.

When Dad and his men went back later that night to collect the doors as agreed – creeping around the jungle at 3am with some hastily chiselled replica doors they could switch them out with for – they were surprised by warriors from the tribe wielding their own machetes.

With two chunky wooden grave doors between them, Dad and his guys ran for their lives. Just making it back to their canoe. As the only white man anyone had seen for years, Dad had probably stood out as suspicious to the village. Perhaps not unfairly so.

★

Our situation couldn't have been unique, but we didn't see anyone else living like we did. If we saw other western kids, they were on holiday. On their way back to their schools and homes, and regular lives.

We would have been well up for playing with local kids, but that didn't happen. Mainly, probably, from shyness: they never asked us and we never flung ourselves on them. We'd see children in places like Indonesia and India, so sweet-looking, marching off to school in their spotless white uniforms. They all looked so neat and even. No one was fat or particularly tall, they all had the same colour hair. Wisp-free. Standing next to them we would have just looked messy and weird. Plus, there was the language thing.

So friendships were rare. The brilliant exception to this was a Dutch family we first met in New Zealand. Two parents and two daughters. Just like us… If you overlooked their healthy family discipline and structure. Oh, and they didn't do drugs: Lars and Liva hardly even drank alcohol.

Sofie and Hana didn't go to school either, but Lars and Liva home-schooled them. *Really* home-schooled them. Tobey and I were meant to tell anyone who asked that we did school via correspondence, but for Sofie and Hana it wasn't just a cover story. They actually had lessons. Every day.

As well as their native Dutch, Sofie and Hana spoke English as well as we did. Some French too. They did things as a family. They sat for mealtimes and talked things over. Sofie and Hana were expected to have opinions. Lars and Liva were strict, but they invested time and effort into raising their daughters. They even sat together on planes. It was weird.

Mum and Dad were always going on about how good Lars and Liva's girls were, and how crap we were in comparison. I could see what they meant. Sofie and Hana *were* incredibly polite and always so clean-looking with their perfect skin and bright-white Dutch smiles. Sofie would never have mud-scrapped knees or bits of leaves in her hair. Hana wouldn't dream of peeing in a pot plant.

Sofie was a year older than me, Hana a year-and-a-half older than Tobey. There wasn't much in it, but almost immediately Sofie and I decided that our little sisters were babies and we were the mature ones. Mostly the four of us hung out together, but there was a constant undercurrent: Sofie and I always looking for an opportunity to slip away and be sophisticated together. A key driver in this was that our sisters were blabbermouths. Anything even slightly questionable would be reported back in grinding detail to our parents. For a rock-n-roll nihilist, Tobey was a real tell-tale. Sofie had similar problems with Hana.

Sofie was going to be a famous international fashion model when she grew up. A lot of people were going to take photos of her, she told me. Sofie was stunning so this didn't seem a stretch, but Lars didn't believe in objectifying female beauty. He had funny ideas about things. He said it didn't matter how we looked; we should be working on improving our brains, not our faces.

It was different in our family. Mum was beautiful. And clearly there was value in that. Dad loved Mum because of her beauty; her long model legs and her fiery red hair. Those were the things he complimented her on.

Mum seemed relaxed about this, but there was never, ever a day she didn't wear make-up. It was pretty natural: beyond the eyeliner, mascara and lipstick, there wasn't a lot of grooming. No foundation or blusher. She never owned a hairdryer. But what make-up she did wear, went on the minute she woke up. No matter what else was going on, whatever high-pitched drama might be unfolding, Mum dealt with it through dark lashes.

She saw the art of fashion and wore it well. Comfortably. For her fashion was fluid, like fast-moving rivers, to be appreciated but not held onto, never overthought. There'd be a handful of clothes, worn for weeks, then left behind for someone else to enjoy. No clothes were reserved for any particular activities: you'd see Mum out with the axe, chopping up wood for the fire or mowing the lawn in the same dress she'd wear to visit the bank manager or on a night out.

She would tear pages from *Vogue* – she was especially fond of the French and Italian editions – and take them to tailors in bazaars to reproduce with her amendments (adding pockets mostly). Often she'd draw up her own designs altogether. A lot of mine and Tobey's clothes were made to measure too. We weren't fans of these clothes. We wanted t-shirts and shorts, not lurex-striped disco jumpsuits.

Poor Mum. Her style was entirely wasted on us. She'd dress us up in scarves and jewellery that we'd shrug off and lose. Earrings especially. I don't know what it was about my earlobes, but they *could not* hold onto an earring.

Lars had banned Sofie from reading fashion magazines or practising 'her angles' in the mirror. She had to do this secretly at our house. It seemed a dull way to spend your time. But Sofie was older than me, so I figured I'd understand in time.

'Why do you even want to be a model?' I asked her one day, watching her perfecting her Jerry Hall arched eyebrow over and over in Mum's mirror.

'A *top fashion* model.'

'Why do you want to be a *top fashion* model?'

'I'll get to travel the world and make lots of money.'

'You already travel everywhere!'

'This will be different. I'll have beautiful clothes and be famous.'

Poor Lars. He and Liva had met in the Netherlands, doing karate. They were both seriously belted and would often still practise together. They weren't doing it to be sexy. It was a good thing for a woman to be able to protect herself, Liva explained to me when we all met up again in Indonesia. 'We travel in dangerous places,' she said. 'But also, for a girl, the whole world can be dangerous.'

★

Wherever we were. Night or day. Any chance we got, Tobey and I were in water. Surf was our favourite, but any body of water would do: swimming pools, tiny creeks, a bucket and scoop. We'd be there, splashing around for as long as we were allowed. We couldn't get enough of the feeling of water on our skin. Learning how to swim in an icy river hadn't put me off in the least.

We lived by the sea a lot. Neither of us had swimming lessons or a clue about currents and rips, but we always seemed to bob back up fine. Luckily Mum and Dad didn't believe in overly vigilant supervision. They were parents, not police, I heard Dad tell someone once. They trusted we'd come back safe, and we always did.

There were a few close shaves. Early on, years before the Buller River, there was the embarrassment of almost drowning myself a few yards from Mum's feet. She was with her friend Nancy, sharing some wine on the deckchairs. It was a large pool and I'd decided to leave the paddling area to undertake a detailed investigation of the deep end. I was crabbing my way around the pool's edge when I choked on some water, got distracted and lost my grip on the ledge.

Adrift, I started sinking towards the dark blue tiles under the diving board. Panicked flailing got me back to the surface where I bobbed about. I could hear Mum and Nancy laughing just yards away, but I was swallowing too much water to call for help. For a few minutes, or the whole of my life, I splashed about, mostly underwater. Finally, somehow, I managed to splutter myself back to the ledge and put the whole awkwardness behind me.

One morning in Sri Lanka, it was different.

It was a beautiful, wide-open beach with miles of space. You could walk for ages without seeing people, just stretches of sea, sand and sky. There was not a hint of lifeguard or yellow-and-red flag, but it never crossed our minds that we needed either to get in the water.

Straightaway Tobey and I could feel the undertow pulling around our legs. The waves were also coming in stronger than usual. With Mum and Dad back at the guesthouse, the rule was that we weren't to go in past our waists. I liked to keep to rules, but that one was a bit unrealistic. Firstly, each wave coming in meant we'd be in water up to our necks. Secondly, this morning the sand bed was dipped in places, like potholes, so we'd take a step and suddenly be treading water. But most of the time, we could both stand, which felt close enough to the rule.

There was a decent surf up. Each time a wave rolled in, we'd look at each other like two serious newsreaders, nod our heads gravely, then yell 'over' or 'under'. Over to jump up, gliding over the lip of the wave before it broke. Under to dive through, clean as two butter knives to the air on the other side.

We were vaguely aware of how far down the beach the current was carrying us, but not concerned. We'd just walk back up the beach when we were done swimming.

'What about our sarongs?' I fretted at some point. Tobey: 'Who exactly do you think's going to nick them?'

We looked up and down the beach and both laughed uproariously. There wasn't a speck of another person. We had the beach to ourselves.

Each set of waves was coming in a few minutes apart. Three or four waves would crash around us like foamy milkshakes in quick succession, then it would be calm again. You'd see the waves begin as wobbling bumps on the surface out at sea. Rising and curving up as they reached us.

We noticed a bump coming towards us that was bigger than the previous ones. Even at a distance it looked big. I realised we'd edged quite far out. With the tide coming in, it was a shock to see how far we were now from the shallows. We started wading backwards. Both paddling with our hands, scrambling to get back to waist-height water before the wave hit us.

The wave kept getting bigger. The pull of water being sucked up into it was dragging us out deeper towards it.

'It's fine,' I yelled. 'We'll just dive through.'

In my head I was screaming. *Shit, shit, shit.* How could I let this happen? We were way past our waists, this was very bad and all my fault. Hideous big-sistering.

Drawing itself up like a body filling with breath, the wave towered above us. I couldn't even grab Tobey to keep hold of her, because we'd need our hands to dive into it.

'Under, under!' we screeched at each other.

'Hard as you can!' was the last thing I shouted at Toby's panicked little face before the wave was upon us.

It came down like a thundering avalanche. Too big to dive through, we were tumbled and tossed, head over heels, like ragdolls in a giant washing machine.

I surfaced gasping for air and spun around, searching for Tobey's head. She'd been carried right back to the shallows. I saw she was safe, clambering to her feet in knee-high water. There was a split-second of relief before the next wave crashed down over me.

My face scraped along the sandbank, then up and down again. Head over heels, and over again. Arms and legs cartwheeling through the whitewash. I pushed against the sand and there was a flash of blue sky. I gulped for air, but swallowed saltwater as I went under again.

There was no chance for air before the third wave came. I got another mouthful of seawater as the churning white collapsed over me. Hitting the sand bed hard, my lungs were pounding and my nose was stinging with seawater. Arms and legs everywhere, everything screaming for air. I bounced along the sandbank again. Tonnes of water, hard as a muscle barrelled over me.

There was an absurd realisation that this might be it. That our fun little swim might be the last thing I ever did. Then everything went murky.

I came to on the wet sand. My sister and some stranger leaning over me. I blinked at their worried faces, then choked up a stomach of seawater.

The man smiled warmly, squeezed my shoulder and ran off down the beach, like this had been a minor interruption to his morning run.

I rolled on my side, coughing up more slimy water.

'What happened?' I sputtered.

'He just carried you out,' said the normally nonchalant Tobey, now bog-eyed.

From an otherwise empty beach, a man, a tall, long-haired westerner, had materialised. He'd seen Tobey standing on the edge of the water, taken in the whole scene, and dashed in to save me.

There couldn't have been more than a handful of other westerners on that part of the island. He'd been running past at the exact right moment *and* known what to do. Apparently, he'd carried me out from the waves in his arms, laying me down on the sand like he was a hero in some Hollywood movie.

Tobey and I looked down the beach in the direction he'd run, but he'd already disappeared in the morning haze. The whole thing was pretty strange. We walked back to our sarongs, my legs all rubbery.

'Don't tell Mum about this.'

'I won't.'

We were back the next morning, and the sea was smooth as glass. Even the sand looked serene. It was hard to believe there had even been waves.

1979

The year we bought a house

We were back in New Zealand and putting down roots. Buying a freaking house. Just like a normal family. Whoohoo. I was pretty excited.

With Poppa's help, Mum and Dad had got a mortgage and bought a rambling 10-acre property an hour into the agricultural wilds outside Auckland. Waimauku was going to be our forever home.

The house had been purpose-built at the turn of the century for a country doctor. There was the house itself, tucked away in the pine forests up the top of a long dirt driveway, then a two-bedroomed cottage, which had been his surgery, a ten-minute saunter down the hill, where the driveway met the public road.

By 1979, the property had fallen into hard times, and some pretty rough hands.

The sellers were a family of about a dozen closely related adults who'd all been taking a rugged stance against cleaning or household maintenance of any sort. They smelt bad. The house smelt marginally worse, like blood and rotting garbage, and you could see why.

They'd turned the kitchen into a makeshift butchers. There were full animal carcasses strung up and dripping onto the floor. There were buckets of congealing blood and offal. The living room was full of car and bike parts, and what looked like half a tractor.

Outside, the grass was strewn with beer tins, upturned fridges, car tyres and bits of rusting junkyard rubbish. Fat green blowflies droned through the air.

The 'mother' came to the door holding a meat cleaver that was slick with blood. There were sprays of blood across her dress. Both hands up to her elbows were stained and dripping like she'd been soaking them in the buckets of blood.

It was the stuff of nightmares. Mum and I had walked into an actual horror movie.

I grabbed Mum's arm, genuinely fearing for our lives. We needed to back away, keeping our eyes on that cleaver. We needed to jump into the car, and put the pedal down hard.

But Mum saw the bones of the place and, once we'd dragged out the tyres and rubbish, the outside space was lovely. I didn't think Mum would ever be able to get the inside clean. But she did. Room by room she swept through, pulling up the carpets and sanding down the wood floors, peeling back layers of wallpaper. Litres and litres of pine-scented disinfectant splashed through the house until the whole place shone.

The floorboards in the kitchen were beyond saving (the wood was literally too blood soaked), so fresh black-and-white tiles were laid.

There were plenty of hideous surprises along the way, but some nice ones too. Under the newspaper that had been glued to the windows in the upstairs bathroom were stained-glass art deco flowers. The plumbing actually worked fine in the bathroom: the taps just hadn't been run for a while. Outside, we found an elegant old brass bedframe in the tall grass. Once it was cleaned and polished up, it became Mum and Dad's bed.

Gradually the house and garden came together. Dad had a man with a yellow digger come and scoop out three large waterlily ponds (inspired by Monet's landscaping and painting efforts at Giverny). We helped Dad plant out the back field with neat rows of vegetables.

There was a hen house. We could have our own fresh eggs and live off the land entirely! After we cleaned it up and repaired the coop, Dad invested in a dozen beautifully fluffy white hens. On a similar self-sufficiency vibe, Dad also planted out a large plot of cannabis. For camouflage, he planted similar-looking tomato seedlings between the illegal ones.

Organic was hardly a buzzword in 1979. But the marigolds threaded in between the crops meant we didn't need to spray our vegetables with pesticides. There was sage growing with the carrots and cabbage. Angelica and scented geraniums attracted the ladybirds, and those cute little ladybirds hunted down aphids and mites for us with deadly precision. Apart from the odd rabbit, we had few issues with pests.

Dad had transformed into an expert of soil quality and natural fertilisers, and all the crops were a great success. The peas were sweet as lollies. The yellow beans bright and crunchy as apples. But the most discussed of Dad's triumphs were his cannabis plants. Like Jack's beanstalk they grew and grew, thicker and fuller each afternoon. Everyone would troop out to marvel at the lusciousness of them. Flopped out on the cushions afterwards, a few puffs in, everyone would croak on about how it was the best weed they'd ever had.

Interlaced with the cannabis and getting the same mulch and fertilisers, the tomato plants were also taking off. We had hundreds of red globes, dangling off every furry branch. More tomatoes than anyone could eat or carry away. Enough tomatoes to sauce an Italian village.

Dad would be desperately thinning out the tomato vines. Mum cooking with as many of them as possible. But much like their reason for existence in the first place, Mum's work had to be covert. Dad didn't like tomatoes. Couldn't stand them.

Equally tortured by the idea of wasted food, Dad would drop overflowing boxes of tomatoes at the local fruit and veg shop whenever he was in town. All our guests left staggering and laughing under the weight of tomatoes (happily patting their smaller bags of weed). Still, we couldn't keep up with the tomatoes.

Out front of the house, there was a delay on Dad's Monet ponds. The cement had been laid, but the waterlilies and goldfish weren't going to be delivered for another fortnight. Sad for Dad, but yay for us. Tobey and I had three swimming pools of our very own. All our dreams come true.

Even after the boxes of lilies and languid koi were put in, we could still splash around a bit when Dad wasn't home, the koi didn't seem to mind (they were languid). Then the freshwater crayfish arrived (to eat the algae and maintain superior pond health, said pool-hating Dad, cruelly).

We watched the crayfish, the size of lobsters, snipping furiously as Dad took the bands off their pinchers. They arrived in bad moods and only got angrier as time went on. I don't know how they got on with the fish, but any time we even *dipped* our feet into the water, they'd come scuttling over with their claws clicking.

It was still nice having the ponds though. My room was upstairs overlooking them, and first thing in the morning with smudgy sleepy eyes, they did look quite Monet-esque when the sunshine glinted off the water and all the pink waterlilies bloomed.

★

Like most of our other homes, there was usually someone around, staying with us at Waimauku. Usually interesting and well-travelled people. Staying up all night, smoking and laughing, sparkling and glowing around the fire. If I was very quiet, sometimes I'd be allowed to sit up listening and watching. One night a stoned adult announced that the kid should choose the next cassette.

I looked around. Everyone was gazing at me expectantly like the choice of a nine-year-old might provide some cosmic insight. Dad nodded that I was allowed.

I could feel my face burning from the pressure, but I knew my choice straightaway. I scrambled up, fished out the green spine of Nina Simone's *Baltimore* cassette that a guy in an underground record bar off Queen Street had recommended to Mum and me the week before.

I slid it into the stereo. The first bassy bars bounced across the room, Nina sang about a beat-up little seagull on a marble step, trying to find some ocean... Someone cheered, and I experienced the proudest moment of my life.

The next morning found me hopping up the concrete steps outside the kitchen. Imagining what it would be like to have no arms like a beat-up little seagull.

You'd think I'd have learned about stairs after careening off the back steps at the retirement home in the baby chair. Or another time when I'd sliced up my kneecaps running down escalators with a stack of library books. Alas, I had not. With all the beautiful nature to play in at Waimauku, I was seeing how many steps I could hop up in one go with my arms glued to my sides, seagull-style.

Hop, hop, hop. *Splat.* Right on my mouth.

There was the beat of shock, then a rush of pain. Before I could wail, the blood came. Mouthfuls gurgling out. As soon as I opened my mouth, it poured all down my dress. I staggered up the last step and into the kitchen. Gargling and spluttering blood.

Poor, poor Grannie May was in the kitchen, making lentil soup at the time. Thirty years of nursing hadn't prepared her for the sight of me standing there: the whole front of me, mouth downwards, drenched bright red, like a miniature Carrie.

I was carried through the kitchen and up to my bed. Spluttering up mouthfuls of blood across the black-and-white tiles as I went. A few hours later, now soaked in Dettol, I was carried back down and laid out on the kitchen table. One of our friends staying from the night before was a doctor from Africa. Along with a cassette by someone called Rodriguez that everyone was really digging, he'd brought his black medical bag.

The sensation of thread pulling through my face was weird, but I kept still and it was over quickly. Everyone was worried I'd be hideously scarred for life, and that whatever goodness there was of my face would be entirely ruined. But the doctor did a lovely job and the scar was soon barely noticeable. Half a fresh-grown front tooth had also been lost on the step. There was talk of a gold replacement, like Dad's, which I'd always thought fetchingly pirate, but Mum vetoed this, so I got a plain, boring white one.

★

Dogs liked Waimauku as much as I did. Our two terrific Dobermans moved in with us, but with all the space inside and out, Mum felt we should also be providing a home for a really big dog. The dog of her childhood dreams. Auckland appeared to be all out of Great Danes, but our new Irish Wolfhound was adorable.

Dad and animals went together like cheese and crackers. As a family, we were all big fans of animals. Almost all of them liked Dad best. Mum and us kids would feed them and clean up after them, I'd spend hours teaching them tricks. Dad would waltz in, give them a half-hearted pat and they'd fall over themselves in a heap of adoration.

Alfie was the first exception. He was friendly and doggy-nice to Dad, but you could tell from the first afternoon he bundled himself out of the truck and onto our lawn, that Alfie was a ladies' man. He was all about Mum and us girls. So probably the cards were stacked against him from the start.

He looked amazing. Part-dog, part shaggy polar-bear. He was large even for his breed, and his breed had originally been developed to drag men off their horses during battle. Alfie had such a chilled, sweet personality you couldn't picture him enjoying that kind of thing much though. Tobey would ride around on his back and he didn't mind in the least.

He was a bit clumsy: he'd come sit next to you and completely knock you over, but you could tell he just didn't realise how colossal he was. He thought he was normal size.

Every morning we'd hear him wake up downstairs and gallop up the stairs to see Mum. He'd run at full pelt down the corridor to Mum and Dad's room, and leap, sailing through the air onto their bed with them. It was a great sound, Alfie's massive white paws on the wood floorboards. You'd hear the bom-de-bom and then nothing for a second as Alfie was airborne. Then the shriek of the bedsprings and Dad's scream, followed by Mum's laughter. It was like clockwork: Tobey and I would be giggling in our beds listening to it every morning around 7am. Mum and Dad would tell him off, but Alfie never got the hang of not jumping on the bed and it always seemed to catch Dad unawares.

Things came to a head the week that Mum's beloved French lavender bushes all went yellow and died overnight (Alfie had peed on every single one; he must have gone down the row of them quite methodically) and Alfie broke the bed.

It was the same routine as every other morning: the paws galloping down the corridor, the shriek of bedsprings, the scream. But with the laughter, we heard a screech of straining metal. Then an almighty crash.

I ran to see what had happened. Mum and Dad and Alfie were lying on the floor in the remains of the bed. Mum was still laughing. Dad was fuming.

'That's it, Vivienne. That fucking dog has got to go!'

Poor Alfie. Tobey and I were very sad to see him go.

Next came a caramel-coloured Standard Poodle. We couldn't stop running our fingers through his teddy bear curls. Tobey said the bumps made him look like a camel, so we named him Tamel. Tamel the Camel was great fun, but very naughty. He didn't listen to any training and only ever wanted to play. He was also the Houdini escape artist of canines.

One night, Tamel the Camel somehow managed to slip out of the house and into the chicken coop. When we woke up, all twelve hens were dead. Murdered in their own home. There were red-slashed white feathers everywhere. It was hard to believe such a goofy dog had been such a hardened killer. He hadn't even been hungry. He'd done it for kicks.

Dad tied one of the poor dead chickens around Tamel's neck. Murderous Tamel was chained up with his victim for days. Tamel suffered greatly for his crimes and whined piteously. We begged Dad to set him free, but Dad was adamant, this was the only way to stop him from biting more birds.

Tamel was put on notice and now had to sleep on the end of a rope. New brown chickens were reinstalled in the coop. Dad sunk the chicken wire down into the ground so Tamel couldn't burrow under it. But it was no use, the taste of blood had taken hold and Tamel was now a crazed addict. Within a week he'd chewed through his rope and managed to dig a tunnel deep enough to squeeze under the chicken wire. We woke up to another gruesome massacre and Tamel the Camel had to go, given away to a non-chicken-owning farm.

★

It had been almost three years since I'd been to school.

I wasn't too fussed, because I could read. Ursula K. Le Guin's *Earthsea* series, the crime-solving adventures of Trixie Belden, Nancy Drew and Hercule Poirot and anything by C.S Lewis, M.M. Kaye or James Cavell were big favourites. Everywhere we went, I scavenged for reading material. All the hotel shelves, any library anywhere. All the magazines. All the novels. The thicker the book, the better. I'm not sure I completely understood the jokes in the *Catch-22*s and the *Shoguns*. Maybe not as much as the ones in my Narnia and Faraway Tree books, but I enjoyed them.

Every so often, I'd get a shiver down my spine thinking about what I'd be missing if Grannie May hadn't taught me to read. For me, reading was like the scarves Mum put up. Books made a room feel like home. They weren't just full of experiences I had no idea about; they were a way to go somewhere you had power. Whatever happened in a book, if it got too grim, too out of hand, you could just turn the page.

I was keen to get Tobey involved. She didn't mind me reading her stories, but had no interest in doing it herself. Tobey liked more practical things. She was always up for damming creeks, building huts or turning our hotel rooms into forts, but sitting quietly with a page of black squiggles was just not her bag.

Dad had high hopes I was giving myself a sound education with all this reading, but Mum could see it was just novels I picked up. Knowing how to poison someone with a cup of crushed apple seeds was only going to get me so far in life, so I was enrolled at the local school.

Much like the posh girls of St Cluny, the country kids at Waimauku Primary weren't particularly impressed. They took one look at me, and my pristine set of 72 Cumberland pencils, and decided I was up myself. That I lived in the old doctor's house probably didn't help. Nor the fact that I thought I could rock up in the middle of the school year when everyone else had known each other since before they were even born.

I read books during lunchtimes. I had strange packed lunches. I went bright red whenever anyone said hello. I wore suspect bits of jewellery. But mainly I was weird. And up myself. Which, in the late seventies in rural New Zealand, was probably the worst thing you could be.

Then, a few months in, I got incredibly lucky and came down with the pox.

There were a lot of cool things about living at Waimauku. The property was encircled with pine forests dotted with scarlet-topped mushrooms like in a fairy tale. We had ponds, gardens of food. It was beautiful. But the best thing that came with the house was the two-bedroomed cottage that had been the doctor's surgery, because that meant Grannie May could move in just down the hill.

She wasn't there more than a few months, but her stay coincided beautifully with me being plague-ridden. I couldn't have been more delighted to be sent to stay with her in splendid isolation. Grannie was a nurse and knew just what to do. The first step was to make up a bed for me on the floor in front of the TV. I lay there re-reading my Agatha Christies and watching *Days of Our Lives* and *Young and the Restless*. Then *Bewitched, Mr Ed* (the talking horse) and *M*A*S*H* when the proper TV came on after 5pm.

We chatted and watched telly together. I remember being itchy and caked in chalky pink calamine lotion, but I don't remember the sickness. I was too happy. At one point, Grannie even whipped up a batch of melted sugar and water that hardened into rock-like candy. Bliss.

I was gutted when the pox cleared up and I had to move back up the hill. But back at school on Monday was more outlandish good luck. The chicken pox couldn't have timed things better. I'd missed two of the three biggest events in the school year: Sports Day (no loss there) and the annual field trip, where the class had bussed into town to visit the Museum of Auckland (I'd already been there so many times I could have sketched the teacher a floorplan, but I kept that quiet).

The great luck was that, somehow, miraculously, the most popular girl in school, Raelee Redwood (Redwood as in where Neil Young searched for his *Heart of Gold,* although this was unrelated), had been off sick during Field-trip Day too.

Half the project work for that term was centred around this field trip, so Raelee and I had to sit together poring over a visitor's guidebook, to help us better understand what the museum might look like inside.

Raelee was brilliant. She even had little layered bits around her ears like the blonde singer from Abba. It turned out she was nice too. We stayed friends even after she didn't have to sit with me anymore. With Raelee's kind endorsement, I suddenly had friends to play with at lunch and someone to sit with on the bus home.

Thank you, pox! Life was magic. Plus, I was back at school for the event that *really* mattered: the school's Fair & Farmland Beauty Pageant.

I had guinea pigs. There was Tuxie Tuxedo, a sleek, jet-black one who considered himself a bit of a ninja guinea pig, and a pair of long-haired, white-and-ginger ones who had turned out to fancy each other. The pick of their litter was an especially fluffy arctic-white male. Ever creative, I named him Fluffer (I didn't know).

All of my guineas were superb. But I just knew the Fluffer was a prize-winning pig. Once you brushed and backcombed up Fluff's fur, he *was* pretty exceptional looking. Like a beady-eyed snowflake. I borrowed Grannie May's Elnett Extra Hold to maintain the stylings, and the heavily hairsprayed Fluffer and I set off.

That morning the school bus looked like an all-cast scene from *The Muppet Show*. The rule was that anything larger than a mid-sized goat had to make alternative transport arrangements, but the driver wasn't a stickler. Most kids had something on a rope or in their laps. It was glorious.

The judges were meant to reach the Guinea Pig & Other Rodents section by noon. But being a country school, there were a lot of animals to appraise. I'd needed a pee since mid-morning. By 1.15pm I couldn't hold it any longer and made a dash.

Fluffer did take first prize, but I was in a toilet stall during my moment of pet ownership glory. Having bestowed the award, the judges had moved on. Leaving him chewing his stalks of dandelion like he couldn't give a fig. A shiny blue-and-gold rosette covering up the 'I'm the Fluffer' sign I'd written in big, proud letters.

★

Generally, my guineas seemed happy in their hutch, but it was hard to know for sure. Their furry little faces, impassively chewing, weren't easy to read. Every so often one of them made a bolt for freedom, but who wouldn't?

An escape meant the rest of my day could be spent lying in the grass on the end of a piece of string. The other end tied to a stick, propping up an upturned cardboard box. Under the box would be a piece of apple or carrot. Once the fugitive was lured out of their lavish new grasslands by the browning chunk of apple, I'd pull the string, bringing the box down to safely trap them. None of us ever learned. The guinea pigs always fell for the irresistible taste of familiarity, and I kept trusting them to be sensible when I dragged the hutch to a fresh patch of lawn each morning.

It was here, on this grass, where the third, most disturbing massacre of Waimauku happened.

A local farmer popped by with a litter of bunnies. Did I want them? He'd shot their mother and now they were all alone. Dad wasn't happy about it, rabbits had been at his lettuces too, but I promised to keep them securely contained in the hutch with the guineas.

These bunnies were *adorable*. Super-cute, super-fluffy. I fed them all carefully and made up a special bed in the hutch with one of my woollen jumpers. The guinea pigs weren't exactly thrilled with their new hutch-mates at first, but after some high-quality food bribery, everyone was snugged up together peaceably enough.

Heart bursting from the cuteness, I promised my little guys I'd be back first thing in the morning and we'd look at building a bigger hutch. I fell asleep smiling.

Eight hours later, I opened my window to wave everyone a very good morning indeed.

The lawn was a carnage of blood and fur. In the space between the house and the ponds there was barely a blade of grass not smeared red with guinea pig and bunny body parts.

From what I could piece together, two of the rabbits had made it out. There was no sign of ninja Tuxie's fur or little legs either. It didn't take a crime-solving Hercule Poirot to put the clues together. What we'd forgotten was that, like Tamel the Camel, rabbits burrow. The bunnies had tunnelled out an escape, the guinea pigs had followed, and the dogs had gone for the lot. It was especially distressing that all of this had happened just beneath my bedroom window. Instead of saving my little friends, I'd slept through their gruesome murders.

I cried and cried. Dad said the dogs were just following their natures. You could tell they felt bad. Standing there, looking at me with their big brown, sorry eyes. They'd never shown interest in the caged guineas, but once the guineas were out on the lawn and smelling of rabbit, the dogs had lost their minds.

A thoroughly traumatised Tuxie *had* survived. After a week of lying around with a box, I was finally able to lure him back from the woods. He didn't want me to hold him for days, and I didn't blame him one bit.

★

About fifteen minutes' drive from the house was Muriwai, a thirty-seven-mile stretch of windswept coastline, where waves rolled up fast and strong out of the Tasman Sea to break on the black sands.

Tobey and I were drawing in the lounge one rainy afternoon when Mum danced in and told us we were going to the beach. Whoop! Suddenly there was electricity in the air.

It was a grey stormy day. The kind where there's no distinct line between the sea and sky. Rain was coming down horizontally. Lashing the windscreen. Mum was in a fun mood. Singing along with the car stereo and driving fast. Tobey and I sliding about in the backseat.

Mum turned off the sealed road and into the sandy lane leading to the beach. The three of us laughing as we bounced in and out of the potholes along the way.

When we got there, Mum yanked the keys out of the ignition and sprung out of the car.

'C'mon kids.'

We kicked off our shoes and ran after her as she sprinted up and over the sand dunes.

Once we cleared the tuffs of long grass, salty wind whipped us full in the face. The long beach lay out before us. Cliffs to one side, then miles of beach curving out to the distant mouth of Kaipara Harbour.

The black sand was piled with dark seaweed washed up from the sea floor and the waves were high. Stormy chargers pounding in. Furious and foamy. It was a surfer's spot, but no one had come out today. Mum was already quite a way ahead.

We were pretty used to the sight of our mother's disappearing figure. Subscribing to the herbivore ethos that survival depended on the young finding their legs as soon as possible, Mum didn't suffer slow walkers. Wherever we went, Tobey and I would be doing a part-jog shuffle behind her, nervous of being left behind and perishing on the trail.

Up ahead, and always just out of reach, Mum's strides would be effortless and lithe. Her long hair swishing from side to side, catching the light.

Mum had a great walk: it was confident, charismatic and super classy. Men would stop what they were doing just to watch her travel down the street. Bobbing along a few yards behind her like two corgis in pursuit of a greyhound, Tobey and I had the best vantage to take in their cartoon-like gazes. She either didn't notice them or thought it inelegant to acknowledge the attention.

On the beach ahead presently, Mum's walk had sped to a dancing run. Her arms were stretched wide, and she was spinning around. Her face tilted up to the rainclouds. Her dress and long wet hair whirling out like Stevie Nicks. Snatches of singing came back in the wind.

She stopped suddenly. We peered across at what she'd spotted out in the water.

With the rain coming down so hard, we couldn't see clearly. Out in the crashing breakers was a large black tangled thing. We blinked, trying to get the water out of our eyes.

A sea monster, a kraken of the deep, was coming out of the waves. Sea monsters might not exist, but what we were seeing didn't look like anything else. It had long dark tendrils, like an octopus, that were snaking out, reaching even higher than the waves. It was fighting with the waves. And, high and strong though the waves were, the creature seemed to be winning. It was massive.

Up ahead we realised Mum was pulling off her Fry boots. Then her jumper was off and she was running down the wet sand. *Towards* the monster.

I raced after her, screaming for her to stop, but my words were whipped away in the wind.

The seawater felt warmer than the rain and wind, but the current was strong. Even at knee height it was hard to wade against. After a few steps the sand bed dipped away sharply and the water was deep, already over my head.

I'd lost sight of the monster; it must have dived under. Mum was at the spot where it had been, and I was gaining on her, nearly there too.

The waves suddenly sucked up, preparing for a big set of breakers.

As the first wave curved up above our heads, I saw the monster in the water with us was actually a dark, barnacle-and-seaweed-covered tree. A tree! In the surf! A kraken would have seemed less out of place.

In that split-second Mum looked back, saw me, and we both realised that the tree would come crashing down on top of us with the wave. The strength of the wave, sucking back the water into itself, was pulling us closer to the tree. Yards apart, we both tried to paddle sideways as it towered above us. There wasn't much we could do. It was a massive, full-grown tree, its branches wider than our bodies. It was going to hit us.

The wave crashed down. We were sent tumbling through the water, I felt the weight and scratch of branches a few times as I was somersaulted head over heels, but by some miracle, Mum and I both bobbed up unscathed among the branches of the tree. The second wave hit, and again we were thrown against branches. When the water drew up for the third wave, Mum managed to grab me and yank me across to her. We swam sideways away from the tree, then back to the shore. Once Mum could stand, we were safe. She dragged me in and we collapsed on the wet sand. Looking back at the tree rising up against the foamy dumpers.

The next time we came down to the beach, a few days later, it was blazing sunshine. The sand hard and smooth. Up on the beach was the tree. The stormy waves had left it beached up past the hightide mark. It was a 20ft oak tree. Its trunk at least 5ft wide. We all sat on its truck and laughed at the outrageousness of Mum thinking she could have dragged it in by herself.

From then on that was our spot. The tree stayed there. Its roots washed clean by the salt and sun, and became a marker for a good spot to swim. It might still be there.

★

That summer Mum had a Saturday stall at the indoor hippy markets in town. Mostly she sold sarongs that she and Dad had shipped back from Indonesia, and earrings and necklaces she was making up with a set of jeweller's pliers. Mum would wind stainless-steel rods and semi-precious stones into these cool pieces that a lot of people wanted to wear. It wasn't acknowledged as such, but there had been times back in the Kombi days, when Mum's designs had been our sole income. She'd quietly make them when we stopped at night, and then sell them for petrol and food in the next town.

At some point, talk filtered through the markets about a music festival being set up on a farm outside Waihi, about two hours south of Auckland. Mum and Dad decided to get involved.

Nambassa would go down in New Zealand history as its counterculture peak, but no one, including the organisers, expected it to be as big as it was. It was described in the press afterwards as NZ's answer to Woodstock. But actually, per capita, Nambassa was estimated to be ten times bigger. On an otherwise nondescript sheep farm in the middle of nowhere, people came together from all over New Zealand and beyond, just to be together and listen to music.

In front of our eyes, it kept getting bigger and bigger. The organisers had to keep opening up more paddocks as the crowd swelled out over the fields. Cars and vans were crawling back-to-back for miles from all possible directions.

As vendors, we were told to get there a day before anything started. Uncharacteristically, Mum and Dad had followed orders, so we were safely setting up shop during the worst of the queues. Our spot was meant to be on the far edge of the site, but by the second day the festival had expanded around us so much that we were now in the middle of it.

Cars and Kombis arrived, having picked up hitchhikers along the way, and people just *poured* out of their doors. No one had seen anything like it.

I don't know what the festival profits were, but after a while the organisers threw away their site map and stopped charging entrance. Beyond the stages and a row of cabins set up for the organisers, there wasn't much structure: just a vast sea of tents. A lot of people didn't care where they slept, they just wanted to be part of the experience.

Around the organiser's area, there was a palpable atmosphere of managed hysteria. They were making desperate callouts for more water, tarpaulins, bundles of hay (at first to make paths for people to walk through the mud, then to lay down for people to sleep on)… Everything they had, they needed *a lot* more off.

Mum and Dad had the idea that festival goers would be the perfect customer for their sarongs. Turned out, they couldn't have been more on the money. Sarongs aren't just clothing, you can use them as towels, bedsheets, hammocks, baby blankets. They're pretty nifty. And these were authentic, beautifully Batiked ones from Java. They were priced fairly and selling like hot cakes. In fact, probably the only thing that would have sold better at Nambassa would have been actual hot cakes.

In the spirit of peace and harmony, no alcohol was sold on site. You could bring your own drinks, but the drug most people were carrying in was green. Any vendor selling cookies, biscuits or anything remotely snack-like was working around the clock; frantically trying to cater for the collective need to munch.

The air was hazy with cannabis. It was being openly passed around. Handfuls of pre-rolled joints were tossed off the stage into the audience. People were sitting around in circles sharing bongs on the muddy hay. Everyone high as peacock feathers.

It was like being in another world, one where the strict drug laws of a conservative late-seventies government didn't apply. There were police: they'd tried to be hardline. But after a mass protest the uniforms had agreed to back down. They were ridiculously outnumbered, probably far from backup. I'm not sure of the legalities but suddenly walking around puffing a massive doobie and being nude except for a pukka-shell necklace was the new normal.

The clothes-optional site policy was something a lot of people were getting into. First it was just a couple of beardy types wandering around with their junk flopping out. Then more people started peeling off. Enjoying the natural setting was part of the advertised Nambassa experience and who needed clothes for that? Plus, everything was muddy. People tiptoed through the mud to begin with, trying not to get too covered, then stopped caring and just took their clothes off.

Whole families were squelching about. Not a stitch on. Bum cheeks and wobbling bits everywhere.

I kept my clothes on, apart from when we were down by the river swimming. Thankfully so did Mum and Dad.

Even on the last day people were still coming: on foot, crammed into cars and vans, on tractors. There were people riding in on horses. No one seemed to care where they were sleeping or whether there'd be toilets or food for them when they got here. No one cared about the rain or the mud. They just wanted to be here. Everyone was sharing drugs and food. Mum gave away sarongs to people who had nothing to sleep on.

There was also no meat served on site. By the end of the second day, nudity looked normal to me, but it never stopped being shockingly brilliant to sidle up to any of the stalls and be able to eat anything they had for sale.

★

By the end of 1979 we were back in airports. Running late for planes and checking into hotels. We still owned Waimauku, but some other people were going to live there now.

I was sad to leave. We'd put a lot of ourselves into this place, and most of the good things we had here wouldn't fit into my little blue case. But anyone could see we weren't the kind of family who stayed in their forever home. And we would always have 231 to go back to.

Part 2: The Eighties

Where everything went wrong.

1980

A very bad year

We were in London, catching up with Owl. It was a cold winter and things weren't going well.

After years of paperwork and a stunning amount of Owl's cash, Ireniska's mother had come to live with them in north London. Owl sold his lovely Hampstead flat and found somewhere bigger to accommodate the three of them. But, instead of making Niska happier and more at home, her mother's presence made her crabbier. Niska and her mother argued constantly. All they could agree on, it seemed, was a shared longing for goulash and loathing of England.

Then, the mother *went back*. Back *behind* the Iron Curtain. There was a cold war going on, but she preferred totalitarian isolation to modern Britain.

Then, just two weeks later, Niska *followed* her. The whole thing was mindboggling. Owl had gone out to stay with Niska to try and save his marriage. He'd just got back from Czechoslovakia when we saw him.

He looked deflated, like a bicycle tyre that someone had left in the shed. Even his magnificent Sam-Elliott-esque moustache seemed to droop. The marriage was not going to make it. He had been neglecting his gallery. He looked like he needed a lot of hugs. Poor Owl.

Late January it was decided Mum and I would be leaving. There were problems back in New Zealand: issues with the mortgage at Waimauku. Mum needed to fly back to tidy things up there, and also see Grannie May, who hadn't been very well. Dad and Tobey would stay in London with Owl, then meet us in Australia in a month or so.

As Mum and I were taking off into the grey skies above Heathrow, beginning our long journey back to the other side of the world, Owl and Dad were arriving at the door of their first party. There weren't many doors in London closed to Owl, and the two men had decided to take advantage of their newly women-less freedoms.

Tobey wasn't cramping their style: she'd make a brief appearance, feast on cocktail-sticked snacks then crash out on the bed with the coats. By all accounts, the three of them were having a once-in-a-lifetime good time. There were so many parties that Tobey went to one by herself. An eight-year-old girl's birthday in a big house in Primrose Hill. The party theme was fairies. *Fairies!* There was a wardrobe assistant to dress the attendees like fairies and a make-up artist to paint their faces with stars and glitter. When I heard about this later, I was sick as a parrot to have missed such goodness. I gripped the memento the girls had each been given – a beautiful black-and-white print of the group, shot by the photographer on hand to capture the day – and did my best to smile graciously.

At another party they went to, a woman stood up on the kitchen table and sang. Everyone got super-excited about how good she was and made her stay there and keep singing. Later, the woman gave Dad and Tobey a lift home in her banged-up old car. She couldn't remember where she'd parked, so they traipsed about for ages in the dark, drunk and laughing, up and down north London streets that all looked the same. Dad had a strict, thin-women-only policy, but even though this woman was not thin and Tobey was conked out asleep over his shoulder, Dad said he thought about having sex with her because her voice was *that* good. There was never a part of the story that included whether the woman with the voice had shared his romantic musings.

Years later when her album came out, we all loved it. Even Mum. She'd bought the cassette before she knew the story, but still all of us would be bopping along in the car. The woman really did have an amazing voice. Her album was number one for ages in the UK. For years you'd hear songs from it in shops and bars all around the world. The fact that Dad had met her just made it better. It was like when we'd made friends with a little boy in Devonport in New Zealand, who had told us about how his auntie Kate Bush in England sent him parcels of toys and clothes that sparkled with glitter. Somehow knowing these things let us be part of the story when we listened to the music.

After a month of partying in London with Owl, entirely on a whim, but possibly also inspired by Leonard Cohen's time at Hydra, Dad decided to go to Greece. He and Tobey flew to Athens, then hopped the first ferry out of Piraeus. They spent two weeks sailing around the islands, baking in the historic sunshine and eating nothing but crisps and olives.

Meanwhile, the trip back to the backwaters of New Zealand was less glorious. I'd lost track of all the planes and trains and buses and taxis Mum and I caught. All I knew was that it was taking a *long* time.

I remember sitting in a place called Whanganui and being more tired than I'd ever been in my life as we waited for our connecting train. It was sometime in the night and I was shivering on the platform bench. There was no one there but us and some old guy who was trying to tell me about the war. Mum kept nudging me to be polite, but I couldn't keep my eyes fully open. And I just could *not* get warm. Jetlag cold is the worse cold.

The first leg of the journey had been the flight Mum and I caught out of Heathrow. It had gone via LAX for refuelling. I'd never been to America so I was pretty excited. We were only scheduled to be there two hours, but I figured that was enough time to have a look around and get a feel for things. America was where *The Brady Bunch* and *Happy Days* and *Wonder Woman* and all my favourite shows came from. It was obviously the heartland of normal. I was expecting tremendous things.

Peering out the plane window, Los Angeles was bizarrely underwhelming. The Hollywood sign looked small and grubby on its dusty brown hill. The city sprawl looked endless. Some skyscrapers bunched together in the smoggy distance, but mostly it was flat. A long crawl of drab buildings and highways stretching out past the horizon. I couldn't see a sprig of green. Even Bombay had more trees. I couldn't get over how grey it looked.

As we were landing, the captain announced the layover would now involve a seven-hour wait.

The reality of that sunk in after we'd disembarked. There had been no vegetarian meals available on the flight: we were hungry and thirsty and we had no American money. Transiting passengers were not allowed to leave the airport. We still had to trudge through immigration though, which seemed harsh.

In the queue ahead of us was an incredibly glamorous group of people. So charismatic I couldn't take my eyes off them. Three men, four women and an entourage of children. All dressed like rockstars. The women in gold hoops and platform heels. The men in leather and flares. All the adults wore oversized shades. But it wasn't just their fashion. I'd seen wide halos of hair like theirs on TV but rarely in real life. They just looked so cool, even the little kids looked cool.

The group gravitated around the tallest man, who was wearing such a large sheepskin jacket I figured a whole sheep must have been involved. We trailed the group through immigration. Then lost sight of them, as we went looking for an airline desk to see if snacks and juice were being provided during the delay.

At the counter Mum explained our situation. The staff said no. Could we access the bureau de change out in the Arrivals Hall then? Nah. That wasn't going to happen either. They were trying to wave us away, basically telling Mum to bugger off, when we heard a voice behind us.

'Why aren't you helping this woman?'

It was the man in the big sheepskin jacket from the rockstar family. He hadn't spoken aggressively, but there was something in his tone that conveyed a lot of pent-up frustration. There was a decent way of doing things, and these airline people were falling short.

One of them said something snippy about how they simply weren't required to. Which wasn't the right thing to say to this man. He stepped forward and drew himself up to his full height, the sheepskin collar snow-white against his skin.

Up close he was so handsome. He seemed to glow.

'How long is the flight delayed?' he asked Mum.

She told him.

He turned back to the airline staff, his voice now even quieter, 'You *are* required to provide food on a delay that long. You're *required* by law.'

He may as well have been shouting at them. The three of them visibly shrunk behind their counter.

'And you *know* that,' he added.

A lot of people were looking over now, leaning in to hear, staring at him. Still he didn't raise his voice, he didn't need to. It carried beautifully across the airport hall.

'This is a mother trying to feed her child. She's not asking for anything you can't easily do. All she wants is to feed her daughter. It's not difficult. It's her right. Why are you making it hard for this woman, trying to bring her down, when what she's asking for is her *right*?'

He made it sound so simple. And he made sure one of the airline staff had scurried off to get us lunch vouchers before he went back to join his family. He was so nice.

Later, when Mum and I were happily digging into two of the most oversized salad bowls I'd ever seen – bowls literally bigger than our heads – Mum told me the man in the sheepskin coat was a famous fighter called Muhammad Ali.

★

The journey from London to Feilding, the small town near Palmerston North where Grannie was staying with her sister, took so long, I'd figured she would be all better by the time we arrived.

But when we got there, Grannie was lying in a single bed in a small dark room. Curtains drawn. The air close and still.

I sat on the edge of her bed. Grannie was very thin now, her body a shallow ridge under the bedspread. When I hugged her, she felt bony and fluttery in my arms, like one of the injured birds I'd carried home. Even in the gloomy light you could see blue veins, reaching out like tree branches under her skin. She was smiling to see us, but her eyes were all sad and smudgy. She didn't look like herself.

She didn't act like herself either. I couldn't remember ever seeing Grannie in bed during the day. She was usually busy: out and about in her little car, tidying and organising things around the house. Now she was so still. Like it was taking all her energy just to be here. Even with someone helping, she could barely move her own pillows.

She was just as sick the next day.

Having been a nurse all her career, Grannie would have known exactly what was coming for her. She had cared for hundreds of people with cancer. It was the death she feared most.

Bedridden and frail. Her hands knuckled with hurt on the quilted bedspread. She would have anticipated all the pain, the indignities of depending on other people's care for even the most private bodily functions. It was the fate she deserved least of all. But if she was angry, she kept that from me. Like everything else she'd ever dealt with, Grannie faced her situation with grace and love.

A nurse came twice a day to administer her injections. Grannie's arms and legs were patched with black, purple and yellowing bruises. She was too weak to talk much, but she always smiled at me.

'Are you feeling any better today?' I asked stupidly. I just didn't get it. What this sickness meant. No one explained how precious this time was. Probably it seemed too obvious to need saying. But I was too full of dumb kid-thoughtlessness to realise Grannie would never get out of bed or leave that room again.

'Don't you worry about that,' she answered. 'You go and meet your cousins.'

So I ran around on the lawn, laughing and swerving about in the sun under a clothesline. Playing tag, an orange ice-block dripping in my hand, while Grannie lay inside alone in her bed.

It wasn't just Grannie being so sick that felt wrong. Nothing about life in this house felt OK. The town it was in: laid out all square and even. Each brick bungalow with its net curtains and identically trimmed lawn. We were in the country but all the food came from a factory. The whole town felt defrosted and overboiled. This was no place for Grannie. The dark little room with its bare walls. Curtains drawn over its view of brown-painted, weatherboard fence.

Poor Auntie June, Grannie's sister, had lived in Feilding all her life. She had a perfectly good car, but she'd never thought to drive it past the town limits sign and just keep going.

I'd only met grand-auntie June a couple of times. She was doing her best, but she was working in an office all day, and a long way from her comfort zone when she was home. She served boiled cabbage in thick mayonnaise and called it salad. Mum told me I didn't have to eat it, 'No wonder Mum's sick,' she whispered.

This was all a bad dream that would pass. It had to be. Mum probably didn't know how to deal with it either. She was only twenty-eight. We stayed a couple of days. Certainly no more than a week, then travelled back up to Auckland to sort things at Waimauku.

I don't have a clear memory of my last moments with Grannie, I know we didn't say goodbye like it meant anything. We'd hugged see-you-later so many times, I figured this was just another of those times.

I didn't thank her for all she'd done for us. I never told her what she meant to me.

Grannie was the person who shaped me the most and expected the least. I never had to worry about how boring or weird I was around Grannie. Either she didn't notice or didn't care, she loved me anyway. But I didn't like seeing her ill, and I was an ungrateful little brat.

Back at Waimauku I had trouble getting to sleep. I was back in my own room, in my old bed, but for the first time ever, I was scared of the dark. I couldn't explain what I was scared of exactly: something shapeless and horrible that had no words. Mum would switch the light off and suddenly I was terrified.

I'd creep downstairs and sit on the stairs, just so I could be near people and light. Mum would yell at me to get back to bed, and I'd lie there, literally shaking with fear.

Night after night it went on. I couldn't be on my own in the darkness. Then Mum brought up a cassette player and let me play Harry Nilsson's *A Little Touch of Schmilsson...* Clutching the cassette case tightly, I'd peer at the photograph on the cover. I couldn't really see it in the moonlight, but I knew it was a black-and-white shot of Harry, inexplicably lighting a cigarette with his thumb, a reassuringly irreverent glint in his eye. Harry had a really kind voice. One side of the cassette would click off and I'd fall out of bed in my panic to get him back in the room.

A few weeks later we flew out of Auckland to meet Dad and Tobey in Sydney. I was excited about that. I'd missed Tobey. And I'd been wanting to see Australia for as long as I could remember. It wasn't just that it was where I was born. Australia always seemed cool. Like New Zealand's cosmopolitan big sister.

Mum and I arrived sometime after 10pm, jumped in a taxi and drove to Kings Cross. Dad had got there first and picked a hotel almost directly across the road from the famous 135ft-long Coca-Cola sign.

Walking into the hotel room, Mum flew into Dad's arms. They held each other for the longest time. Tobey and I stared at each other, grinning like loons. She looked different, very brown and quite grown-up, telling me all her adventures. How she'd gone to a magic fairy garden party, and then Greece.

The next morning, we moved to a different hotel. Tobey and I had our own room. The breakfast buffet downstairs served gloriously trashy cereals and four different styles of egg. The TV in our room had three different channels. *Three.* Australia was ace.

We were back in Auckland, staying at 231 in the flat next to Poppa and Nanny Starling's, when Grannie died. She had been alone in her dark room with its bare walls and drawn curtains. The nurse had found her dead when she'd come to give her the evening shots.

We were standing in the lounge when I found out. Mum, Dad, Tobey, our aunt Erin and me: all of us clumped together by the door. We must have been about to go out.

I burst into weird tears. I wasn't making any noise, just water pouring out of my eyes like two taps.

Erin was looking at me. 'What's got into you?' she asked, genuinely curious.

'Grannie died.'

She stared at me blankly, not understanding my reaction at all. 'You knew she was going to die.'

But I really didn't. It hadn't occurred to me that I'd never see Grannie again. That she wouldn't always be there. Back in New Zealand somewhere, waiting for us to come home. Sometimes I really wasn't the sharpest kid in the shed.

All I could think about was how I'd been running around on that stupid lawn in Feilding, laughing in the sun with a sticky orange ice-block. I could have sat with her. Held her hand, and just breathed with her as she lay there.

For those last months of her life Grannie had been alone in that room all day. While we were there, I could've read to her. That would have been the *least* I could have done for Grannie. I never saw those cousins again, what did it matter whether I'd played with them? Every second with Grannie had been more precious than anything in my whole life and I'd let it blow away through my hands, without even trying to hold it safe.

I walked out the back door of 231 and into the garden. The sun was blazing. I couldn't understand how everyone else seemed OK. Even Mum was OK, a bit sad sure, but not devastated. How could Grannie be gone and everything else was the same? Everyone was just cracking on. Making toast and talking about ordinary things. Like the worst thing in the world that could happen, hadn't just happened.

I sat under the grapefruit tree. It looked the same as it had yesterday. I could smell sweet white blossoms. The long grass felt the same scratchy green on my legs. Cicadas buzzed around me. How was it even *possible* that Grannie wasn't here anymore? I just didn't get how any of this was real.

I wasn't allowed to travel back to Feilding with Mum and Dad. The funeral was for adults. And it was Mum's mum, so her loss not mine. With all the grave doors and skeletons, the close shaves we'd had and the actual dead bodies I'd come across, I thought I had a handle on death.

This was utterly incorrect.

When you're a kid and death has not yet come for anyone you love, you really have no clue.

That week Mum and Dad sold Waimauku.

Just after that, Mum found out she was pregnant.

I didn't tell anyone, but before falling asleep each night I'd pray the baby would be Grannie's spirit come back to be with us. Reincarnation was a regular expectation in much of the world, why couldn't it happen in our family? Not seeing Grannie for long stretches of time was something I was used to, but never seeing her again wasn't something I could get my head around.

1981

Griffy

I was ten now and it was the eighties. Grannie was dead. We didn't know it, but other bad things were coming. Blowing down the horizon towards us like bad seeds.

We were back in India. Living like castaways on the high sloping sand dunes on the edge of a beach in Goa. Our accommodation was essentially a handful of coconut palm leaves held together with blue twine. No plumbing, no electricity, the floor was sand. At highest tide we were nine steps from the Arabian Sea. The waves were crashing dumpers, the beach was long and clear. Tobey and I couldn't have loved it more. In the hut there was sand in our beds, salt on our skin. Our dreams were full of ocean when we slept.

It was like being part of the sand and water. Our hair, our clothes, everything smelt sun-bleached and salty. You'd lie in bed, half asleep, drifting with the curl and draw of the waves. Imagining foaming water between your fingers, pulling around your ankles. Washing over you, soothing your family into the dark depths of sleep.

When the tide was out, you could see people walking along the flat wet sand for miles. There were two distinct types of people on the beach. Hippies who were sunbathing and local men who had come to see hippies sunbathing. Presumably the local women were all too busy with their lives to bother with hippies.

The local men were dressed almost exclusively in seventies-era safari suits. They would be holding hands and hugging as they walked along in clumps, pointing and giggling at the hippie breasts. They looped their arms tightly around each other like lovers did in western countries. Their closeness didn't seem to be about being gay: they were only interested in gawping at the female bodies. Personal space was just different here.

Once our cashflow improved, we moved into rooms ten minutes back from the beach. Living in a house again wasn't so much fun, but having cool tiles underfoot and a lazy fan circling above had its advantages too. The rooms we rented were in a large family house where all the men had either died or just got up and left. There was an old guy who came every morning to rake up the leaves and tweak things in the garden, but otherwise the household was female. The women of the house were all over fifty and wonderful. There was a *Golden Girls* kind of vibe, but with saris.

Led by great-grandmother Ida, the five women sat out in rattan armchairs on their wraparound veranda most afternoons, gossiping and playing dominoes and cards over a rickety card table. They'd sip tall glasses of lemonade made with fresh-picked limes and palm sugar, and wisecrack each other in a blend of English, Portuguese and Konkani. Once Tobey and I had proven we could be appropriately respectful, they let us sit and drink lemonade with them and taught us how to play dominoes and gin rummy.

The ladies' garden had two interesting trees: a large tamarind out front, and a cashew around the back. Both were thrilling discoveries. The tamarind fruit fell from the tree in crackly skinned pods. Once you peeled off the skin and the ants, you were left with a face-wincingly tart paste, like a super-tangy lolly. According to the ladies, the sticky brown paste was strictly for cooking and would whip the enamel right off our teeth. Tobey and I had no time for that advice.

We'd not seen a cashew nut growing before. First there was the apple-sized fruit – bright red or glossy yellow. Hanging below that, in a mottled green-grey kidney-shaped casing, was the nut. Such elaborate measures the tree went through to grow each individual nut. The cashew fruit looked great. Unfortunately, it was inedible. We gave it a good go, struggling to believe a fruit could be so serious about tasting so bad. Not only was it awful, each bite left a weird feeling that furred up your mouth for the rest of the day. Perhaps it was this quality that helped it ferment so quickly: locals made a kind of fast rum from cashew fruit called feni. Drinking that, said Ida, would take your tooth enamel *and* any sense you had left in your head.

All the ladies at the house loved Griffy.

While Mum was pregnant, I'd imagined the baby inside was a girl. Wouldn't Grannie feel more comfortable reincarnated in her previous shape? But when the baby came out it was Griffin.

I understood from my Indian comics how our spirits are above such mundane considerations as gender, so I knew this didn't rule out the possibility of our new family member being someone we already loved.

Right from the start Griffy seemed his own person, but then both he and Grannie *really* liked barley sugars. I kept looking for signs. There were many, for both possibilities. I didn't remember Grannie ever being interested in cars and trucks. Griffy was obsessed. Both Grannie and Griffy were brave, but quietly so. They weren't flashy about their goodness. And Griffy was a joy. He couldn't have been easier to love. Smiley and sweet-natured: he was a breeze to look after.

Either way it was so nice to have him in our family.

With the skills I'd perfected grooming Fluffer, the prize-winning guinea pig, I'd brush Griffy's hair up into a soft Mohican along the top of his head. Tobey and I wore glass bracelets up our arms and silver anklets looped around our ankles like the local women and girls did. Babies wore anklets here too. Mum bought Griffy a pair and he'd toddle about tinkling and giggling with his fluffy spiked hair. He was adorable and very loved by everyone. The ladies all made a fuss of him. His whole day was spent snuggled up getting hugs in someone's lap. He was just the cutest kid.

Most Sundays we'd go to the markets at Anjuna and buy food from the westerners who were living in Goa permanently. They'd be selling homemade bread and hummus to fund their life here. The Anjuna Markets weren't famous yet. They were just a dozen or so stalls along Anjuna Beach then, but they were well known among the travellers. You got to them by walking a dusty goat trail through coconut fields. Everything for sale was highly mung bean, but pretty delicious. There was a woman who always had a few different types of chocolate cake on display and a platter of organic hash brownies under her counter. Probably you could get most things, drug-wise, if you asked the right stall.

You could also buy things like tied-dyed scarves and handmade incense and jewellery. Most weeks there would be people selling the entire contents of their backpacks. Well-thumbed paperbacks, clothes, half-used bottles of shampoo, sometimes even their passport would be spread out on the sand: anything to stay here longer. These were the real people. The proper travellers. To them, we were just tourists passing through. I didn't like to think of them trapped here without a passport; a stranger travelling around under their name, but probably they felt free.

One night Mum and I went to one of their parties. Sometime after midnight she'd woken me up and we'd stolen out of the house. I loved these adventures with Mum. As Dad, Tobey and Griffin slept back at the house, there was nothing more thrilling than to be racing with her across the sand dunes.

We were heading towards some distant bonfires on the horizon.

'Mum, what is that? What's happening?'

She did one of her classic, one-eyebrow-raised half smiles, 'You'll see.'

As we neared, I could see figures swirling around the fires. People were dancing, hand-in-hand. Westerners. Or mostly westerners. A few hundred people like the ones at Anjuna Markets: thin and brown with beaded necklaces and feathers in their hair, and here to stay for as long as they could.

There was music, people beating hand drums between their legs and someone was singing. Torches of fire were staked out, burning along the sand dunes. Most of the people were dancing or sitting in groups together, watching the musicians play. Some people were just lying on the sand, faces pointed up to the stars. There were naked and topless dancers, and everything felt relaxed and friendly. Everyone was sharing and smiling and laughing.

Trays of chocolate brownies were being carried around. The woman said something to Mum as she offered us some.

'Hash?' Mum asked

The woman nodded.

'Strong?'

The woman shrugged casually, 'Fairly.'

'You can try it,' Mum told me, 'But just a bite.'

The brownie was delicious. I was gutted I couldn't have the whole thing.

There was also a drink going around. It was being ladled from an enormous pot and everyone was sipping it from coconut shells. It had a lovely, creamy-tropical smell and I was really keen to try some of that too, but Mum gave me a firm headshake no. It was a strong rum pina colada. The rum wasn't a problem. But the man ladling it out warned her it was laced with LSD, which unfortunately I wasn't allowed.

It seemed very clear these people were living their best lives, drinking pineapple-sweet acid out of coconut shells on sand dunes under a starry, velvet-blue nightsky. They looked beautiful dancing and singing with their tassels and necklaces twirling. Maybe if I was having this sort of life, I'd sell all my things too.

I wanted to get involved and dance and sing with them, or even just lie down on the warm sand with the ones staring up at the stars – the hash brownie must have been kicking in – but we had to get back to the house before anyone woke up.

★

At Anjuna there was talk of a secret beach, where a colony of westerners lived completely off the grid at a magical fresh-water lagoon. Word was, they had the best hash in India. Every taxi we climbed into, Dad would ask the driver if he knew the secret beach.

No one did. He'd ask people everywhere. No one even knew if it was north or south. Secret beach was some kind of frustrating Goan mythology.

Then, one afternoon, we got into a taxi and a driver with an arrestingly oversized quiff said yes, he knew *the* secret beach. Yes, it was real. Most definitely the beach existed. For a special price, the driver could take us there right now. Just an hour's taxi-ride up the coast he said.

The driver pulled out onto the highway and put his foot down hard. It was a scorching day, even for southern India. We drove and drove. Our skin glued to the thick plastic covering on the backseat. The air roaring in from the windows raspy with heat. Our hair whipping around our faces like we were in a heavy metal band.

Outside the landscape was getting increasingly dried up and desolate. Onwards we drove.

Just a moment longer, the driver promised. Most *definitely* just a moment longer.

Three more hours of high-speed driving later, he veered abruptly onto the shoulder of the road.

It felt like we'd pulled up inside an oven. Sweat sprung up in bubbles on our skin the second the car stopped. Our ears were ringing from the buffeting winds. Everyone's hair had been blown into bird's nests. The driver's quiff was in long strands down one side of his head.

There was nothing here. Just the husks of long-perished weeds and a bunch of disheartened rocks.

The sun beat down, making the road ahead look oily and distorted.

We looked doubtfully at the driver.

'It's here. Yes. *Most definitely*. Secret beach! Secret beach! Come, come.'

God knows how he'd recognised the spot, speeding past it at 70mph, but a few yards back there was a thin rocky trail that had been obscured by the roadside weeds. There was no signposting. There was no sound of a beach, no buzz of cicadas. No sign of any life at all. It was too hot for even lizards to bother coming out. I thought about the lovely cool lemonades we could be having back home on the ladies' veranda.

We started down the path, Mum and I taking turns to carry Griffy. Dad and the driver loaded with bags of mangos and dry foods to trade for India's best hash.

After a while the rocks started getting bigger. An hour in, we were clambering over them with our hands and feet.

'Just a bit further,' promised the driver, the back of his shirt dripping with sweat. 'Smallest bit.'

Finally, we heard the faint sound of waves breaking.

Further down, the trail seemed to end at two large boulders. The driver showed us a crack in one of the boulders just wide enough to wedge ourselves through sideways. We passed Griffy and the bags through to each other.

'See! It's here! Secret beach!' announced the driver; flicking his hair aside and extending an arm out like he'd conjured the view from a top hat.

We stood there, catching our breath and taking it in. The beach looked good, a nice sandy bay with decent waves. The magical lagoon was less impressive. Murky brown rather than the sparkling blue I'd been imagining, and all manky and slimy around the edges.

Then we saw the people.

We were fairly trim. Most people in India were. But these guys were *thin*. Gaunt. Their eyes looked too big and their bones were showing through. Men, women and children: from what I could see under the dirt and tan, all westerners. Maybe three dozen people. A lot of them were naked and everyone had long hair. The men were aggressively bearded. In fact, hair seemed to be the only part of these people getting regular nourishment. There were a lot of young children. They were too thin too.

Along the opposite side of the pond-lagoon was a horseshoe of messy lean-tos, fashioned mainly from plastic bags and sticks. We'd been staying in a beach shack recently that had no running water, electricity or even a proper door, but these guys were living *rough*.

They did not look happy to see us. We were staring at them and they'd been staring back at us. But they looked angry, like we were invading colonials come to nick their plastic-bag roofs.

Two of the beardy guys stomped over.

'There's no more room,' said the first one

'Yeah man, you'll have to find somewhere else,' agreed the second.

'No, no. We just wanted to say hey,' said Dad, shaking his bags of food encouragingly. 'See if you guys had anything you wanted to trade?' he added, meaning their hash.

They glared at us a bit harder. For a long beat there was no sound apart from the waves. They knew exactly what Dad meant, but they clearly didn't want any part of us, or our offers to trade. They didn't even need to discuss it with each other.

Their stash was only for themselves said Beardy One. They were *not* cool with anyone else knowing their location, so could we keep that to ourselves?

'And, don't go near the pond, man,' added Beardy Two. 'That's our drinking water.'

I looked at the muddy reeds. I really hoped they were boiling that water.

We walked down the beach away from the colony and had a quick swim before trekking back up to the taxi, leaving Dad's bags of food for the poor pond children.

★

Having been in hundreds of antique shops, Mum and Dad had an idea for an antique shop that wasn't like any antique shop they'd ever been in. Mum and Dad never let the fact that other people weren't doing something stop them from deciding it was a capital idea.

This antique shop would display carefully chosen pieces under angled spotlights. High white walls and crisp black stands. No dust. No clutter. Full minimalism. An antique shop that was cool. Like a New York art gallery but with antiques. Not for grandmas. Not a speck of chintz. Dad always thought antiques were sexy. To him they were doorways back in time: relics of lost civilisations, maps to different ways of life. What was cooler than that?

This gallery/antique shop would be called Artaffection – get it? Affection for art? I thought that was genius. Don't forget this was 1981. For 1981 this was classy AF.

We flew back to Auckland to make it all happen.

A derelict factory building was found just up the hill from the heart of the city. The building would need a major clean up, including new floorboards where the floor had rotted through to the basement, but that had never put Mum and Dad off either. To save costs and help get the job done quicker, we'd live upstairs.

Chase and Pam put up most of the cash and Mum and Dad supplied the expertise and style. Dad would be the collector; Mum was going to manage the gallery floor. Chase would sort the accounts. What could go wrong?

Chase and Pam were upstate New Yorkers who were inexplicably living in rural Auckland. For the life of me I couldn't work out why anyone would move from America to a remote beach in New Zealand.

Everything in Chase and Pam's house was the same shade of sandy blonde as Pam's hair. They had cool gadgets in the kitchen and furniture that wasn't meant to be sat on. There were lights outside in their garden, like in a posh hotel. Chase said the only way to drink 'OJ' was freshly squished on his three-legged spaceship. We knew he meant orange juice and he was American, so he had to know about OJ: they drank nothing else on TV.

Pam 'wasn't used' to children. What she said was nice, but there was something about how she spoke that made you wonder if she hated you really. Her hair was the texture of candyfloss, all pouffed up on the top of her head like the prime minister of England's. Chase talked loudly and laughed a lot. After a couple of beers, he'd get intense eyes and hug Tobey and me close, telling us what special blessings we were and how he'd do anything to be a dad to a pair of kids like us.

Chase had a finance background and had made smart investments. Pam was an air hostess, but didn't fly anymore because

Chase also 'came from money'. They had perfect smiles and Barbie-and-Ken matching outfits.

Artaffection was going to make everyone rich, or richer in the case of Chase. When it was finished, it looked tremendous. Inside was black and white. Outside had been painted a discreet olive green. All the artefacts were lit beautifully. Dad had black wooden display stands handmade for each piece.

On the first month of business Alan Alda from M*A*S*H – only the highest-rated TV show in history – got his driver to bring him by during a publicity tour of Auckland. Tobey and I couldn't believe we'd missed Hawkeye. We loved M*A*S*H, and always watched it eating dinner. We didn't mind in the least that half the scenes involved spaghetti-style surgery. Probably no one did, because it aired during most people's dinnertime and everyone watched it.

Living above the gallery was fun. It was only one room, but it was a massive space with big sash windows and high ceilings. Mum and Dad slept in one corner, Tobey, Griff and me in another. Someone looped a rope over one of the industrial beams and Tobey and I took turns swinging high as we could, looking out on the cars whizzing by in the street down below.

We didn't last long above the gallery. The building wasn't cleared for residential use and Chase wouldn't let us build any kind of kitchen, so everything we ate was raw. Also the toilet was shared with the dodgy photography studio next door. The studio had been handy for getting our new family passport photos done, but at night they'd make films and you'd go to pee in the morning and find condoms and tissues and some girl's knickers on the floor. But mainly, in an unusually good business move (this must have been Chase), it was realised that renting out the second floor would be a decent revenue spinner.

Mum, Tobey, Griff and I moved an hour-and-half north to an old bungalow Mum found about twenty minutes' outside the sleepy coastal town of Waipu. Dad would stay with the business during the week. He'd sleep in the back office, then drive up on Friday to spend the weekend with us. The back office was officially his work area, but it was also a 600sqft space where everyone socialised and hung out. It had desks, sofas, a couple of low-slung coffee tables, mood lighting, a fancy stereo and a lot of tea chests of antiques. It later emerged that there had been more entertaining in the back office than was strictly necessary, but we didn't know that till later.

I don't know if he deemed it a particularly dangerous town or if he was expecting something specific, but Dad bought Mum a shotgun when we moved up to Waipu. The only thing that got shot with our gun was an unfortunate possum that Dad blew out of existence one night after it had been tramping back and forwards on loop across our corrugated-iron roof.

The Waipu bungalow was on a rocky coastline. A steep hike down through slanting grasslands took us to the sea, where the waves washed directly against rock. There was no beach and the undertow was fierce, but we could still wedge ourselves between the sea-urchin spiked rocks for a splash around.

There were lots of dramatic storms while we were there. After a particularly blowy night, we came down to find the rocks had moved around a bit and left us a miniature sandy inlet of our own. About six yards across, framed by boulders. It couldn't have been cuter.

'Good spot for you two to learn how to jump properly,' said Dad, sitting down and leaning back on a log of driftwood.

No one questioned why we'd need to do this, and Tobey and I both happily clambered up the 10ft boulder and took turns springing off onto the new sandy area. The first few leaps were a bit scary but we never doubted Dad's instruction. It was too thrilling to have his attention. Again and again we scrambled up and leapt off, perfecting our ninja-roll-on-impact landings.

Dad was right about the rolling: it really must have been taking the strain from our knees and ankles. The next time we came down, Tobey and I built a sandcastle and discovered we'd been landing on a rocky ledge, lightly dusted with about two inches of sand.

The other thing we learned at Waipu was handwriting. Mum decided mine and Tobey's was atrocious. She had a point. We both printed in the standard, robotic block lettering we'd been taught at school.

'Easy to read,' we told her.

'But hard to look at,' she said.

Her own handwriting swept stylishly across the page, Dad's was jaunty and rebelliously upright. It was time we learned to write like humans too.

Mum got some exercise books. She drew up lines on the page, and showed us how each letter should lean and where it joined up to the next letter. Then we just had to practise. As simple and impossible as that. Neither Tobey nor I had done much practise before. The idea of repeating something that we were rubbish at – over and over again until we were less rubbish at it – was hideous. It made you want to combust in a puff of defeat.

One of Dad's friends, a six-foot-four biker who specialised in delicate watercolour illustrations, told me that practising a slant would help with my drawing too, so I actually did practise, for a few afternoons at least.

Mainly what Tobey and I did at Waipu was make tunnels. The house was surrounded by areas of strangely dense grasses: thick as bales of hay, over three-foot tall. Not having a creek to dam, we decided the best use of our time would be to construct long tunnels through the grass. The trick was to hollow and curve it enough that we could crawl through, but still have covering over our heads. If you could see the sky, it was a failure tunnel.

Some days we'd be carefully flattening grass for hours. It must have been really annoying for anything living in the grass. Luckily it was New Zealand so there weren't any deadly snakes, spiders or scorpions, otherwise we'd probably not have lasted the first morning.

In addition to any novel I could find, I'd switched from reading comics about Hindu deities to magazines. Or just the one. For Australasian teens, there really was only one magazine. An amalgamation of fashion and lifestyle, *Dolly* was basically a how-to on being normal. I'd pore over each issue for hours – every page studied like the map to a country I'd be visiting soon. Then stack them up for later reference. I liked to keep them in pack-fresh pristineness, running my fingers down their precious pastel-coloured spines.

Tobey was into my *Dolly*s too, but for different reasons. She was allowed to look through them. If she had clean hands and was careful. She was not allowed to draw moustaches and goatees on the sweet-faced *Dolly* models. She was not allowed to give them speech bubbles with her own insights on my personality defects. Or cut out their model bodies and stick them on the walls doing silly poses. Or leave their poor severed model heads between the pages of the book I was reading, on my pillow or taped to my toothbrush. But she did.

Dad was the advertised genius of the family, but Tobey might have been the real brains. Probably she could have ruled the world. It was hard to get Tobey to do anything she didn't want to. Even harder to stop her from doing what she wanted. Sometimes I'd get all caught up with the unfairness. She'd be flopped over the sofa watching morning cartoons, I'd be vacuuming the house, how was that fair?! But she wasn't particularly interested in order. Tidiness was a bore. Whether it was the backseat of a taxi or our bedroom, whatever space we shared was cut down the middle: one side prissy as a pin, the other raging chaos. In sixty seconds flat she could make a biblical mess out of a hotel bed, two hairbands and a bag of crisps.

When it came to what interested her, Tobey had the discipline of a Buddhist monk. Her pranks were the stuff of face-sweating nightmare. She'd spend hours lying in wait for the right opportunity. For years she was captain of the SOS club. Full name: the Spy on Saylor club. Its members (Tobey, any kids and pets she could rope in) would lurk about, hiding in bushes, behind sofas, watching whatever I was doing and taking detailed notes. You'd hear a shuffle, then giggling, and realise your private moment of rearranging the cutlery drawer or comparing arm hairs had been scrutinised by a gaggle of scoffing kids.

Always with the trusting optimism of a Labrador, I didn't exactly help myself. Part of my predictable routine was waking early. With everyone asleep and the house quiet, I'd read in bed before getting up. One morning, after a cosy half-hour's read, I realised I couldn't hold off a trip to the loo any longer. I marked the page I was on, and swung my legs out of bed.

As my bed-warm feet landed on the floor, two icy, undead hands clasped tightly around my ankles.

I screamed. It was the creepiest, most blood-curdling sensation I'd ever felt.

Tobey. Seven-year-old Tobey, who despised early mornings and struggled to sit still ordinarily, had willed herself to wake up even earlier than me. She'd puffed up her bedclothes to look as though she was still sleeping. Crept to the fridge and emptied the ice trays she'd filled the night before into a bowl. Then she'd tiptoed back into our room, wrapped herself in a blanket and ninjaed under my bed to begin soaking her hands.

After that I slept in socks.

It was Tobey who called things for what they were. I'd be too busy trying to work out the rules to question whether they were worth following. But Tobey saw the big picture. She was the dissenter. Why was everything all about Mum and Dad?

'Why,' she'd whisper to me in the backseat of the car, 'should we always be waiting around for them?'

'Won't be long.'

'Goody-two shoes.'

I'd be all, yay: we're getting dropped off at the museum. 'Only because it's cheaper than coughing up for a crèche', she'd say, deadpan eyes.

A true Darwinist, she always got the survival theories. For Tobey, it just made sense. A year earlier, when she was six, she'd decided to protect herself from the variables of our fortunes.

She took in the scene and decided that she'd best start putting away a safety net.

She had been taking money for some time when she was discovered. She'd been going for the good stuff, mostly twenty-dollar notes with the odd tenner. No time-wasting with any smaller denominations. No coins: not just because they were worth less, they'd be heavier to carry. This was before New Zealand introduced its $50 note, otherwise that would have been Tobey's key target.

Her main harvesting areas were Mum's purse and Dad's pockets. She kept her thick roll of notes in a velvet bag (also stolen) under her mattress. It wasn't until Mum noticed the drawstring of her lost velvet bag dangling from Tobey's bed that any depletion of funds was realised. But by all accounts, it was a robust stash.

I had no knowledge of Tobey's plans, so they couldn't have included me. A scheme like this would never have occurred to me. Thinking about it though, who could blame her? Ensuring her own food money was smart.

Of course, Dad didn't see it that way. Tobey had been stealing from her own family and this was very serious. Diabolical. Up there with smashing a Ming plate. How could Tobey rob her own mother and father?

Tobey usually got away with things. She was the outrageous one. The fun, rulebreaker who didn't give a toss about all the boring things. I was the one who hated cigarette smoke. It totally made sense.

But this time Dad wasn't making any allowances. He was furious. Scary angry. This was a crime against her family. Against him. The very height of dishonesty and ungratefulness. After he had clothed, fed and cared for Tobey for six years, how could she turn around and stab him in the back like this?

And of course, Mum backed him. It was always us Starlings, together against the world. But within the Starlings, it was them against us kids. Mum and Dad stuck together like UHU superglue.

There was talk of boarding schools, orphanages, going to live with Nanny, maybe adoption. At one point Dad told me to say my goodbyes. Tobey never went to live with Nanny; she didn't end up being sent anywhere, but it was a terrible, terrible time.

★

Waipu was actually the second time we'd lived separate from Dad.

In a time that was never talked about – at some point when Tobey was still a baby – Mum, Tobey and I lived in a caravan on a beach. About three hours north of the city where Dad lived.

Our caravan was basic: one narrow room with a cupboard-style toilet/shower. It was one of five caravans in a line facing the water. Each one propped up on concrete cinder blocks in case of high tide. Mostly, the other caravans were empty.

Behind the caravans were chalky white cliffs and a steep dirt road coming down to a flat, grassy plateau that ran to golden sand and smooth water. I don't remember much of life here, other than it being peaceful. There weren't many other people around.

I think it was winter when we lived here, because we wore woolly jumpers and didn't do much swimming. One time a storm came in from the sea that rocked our caravan back and forth. It was exciting watching the waves come up over the grass and splash against our door, but Mum worried the tide would knock us off the cinder blocks. Afterwards there was a lot of driftwood for our fire.

We always got up early. Most of my memories of this place are sunrise: golden and all-encompassing. Mum would have already been awake. I'd shuffle out to find her, sleepy and rubbing my eyes, and she would be meditating and practising yoga on the grass out front. Her hair in one long plait down her back. Her face radiant in the dawning light.

Mum was always slim and flexible, but here she was whisper-thin and all supple muscle. She would spend hours perfecting increasingly outlandish poses. She'd curl around herself and balance effortlessly on two fingers. Lighter than gravity, she seemed to float on air.

She would have been around twenty-three. A lot of people that young might have hated living somewhere so isolated, but I think the simplicity suited Mum. Or at least it did then. She seemed so much herself. There was no drinking, no drugs, I don't know if she was even smoking cigarettes at this place. Maybe this was her in her realest, most true self – glowing with health; capable of anything – skipping out of bed at 4am to practise yoga. I like to think so.

I don't know how long we were there for.

★

We'd been friends with Nils and Baz for ages when they came up to Waipu to stay the weekend. I don't know how connected they were with drugs at this point. Definitely they had interesting lives beyond importing cocaine. Dividing their time mainly between LA and Auckland, they knew famous musicians and had fascinating girlfriends. Baz had Cleo and Nils had Krista. God knows how. Both women seemed ridiculously out of their respective leagues.

This was the weekend we met Krista. She hadn't been around much due to her constant jetsetting. She was Dutch or Swedish or half of both, and always modelling on location somewhere. She did TV commercials for yoghurt. Nils said Krista ate only raw vegetables and the occasional nut. Baz said Krista was taller than Nils. Tobey and I were equal parts thrilled-anxious that this near-mythical creature would be arriving at our place soon.

But we needn't have worried. Krista was a pussycat. A six-foot-one, Viking wonder woman pussycat. Everything about her was larger than life and flawlessly symmetrical. Perfect teeth, glowing skin: she was so attractive that looking at her full in the face made you blink. I can't remember where she'd flown in from, but it had taken her two days of travel to get to Waipu. After her long journey, rather than hang out with the adults, the first thing she wanted to do was go swimming, Tobey and I happily took her down to the rocks. She stripped off with a startling lack of self-consciousness. Not for Krista was hiding behind a towel sneakily exchanging bra for a bikini top. She stood there starkers, so comfortable in her own gloriously tanned, natural blondeness that she didn't even notice our awkwardly averted eyes.

'The water. It is deep here, yah?'

We nodded, eyes clamped tightly to somewhere higher than her faultlessly round breasts.

With a smile, she stepped lightly across the rocks and dived in, a perfect arch into the water.

Tobey and I looked at each other. My sister, the nihilist, was impressed.

'She even took her knickers off!'

'I know.' Keen to demonstrate I was also a woman of the world, au fait with European customs, I added, 'She's Swedish.'

'She's got massive boobies.'

'Ssh. Be cool.'

Cleo was a different kettle of fish. Also absurdly attractive, but in a different way. Where Krista was a wholesome, friendly giant. Cleo looked like the pages of Mum's French *Vogue* come to life. She was more angular and far more fuck-you. There was a kind of saucy Marie Helvin vibe about her long ringlets. She was also quite tall.

Suddenly Mum wasn't the tallest, most glamorous woman in the room but she didn't seem to mind, and all three women got on well. With Dad being the way he was, you could understand why other women were usually perceived as competition. But you couldn't deny how fun Cleo and Krista were.

Both women had hilarious, scandalously unflattering stories about their men. Cleo told us about the time she and Baz were in Belgium and he was dumb enough to get busted for holding – 'just a fold of coke,' she said, with a shrug. 'Nothing really. But ah, what a klutz.'

He was fine, Belgium jails apparently being as pleasantly appointed as a cheap hotel anywhere else, but after a few weeks their money ran out. Cleo didn't want to leave him in Belgium. Local modelling assignments were scarce, especially as she only had a smattering of French and didn't speak any Dutch or German at all. So she did the obvious thing and advanced their income with a stint of high-class hooking.

'What?!'

'Just sex,' she told us nonchalantly. 'No big deal. Baz knew it was nothing. Anyone in my position would have done the same.'

Laughing at our lack of sophistication, she added that sometimes she didn't even need to have sex. The clients who paid the most didn't actually touch her.

'Whaaat?!'

'The coffee-table guys,' she smiled.

Apparently, there were men who would pay a 'crazy amount' of francs to lie under a glass coffee table and watch Cleo doing a poo above them.

'What do you mean exactly, doing a poo?'

'Oh you know, you squat over the table, one leg on each side and just do it. They lie underneath watching.

It blew my mind.

Krista and Cleo were breezy and independent. Getting married or having children were not on either of their tables, glass or otherwise. Cleo looked at us with speculative interest. What did we *do* exactly? You children? But Tobey and I weren't doing anything, just sitting there quietly, fascinated out of our skulls. Scared of asking too many questions in case we'd be banished from the room.

Cleo was so fashionable, she was ahead of *Vogue*. 'Of course!' she laughed. 'Magazines are *months* old!'

One time we went around to Baz and Cleo's house and she opened the door in a pair of skin-tight leggings. Baby pink with purple and gold-lurex stripes. You could see her crotch! You could see everything! And she'd been out of the house like that – all the way to the shops. Sashaying down the road to buy milk and cigarettes. With her *whole* bum showing! This might have been more shocking than the coffee-table story.

In the car driving home, Mum voiced all of our amazement.

'It was like she thought she was wearing a pair of jeans.'

A month later Mum was wearing a similar outfit, having made the first of many trips to Bloch's ballet shop for the soft-jersey footless tights. They were 'just so comfortable'.

Leggings are normal now, but Cleo was there first. Decades ahead.

Krista had good stories too. She told us about the time Nils took too much acid and blacked out for three days. We'd heard a version of this story before. He'd told us that he'd been a bit out of it.

Krista snorted with laughter, 'Out of it? He was *out cold*. Unconscious.' She waved her hand across her eyes, mimicking lack of vision, 'Nothing. Blackness. Kaput.'

She laughed about it, how she'd had to drag him into the bath and hold his head up so he didn't drown. There was no consideration of taking him to the hospital. She checked his heart, it was beating OK, as far as she could tell.

'What did it feel like?' I asked Nils, amazed.

'Don't remember much of it. You kind of climb into your head. Or maybe you float over the top of it.'

How brilliant. I couldn't wait to try acid.

I sort of knew what he meant.

One time we were sitting in the back office of Artaffection. Tobey, Sofie and Hana and me. Lars and Liva had just flown into town with their daughters, and we kids were catching up on all our news and where everyone had been since we'd last seen each other. They'd been back to Holland and a few new places.

There were these little pine stools. Wide seats and short legs: perfect for dwarves. The four of us were sitting on them in a tight circle, chattering away at each other like parakeets. We were drinking tinned fruit juice, apricot, I think. Something very sweet. There were adults there too, over by the sofas. Maybe twelve or so people in the room. There was a flurry of coming and going around us as a new shipment of tea chests were being unpacked.

And there in the middle of all this activity, I felt a soft tug, like being gently pulled upwards. I thought I was going to faint, but then realised I wasn't dizzy. I stopped resisting the feeling and sort of peeled up and out of myself until I was looking back down on the top of my head. It was a weird, fuzzy-edged sensation. I realised I could affect the fuzziness: just by thinking of going higher, I could go higher.

I lifted to the top of the ceiling and floated around the room a bit, looking down on everything with a kind of hazy detachment. It was like being in a dream, but I got a sense I could go anywhere. Location and maybe even time could be travelled. Just by thinking about somewhere, I could be there. It was all possible. Instead of doing anything interesting or having an epiphany, I just floated there, looking down on my own small head. Would I be able to get back in there? I didn't want to leave my family. I wondered again if I was sick. Was this dying? Was I about to die? For some reason I felt pretty relaxed about it.

I heard someone on the stools below ask me – other, *actual* me – if I was OK. I realised they'd already asked me twice. I saw them shake my shoulder.

Then, like losing balance, I toppled downwards and folded back into myself.

I blinked and looked out of my own eyes again.

'Yeah, fine, why?'

'You looked weird.'

Whatever that was. It never happened again.

1982

Sydney

With all the travel – so many different landscapes swirling past – I'd not been paying attention to the biggest changes. The ones that were happening right in front of my face.

Peace and love and burning incense were old fashioned. Hippies were over. Times, they were a-changin' again. Things were headed up. Up and out. Natural was dreary. Fast and shiny was where it was at now. Everything was big and bright and larger than life. Neon, neon, neon!

We'd sold our share of Artaffection, traipsed about Asia for a bit, and were now back in Australia. The drugs had changed too. For Mum and Dad, it wasn't just about smoking dope anymore. Which didn't seem like a big deal at first.

For some reason we were living in Surry Hills.

This was before it was the coolest part of town. Surry Hills had been a warehouse district. Now many of the old warehouses stood vacant and dilapidated, their walls graffitied and bill posted, windows smashed.

A few years later those warehouses would be on their way to becoming expensive blocks of flats. Some of them would be producing fast fashion: blasting Madonna's *Borderline* from their loading bays and selling racks of oversized t-shirts on the footpath out front. The t-shirts would all have capital-lettered slogans, urging you to RELAX! DON'T DO IT! and CHOOSE LIFE! There'd be a vibe happening on the streets. Coffee bars and pan-pacific brasseries would be edging in. The streets would smell of fresh-roasted flat whites and grilled focaccia.

But in 1982, inner-city industrial wasn't all that chic yet, and Surry Hills didn't smell so good. Mainly it was a place for degenerates: alkies and junkies, rent boys and hookers. The footpaths were gritted with broken bottles. People were slumped in urine-soaked doorways.

The flat we were renting was in the heart of the chaos, just off Crown Street. The building had been a church, and still looked that way from the outside. Apart from the extra-thick bars on all the downstairs windows. Inside, it had been whitewashed over and sliced in half. Our flat was in the back. A real estate office took up the front. Apart from the mournful biblical scenes in stained glass on all the upstairs windows, everything in our half was white.

Our landlord was a well-known radio DJ with a super-conservative image. Dad knew his dealer, who gossiped that the radio DJ also had a massive coke habit on the side.

There wasn't much greenery at Surry Hills. Our backyard had been paved over to make room for a carpark, just like in the Joni Mitchell song. There was a kid's playground a few streets over, but it was basically a few stalks of grass and two broken-down swings. The bins were always overflowing with empty beer bottles and there were a lot of cockroaches: glossy brown ones a few inches long, that would be scuttling over everything.

I'd take Griffy and our little dog, Mick, there, because otherwise we'd just be walking past warehouses and grilled up shopfronts. Griffy preferred to be carried, like a koala bear, and I was fine with that. Even when we got to the park, I didn't like putting him down or letting Mick off his leash, because the grass was flecked with cigarette butts and the bright-orange caps that came from the syringes that junkies used to shoot heroin with.

Sometimes the junkies left their syringes behind too. You'd see them lying in the grass and under the bench. You could tell they were used from the rust-coloured blood left in the barrel. The cockroaches would often be bunched around them.

The junkies themselves you'd see staggering in the street, nodding out and collapsing into doorways. It was hard to even look at them. How had they let their lives get so sad and messy? I couldn't understand how there could be so many of them. You'd think one would be enough. Who would take a look at that lifestyle and want any part of it?

I was obsessed with how easy it would be for the needle of one of those syringes to puncture Griffy's shoe or get stuck in Mick's soft paws. I'd rush around scanning the grass, but even then, I couldn't relax. Who could when there was a hideous disease, sweeping the city like a modern-day plague?

We'd learn more about it in later years – the big disease with a little name as Prince would call it – as it burned across the globe, taking out millions of people. Newspapers would eventually report that it had come from people eating chimpanzees in Africa, not dancing in discos in America. We'd learn how it was transmitted. But in 1982 people were scared. Young people were dying, there was no cure and a lot of confusion. Was it like a flu, could you catch it just from being in the same room?

We didn't know much about AIDS then either. But we knew used needles like the ones lying around in the park could give it to you, and that you didn't have to be gay, because Jimmy, one of Mum and Dad's friends, had AIDS. Jimmy had caught it sharing needles. He'd gone home and given it to his girlfriend before he knew he was infected. And his girlfriend had been pregnant.

Their daughter was born with HIV. It was the saddest thing to think about. Isabelle was a ridiculously cute kid: big blue eyes, dark curls, the sweetest personality. She wasn't allowed to go to nursery or spend time with other toddlers. Jimmy said the only person who ever picked her up apart from himself and his girlfriend was Mum. Mum refused to believe anything bad could happen from hugging Isabelle.

'You're just a little baby,' she'd tell Isabelle, who'd be beaming up at her. 'Such a sweetie. How could *you* hurt anyone?'

I really, *really* hoped Mum was right. People said you could get infected from saliva and Isabelle was one of those extra-droolly babies. It was hard not to stare at her happily gurgling little mouth.

I'd watch the slippery, shiny dribble run down Isabelle's chin and drip onto Mum's hands, and really hope my mum was going to be OK. And also feel guilty about thinking suspicious things about a poor, blameless baby.

★

Things weren't great all over. Mum and Dad were going through a weird stage at Surry Hills. Mum had just found out she was pregnant again. A new Starling was on their way. Which was always terrific news. But otherwise, things felt a bit tense. Mum and Dad were fighting more than usual. Big rows would flare out of nowhere. And they'd got really into cocaine and martial-art movies.

In a remarkably short time, Mum and Dad had escalated from enjoying the odd line here and there, to hoovering up long bumps with their morning tea. Mirrors were off the walls and stretched across the coffee tables. Asian battle cries and anguished death gurgles echoed through the apartment night and day.

So family life was already a little off-kilter when Bridget, Dad's youngest sister, arrived.

She rocked up high as a kite, broke and 'going through some stuff', and of course Mum and Dad said she could stay. She'd stayed with us before. Everyone had. But her being strung out on speed put a new edge to things.

There wasn't a spare room. Mum and Dad moved out of the main bedroom and Etty and her on-off boyfriend, Ivan, moved in. Ivan didn't talk much to us kids. The key things to know about him were that he liked to pee sitting down and was most likely the hairiest man alive. From neck to ankle the man was furrier than a chimp. I wished dearly that I didn't know these things about Ivan, but the toilet was off the corridor and he kept leaving the door wide open.

The whole upstairs was now Mum and Dad's bedroom. Mum bought a king-size futon and turned the open-plan lounge-kitchen space into a huge den of bedroom, like a luxurious desert tent.

The TV was directly in front of the bed, blasting Kung Fu on loop. For a sub-genre, it had a surprisingly extensive back catalogue. Every time you looked at the screen a horrific injury was playing out. I sat down with my breakfast one morning just in time to see some assassin backflip through the air, come to a stop nose-to-nose with their opponent, then skewer out both his eyes with a pair of chopsticks. Eyeballs and eye-tendons ricocheting away in hyper-realistic close-up. It kind of put you off your muesli.

The dining table had been pushed against the far corner, so generally Tobey, Griff and I ate our meals in a row facing the back wall, which was probably for the best. Mum and Dad weren't doing meals at the moment. Pregnant Mum would pick at things and say it was what the baby wanted. The baby liked stuffed green olives and baked rice pudding.

With all the low tables and Gujarat rugs, the lounge/main bedroom reminded me of *Lawrence of Arabia* or possibly the tent Brooke Shields was kidnapped to in the recent movie *Sahara*. Instead of Brooke's dishy French sheik, there was an entourage of shouldered-padded, fluffy-haired guests. Mum and Dad received everyone from their bed, draped in tasselled scarves, like a colourful homage to John Lennon and Yoko Ono's Bed Peace.

Everyone else lay propped on cushions on the floor, tapping their feet to Talking Heads, Duran Duran and John's bits on the *Double Fantasy* album. You had to thread your way through the bodies and wineglasses and mirrors to get to the kitchen. The air hazy as always with smoke.

One of the regular guests was a friend of Etty's who taught at a private school for girls during the day and snorted lines through the night. He didn't look like any teacher I'd ever seen. Handsome, his hair feathered stylishly, a pencil moustache and a permanently loosened tie, he was working a Bryan Ferry *Let's Stick Together* kind of vibe. He was also one of the few visitors who seemed interested in us kids. I couldn't believe how lucky the girls at that school were.

One afternoon he grabbed my leg. I'd been concentrating on getting back from the kitchen: trying not to spill my glasses of apple juice or tread on any bits of flopped-out guests, so it caught me by surprise.

He smiled up at me lazily from the cushions, both his arms wrapping slowly around my leg. There was drug haziness to his face, but his eyes glinted with sharp meaning. I tried to squirm out of his grasp, but he held me fast.

'Hello there you,' he said.

I understood his attention was intended as a compliment. He'd taken time out of his adult socialising to see some value in me, but I was gawky and self-conscious. Not knowing what to do with the attention, I did what I always did, and made everything worse by going bright red.

I'd seen a documentary on strange creatures of the ocean. The scientists were particularly excited by octopuses. They were the strangest creatures of all. Three hearts, eight back-up brains, galaxy-blue blood: deeply mysterious. According to one scientist, octopuses didn't belong on earth; they were so genetically different from all other species living here, they may as well be aliens. But look, said another scientist. They camouflage themselves so well, they can fit in anywhere they go.

What a dream. But, instead of merging quietly with the carpet, when it mattered the most, my survival technique was two burning red cheeks.

The teacher smiled wider, enjoying the reaction.

'Let me go.'

He shook his head no, chuckling as I squirmed more, one of his hands now high above my knee, tracing circles on my inner thigh, 'How old are you anyway?'

'Eleven.'

He tsked, 'An eleven-year-old's got no business wearing those jeans.'

He sounded petulant, unfairly provoked. They were just an old pair of Levi's that someone had given me, so I wasn't sure exactly what he meant. But I figured this was a variation on the 'mature for my age' line that adults often said. Like I was a bizarre cheese. Sometimes I was 'precocious.' Women made these pronouncements too, but it was only men who said it like you were being that way deliberately, to them personally.

'Let me go,' I asked again, all super-awks and trying not to cause a scene.

'Sssh, be nice,' he said, the smile back on his face.

'These'll spill,' I held out the three glasses of apple juice to show him how full they were.

He glanced over to where Mum and Dad were in deep conversation at the head of their bed, and let his hands fall away.

I skittered off with the juices, down the stairs to Griff, Tobey and the jigsaw puzzle we were putting together.

He went back to his high-school girls.

★

The best thing about Surry Hills was the Surry Hills Library. Conveniently situated fifteen minutes' walk away. Most mornings I'd take Griff and Mick there. My two little favourites, one on each side. Mick on his leash, Griffy doing his koala-bear impression on my hip. We'd go to the newsagent, officially for the papers, really for Griffy's daily Matchbox car.

Griff's memory for the model cars was mind-bogglingly precise. As we walked through the shop door, the entry bell chiming behind us, he'd already be frowning with deep concentration. I'd lift him up, so he could take in the whole revolving stand of miniature vehicles. It only took him a spin or two to settle on one he didn't already have, and he rarely got it wrong.

On the way back we'd pop by the library. Mick would lounge on the steps outside, getting some much-needed sunlight – Surry Hills not being super conducive to outside living. Griffy would leaf through the kid's picture books and I'd hit up Fiction. We'd be in and out within minutes.

With a whole library at my disposal, I'd started to read like it was a lucrative sport worth training for. Shelf after shelf I burned through. Two, sometimes three books a day. Classics, moderns, all the James Clavells, twice. Great stories, boring ones. Most had something you could sink into and get lost in.

The 'women's section' was a stand of well-thumbed romance paperbacks. That was where I drew the line. One look at the couples on the covers, shirts unbuttoned, eyes shut in gaudy sunset rapture and you knew to leave well alone.

In the beginning, the librarian scowled and tutted at the age-inappropriate choices I'd bring up to her counter. She wasn't buying the whole, 'they're-for-my-bedridden-mother' routine. But after a few weeks, we were exchanging opinions. She liked the love stories and I preferred war, but we came together on the Agatha Christies.

By the time we left Surry Hills, Griff had at least 200 Matchbox miniatures, Mick's paws were miraculously still intact and the librarian was telling me to give the romance stand a spin, because there weren't any other novels left.

★

I wasn't in on the chats, but it must have been around this time that Dad started thinking about how his import-export business model could work just as well, if not better, with other products. Swapping tribal artefacts for cocaine wasn't a huge stretch. The principle was the same. There'd be international travel; both products were outside the law. Narcotics came with higher risks, but also wider demand. Dad had always been pretty casual about risk, so probably what's surprising is that he didn't think of it sooner.

Like the general mood, Mum and Dad's friends had been changing. No one around the futon was lighting incense or talking about spiritual enlightenment anymore. Someone introduced Mum and Dad to Ramona and Alvaro, and we were working with them now. Most of the family flew out to Fiji to get the ball rolling.

Mick, Aunt Etty and I would stay and mind the house.

I'd always liked Etty, but you had to keep your wits about you. She had a track record of creating havoc.

Being the youngest of Dad's siblings and only ten years older than me, Etty had been my main babysitter when I was little at 231. She would take me out on the kind of excursions that required a lot of promising not to tell either of our mothers. Sometimes she'd pin me down, dangling trails of spit from her mouth over my face to ensure my silence. I didn't need any incentivising not to blab, but she liked to be certain.

Etty had once convinced Poppa to buy her a crazy ex-racehorse. A magnificent-looking stallion: glossy as black oil and seething with rage. Ike's previous owners had deemed him un-rideable. Etty had saved Ike from the glue factory, but he wouldn't let her ride him either. Anytime she managed to get him still enough for her to climb up into the saddle, he'd just buck her off.

She took me to meet him just after I'd turned four. We had to catch three different buses out to the rural fields where he lived, so it seemed a great adventure.

Her thinking was probably that Ike wouldn't mind such a little load, and to be fair, he didn't buck me off. Instead, as soon as I'd been lifted up and plonked onto the saddle, Ike bolted like his backside had caught fire.

I didn't know about stirrups and reins, but I wouldn't have been able to reach them anyway. I grabbed at Ike's mane like my life depended on it, which it felt like it did.

I looked down at Etty for help. But she'd suddenly become a tiny figure behind us. A distant voice came over the field, 'Tell Ike to halt, to HALT!'

I was bouncing too hard to be able to tell Ike anything. Jolting and sliding around somewhere near the beginning of his neck. He was thundering down the fields, going so fast the grass below us was a blur. It did not look soft. I couldn't see Ike's hooves, but I knew I didn't want to fall anywhere near the source of the pounding sound that was throwing up showery clumps of dirt.

There was plenty of land for Ike to run off his fury and he was really going for it. Each time I came down onto the edge of the saddle, I was thrown up into the air again. The only part of me properly on the horse were my hands gripping his hair. I didn't know if I could keep holding on. I wasn't sure I liked horse riding.

Then I saw a dark shape of brambles up ahead. With desolate, sparse field on either side, Crazy Ike was heading straight for the brambles, as if magnetically drawn to the razor-sharp thorns. A bramble mound the size of a house and we were roaring towards it.

'Ha-a-alt! Ple-ase. Ha-a-a-a-alt'.

The horse couldn't give a fig, he gave no sign of slowing down.

I braced myself for certain, scratchy pain. Maybe death. I shut my eyes.

But, at the last minute, Ike pulled up. Rearing up on his back legs like a movie horse, me clinging on like a tearful starfish.

Meeting Ike had been one of the Aunt Etty excursions that had to be kept quiet about.

Here we were alone together at Surry Hills. Mum and Dad had left us both with money. Etty had most of it, and I had some back-up notes, just in case of emergency. By day three, Etty had blitzed through her amphetamines and all the money she'd been given to buy our food.

She needed a fix and knew I had some cash hidden away. Things got scratchy between us when I wouldn't hand it over. Negotiations spiralled to the point where she was chasing me down the stairs. I made it to the outside of my bedroom door before she reached me, pushing me up against the wall.

'Just get the money you little brat!'

'No. I won't.'

Why should I? I thought. Stubborn as an eleven-year-old mule. How was *this* an emergency? Plus, Etty had had friends over partying all night and the cupboards were pretty bare. Mick needed dog food too. As it was, unless both Mick and I skipped our treats, my money probably wouldn't last the fortnight.

Etty had her hands around my throat and started to grip tighter in frustration. She was drunk and reeling, her eyes bloodshot. I don't know when she'd last slept. I guess she was thinking that the only thing between her and good times was the little brat in front of her.

I was thinking, I'd *die* before handing over my money. There was no way Mick and I were going hungry, just because Etty wanted to party.

Etty was foamy in the corners of her mouth and had pretty much lost control. Legitimately manic. She kept squeezing my throat, the weight of her body pinning me against the wall. I couldn't breathe. My vision was blurring. Somewhere in the background she was yelling at me and Mick was barking.

Then Mick bit her leg.

Etty screamed, kicked at him and loosened her grip long enough for me to wriggle free.

Mick and I scrambled into my room and I slammed shut the door. Luckily the ultra-conservative, but coke-loving radio DJ landlord had opted for doors with solid locks when he'd signed off on his church renovations. Etty banged against the door for a while, but we were safe. Me heaving for breath. Mick growling at Etty under the gap. He'd never even pretend-bitten anyone before.

The rest of the fortnight, the two of us holed up in my bedroom, stealing out for food and a quick walk first thing in the morning when Etty was asleep. When we heard her go out, we'd make covert reconnaissance dashes. Occasionally she'd bang on the door and we heard other voices upstairs, but I only had to look at the necklace of bruises around my neck to stay put. Mick seemed happy with that plan too.

Mick had always been superb company. He just got things. No one could read a room like him. All the dogs we lived with over the years were ace, but Mick was the most loyal friend we ever had. Heart big as a house. Smarter than a lot of people I knew, easily twice as brave. He was such a good dog.

Dad had come home with him one morning when we were living in Devonport. He'd walked in with something moving inside his inner jacket pocket. We crowded around to see what it was. Dad reached in and there, sitting in the palm of his hand was the cutest little guy ever. Black and brindle fur with a soft triangle face. The tiniest Staffordshire terrier puppy. He'd been the runt of his litter. Too small to sell, and the guy had owed Dad some money.

'Aww, what's his name?' we asked Dad.

Dad thought for a second, 'Mick.'

Dad put Mick on the floor. The puppy looked up at us, gave us a jaunty tail wag and marched past us, down the hallway and straight into the airing closet, as if he'd been in our house a million times. We all looked at each other and laughed. The whole family was in love. Mum got him a towel to snug up in, and the bottom of the airing closet, next to the warmth of the boiler was now Mick's home.

Years later we were living in Bilgola Plateau, Sydney, in a house perched atop a near-vertical driveway leading to a busy road: a 30ft cliff drop on the other side. The driveway was so steep we sat in the car like a team of astronauts about to launch. God knows why we lived in all these precarious places, but we did. Anyway, one afternoon Dad and Griff were in the car waiting for Mum, Tobey and me to lock up the house.

Dad got out to yell at us to hurry up. Griff climbed into the front seat to follow him, knocking the handbrake. The car lurched backwards, reversing at speed down the driveway towards the traffic.

Dad had fast reflexes, but before he could react, Mick had already propelled himself from nowhere, up through the air and into the car's open window. I don't know how he thought he could stop the car with no opposable thumbs, but he was clearly trying to save four-year-old Griffy.

A split-second later Dad pulled a similar move, launching himself horizontally through the air at the handbrake, half his body in the car, the other half being dragged down the driveway. The car came to a juddering halt in the road, traffic on both sides slamming their brakes and screeching to a stop.

Five minutes later we were all in the car, driving into town. Windows down, wind in our hair, sunset in our eyes, bopping along to Roxy Music. I looked over at Mick on the seat beside me and patted his head. He looked back with an easy smile. That was just the kind of dog Mick was, he'd do anything for you and not think it any big deal.

When Dad and Tobey got back from Fiji, the atmosphere between Etty and me was laughed off as family scrapping, which was fine by me. I didn't want to think about it anymore either. Besides, Dad had some great news: I was going to fly over to help Mum. I'd never been to Fiji before and I was well up for getting out of the house for a bit.

The next morning Dad drove me to the airport and off I went. Trotting through passport control. I was waiting quietly at my departure gate, boarding pass clasped in hand, when one of the check-in staff stalked over to let me know I was an 'unaccompanied minor'. They'd need to supervise me in the air, she said, eyeing me warily. This seemed dramatic: I was a kid, not a raving imbecile. It's not like I'd be flinging open a window.

An hour into the flight, one of the attendants asked me to move to first class. Instead of being thrilled with delight like any normal person, I felt a bit singled-out. To be yanked from my seat and taken to an otherwise vacant part of the plane seemed weird. The attendant didn't explain why, she must have thought it was obvious. She flashed a double-decker grin and told me to enjoy the view.

Sat in my massive, creamy white leather seat, I looked around. Instead of the sardine-packed rows I'd come from, there was literally no one but me. I was right in the nose of the plane. The pilot was either directly above or the plane was driving itself. In front of me was all window and sky.

The view was incredible. It was entirely wasted on me. Instead of loving the experience, watching the clouds part exquisitely ahead, I sat perched on the edge of my seat fretting. Finally, the captain announced our descent. I buckled my seatbelt tighter, relieved the ordeal was over. We landed and taxied along the tarmac.

As the plane came to a stop, I looked up to the terminal and gasped in horror.

I'd never been to Fiji, but I knew vaguely what a Fijian looked like. I'd been looking forward to seeing Afro hair, red hibiscus flowers, big smiles, possibly the odd grass skirt. What I saw was saris. It was a small airport with an outside viewing balcony out front. Jammed on the balcony, elbow-to-elbow, down the length of the building, were people of unmistakably South Asian origin, pretty saris billowing wide in the wind. Not a single Afro among them.

I didn't have a scooby about the ethnic split of Fiji: the mass immigration from India, the indentured labouring in the sugar cane plantations, the complex and questionable British involvement. I'd no clue that indigenous Fijians were currently an ethnic minority in their own country.

All I could see were Indian people.

I'd caught the wrong plane and flown to India.

Mind shrieking with panic, I scuttled off the plane with the rest of the passengers. Somehow I'd have to get myself on another flight. How? I had no money. Did flights even go between India and Fiji? Mum and Dad were going to kill me.

There were no public phones in the immigration hall. I would have to get through passport control first. Screaming panic! That made everything official. Was I going to be arrested for being in the wrong country? What would they do to me? How could I have been so stupid? Those flight attendants had been right about me. What an imbecile.

At passport control, the Sikh immigration officer flicked through my documents. I looked past his turban to the three heavily armed Indian guards standing by the wall, and tried to look normal.

He stamped my passport and I bolted. Running through the hall, searching desperately for a phone.

'Saylor, *Saylor*!'

I spun around. There, against all probability, was my mother.

Apparently, Fiji is delightful. I didn't see much of it. On the cab ride to the hotel, it started raining. It didn't stop raining. For the duration of my stay, it just kept raining. I'd never been anywhere in the world with such committed wetness. Even up on Sai Baba's mountains in Puttaparthi, there'd been the occasional breather.

The precise detail of why we were in Fiji was murky, but the jist of it was that we were helping Ramona and Alvaro bring a consignment of their cocaine back to Sydney. I'd only met Ramona and Alvaro briefly, but they seemed a little highly strung. The story was that they'd had a tough life, so we should make allowances. They had seen things that would make anyone go batty (these 'things' allegedly included gruesome murder. It was never clarified, least not in my presence, who had been doing the murdering). Also, their contacts were superb.

Ramona and Alvaro might not have been the most stable of tables, but they did make a compelling argument for drugs being a high-return business model. Growing up dirt poor in the backwaters of Caracas, Venezuela, life hadn't been easy for Ramona and Alvaro. But, thanks to cocaine importation, they had turned their lives around and now travelled the world, staying in fancy hotels and living their best lives.

Ramona and Alvaro had a son called Miguel. Normally, Tobey and I would be thrilled spending time with another kid. But Miguel wasn't the least bit interested in playing with us, and to be honest, we weren't crazy about him. The kid had two emotions: high-pitched sorrow or explosive anger. He was endlessly kicking things: tables, walls, hotel staff… anything that stood in his way was rewarded with a sharp hit of his eight-year-old boot. Ramona would just shrug her shoulders noncommittally at the limping waiter or the weeping receptionist. Alvaro didn't bother noticing at all.

The family's hotel room was a Jackson Pollock of strewn clothes, food-splattered toys and leftover room service. No one with even the slightest sense of smell could go near the bathroom. There was a panel of wallpaper by Miguel's bed that had been ripped off just to spite it. Deep tracks of a recent breakfast had been driven into the carpet pile under the wheels of Miguel's Tonka truck. You could tell it was the Tonka, because there were matching egg and beans still wedged in its tyre treads.

Ramona and Alvaro's lack of parental embarrassment was bizarre and exotic. Miguel seemed to live entirely without consequence. He did whatever he wanted. He ate pancakes with chocolate sauce for lunch and Coco Pops with ice cream for dinner. He slept long into the day and stayed up, rollercoastering sugar highs and lows, late into the night.

After midnight he'd be zigzagging his remote-controlled cars into walls or anyone unfortunate enough to be caught walking the hotel corridors. Back in their room, his parents would be on their own rollercoaster: blasting their ghetto box and feverishly razor-blading the glass coffee table.

Miguel often smelt like pee and I wondered what his bathing routine was like. He *didn't even have to take a bath*. It was anarchy.

At Fiji there were delays with the shipment. By the time I got there, siege mentality had set in. What was meant to have been a two-day turnaround was now deep into its third week. The hotel was nice, but nowhere you'd want to be stuck.

Mum and I weren't out exploring the island. Besides the matter of pouring rain, we were here to work. And it was a fulltime job keeping Ramona and Alvaro from getting arrested. For successful international drug dealers, these people were *not* cool. They attracted a lot of attention. Besides being wincingly rude to everyone they came across, Ramona and Alvaro had crazy-white capped teeth and wore a lot of clashing Versace and Gucci prints. They were both short, so the overall impression was two tropical parrots out for a night on the town in novelty Bee Gees chew-sets. All three of them – Miguel included – jangled about under kilos of gold jewellery.

But really, the biggest problem with Ramona and Alvaro was the amount of marching powder it took to keep them on track. Their own supply of coke had run dry two days in. Some local gear had been sourced, but being of inferior quality, it had almost immediately run out. There had been house calls to the hotel's doctor for various pharmaceutical alternatives. Then, increasingly desperate, late-night excursions to other doctors' surgeries across the island.

Meanwhile the rain kept sheeting down. Everything was damp and soggy. Everywhere in the hotel I went, the staff and guests were talking about the weather. Nobody could believe how much it rained. No one had seen anything like it. The hotel staff were friendly at first, but once they realised Mum and I were friends of the party in room 106, the smiles were more like shuddery grimaces.

Day after day, I pulled back the curtains to reveal grey gloom. I read the books on the guest sharing shelves. Even the mouldy old Danielle Steels. Between meals I'd slump around to the deserted pool and do some rain swimming. Pools weren't as fun without Tobey. There wasn't much point diving for pebbles on your own, but I tried to make the best of it.

One afternoon after splashing about for a bit, I noticed something in the water with me. Something long and rippling down the deep end of the pool. I couldn't see clearly in the driving rain, but I could tell that whatever was down there, was something big and entirely out of place.

It wasn't until I was almost directly above the dark shape that I saw it was a body. Someone was lying face down, under about 12ft of water on the bottom of the pool.

I screamed for help, waving and swallowing water in my panic. A raincoated gardener who had been forlornly raking up soggy leaves on the other side of the garden headed over.

I dived down. It was Ramona. How long had she been in the water? I'd been in the pool for minutes, how had I not seen her?

Reaching around her arms underwater, I tried to pull her up. It wasn't easy to get her off the bottom of the pool; she was heavy and her skin felt slippery. Using the pool floor to push against, I finally managed to propel her to the surface. Struggling to keep her face above water, I splashed and choked my way to the edge of the pool where the gardener was standing nervously. Ramona was lifeless: her mouth was open and full of chlorine-y water.

'Help me pull her up,' I spluttered at the gardener.

He didn't move. His eyes round with horror. The poor guy didn't want to touch her. Mainly because she was topless, but also because her tiny pink bikini briefs had gone brown. She'd pooped herself.

'You have to! I can't get her up by myself.'

After he'd finally dragged her out over the lip of the pool, he jogged away to get help. Ramona lay on the tiles on her back, all pruned up and not a sign of life. She felt cold. Why on earth hadn't I seen her straightaway?

I listened at her chest. All I could hear was my own heart hammering.

Anyone who had watched the slightest bit of TV knew this was where you started mouth-to-mouth resuscitation. But how did that go exactly? There was special timing you had to do. What if I counted wrong and hurt her? I tilted Ramona's head sideways and pushed down on the part of her chest that wasn't breast. Was she dead? It seemed like she must be dead: there was no way I could hold my breath underwater that long. I kept pumping her chest. It didn't seem like it was helping, but I couldn't bring myself to stop.

Then, as the gardener jogged back with some other hotel staff, Ramona started coughing up water.

She was wrapped in hotel towels and wheeled off to her room. The official story was that she'd had a leg cramp and blacked out, but really their coke had finally arrived and she'd overdosed.

Ramona was back at the dinner table that night. Laughing and drinking as normal. Nothing was mentioned about the afternoon's escapade, other than to say the consignment had been tested. It was good, 'very good,' she said. 'Maybe a leetle stronger than usual.'

Mum and I were on the flight back to Sydney the next morning.

When we got back, we were living in a different place.

At some point during the time Mum and I were in Fiji, Etty had convinced Dad that a serious international entrepreneur such as himself should not be cooped up in an inner-city apartment. Entirely unsupervised, they had packed up our whole apartment and moved everything up the coast to the deluxe Palm Beach peninsula.

The move happened in the dark of night. God knows what state the two of them left Surry Hills in, or how much of our stuff they left behind. Dad liked a pristine home as much as Mum, but he didn't involve himself in the actual cleaning, and Etty was never too fussed about such details.

Dad met us at the airport. Surprise! We had a new place! Right on the water! A house with its own jetty! Our backyard was a whole ocean! He was practically doing jazz hands around the steering wheel as he accelerated out into the freeway.

Mum didn't need much convincing. We weren't exactly a family who feared change. But Dad was still feverishly explaining the move. And it wasn't just a move. Dad said this would be a new start. He and Mum would quit the coke. Or maybe just save it for special, *special* occasions. We'd all get healthy. He spun around to look at me in the backseat, the road in front of him unmonitored.

'When was the last time we had a family dinner?' He demanded, eyes as manic as a man who'd been awake for a week; snorting lines and cooking schemes with his naughty little sister. 'WHEN?!'

I did love the sound of what he was saying though.

'Dad, is Mick there?'

'Mick..? Yes! Mick loves the place. LOVES IT!'

I settled into the backseat and looked out the window, listening to Dad raving to Mum about how great our new life was going to be, as the city swept by.

It was strange not going back to Surry Hills. I thought about the room Tobey and I had shared. The metal bunks we'd slept in. It wasn't the best place we'd lived, but we had been there an awfully long time. Six months at least. If I was honest, I was feeling robbed, not of the place, but of my goodbye. That weirdo little moment I liked to have standing in the empty rooms after everyone had left. It felt like quite a lot had happened at Surry Hills.

Then I heard Dad say something about 231.

I pricked up my ears at the good news, 'Dad, are we going back to Auckland soon?'

'Everyone's moving over here!' More jazz hands from Dad.

'What do you mean?'

Nanny and Poppa Starling were selling 231. They were formally separating. They were both moving to Australia, but to different houses. Maybe different states. We wouldn't be seeing 231 again, and anyway it had already been sold. The new owners already had it. It was gone.

'Onwards and upwards!' cried Dad. 'That house's been a weight round our necks for years.'

I thought about my weedy little macadamia tree outside the washhouse. Suddenly it seemed really precious. I'd never given it a chance. Why had I been so harsh with it? Would the new owners even know it was a macadamia tree? Would they look after it properly? What about all the other things? The rockery, the pear and grapefruit trees. The potholes on the driveway, the toast-smelling hallways. Where would we live now? When we ran out of money again, there would be nowhere for us to go. We didn't even have Grannie May to help us anymore.

It was late night when we arrived at our new home. We swung into the carport and the headlights beamed across a riot of salmon pink concrete and deeply brown tiles. Dad wasn't kidding about it being on the water, I jumped out of the car and ran to the edge of the carport. Directly below, a long way down, was dark water. The house was chiselled straight into the cliff face.

It looked precarious, but once you walked in, the place felt solid enough. The walls were spiky stucco, the floors light pink shagpile and there were oppressive amounts of brown tiling, but also loads of space. Most rooms had a balcony. Bedrooms had their own bathrooms. At Surry Hills there'd been one bathroom between everyone. Here I had a whole bedroom to myself *with* a balcony *and* a bathroom. We were living the high life. Like sixties-era James Bond villains.

Exploring the perimeters first thing the next morning I discovered there was no garden whatsoever. We were a hundred percent dangling off a cliff, clinging on for dear life over the Pittwater. But clinging below us, under the last floor of the house were four flights of steps that took me to a jetty (tiled brown to match the kitchen, bathrooms, carport and everything else not stuccoed or shagged).

Sitting on the jetty were two kayaks. I figured they must have come with the house. I'd never been in a kayak, but how hard could it be?

I dragged one of them across the jetty and popped it into the dark green water to find out. Not learning a thing from my Norfolk Island errors, I jumped in and paddled off. Right out across the bay into the morning mist.

Later I found out they didn't come with the house. Someone had owed Dad money and he'd collected it in kayak. No one else at the house was particularly interested, so they sort of became mine. I paddled out most days. The Pittwater was deep enough for the occasional ocean liner, but usually quite smooth. Kayaking was easy-peasy, lemon-squeezy.

At least once a week, I'd take my two-year-old brother and Mick the dog: Mick tucked into the hollow nose and Griffy sitting on my lap in a raincoat. They loved it. When they were with me, I kept to the tidal coastline. Mostly we paddled through the mangroves, avoiding raw open sea, so I must have had a speck of sense. But it wasn't until I saw some adults struggle to stay afloat a year or so later, long after we'd moved out of Palm Beach, that it even occurred to me that you could capsize a kayak.

Watching the adults flapping about in shallow water, I saw how easy it would be to flip over and get stuck, trapped upside. A shudder ran through me thinking about Griff and Mick. What an idiot, terrible big sister I was. We'd been very lucky.

★

Palm beach was a weird house. But it wasn't the house's fault some of us went crazy there.

The first problem was that money was pouring in. *Pouring* in. Fiji had turned out to be a good move. The deal had gone great. Dad couldn't put all the cash in the bank, so he bought a safe. And an automatic handgun, to be extra safe.

On the second morning we were there, the entrance chimes pealed majestically through the house. Mum and Dad were still in bed, so it was me who answered the door to an extremely tanned man in expensive leisurewear.

Our landlord apparently. 'And what's *your* name, little lady?' he said.

'You don't say? Well *hello* Saylor,' he grinned, and bobbed his head forward into my face.

I blinked in horror. I'd felt his actual lips! All prickly and old.

On my mouth. My actual mouth! The man was at least forty. Older than Dad. *Ewww.*

The landlord sailed on with an explanation about his own house being directly across the Pittwater. He could see us clearly, he said with deep meaning. If there was anything I needed, just give him a little wave and he'd be back over in a jiffy... So, did I like my room?

I nodded mutely. My room was glass windows from ceiling to floor. Entirely see-through. Most of the house was.

'OK then, tell your parents I said hi.'

He leapt back into his sportscar, winked extravagantly and accelerated off.

Everyone thought my story of meeting the landlord was hila-riiiii-ous, but after I said he might have a pair of binoculars, our curtains were pulled more often than not. With all the windows we were like goldfish in a bowl. It wasn't hard to feel watched.

I was also a bit uneasy about the handgun. Yes, it felt cool to hold. So solid and neat in your hand. Surprisingly heavy. But Griffy had always been desperate for a toy gun. I'd never let him have a pretend gun, so us now having a real one with a jumbo box of live bullets in the house seemed unfair.

Also Mum and Dad had been arguing more.

They'd never been the kind of couple to settle disagreements with a calm exchange of viewpoints, but since Surry Hills, the rows had been fiercer. It seemed a long time since I'd seen them be all cute with each other. Exchanging those secret little smiles like they used to.

Stuff had been coming up from the past. Things that Dad had done behind Mum's back. There were also things Mum had done behind Dad's back. But mostly it was Dad doing the things, and mostly what he'd done was other women. Dad called Mum terrible things. Mum reminded Dad he'd had a threesome with two of her friends – who were sisters! *Sisters*! – one night while she was asleep in the room upstairs. *Upstairs*!

It's not like I thought they'd shoot each other, exactly. But things could escalate fast.

At Surry Hills Mum and Dad had started throwing cups and plates at each other's heads. Now there were heavier, more hurtful things being hurled. I'd find shards of chunky glass ashtrays in the rubbish bin. The occasional unlucky lampshade or chair that Dad had kicked in, or swung against a wall. Paintings with a fist-shaped rip through their centre.

I worried how easy it would be for things to get out of hand if that gun came out of the safe.

One night we heard Mum and Dad screaming at each other especially savagely. Mum shouting that she didn't want it in the house. Dad roaring back that he just wanted to fucking try it, alright? Whatever it was that Dad wanted to try, apparently it was no fucking worse than all the fucking coke. Which they were still doing every day.

Usually, they'd be fine in the morning. All happy and made up again. But this row raged on, for days and deep through the night. You'd wake up with a start. Realise it was just another piece of furniture being smashed. Look at the clock, see it was only 3am, burrow under the covers and try to get back to sleep. Any time you got up and tried to intercept, they'd both just turn and yell at you to stay out of it.

On and on it went. Things felt tense.

Tobey, Griff and I tiptoed around during the day, whispering, not wanting to wake them up and have it all start again. I'd check the gun was still locked in the safe.

Then, after about four days and nights, it all went quiet.

At the time that seemed like a good sign. It took me a while to realise what they had been arguing about. What it was going to mean for all of us.

Hash, grass, tobacco, alcohol, the odd magic mushroom, lately a lot of coke. There were always drugs around, always had been. Sometimes drugs were interesting – I'd always liked the sound of LSD – but mainly they were stinky and inconvenient. A drug-free homelife would have been preferable, obviously, but I don't remember actively hating drugs. Tobey and I didn't think too much about them. Not until Palm Beach.

Dad had won the argument.

Behind their locked door, in the quiet, Mum and Dad were trying heroin.

It's not like anyone could stop them from doing what they wanted, least of all me. But by the time I'd understood what was happening, they were shooting it into the veins in their arms.

I walked into their room and they were both passed out, mouths open, out cold. There were syringes on the bedside table. Dad had one in his hand. Mum's thin leather belt was still looped around his elbow. There was a long, wet smear of blood down his arm.

I saw the plastic syringe caps on their bed – the same bright-orange ones that had littered the Surry Hills grass – and didn't know what to do.

I just stood there with my mouth open too.

Heroin was what Jimmy had got AIDs from. Heroin was why baby Isabelle might never have a third birthday. It was in all those blood-smeared needles in the Surry Hills park. It was why all those junkies were slumped in filthy doorways, rotting from their insides out. Heroin was the stuff of nightmares. How could it be in our house, *inside our home*?

Maybe if Mum and Dad had just been snorting it, it wouldn't have been so bad.

When I found out that you don't need to stick needles into your veins to take it, I couldn't believe my parents were. There are other ways. Assuming you *need* to take it at all. Heroin (or smack, junk, horse, H, brown sugar, Chinawhite, etc, etc) becomes a vapour when heated, so you can smoke or 'chase' it. You can snort it. Probably you can add it to tea and sip it down with a slice of lemon and a digestive biscuit.

There was a lot to learn about heroin. None of it good.

People shoot it because the hit is stronger, but injecting is gruesome. First, you have to put aside your fears about needles. Which, in 1982, were pretty legit fears. AIDs was associated with the gay community then, but all the junkies knew it was just as likely to come for them. Individuals who injected heroin were 28 times more likely to contract HIV. In 1982, contracting HIV meant a sad, painful death. Wasting away in a hospital bed with big purple lesions and no one wanting to touch you.

But, if that didn't put you off needles, mainlining your heroin into a vein was the popular way to do it. Like Mum and Dad, the crook of the arm, or cubital fossa, is where most junkies start injecting. The veins here are close to the skin's surface and, given their large size and distinctive, bluish colour, easy to see. If you tie a belt around them real tight, they'll helpfully bulge out a bit for easy access.

Once the walls of the cubital fails – and if you keep injecting the same spot without letting the constant bruising and red abscesses (track marks) heal, most likely they *will* fail – you'll have to move on to veins in your groin, between your toes, even inside your eye, just under the socket.

Intravenous heroin use can destroy muscle, organ and skin tissue. You also have to be careful not to include any air bubbles in the shot. Just 1ml of air in the wrong vein can be fatal in seconds. Think: air embolism, stroke and complete cardiac arrest.

Then there's the heroin itself. As with any illegal, non-regulated drug, it's tricky to know what you're actually putting into your system.

If the heroin is purer than your body is used to, you could be overdosed and dead in minutes. Street heroin is typically less than fifty percent pure though, so the more pressing concern is what your heroin's been mixed with. Excluding the impoverished poppy farmers working in the fields, you have to imagine that every dirty little pair of mitts who's been handling your drugs has added something to step up their profit margin.

Common powders to cut heroin with include, but are not limited to: baking soda, baby laxative, talcum powder, powdered milk, flour and sugars, caffeine, paracetamol, fentanyl, laundry detergent and rat poison. Nothing you'd want near a major vein.

Also, hygiene. No one talks about this. I don't know why. Aside from the high probability that your score has spent time being carted about in a series of bum holes, there's not as much handwashing in the drug trade as you'd hope.

Junkies have a terrible life expectancy. If you classify heroin as a disease, it's up there with cancer.

If you're *still* not put off, try watching someone actually take heroin. Someone you love.

You see them tie off, tap up their poor vein until it bulges. Then sink the needle in. There's a spray of blood – arcing up the wall, across the bedding, the wall or wherever they're sitting – as they flush the syringe, because heroin is now far more precious than anything else, including their own blood.

A second later their eyes roll up and they collapse backwards or sideways into the wall or cushions or whatever's there to take their weight. Apparently, it feels euphoric, like the best thing they've felt. Better than food or sex or swimming in the ocean. But it *looks* like you're watching your Mum and Dad dying, right in front of you. Every time. And every time you know that you might be. If you're around junkies shooting up, you spend a lot of time thinking about death.

Then comes the hours of nodding off where they're not quite out cold, definitely not awake. While there's plenty of drug in their system, they're very sleepy, like overtired toddlers. Their head gets heavy on their neck. It starts to droop. Their mouth hangs open. Maybe they drool. I don't know who wants to see their own thirtysomething parents dribbling.

Fun fact. When Bayer were synthesizing their latest painkiller back in 1897, they apparently coined the name heroin after some of their test subjects said they felt like heroes while they were on it. Were those Bayer scientists out of their white-coated minds? Did they even look at their test subjects? Slumped over, a burning cigarette in their hands, eyes half-open, head all-gone: it's hard to understand anyone thinking *that* looks heroic.

Later there's the itching as they start to hang out. Which gets worse as the gap between their last fix widens. Some people will scratch so much, there's little halfmoons of blood and skin permanently under their nails.

The more I learned about heroin, the more fun it got. There were so many details. The big detail was how much it changed our lives. Overnight. It was like going to bed in one life and waking up in a completely different one. Things looked the same, but they were not the same.

This wasn't just a hobby for Mum and Dad, like the other drugs. This drug they couldn't do anything without. They'd shoot up before getting out of bed to pee in the morning.

I kept remembering all those cockroaches clustered around the syringes at Surry Hills and that was how I pictured heroin. It was a filthy, sticky-blooded cockroach that had our parents in its grip.

Maybe it's unfair to blame a drug for all the trouble that came. Like guns and money, maybe drugs are just a means to an end. Maybe we were already tinder waiting to burn.

But how it felt was that we had an arch nemesis. Grannie May was gone. 231 was sold and now we were alone with this monster cockroach stalking us through the house, its long antennae flicking and foul.

★

There weren't many guests at Palm Beach. Aunt Etty had moved out after a couple of weeks. It wasn't the fights or the drugs she had a problem with: the house had just turned out to be too far from the city. Aunt Erin came for a few weeks, but left suddenly. No one else was invited around to hang out.

Craig moved into the bedroom upstairs: he'd help with security and driving. He didn't look especially threatening: six-foot-three, but with the kind of floppy blond hair and super-even smile that made you think of TV ads for secretly unhealthy muesli.

Craig was very nice, and also a raving alcoholic. It seemed such a shame. His pretty blue eyes always being red-rimmed, like some cruel beauty company had tested their mascaras on him. He drank Napoleon brandy, in various-sized bottles. There were always a handful of empty ones on the floor of the Range Rover. Each time we took a corner, there would be a tinkling as all the little Napoleons rolled together.

We'd never been a family with much of a schedule. Mum and Dad laughed at the idea of circadian rhythms. Night-times weren't necessarily for sleeping. But now that they needed a fix every four hours, things were a lot more predictable.

Besides the sprays of blood, the blackened tablespoons, the cigarette burns on everything and all the plastic orange syringe caps, the other thing the cockroach nemesis brought to our home was routine.

Pretty soon, we all knew where we'd be and what we'd be doing at any given time.

Mum and Dad were mostly either asleep or shooting up downstairs in the grand bedroom. We didn't see much of them during the day. Their stunning view across the bay obscured with blackout curtains.

Upstairs, we'd be creeping around with worried eyes. I'd always liked the idea of a family routine, but it hadn't turned out to be as calming as I'd expected.

Tobey mostly went to school. Griffy mostly played with his Matchbox cars. Craig would be scarfing down brandy in the top-floor bedroom, and I'd mostly be baking.

Baking. Even I could tell the baking was a bit odd. But it started reasonably enough.

One morning I got out of bed, walked upstairs and looked around. If proof was needed that things were not OK with our family, here it was. There were overflowing ashtrays, puddles of spilt red wine, an overturned chair. But it wasn't just the usual clutter of mess that happened in the night.

In the kitchen a track of ants was marching cracker crumbs across the floor, up the bench and out the window. The sink was piled with dirty dishes and leftover food. The fridge was empty and the rubbish bin was overflowing. Things looked bad, *out of control* bad.

Mum had always made sure our homes were clean. She'd done it so easily – all swishy and fast, like she walked up a road – that I'd not understood the importance of her work. Clean was safety. Having a neat house had been keeping a tumbling avalanche of chaos from overwhelming our family.

Probably I didn't think too deeply about it that morning. Mum usually did the tidying up. Now she wasn't. As the eldest, I needed to help get us back on track.

I started disinfecting down the benches.

From then on, I'd be springing out of bed early to sort things out. On some weird mission to lemon-fresh the world. But I lacked Mum's finesse, and there was always something more to polish or scrub. Every day there was new dust. The closer you looked, the more dirt you saw.

The first thing I always did was look for the little orange caps. I started getting awfully particular about eradicating all signs of cockroach. Dad used to hate plastic. There was a time when plastic had been banned from our home, now it was wedged in the carpet, down the back of the sofa, rolling across the bathroom sink, scattered through Mum and Dad's bed, in Dad's pockets, caught in the rubber lip on the door of the washing machine…

Tobey would leave for school and Griffy would follow me around the house happily playing with his cars as I looned about. I don't know how much Mum and Dad noticed. Griffy was just a toddler. Neither Mick the dog or Craig the driver enjoyed my vacuuming, but they both politely kept their views to themselves.

Then came the cooking. Just a few omelettes and soups at first, to give Griff and Tobey a break from toast and beans for dinner. Because I didn't know how to cook many things, I bought some cookbooks down at the bookstore in town.

One, then two cookbooks. Then lots of them.

The *Women's Weekly* range was my gateway, but I soon moved on to fancier-looking books. I'd flick through the pictures and try out a couple of different dishes every night.

With the fancy recipes came more intricate ingredients and instruments. I'd be merrily buying saffron strands and star aniseed. Special measuring utensils, flour shifters, tart tins with easy-release bottoms, weird little beads to weigh down the pastry inside the tart tins… who knew there was so many types of baking flour!

Most days went like this: dress Griffy and myself. Make breakfast.

See Tobey off to school. Do tidying. Grab a wad of cash from under the gun in the safe and go wake up Craig.

Bleary-eyed, Craig would drive me to the shops where I'd spend an increasingly ridiculous amount of money at the greengrocer, the supermarket and a boutique, speciality cook's store. Craig waited in the carpark, surreptitiously sipping on a brown-bagged 750ml Napoleon.

We'd come home. Unpack. I'd go for a kayak. By about 3pm, I'd be back in the kitchen, whisking and double-baking like a maniac. I'd spend hours, *hours* cooking these weirdly overblown meals.

I'm not sure how it all got so out of hand.

I thought about Grannie May a lot when I was in the kitchen. Maybe it was the smell of all the baking. Cookies in the oven. The sugary rise of sponge cake...

It was clear Griff was his own, brand-new person. Much as I adored him – and probably I couldn't have loved the little Griffster more – as soon as he'd started talking in full sentences my reincarnation scheme had tanked. Griff wouldn't be morphing into a grandmother anytime soon.

So I knew Grannie was gone, and gone for good.

Still, I'd be imagining these conversations that she and I might have about all the things I could bake on my own now. Without messing up the kitchen floor! Oh, how we'd laugh.

It was soothing too, the reliability. If you followed the rules – measuring the ingredients exactly, using the right amount of heat, at the precise time, being all patient and just-so – everything always turned out OK.

Our family dinners started getting more outlandish. I was plating up intricate entrees, mains with side dishes, vegetables peeled and trimmed to à la carte standard. I'd make sauces and jus. Food we'd never eaten before, not even in restaurants. Few dishes were repeated. Thankfully Craig had a hearty appetite. Mum and Dad were eating lightly at best. We weren't exactly having those family sit-downs Dad had promised when he picked Mum and me up from the airport after we flew back from Fiji.

For dessert, I'd do soufflés (not half as difficult as advertised), tarts, all sorts of biscuits and squares, but my speciality was cakes. Ones with piped rosettes of icing and whipped cream layers. Having realised an allergy to cow's milk, I wasn't eating much of them myself, but I thought this was what normal people ate. Alice and Mrs Brady from *The Brady Bunch* served up this sort of thing. This was how normal people's homes smelt.

I was trying to bake together some kind of normal for Tobey and Griffy. But, as usual, I was getting normal all wrong. In my head, having layered cake and a tidy house might save us from what the cockroach was tearing apart downstairs.

What an absolute banana I was.

★

The other thing that had been happening downstairs was that the baby was getting ready to be born.

The problem with this, from Mum and Dad's point of view, was that you couldn't really take heroin into a hospital. Drugs aren't considered a BYO situation on the labour ward; you're meant to use the ones they have there.

Mum could obviously sneak her gear in and find a way to take it on the sly, but the hospital would do routine blood tests that would almost certainly lead to difficult questions.

A Palm Beach birth was decided on. A top obstetrician was found who would deliver our new family member at home. Labour started around 6pm.

The doctor was called for. By 8pm he was doing all the kind of checks and heart monitoring you see in movies. Mother and baby were dilating and beating well.

By 11pm Mum had sent everyone out of the bedroom, she just wanted to breathe and listen to music. I could hear her pacing back and forth between her balcony and the ensuite bathroom. Mum wasn't worried. She'd done this three times before.

Upstairs in the lounge Dad and the doctor were flopped on the couch, getting tipsy on Portuguese sherry and rallying themselves with the fat bumps of coke Dad had lined up across the coffee table.

I don't know how much the doctor knew about the alternative pain relief Mum was using, but he must have had some inkling about the bruising in the crook of her elbows. He was an expensive doctor with private chambers in the most exclusive part of town, but you could see Dad had charmed him. He was loving all the paintings and artefacts. The whole luxe-bohemia vibe of Mum's decor. Dad was spinning his tales, showing him some tektites from Rizal. The doctor kept going, oooh, really? How *fascinating*?

Downstairs Mum had the grand bedroom kitted out for the birth with flickering candles and extra-soft sheepskin rugs. All the usual tassels and scarves. She was making increasingly worrying noises. Every so often the doctor would trot down and redo his checks.

Childbirth sounded like off-the-charts suffering. I knew Mum had a high tolerance for pain and, since it was made from morphine, I figured whatever else heroin was, it had to be a decent painkiller. But the sounds coming out of the grand bedroom were getting scarier and scarier.

According to the doctor though, everything was all going swimmingly.

Until suddenly it wasn't.

Either he'd finally turned the lights on properly or Mum had dilated enough for him to see that the baby was upside down. It was going to be a breech birth. Then he, the fancy paediatric doctor, panicked. He'd drunk too much. He was too high to deal with this. We needed to call an ambulance, he said. *Right now.*

Even if an ambulance arrived immediately. Which it wouldn't (how could it? They didn't just drive up and down the peninsula waiting for house calls). We were still an hour, maybe more from the closest hospital. There was no back-up plan.

Mum's breathing was getting faster, more frantic.

Dad took a long look between Mum's legs. His eyes were wide, but his voice stayed calm.

'Saylor, go get some olive oil.'

'What, from the kitchen?'

'Yes. The one you use for salad dressing.'

I bolted off to get the large green bottle of cold-pressed extra-virgin.

When I got back, Dad was between Mum's knees and the doctor was slumped into the Eames.

'Why did you get him so drunk?' Mum hissed between the contractions.

'Should I call an ambulance?' I asked. 'I think I should.'

'No!' yelled both parents in unison.

'Go back to your room. We're going to be fine,' said Dad, not taking his eyes off Mum's face.

Back in my bedroom I sat on the bed. I stared at the reflection in the window. I closed the curtains. Then I stared at the curtains. At the floor. The ceiling. The cries and moans got worse. I got into bed and hid under my blankets. I bit my nails. I flung off the blankets and stared at the door.

I snuck back to the grand bedroom's closed door and sat on the carpet. It often felt like dangerous things were going on beyond this door, but this was absolutely the worse. The pain sounded so bad.

I went back to my room and hid under the covers again. The cries got faster, and then stopped.

I waited a second, then ran back to the door and stuck my ear against it, my whole body craning to hear something. Listening desperately.

I couldn't hear anything. No yelling, no moaning. Nothing. Then I heard a baby crying.

I knocked on the door and Dad called me in to meet our little sister.

The baby hadn't just been upside down, she'd had the umbilical cord wrapped around her neck, twice. Dad had poured olive oil, and literally spun the baby out, looping the cord twice over her head to free her as she was delivered. Both baby and mother were fine. Mum didn't even need any stitches. Dad had totally stepped up and saved the day.

Now the emergency was over, the doctor had flickered back to life, he was listening to the baby's heart, checking all the things he needed to check. He was literally shaking with relief. You could see in his eyes that we were very, very lucky to have all made it. The Starling luck had pulled us through yet again.

And now we had Palomino Starling. Dad said when he'd seen her hair glint like pale gold in the candlelight as he'd lifted her free, he'd known she was meant to be. Even before she cried, he'd known she was going to be fine. Her name had just come to him.

The next morning, I was putting the empty bottle of sherry that Dad and the doctor had polished off in the bin when something caught my eye. The gold writing on the label described itself as an artful blend of Palomino and Pedro Ximénez grapes. Strange coincidence.

We always called her Lola anyway. And there was no doubt Lola was meant to be. Dad was a hundred percent right about that. She was bright as a spark and cute as a button with her upturned nose. If ever there was a kid who embodied the line from *A Midsummer Night's Dream* about being little and fierce, it was Lola. She had the face of an angel – grannies would stop us in the street to say so. But, if you ever tried to tidy away her things, she'd come at you like a spider monkey. Lola was an excellent addition to the family. We were all a bit scared of her.

★

It didn't take long for the money to dwindle at Palm Beach. The stacks of notes in the safe got lower and lower, until all that was left were a few crumpled fifties and one very secure handgun. Given our lavish culinary and heroin expenses, the money probably lasted longer than it should have.

A scheme was developed. With Nils and Baz, we would be bringing a chunk of coke back from the Netherlands to Sydney. The Fiji run had felt high risk, this time the stakes would be substantially higher. We'd be carrying more cocaine. Instead of one quick flight, we'd be smuggling illegal narcotics through both hemispheres and a bunch of different security measures. More moving parts – including a relatively new baby – and a lot more that could go horribly wrong.

Mum and Dad would really need to pull themselves together.

1983

Amsterdam, again

Having paused enroute for a month-long hit of tropics, we arrived in Amsterdam in a waft of jasmine, silk and flimsy sandals. Somewhat unprepared for a European cold snap. Baby Lola and Dad were the only ones with a pair of socks.

The doors of Schiphol Airport slid open, we inhaled the first breaths of northern winter we'd had for a while, stepped out into the concrete grey afternoon, and froze into six blocks of human ice.

Coat-less, jumper-less, scarf-less and (mainly) sock-less, we bundled into a cab. At the hotel we cranked the radiators up to max, wrapped ourselves in duvets and took turns thawing out under the hot showers.

Generally, we were a bit smarter with climates. I'm not sure what went wrong. There was also an issue with our finances. They'd been wired to the wrong place and wouldn't be with us here, in our current hemisphere, for at least five working days. We'd had delays with bank transfers before, but being broke seemed more extreme in minus-five-degree weather.

You could drink the tap water here and the hotel made toasted sandwiches, so we knew we could survive on room service. But even if we layered on every piece of clothing we currently owned, leaving our rooms would be problematic.

There was a big department store a few streets away. I don't remember the group strategy being discussed. Certainly, it didn't seem there was any other option. Getting warm felt like a matter of survival. Probably the ten-minute walk there had already given us all a slight case of exposure.

We hit that poor department store like a plague of tropically clad locusts. Every Starling for themself, we split up and went through level by level. Ground floor first, I tried on a white bobble hat and matching scarf, and just kept them on. Next to me, Tobey was jamming her iced fingers into a pair of gloves. Then up the escalator to the children's department, where we saw Mum buttoning Griff and Lola into all-in-one padded suits.

Tobey and I easily found coats that didn't have security tags. She opted for bright orange. I went for a blue one that was a bit big, but looked nice with my hat. There was a stack of little fake-fur trimmed boots, both lefts and rights. No one noticed the two empty boxes we left tucked neatly under the bench.

It seemed incredible that we were getting away with it. But we were. The shop attendants were serving proper customers, adult mothers with children. No one asked the two of us unaccompanied children what we were doing or if we needed help. I saw a drawstring bag with a sparkly pony on it, and filled it with socks and a thermal vest each for Tobey, Griff and myself. Tobey and I pulled jeans on over the top of our skirts in the change room and just wore them out like we weren't doing anything wrong. It didn't feel like we were, really. We were so cold and it was a faceless corporate department store, it didn't feel like we were robbing anyone exactly. The two of us breezed out the main doors downstairs, casual as cats, and no one stopped us.

Back at the hotel we all looked at each other, amazed at how different we were in our new clothes. We looked almost normal. An ordinary, if slightly mismatching, family.

Mum wasn't crazy about the conservative looks, but she and Dad were both impressed by my haul. I'd stolen the most. Poor Mum and Dad, it must have seemed like I was coming round to my DNA: finally doing something bold. Their approval felt as good as the warmth coming off the radiator, but I knew the truth. Nothing had changed. I was still me: the urgent necessity of cold had just swept me a bit beyond myself.

Mum went back to the store a couple of days later and really outdid herself: Lola and Griff needed a change of clothes. Dad had dressed himself very impractically. Mum started at the top of the store in the luggage department. Smiled charmingly at the male attendant who passed her a family-size suitcase down from the shelf. She then made her way floor-by-floor back down to ground level, filling it up with bits for each of us. Mostly clothes to keep us warm, but there were also nappies and some teething rusks for Lola and a *Vogue* for her.

She regularly spoke to the attendants, asking each one if it was OK to settle up in one go at the ground-floor cashier. It was an expensive store, she was selecting quality items and only checking the sizes, never once the prices. Mum would have seemed an ideal shopper. No one batted an eyelid.

At the exit on the ground floor, she took a deep breath, leaned down to whisk off the price sticker on the suitcase, smiled serenely at the security guard and wheeled her now-heavy suitcase out.

That afternoon it snowed. We raced outside in our new coats. Little flakes were spinning and falling through the air, settling everywhere in lacy piles. Tobey and I didn't know much about snow. You kind of expected it to taste sweet, like lemonade ice lollies, but we couldn't taste it at all.

At the hotel we lived on hot chocolate and toasted cheese sandwiches. I got a cold almost instantly from the cow's milk, but the hot chocolate tasted straight out of Narnia and was well worth the snot.

Amsterdam was brilliant. We liked it a lot. The people seemed ace. Tall, straightforward. Deeply reasonable and immaculately teethed. Everyone we spoke to knew our language as well as we did (possibly better).

Being here in their homelands, I kept hoping we'd bump into Sofie and Hana and Lars and Liva, but they were probably far away on another continent, practising their karate kicks on a beach.

Walking around, looking in the shop windows and on the streets, I saw the Dutch girls were all very cool with their feathery hairstyles. I was twelve now, and totally weighed down by my dreary long hair. Back at the hotel, Mum agreed to do some slight trimming.

We borrowed a pair of scissors from the reception downstairs and Mum cut my hair as I sat on the edge of the bath. Chunks of hair started falling into the tub. The haircut was going better than I'd hoped. Mum kept snipping one side, then sucking in her breath and going back to the other side to even it up. The scissors kept getting closer and closer to my neck. Then up towards my ears. It was thrilling. When she finished it was short and super-layered. I'd gone from waist-length hair to Nena *99 Luftballons*.

I loved it. *Loved* it.

Dad hated it so much he couldn't even look at me. Mum was a bit sheepish, but Nils and Baz had just arrived and Nils said I looked less catholic, which seemed a great compliment.

The next day the money came through and we moved out of the hotel and into an apartment a few canals away on the Prinsengracht.

The more we saw of Amsterdam, the better we liked it. There were so many adorable details, like when the neighbours next door moved out, they did it via rope and pulley from their windows. All the furniture hoisted down the front of their house from a hook just below the roof. The next day, the new tenants did the same in reverse. A table went up on ropes. Some armchairs. A piano! All too wide for the narrow flights of stairs inside.

We liked the cobblestoned roads looped with bridges and canals. We liked that half the traffic was bicycle. Where we were staying was on one of the central canals curling around the epicentre of Amsterdam, just four bridges from Dam Square, so it felt like we were in the heart of things. Everywhere we went, we walked there.

We liked the flat we were living in too. Nico, Nils and Baz's friend, who it belonged to, had a kind of androgynous swagger and a slow, punchy way of talking that made everything she said sound naughty. She had a fringe like Chrissie Hynde and always wore skinny black leather and fat lashings of kohl.

Nico's sexy voice was partly due to an emergency tracheotomy that had saved her life, but left her with a hole the width of a fingertip in the middle of her throat. She'd had a silver necklace designed to wear over the hole. When she smoked, which she did constantly, a little flap in the choker lifted, so smoke could drift out from her 'trachie'. Sometimes she put the cigarette directly in the hole and smoked it from there. It held perfectly. Saves time, she laughed. We adored her.

Nico's boyfriend was in a band who were on a global tour of stadiums. Between trips out to see him in exotic places like Buffalo and Birmingham, Nico was looking after his place, leaving hers free for us.

One afternoon she came around to pick up something.

'What are you children doing?' she growled.

'Nothing. Some dusting?' It was just me and Griffy home and I was worried I'd been caught doing something I shouldn't.

'No?! All alone! Poor, *poor* children. Quick, your coats.'

'Should we leave a note?'

'For why? They leave you!'

Nico took us back to her boyfriend's apartment, which was bigger but, for my money not as cool as Nico's. She dressed me up in her clothes. All three of us painted our nails midnight-noir and danced to the Violent Femmes and The Slits. After that we got into a cab to visit one of her friends on the outskirts of town. Griffy and I ate liquorice and dark chocolate; Nico and her friend had hash and champagne. It was a glorious afternoon.

Nico dropped us off long after it had gone dark. Mum wasn't entirely pleased with our unexpected disappearance or my new look, but Nico insisted I keep the studded leather belt at very least. And what could Mum say? Nico *was* our landlady.

The next day the consignment arrived. That night we stayed up late stuffing tripod legs with the cocaine and – one of us at least – completely losing our heads out on Nico's balcony in the snow.

You couldn't be too squeamish in our family, but it always amazed me how messy blood is. When I went out to the balcony the next morning, there were splatters of it everywhere. Door, walls… had I been *waving* my arm around?

To sneak back inside without dripping across the carpet, I'd jammed my wrist with snow and tied one of my socks around it. In the bathroom, I'd managed to bleed through half a roll of toilet paper – smearing the toilet, the basin, and two of the hand towels – before I'd found some proper bandages at the back of Nico's cabinet. The cut was so clean though, it healed like magic, almost overnight.

When Tobey asked about the bandage, I mumbled something shifty about making sandwiches with the sushi knife. Luckily no one wondered why I was sponging down the balcony with steaming soap suds.

In the light of day, the whole episode was hideously embarrassing. Probably I'd never mention it to anyone. Since Grannie May died there had been a bunched-up, sad feeling in my chest. With Mum and Dad taking heroin, the roof of our life could be ripped off at any moment. We weren't safe. 231 was gone. I was weird. And all bratty and itchy under my skin. No school, no friends. All that stuff was true.

But also. Back when I was on Norfolk Island, staying with Nanny and Erin, one afternoon, for no reason whatsoever, I'd taken a pair of scissors and cut my inflatable yellow canoe. I loved that canoe so much, no one could understand why I'd done it. I didn't understand either. Something in me just needed to see if danger really was that close.

I don't know what intervention I'd expected to appear, but I was shocked – open-mouth stunned – that the universe had allowed something so important as my canoe to be lost that easily. But it had. No thunder. No lightning. Just one snip, and my precious canoe was dead, folded up in the rubbish bin.

This was like that. And it was still shocking to see how close you could be to being lost forever.

Once I'd cleaned up the mess, I tried not to think about it. There were other things to worry about. But, like the intoxicating scent of inflatable plastic, that sense stayed with me. The exquisite sadness of Anne Frank's house on a blue-lit winter's night. Snow falling across the frozen canal. That feeling is there. Any time I turn over my wrist and see the thin white line running along my vein, I remember how close life beats to the surface of your skin.

We Starlings could be gone in a snip.

And no one was going to stop us, no one but ourselves.

★

We liked flying. But airports had become stressful. Going into them was fine, but coming out of airports was the worst. More specifically the customs part. Most specifically when they searched our bags. Mainly because there were now illegal narcotics inside them.

Most people wouldn't suspect a family of six to be travelling with a bunch of drugs. But we got pulled aside to have our luggage searched a lot. They always called it random, but you felt like such a little criminal. Standing there, all clammy, as someone rooted around in your things. The other passengers streaming past, looking at you like you'd done something appalling. Which I guess we had. But it's still really embarrassing having everything you own in the whole world piled up on a dirty counter for everyone to gawp at.

On the way back from Amsterdam, we were walking through the last part of customs when they pulled us over. Baby Lola was grizzly from being in the air for 24 hours. We were all overtired and anxious. For various reasons, it had been a long flight.

We opened up our suitcases across the benches, and they started rummaging. One customs officer had just raked past my swirly blue 'Wednesday' underpants, when the other officer started shaking a box of wine bottles wrapped in Happy Anniversary paper. You could hear the liquids inside, faintly slapping against the green glass.

The clammy, bag-search stress sharpened to a white-knuckle, diarrhoea cramp of fear.

Blood pounded in my ears and all I could think was how we mustn't look guilty. The second we looked like anything was wrong, the customs officers would start getting more thorough. And if they checked, *properly* checked, inside those wine bottles, our parents would go to jail for a long time. God knows what would happen to us.

I started talking to Tobey about the colouring-in books we'd been given on the flight. Her eyes were all bogged-out scared, her pupils dilated to black. Looking at her, I knew mine were too. We fake-chatted about the books, but really we were both listening to what the customs officers were saying.

The tripod legs were stacked against Lola's nappy bag. When one of the officers wondered out loud why anyone would need that many sets of tripods, the pounding in my ears got so loud I couldn't breathe.

Could Dad prove he was an accredited photographer? Did he have some kind of ID or maybe a letter from *National Geographic*?

I wouldn't – and this can't be stressed enough – recommend smuggling drugs to anyone.

★

Over the years Mum had found us some great houses to live in. Sometimes it was just good luck. She'd be zipping down a country road and see a beat-up 'To Rent' sign propped against an overgrown hedgerow. Or she'd talk to someone in a health-food shop who happened have an aunt with a cottage to rent on the coast. We'd rock up to live somewhere without even seeing a picture of it. There'd be cobwebs. Sometimes years of dust to sweep up, but the places we lived were usually interesting with plenty of nature to explore.

I don't know what chain of events resulted in us living at the Whitebox house in Bali.

On an unusually beautiful island – an island renowned for its graceful architecture and exquisite landscaping – the owners of this house had made some bold decisions. First, they'd found a plot of uniquely dull land. Then they'd built an outstandingly featureless block. And put it bang on the side of the road.

Financial practicalities would have spoken for the general location. But their reasons for having the house jammed up to the extreme edge of the road, when there was nothing but dry dirt and a few bored coconut trees for miles in every other direction, were unclear.

The other puzzle we never solved was why the owners had gone so hard on brilliant white. Inside and out, there was no other colour. The tiled walls, the polished stone floors, the gleaming ceilings. All of it unrelenting, shiny white.

Tucked away on Bali's southeastern corner, it felt like we were in the middle of nowhere, but not in a good way. There was limited running water, and a hand-pumped well out the back.

Aside from a collection of plastic buckets – to use as kitchen sinks and bathroom showers – the house came aggressively unfurnished. No curtains or blinds. Not a hint of lightshade, just blinding strip lighting and a few 100-watt bulbs, in brilliant white.

Apart from mattresses to sleep on and some basic utensils for the kitchen, we never got around to furnishings. I don't know why Mum didn't decorate as she usually did. There were a few overworked scarves in her and Dad's room, but that was it. Maybe the place was just too overwhelmingly white even for Mum to tackle.

It was a bit like living in a low-budget torture-dream sequence, but we weren't too fussed. Mum and Dad said we wouldn't be staying long. A couple of weeks. A month at the most. Just long enough for Mum and Dad to detox.

Against what felt like considerable odds, we'd got the cocaine safely through to Australia. Now that was in place, it was time to get ourselves together. Turns out, hanging out on long flights wasn't much fun. Besides, Dad told us, heroin was only something to try for a little while. It wasn't really their scene. Time to clean up and get healthy. A spot of Bali heat should sort it. Then we'd head back to Australia. And then maybe London.

Meantime, having no furniture meant the house was basically one big, shiny white dancefloor. The other bonus with the Whitebox was that everything was easy-wipe. I didn't really appreciate this advantage until one morning when I was jolted from sleep by my brother having a bout of tropical diarrhoea.

From what I could tell, he had woken up, realised an urgency and made some attempt to get to the bathroom. He'd taken a whimsical route, around the top of our mattresses lined up on the floor: leaning his backside over our pillows to leave a gruesome trail.

I'd been sleeping with my hair fanned out above my head and that was where most of the horror had splattered.

I opened my eyes just in time to see his little bum retreating.

It took me a moment to understand what I was seeing. Then the smell hit me.

It's hard to feel clean after someone has pooped on your head. Even after I'd shampooed and disinfected a good chunk of my hair down the drain, I was still pretty haunted.

★

There was no fancy cooking at the Whitebox. The kitchen was a white tiled bench, two buckets and a camping-style gas ring. You had to swap over the gas cylinder when it was empty. We had one pot for boiling rice and porridge. Everything else we ate was wok-ed over the high flames of blue gas. All the recipe following was over. Bam. Gone. I didn't really think about it. That was something we'd left at Palm Beach. Cooking over roaring flames was pretty satisfying and took two minutes.

I was in the kitchen, flipping krupuks for dinner one night, concentrating on getting their edges just so, when something clanged loudly on the tiles behind me.

I spun around in fright, almost spraying my wok of smoking oil.

Tobey was standing in the doorway looking triumphant.

The aluminium ashtray she'd just frisbeed across the room was still clattering at my feet.

'What are you doing?' I shrieked.

'Just saved your life,' she grinned.

She was right. Under the ashtray was a squashed scorpion.

As she'd walked through the doorway behind me, Tobey had spotted it arching its tail at my bare heel. It must have been hiding behind the gas canister and I'd obviously startled it, as stepping forwards and back, tilting the wok. Tobey's aim had been freakishly perfect. Lucky for me, but tough break for the scorpion. Who expects to be wiped out by a hurtling ashtray?

When we lifted the ashtray, we saw the scorpion had been a dark female, one of the deadly ones. Its tail had been arched up to attack, if Tobey had come in seconds later, I would have already been stung. If Tobey had missed, I would have been stung. There's no way we would have got help in time; we didn't even have a car. Tobey had totally saved my life.

★

Our daily routine was pretty basic at the Whitebox. I'd make us sliced fruit and porridge. We'd chill for a bit, then go for a walk somewhere. Griff still wasn't super inspired about walking. He had great little legs, they worked fine. He was just saving them, so mostly I carried him. We didn't go far.

Some days it was only as far as the local warung for a bowl of ais kacang – shaved ice, red syrup, condensed milk, black grass jelly, palm seeds and sweet beans – a lot more delicious than it may sound. Most of the time we had money to pay, but sometimes we didn't, and the woman who ran the warung would give us one to share anyway. She was so nice. She would have been just squeaking by, working hard to sustain a life for herself and her children out of a dirt-floor bamboo shack, but still she gave free treats to the rich westerners who lived up the road in a three-bedroomed house with electricity.

By 2ish, we'd be out of the heat of day and back within the shiny white walls, flopped on the shiny white floor. I'd make us a light snack. Tobey would put a cassette in the boombox and we'd spend the rest of the afternoon dancing interpretively around the lounge.

Not counting the two electric sockets or the mega-watt lightbulb hanging down from the ceiling, the only thing in the lounge was the little boombox we had on timeshare. We had it days; night-time it was in Mum and Dad's room. If the boombox wasn't back, sitting outside their door in the morning, we had to wait till noon before we could knock on their door and sneak it back out.

We only had eight cassettes, played on white-hot rotation. One of them was Chris de Burgh's seminal *Spanish Train and Other Stories* album. Those stories really spoke to us, and tracks like *Patricia The Stripper* were super-danceable.

The music never bothered Mum and Dad. But Baz who was living with us in the third bedroom, was not a fan of the de Burgh rotations. We felt they were fresh enough to be heard ten times a day. Baz disagreed. He'd come flying out of his room, dressing gown flapping.

'Jesus fucking Chriiiiiiiist. Turn that cheesy fucking crap OFF.'

We'd nod our heads and dutifully turn the volume down, but gradually Patricia would edge back up to disco.

Some afternoons we'd come back from our walks and find poor de Burgh in the bin. We'd just fish him out, give him a quick wipe and pop him back into the boombox. We liked Baz, we liked him a lot. But there was no way we were giving up de Burgh. At one point, Baz was desperate enough to yank out the cassette's ribbon, but we just spooled it back in with our fingers and you almost couldn't hear the difference.

We didn't realise it, but at the Whitebox, mostly what we were was bored out of our minds. We'd just come from the buzz of Amsterdam. We didn't have books or paper and pencils. Griffy had a few Matchbox cars – which raced like the clappers on the shiny white floors – but that was pretty much it. Lola was just a cute little baby. As long as she had Mum in her view and a teething rusk in her hand, she was fine, but the rest of us were crazy bored.

We weren't seeing much of Mum and Dad. The Getting Off Heroin plan wasn't going well. They were back being locked away in their room all day, taking loads of it. They had tried getting clean when we first arrived. The strategy had been to go cold turkey, then take a couple of weeks to get healthy. But it turns out coming off smack is hard. A month became two.

I don't know how the arrangements were going in Sydney or how much of a spanner our Bali delay was: those discussions happened late at night. But the vibe around the house was getting increasingly tense, as we sunk into this weird holding pattern of Mum and Dad's next score always going to be their last.

After nine weeks, Baz flew out to spend some time with Cleo.

Mum and Dad's dealer in Bali was a doctor's wife in Kuta. A couple of times a week Dad would cab over to buy the drugs, and two of us kids went with him. It was nice going for a drive and getting out of the house, but once you got there, you usually wished you were back at the Whitebox.

I don't know if people factor this when weighing up future lifestyles, but being addicted to drugs like heroin means some really dull times. Heroin isn't punctual. It doesn't need to be. There's *a lot* of waiting around.

We were used to spending time in the back of parked cars, but heroin-waiting took things to a whole new level. Now there were whole days waiting in parked cars. Mum and Dad went inside, we stayed in the backseat. Sometimes there was a driver, sometimes it was an empty car. Sometimes it was hot and sweaty and we were thirsty or hungry. Tobey and I would bicker. The babies would cry. We'd try and amuse them. Mostly we'd look out the windows, our legs sticky on the plastic-covered seats. Sometimes we'd be parked somewhere interesting. Usually, it was the kind of dingy back alley you'd expect to find behind a drug dealer's house.

I don't know why exactly we weren't allowed out of the car. This was deemed dangerous, but I'm not sure for who. Maybe these were places we needed to be able to leave fast. There might also have been an element of Dad not wanting to get back to the car and have to wait for us if we'd wandered off.

It wasn't that we were ungrateful. We knew how lucky we were. We'd seen the children begging for money and sleeping in piles of rubbish in India. And there were plenty of stories about children who had it far worse than us. The kids who had *really* questionable parents. There was Rayna, daughter of artist Ray. He had taken her to a party, got so off his head that *she* had to drive them home. It wasn't the kind of party where anyone noticed Ray staggering out, needing his ten-year-old daughter's help to get to the car. He'd passed out across the backseat. It was a school night and she'd wanted to get home, so in the early hours of the morning she'd been careening through the red lights of downtown Auckland, sitting on her Dad's paintbox to see over the steering wheel.

There were other stories. Children who were left in the house for days without food. Baby Isabelle who had been born with a fatal disease because one of her parents shared needles. You'd meet these kids and they seemed a bit fragile, a bit beat-up-looking around the eyes. Like poor little Guppy the puppy from Murchison who had gone to the cruel man. Not like us, we were OK. And we had each other.

So we knew we were lucky, but waiting is the worst. According to Dad, only boring people got bored. But waiting is *so* boring. It feels like wasted life.

Anyway. Back in Kuta, Griffy and I were being boring people, waiting for Dad in a taxi at the doctor's. We'd parked around the back as usual. Dad had scrambled out and we'd settled down to wait.

I never went inside, but apparently the doctor's practice at the front of the house was legit, except for the fact his wife, an unusually unattractive woman, was side-hustling heroin out of it.

It was a hot day. Maybe 35, 36 sticky, breezeless degrees. Griff and I had been sitting in the back of the taxi for about two hours. Windows wound down. Playing a loose game of I Spy. The driver was getting antsy. He'd been told it was a regular doctor's visit, but I could see he was starting to wonder.

Griffy was thirsty. I blew on his sweaty little forehead to cool it down and tried to distract him by pointing out, for the twentieth-millionth time, the two budgies flitting about in a tiny bamboo cage hanging by the backdoor.

It was all pretty run of the mill. We'd been here a dozen times. We knew those poor budgies. We knew what was happening inside. Dad was either still waiting for the delivery, in which case he'd be hanging out, each minute dragging by slower for him than it was for us. Or it had finally arrived, and he'd be out any minute. Unless he'd decided to have a hit here, which would mean he'd be nodding out, his belt still looped above the knot of veins at his elbow, and outside we'd have a much longer wait.

When Dad appeared at the doorway, my first thought was relief that this wasn't one of those visits. We'd be on the freeway home soon, the wind blowing in. We'd have water within an hour.

Then I saw there was something about the way he was moving that didn't look right.

Griff and I watched him take another step. He leaned on the gate, smiled at an empty patch of dirt in front of him, half-embarrassed, half-surprised, then pitched forward and collapsed onto it.

I ran to him. His eyes were flickering, he was dripping with sweat, very pale and out cold.

I shook him, screaming for help. The doctor's wife stomped out frowning.

'Go. Take him. Away! Away! He stupid man! He take too much.'

'He needs the doctor!'

'No. This proper doctor. He no can be here.'

She looked down at Dad, shaking her head. 'I tell him strong. He no listen. You take to hospital. Maybe he OK...'

She shrugged her shoulders, then stalked back inside. The door slammed shut. I heard the locks click into place.

The taxi-driver started his engine.

'Wait!' I yelled at him.

In many Asian countries drugs came with the death penalty. In Indonesia, being caught with drugs back then, even modest quantities, meant death by firing squad.

Everyone knew the sentence: After waiting in a squalid cell, sometimes for years, prisoners were woken in the middle of the night and taken to a remote, undisclosed location. Blindfolded, you're led to a wooden stake or chair and tied to it. A line of soldiers then shoot, aiming at a cross that's been drawn over your heart. Word was, only three of the soldiers fired live bullets: if you survived the first round, the commander was required to walk over and shoot you in the brain with his own weapon.

This scenario might have been on the taxi-driver's mind. If Griffin hadn't still been sitting wide-eyed in the backseat of his car, he probably would have hit the accelerator right out of this dangerous mess.

I screamed that my father was having a heart attack. I'm pretty sure the driver knew I was lying, but bless him, he helped me drag Dad's limp body to the car anyway.

'To the hospital?' he asked reluctantly.

In our family the rule was *never* call an ambulance. No matter what. Hospitals could mean police. But Dad was not good. There was no time to ask Mum. The Whitebox didn't even have a phone.

What if Dad got better on his own, like Nils had when he was out for three days on acid, but then the police executed him? Because of me. Maybe he only *looked* bad. Maybe this wasn't as serious as it looked.

But what if Dad's only hope was the hospital? Was the risk of someone there calling the police, worth the chance that Dad was overdosing right now, in front of his two-year-old son? There was no good decision I could make, but I had to make one. Every second I dithered could be costing Dad his life.

'Yes, the hospital, please hurry, thank you.'

I'd read that people go blue. I'd thought it was a figure of speech. But sprawled across me in the backseat, Dad's waxy white skin was now turning blue. His fingertips were blue like denim. I tried breathing air into his mouth. It made no difference. I was twelve. I didn't know what I was doing. Didn't have a clue. I knew I wasn't doing the right things, but I didn't know what they were. I kept talking to Dad, telling him to stay with us, that we were nearly there.

Griffy started crying. I told him it was going to be OK, but that felt like a terrible lie. So I told him to look out the window, not at Dad sprawled, boneless, a dead weight across our legs.

Later I thought all sorts of things like the fact Dad had done this to himself. How could he? How could he have *chosen* this? But in the taxi, with him lying there, all I could think was that I'd do anything so Griffy didn't have to see this.

I'm begging the driver to please drive faster. Dad's whole hands are blue now, his chest still. Every red light, every time we have to slow down for traffic, feels like a chasm of time we don't have. Everything is sweaty white panic and the loudest thought screaming in my head is that seeing his father die like this, spreadeagled across his little legs, in the back of a dirty taxi in Denpasar, could really mess Griffy up.

Dad can't die.

When we got to the emergency door of the hospital, the doctors came out with a stretcher. They could see the track marks on Dad's arm. They didn't need to ask what had happened.

The hospital was a small building. Griffy and I sat in the corridor outside the A&E room. Griffy on my knee. He was so smart and so aware of everything you forgot how young he was, but Griffin was still so little, just a baby really. I wanted to take him outside, away from this, but we couldn't leave Dad. I smoothed down his hair and hugged him close and kept telling him it was OK and the doctors would fix Daddy and everything would be alright. But I wasn't sure.

We weren't allowed in the A&E room, but the door to it had a glass panel. Griffy couldn't see, but I was just tall enough to watch the doctors through the glass. There were six people working on Dad. He had an oxygen mask over his face and they were pumping his chest. Again and again.

Minutes went by and he was just lying there. Gradually the doctors were slowing down. One by one, I saw them straighten up and step back from the bed.

Someone draped a sheet across Dad. When I saw it covered his face. I knew he was dead. I just sat there, holding Griffy. Instead of doing something, all I could think was how could I tell Griff. How was he going to be able to understand this?

We were sitting there like that when Mum swept in, flowing red hair like a furious hurricane.

She took one look at us. My wet face, arms tightly hugging Griff.

'Where is he?'

I shook my head, unable to speak.

'*Where* is your father?'

I pointed at the white sheet on the stretcher.

'No! No he's *not!*'

She flew into the emergency room, shouting at the shocked doctors and whipped off the sheet. I don't know what she said, to the doctors or to Dad. She was yelling at all of them, I couldn't hear and I never thought to ask, if it was threats or encouragement or both, but the doctors started working on Dad again.

There were more injections.

And suddenly Dad was breathing again.

They had already called a time of death, but like a miracle, like a drug-bent Lazarus, Dad rose.

He was back at home with us that night, and he and I were back at the shady doctor's door the next week. Apparently the doctor's wife was our friend because she'd sent one of her men to go get Mum and drive her to the hospital.

I sat looking at the same patch of dirt, same poor little budgies, tweeting in their tiny cage, knowing Dad would be taking the same drugs inside. Different taxi-driver.

★

We were pretty happy to leave the Whitebox house. How we left it wasn't so good.

As usual, we'd come into Bali on the standard three-month tourist visa. The rule was that if you wanted to extend your visa, you had to fly out and go through the paperwork at an Indonesian consulate somewhere else. It felt a bit roundabout but that was the system.

Most people went somewhere close like Singapore, but Dad knew the Chief. Dad would buy special gifts like kitchen appliances, and dressed in our Sunday best we would visit the Chief and his family. It was like a special visa-getting ceremony. After the Magimixes had been presented, he and Dad would make fake conversation for an hour or so, both of them overdoing the smiles. We'd sit neatly listening to them complimenting each other on their well-behaved children (we never saw the Chief's). The

Chief had said nice things about us daughters. But then Griffy came along and the chat became all about how relieved Dad must be to finally have a son.

At some point Dad would gently broach the subject of visas, and the Chief would bat it away as if it was a trifle embarrassing, a topic far beneath such friendship. We would leave our passports with him and the next week we'd drive back and pick them up with their new visa extension stamps.

This time, what with all the heroin-taking and not expecting to be here so long, we'd forgotten to make this visit. Perhaps the Chief had been offended by our neglect. Maybe there'd been rumours about the hospital trip. Either way, Tobey, Griff and I were dancing in the lounge one afternoon, miming out the lyrics to Chris de Burgh's stirring opus on *The Painter*, when there was a sharp rap at the door.

In the driveway were three jeeps worth of officers. They'd come with machine guns. We had ten minutes to pack our bags. For a long second, the three of us stared bog-eyed at the officer, then we scattered like bugs. I ran out to the washing line. Tobey ran to get Mum and little Griff went straight to his Matchbox cars.

We didn't have a lot of baggage, but we still managed to leave a chunk of it behind. As we pulled into the road, I noticed half the family's underwear drying on a bush by the backdoor. Tobey had the boombox with de Burg still in it on her knees, I was hugging a packet of Lola's nappies.

The jeeps sped in siren-wailing convoy to the airport. I'd expected them to just drop us off at the kerb like moody taxi-drivers, but no, this was going to be door-to-door service. They were so keen to be rid of us, they had been holding a full passenger plane on the runway.

It was embarrassing enough being rushed through immigration under gunpoint. Especially in our scrappy, around-the-house clothes. But then we were jogged across the tarmac, surrounded like we were big-time political prisoners. The plane's passengers all staring out the windows at us as we scrambled across the runway.

The whole family sweaty and messy-haired, with our bags banging up and down against us.

The guys with guns even saw us to our seats, making sure we were buckled in. Once they had exited the cabin and the door was shut, the passengers all booed at us. Mortifying.

In the whole scheme of things, we got off lightly, but it wasn't the most relaxing flight. Apparently, the plane had been held for hours on the runway. The passengers had been there, waiting for us, before we even knew we were leaving the island. There weren't seats together, so we were sitting separately, dotted out across the cabin. I wanted to apologise to the couple next to me, but they gave me such dirty looks when I sat down, I was too embarrassed to speak.

It was just one of those days where you wake up and everything seems ordinary. Then you find yourself on a plane to Australia. Nothing ever happened, until everything happened.

Coming back into Sydney airport, the customs officers were not content just searching our bags.

After they'd pulled apart the cotton wool in Mum's tampons, squeezed out the family tube of toothpaste and put a fork through the paste to see if there was anything in it, I felt pretty certain they were going to find Mum and Dad's heroin.

We got taken into rooms. Special window-less rooms with wipe-down tables and plastic chairs. One for us kids and Mum, another room for Dad. They can keep you in those rooms for hours; without water, without being able to go to the bathroom. They have guns and plastic gloves. They can yell at you, lock you up, make you take all your clothes off. You know they're just people doing their jobs, but these people have jobs that give them dominion over you and your body. Whether or not you've done anything wrong.

It's awful how powerless you feel in those claustrophobic little rooms.

There were two female officers. They were polite enough, but if you're female, being put in a room with same-sex officers probably means a body search. Usually if you're a minor, they just pat you down. But this time we all had to strip. Even poor Griffy and Lola.

I was really scared. I knew Mum had the heroin actually on her. Somewhere in her clothes would be a glossy magazine page folded into a little origami envelope and filled with off-white powder. Mum and Dad would have had the chance to get rid of it before we were escorted out of the Whitebox. They hadn't though, because that would've meant a six-hour flight of hanging out.

As we peeled off our clothes for the officers, I caught a glimpse of the shiny paper in Mum's hand. She had the fold of heroin between her thumb and forefinger. Her face was beautifully calm, like there was nothing wrong, apart from this slight inconvenience we were currently experiencing. But the next thing she would have to do is turn over her hands, palms up, for the officers to inspect.

Usually when I was scared, my head was just a mess of shrieking. But what needed to be done here was sharp and clear. I shuffled against Mum, nudging her hand. Without even inclining her head, covering my hand for the briefest moment, she slipped me the fold. I gripped it between my forefinger and palm, then slid it up under my watch strap.

Mum never wore a watch. It was only good luck that mine was on tight enough that day to keep the fold in place. I passed my underpants for inspection. The officer shook them and handed them back. As I pulled my pants back on, I slid the stupid packet of heroin down into the back of them. Then, heart beating like a jack hammer, I took my watch off to show the officer.

When we were naked, each of us had to take a turn jumping up and down on the spot in front of the two uniformed officers. Kind of funny, kind of the most humiliating thing you could imagine. Especially when I realised they were asking us to do this because they thought we might have drugs jammed up our *cavities*.

I don't know who needs to hear this, but I wouldn't – and this can't be stressed enough – recommend smuggling drugs.

An hour later, I was sitting with Dad across a desk from the man who seemed to be in charge. He'd been called down to the airport to speak to Dad for undisclosed reasons, but otherwise things were back to normal. No drugs had been found. There was some paperwork, but mostly we could go back to breathing.

Dad was chatting and laughing with the man like they were old friends. No hard feelings, all part of the travel experience, ha ha, all of that.

I don't know why it was just Dad and me in the office with the man, but I remember thinking the man seemed nice, he'd been nodding in my direction, including me in the conversation. He was older, with grey hair and a well-cut suit. I got the sense his job had importance. The conversation was wrapping up when he turned, looking across the desk very directly at me.

'This all must have been unpleasant?'

I wasn't used to official people acknowledging stuff like that, 'It was fine, thank you.'

He smiled, 'You're awfully level-headed for someone your age, aren't you?

I didn't know what to say. He didn't seem to be meaning it badly, but the man had our passports in front of him: he knew exactly how old I was. I shrugged, respectfully as possible.

'Only a few years more,' he told me. 'Soon as you can, you'll be out.'

It was such an odd thing to say. He was ignoring Dad and looking at me intently, all steely blue, like he knew everything that was going on. Like he wasn't fooled in the least by what Dad was saying. He knew there were drugs on us, and that somewhere else there was probably a lot of other drugs. He seemed very smart. Leaving my family was unthinkable though. I'd literally never thought about it.

Then he got out a business card and slid it across the desk to me, 'If ever you need help, and probably you will, call me and I should be able to help.'

'With airport problems?'

'I don't work at the airport.'

I put the card in my pocket, meaning to keep it safe. Dad and I said goodbye and went out to meet Mum and the kids in the Arrivals Hall. I'd lost the business card within the week, but I thought a lot about what he'd said.

★

A few weeks later, and we were back out in the countryside again.

Tanilba Bay was a small coastal town a hundred or so miles north of Sydney. The centrepiece of the town when we lived there, as it probably remains, was Tanilba House: the first house to be built on the peninsula and one of Australia's oldest buildings.

Things started at Tanilba in 1831, when Royal Navy Lieutenant William Caswell received a grant of fifty acres and an assignment of convict workers. Land was cleared and a house raised from locally quarried stone – complete with three narrow jail cells (which the poor prisoners presumably had to build for themselves).

By all accounts Caswell was a pioneering thinker and he had ambitious plans for the area. He built his house atop the only hill, to best enjoy the sea breezes and a majestic overview of the rest of town. But things went badly at Tanilba House. Two of his children and a very unfortunate governess are said to be buried somewhere on the grounds. The house was left deserted for decades, then taken over by a religious sect. At some point, ten acres of vineyard were planted, a magnificent mulberry tree and what is now considered Australia's oldest olive tree.

Mum wasn't aware of any of this when she arranged to rent No.1 Admiralty Avenue over the phone, sight unseen. She liked hearing that the house stood by itself on the hill. It had been empty for a long time, so the rent wasn't outrageous. Had she known the backstory, I doubt it would have deterred her whatsoever.

Tobey and I weren't crazy about the musty cellars underneath the house or the three jail cells lined up outside the kitchen, but to us it was just another place to live. Admittedly one with 1.5ft-thick stone walls cemented together with lime from burnt oyster shells. But just another place that was home for a while.

We liked the gardens. We *loved* the mulberry tree. We'd never eaten mulberries before and stood under the glorious umbrella of berries feasting like fiends.

The other thing Tanilba had was a ghost. And apparently the haunting was legit. None of the locals would come near the house. Even the kids down the road who Tobey played with would only come as far as the front lawn.

We were on high alert for a while, then forgot about being haunted. Mum and Dad were often in Sydney overnight. We kids would regularly be alone on the hill for a night or two, but I never saw anything or picked up weird vibes.

It *was* a cold house, but how could it not be with all that stone? I imagined our otherworldly housemate was the lieutenant, his dashing sea captain uniform now a bit see-through. But I guess one of the children or the governess or even an unlucky convict would have been more likely.

The house also came with a horse. Part of the rental agreement was to keep an eye on him. The kitchen overlooked the paddock he lived in. Tobey and I spent weeks trying to make friends with him, trying to barter his interest with bright jewels of carrot and apple. He wasn't having any of it. Flicking his mane and snorting in disgust at the very sight of us. There was no question of us riding him, he didn't even deign to be patted. Fair enough. He'd been alone too long and had plenty of grass.

The real problem with Tanilba House was that it was a monster to clean. Dusty, lots of nooks and crannies and nowhere near enough power sockets to run a vacuum cleaner. The kitchen was pretty rustic. A farmhouse-style sink and planks of wood for shelves. In place of an oven was a cast-iron cooker that dated back to another century. Most likely invaluable, but with no dials or a glass door, I wasn't super impressed.

I'd adopted a more haphazard housecleaning approach. Things were still lemon-fresh in the important areas, but there was too much house to cover for me to pretend I could tidy us back to how we used to be. That sort of naiveté seemed childish now anyway.

Every so often I'd get to a proper dusting, but mainly it was about emptying ashtrays, and ferrying wine glasses and sticky brown spoons back to the kitchen sink.

This was the setting of my great Crime Against the Family. Marginally worse than when I dropped the priceless Ming.

Like the Ming, it was entirely avoidable. Hundred percent I should have known better. If I hadn't been so distracted by my own eye-rolling at the mess left behind from the night before, I probably wouldn't have been such an idiot.

I was stomping about in the living room, huffing my way through the tidying up, when I saw an oven tray of dirty water. It was just sitting on the coffee table. But at this point, we were used to seeing things in odd places. You couldn't expect to find a spoon in the kitchen drawer anymore. Bedroom items were all over the house. Pots and pans might have been used for anything, anywhere. Certainly, an aluminium oven tray of water on the coffee table wasn't the oddest thing I'd seen.

Instead of carrying the tray three rooms back to the kitchen sink, slopping water over the ancient carpets, I decided to tip it over the plants under the open window next to me. It was done in a second.

As the last drops hit the agapanthus, I had a slight pang that the stale-looking water might not be ideal for them, but that was the extent of my consideration.

An hour or so later, I was wiping down the kitchen table when I heard Dad scream.

Turns out the water was more than $100,000 of cocaine air drying from liquid to powder form. Dad had been trying out a new method of dehydration.

He couldn't even look in my direction. There was talk of boarding school, orphanages, going to live with Nanny or maybe adoption. Dad was so furious, I think he actually toyed with the idea of getting rid of me for real. I had to sneak about the house, hiding from him.

Dad's disappointment would have lasted longer if it weren't for what happened next.

It was about 2am. Mum and Dad were still half-awake, but the rest of us were sound asleep. I woke suddenly, to see a man in my bedroom. Standing above me with a gun pointing straight down at my face.

He turned out to be one of three men with guns inside our house. They'd been sent by a drug lord.

There was a murky backstory about how Baz and Nils and Dad had fallen out. Some time prior to this evening Nils had made a smaller delivery of cocaine to his contact than had previously been agreed. It further emerged that this may have been in someways due to Mum and Dad tooting through a camera leg of the stash, although Baz and Nils wouldn't have had entirely clean noses either.

What were they all thinking? That an international drug boss was just not going to notice that some of his order was missing? Cripes. We so should have stuck with the antiques.

I knew Nils and Baz weren't our friends anymore, but the first I knew about any of the rest of the story was opening my eyes and seeing the barrel of a gun. The man told me to follow him through to the living room where the other two men with guns were pointing them at Mum and Dad. Tobey and Griff were already there, eyes bogged wide, sitting on the sofa. Baby Lola must have still been asleep.

Last came Mark who was staying with us ostensibly to help with security. Mark looked the part. Tall and square jawed with a ruggedly bushy moustache, like he'd just stepped down from a Marlboro smokes billboard. That night we all learned that Mark slept nude. Instead of making tough-guy moves to wrestle the guns off the men, we heard him asking very sweetly if he could put his underpants on before they shot him.

The men had brought Nils with them. Nils was half-standing, half-slumped against one of them. He had bruises on his face and dried blood around his mouth. He looked like he was about to pass out at any moment. They'd obviously beaten him up, and maybe worse. It was scary to see him like that, but I couldn't believe he had told them where we lived. He'd brought hitmen with guns to a house where a toddler and baby were.

Griffy was sitting there on the sofa. He was keeping very still and not making a sound. Lola was too young to remember this night, but whatever was about to happen, poor little Griff was about to see it all.

Dad was high as a kite. Instead of being sensible, he was saying stuff that was clearly escalating the situation. He was shouting at the men. They were shouting back. All the yelling was going to wake Lola and then she'd be crying. And there weren't many situations that got calmer after Lola started crying.

Mark standing there with his jeans half-buttoned wasn't going to be much help.

Dad started putting his hands up threateningly at the men.

In slow motion I saw Dad's arms go up.

Nils slumped sideward.

And then I saw that the guy who had been propping Nils up had been holding a knife against him all this time. It was a hunting knife with a big jagged blade.

The guy with the knife lunged towards Dad's neck.

I thought, why do they need a knife when they have guns? Then, weirdly, I stepped into the way.

It was clear Dad wasn't going to be able to defend himself. He was staggering and swaying almost as badly as Nils. I'm not sure he even saw the knife coming. It wasn't so much about being brave. More that I figured I'd be fine. Even though they were bad guys: actual drug lord henchmen, it felt like they'd draw the line at stabbing a kid in the face.

Luckily this was the case. The guy swerved and yanked back his knife.

I don't know if they'd even been expecting to find kids at the house. But whatever their plans had been, there's being a henchman and then there's hurting children. You'd have to be pretty hardcore not to be put off doing bad things with a baby and a toddler involved.

One of the men laughed at me flapping about in my pink nightie. Dad had a little wildcat on his hands with this one, he said. Things calmed down a bit.

They left not long after that, taking Nils with them. But none of the drugs they'd come for. The mixture that had been tipped out the window over the agapanthus had been the last of the Amsterdam cocaine, so there was nothing left for them to take. I almost felt sorry for them, they seemed pretty reasonable, all things considered, and it was a long drive back to the city.

Later on we found out that they weren't such reasonable guys after all. Before they visited us, they'd dangled Baz by the ankles out of a two-story window. And then let go. He'd survived, but had spent a long time in hospital.

We never saw Baz or Nils again. Dad said it had all been their fault. Truthfully, I don't know who screwed over who. Or who screwed over who the most. Probably it was us. But that didn't occur to me at the time: you always think you're the good guys.

A week later we were pulled from our beds in the middle of the night again.

The first time it had been by men sent by a drug lord. The second time it was the Australian Federal police. Both groups came armed, but the police had much bigger guns. And seemed to have no problem pointing them at Lola and Griffy.

I heard them at the doors, battering them down with rams. It was a full-scale attack: while we were sleeping they'd swarmed around the house like a nest of wasps. Smashing their way in through all the doors simultaneously at 4.30am. The kitchen door hadn't even been locked.

I bolted up in bed. By the time I understood what the crashing noise was, there were three of them crammed into my bedroom. There were so many of them. They were in all our rooms. They definitely had been expecting to find children in the house, and they didn't give a damn. Instead of handguns, it was military-style guns with high-beam torches pointed at me. They were geared like soldiers or riot police. I could only see their eyes, but their eyes looked all fired up as though our old house was a war zone.

I was much more scared of us getting hurt that night.

They searched everything, breaking and smashing things unnecessarily. They told me to stand next to my bed while two officers pulled out everything from the drawers, my neat folding all over the floor being stomped under their boots. My underwear. My drawings and lame poetry attempts. They ripped out pages from my *Dolly* magazines. You can't work out why they're doing these things, but you get to stand there in your stupid pink nightie, watching them do it.

They even went through my rubbish bin.

Having just turned thirteen, every waking moment of my life was already spent being deeply mortified by something. But the timing of the raid wasn't great. I'd had my period that night. My fourth-ever period. Like most girls having menstrual cycles in 1983, especially those living in houses with antique plumbing, my sanitary care got wrapped up and hid in the bin overnight.

'What's this then?' one officer whooped.

'Oi Sarge, you better see this,' yelled the other, calling in more of his colleagues.

They bunched around my rubbish bin, excited to find a little parcel. I tried to stop them, but I couldn't bring myself to say the words.

Then the officers were yelling eww and yuck, and looking up at me. I felt so ashamed.

Once again, we were all gathered together in the living room. But then we were taken to separate rooms for questioning. The questions went on and on. I don't know if there was meant to be a counsellor or guardian present, but it was just me and two officers. The same questions over and over in different ways.

I sat opposite them, looking down at the little flowers on my pink nightie. I was petrified they would trick me into saying something dangerous for Mum and Dad. But luckily, they just treated me like a stupid kid.

'Look, we just want to know where the cocaine is,' said the first. 'We know it's here.'

'Maybe you've heard your parents talking about coke?' said the second in a fake-nice voice.

Mum had always told us the best way to navigate this type of questioning was to play dumb: pretend we thought they were talking about Coca-Cola, the fizzy drink. Which *was* an authentically outlawed substance in our home.

'Yes', I answered.

'You know about the coke?' they leaned forward, eager.

'Yes sir.'

'Where is it?'

'Oh, we're not allowed coke...' I said with big fake-sincere eyes. 'Mum says it's full of sugar.'

Apparently Tobey was having a similar conversation a few rooms away.

They rolled their eyes and sighed aggressively. Just tell us something, they kept saying. Then you can all go back to bed. Just tell us where the drugs are, *anything*.

I couldn't believe they genuinely expected me to rat out my own parents. I'd have been carted off in a paddy van before being that disloyal. But also, who would be that stupid? *As if* they'd just let us all go back to bed if they found any drugs.

Next it was through to the kitchen where I was told to sit at the kitchen table while they smashed open jars of rice and flour. I couldn't understand why they didn't just open the lids.

Once the riot police had been stood down and the danger of someone in my family getting sprayed with bullets from an automatic weapon had lessened, I got angrier and angrier watching them break all our things. A whole shelf of mason jars labelled with my neatest writing were on the floor, shards of glass sticking out of the piles of flours and grains. Cocaine didn't look anything like brown rice. How could a drug squad not know that?

Each time they asked me if I knew where the drugs were, I told them something ridiculous. At one point there was an officer with his head and shoulders up the chimney, another tasting his baking-soda tipped pinkie finger. A third one was outside, poking sticks hopefully into our car's gas tank.

No one thought to test the agapanthus plants growing under the living room window. The only illegal substance the police found were traces of the heroin Mum and Dad had been using. Luckily, they'd been running low.

I didn't feel the least bit sorry for the drug squad's wasted trip.

The hitmen were one thing, but it took me a long time to feel safe in my bed again after the police came. Even after we'd cleaned up all the mess, it took me ages not to hear the sound of doors splintering open. I accidently-on-purpose slept in my clothes. Being pulled from your bed by state-sanctioned men in riot gear just takes a while to get over.

★

Dad only had one real leg. He didn't talk about how he'd lost the other one.

The past was one of the few countries Mum and Dad had no interest visiting. Given Dad's love of things *from* the past, maybe this was strange, but he and Mum rarely talked about their own histories.

Dad had a slight limp that was more pronounced when he was tired. His 'leg' was a series of artificial limbs in heavy, salmon-coloured plastic. The toes moulded together like Barbie's. Strapped on with chunky leather and industrial Velcro. Probably not a great deal more wearable than the wooden pegs pirates used to hop about on, almost definitely heavier.

There were often red raw ulcers where his leg had been amputated, just below his right knee. They bled through his thick socks if he walked too far in the heat. Sometimes shooting pains from the severed nerve endings made him gasp; his face would suddenly drain of colour. Before an electrical storm there would be aches that kept him awake into the night.

Dad never complained about the pain. He only took his leg off to sleep or bathe. In all the years we lived by the sea, there were less than a handful of days he came swimming with us.

The word disability was foreign. It never occurred to us to park in the spot with the wheelchair sign. One time we got pulled over by highway police because someone had reported a severed leg they'd seen in our back window. It was just Dad's spare leg plonked foot-upwards between Tobey and me in the backseat. The policeman said we should have our disabled sign displayed and we all looked at him blankly. I genuinely had no idea what he was talking about.

We didn't know the full story, but like Mum being adopted, I don't remember a time without the basic facts. The accident happened when Dad was a little boy. Poppa had been mowing the lawn.

A rock got caught in the blades of the lawn mower, clanking and spinning under the guard, building up speed, before ricocheting out across the lawn. Dad had been barefoot in the grass. The rock hit his foot with such force that he was sent flying. When Poppa ran over, Dad's foot was bloody pulp.

We knew that it had been a long drive to the hospital in the pick-up truck. This was when Nanny and Poppa Starling had their farm, so they were in the country. The doctors were unable to save Dad's foot.

Later came other details. That Dad had nearly died. He was drifting in and out of consciousness by the time they got to the hospital. The truck was wet with his blood. It had poured through the towels Nanny had wrapped around his foot and soaked the 1950s-style seat. All three of them were covered in blood.

Much of the way to the hospital was potholed dirt roads. Poppa drove as fast as he could. The old pick-up didn't have much suspension and Dad's foot was attached by threads. Each bump would have been agonising.

There was a first operation, where they amputated Dad's foot. Then another, where the doctors cut away more, so everything below the knee of his right leg was gone.

Then they wheeled him out to a ward of old men and waited to see if he'd live.

He lay there alone. A little body bandaged up under the sheets.

Nanny couldn't bring herself to see him. She couldn't even go into the hospital. The one time she visited, she stood in the flowerbed outside and called out to him through the ward window. She had a nurse take him a bag of sweets.

I don't know why she was like this. Or what was going on in her head. Maybe it was just too much for her to bear. Her first-born son who could run like the wind, now lying broken in a hospital bed.

As a kid, Dad had sprinted everywhere. 'Don't run in the house!' she'd constantly be yelling after him. 'Don't run down the stairs! Wait for your brother.' Now the doctors were saying that if he lived, he would not likely walk without crutches.

Poppa was always strange about the accident too. Decades later, Tobey and I knew we weren't allowed to mention it, or say anything about Dad's leg. Poppa blamed himself. There was a feeling that Dad hadn't wanted to be on the lawn. Someone said Poppa had been yelling at him at the time. Nanny and Poppa had both been in the war, maybe all that blood in the truck had just brought back things they'd travelled a long way to leave behind.

What I do know is that Dad was only nine years old when he lay there alone in a hospital bed. He was there for six months. All through summer and into autumn. There was no TV to watch or books to read. Just staring at the ceiling and looking at the empty space at the end of the bed where his foot used to be.

It was a small hospital with no children's ward. The old men lying in the beds around him came and went. They had phlegmy hacking coughs, waking him up through the night. Many of them died in the time Dad was there. He would have come to recognise the end approaching. After a while he would have seen the signs. The particular rattle to the cough, the flatness around the eyes. Death would have felt close and real.

It wasn't certain he would live either. I don't know how a nine-year-old kid processes all of this. He must have felt frightened and very alone.

No one was talking to him about the situation he was in, reassuring him. There were no hugs, no one trying to make him laugh. I don't know what the rest of his life would have looked like to him, as he lay there, looking down his bed. Watching the curtains being drawn around the other beds in the morning, the bodies being wheeled away.

Maybe he told himself that he was different. Not like those around him. Just to get through those long, lonely months, maybe nine-year-old Dad promised himself that he wouldn't have to live by everyone else's rules and circumstance. Maybe being different from everyone else felt like survival.

The other thing that happened there was that they put him on a lot of morphine. Shots every few hours for six months. Enough that he had a massive habit by the time he left the hospital. At a very formative age Dad learned all about the relief and escape that needles could bring.

I'm only speculating here, but I imagine *that* left a pretty big impression.

★

Our departure from Tanilba House was swift.

We were back in the city, and in disguise.

Obviously we hadn't been safe up on the coast. But exactly how much danger was looming over us now wasn't clear. While Mum and Dad assessed our situation, we were staying at the Koala Inn on Oxford Street. Inside, the vibe was strong seventies and the pool was on the roof, twenty-five-floors up.

We'd checked in under the cover of darkness. Mum hurried out first thing and came back with a bag of wigs and dark sunglasses. Mum and Dad were nervous. Everyone but Lola had to wear their wig and shades whenever we stepped out onto the street. Dad also shaved his beard, and affected a baseball cap. Mum wore a pair of fake glasses.

It seemed like a dodgy disguise to me. Mum looked good in her glossy blonde bob, and both she and Dad had a whiff of incognito celebrity about them. But put a three-year-old in a hairpiece and wraparound shades and all you've got is weird. Plus, anyone looking for a family of six, would still see a family of six. Staying in the heartland of the Sydney gay scene, we didn't exactly blend in. Just the fact we came in a variety of heights and one of us was carrying a baby made us stand out.

'It's not safe to leave the hotel together,' said Dad.

'So what, we do dinner in shifts?' asked Mum.

Out we trooped.

It felt like the shiny wigs and sunglasses were actually attracting *more* attention. We seemed to be getting more side glances than usual, but probably I was just being paranoid. After all, the glasses disguise had always worked a treat for Clark Kent and Diana Prince.

Mostly Mum and Dad went out, and we kids hit the rooftop, sunburning ourselves to tight little tomatoes in the glorious turquoise rectangle.

It was a weird time. I was hyperaware that we might all die. Every time I stepped out of our hotel room and into the long, dark brown corridor, I half expected to feel a bullet rip through the back of my head. But on the other hand, I also remember laughing a lot about how ridiculous we looked in our wigs as we tramped up and down Oxford Street, past all the gay bars and bright rainbow flags, looking for somewhere to eat.

Definitely we were sitting ducks. Small-fry in well over our heads. If the drug boss *had* decided to send his guys back to kill us, or the police had decided to arrest Mum and Dad, we'd have been pretty breezy to locate.

But nothing happened.

For a few weeks Mum and Dad talked about leaving the country, assuming new identities, plastic surgery.

Instead, we rented a house in the suburbs.

Hopefully the tip-off to the police had been the end of the episode. With all the stress going on, Mum and Dad had been taking a lot of heroin, which probably lent a fuzzy detachment to proceedings for them.

They'd stopped talking about getting clean. Any sign that things were spiralling out of control was called something else. They bought a king-size waterbed. With all the porn-star, velvet-headboard trimmings. Dad kept nodding off with lit cigarettes. There were burn holes everywhere, but when you're lying on a 940-litre bag of water, they're harder to ignore. After a week of waking up surrounded in comedy spouting leaks, they decided this was simply a sign the waterbed would be best suited to my room.

I'd been fine with my single bed and having floor space. But what thirteen-year-old wouldn't prefer their bedroom was wall-to-wall, band-aided, gurgling rubber? Just looking at that bed made me feel about ninety-seven.

The taking of heroin – the few minutes of enjoying it, the getting more of it – was taking up all their time. There wasn't a lot of headspace for other things. There didn't seem to be any plans on the table for antiquing trips overseas. There wasn't much socialising. The people they knew were different. Gone were the well-travelled, well-educated bohemians. There were outsiders of a different sort at our house now. Badly dressed and pretty charmless. Other junkies.

I don't know what happened to the interesting people, they sort of just melted away. But who would want to be around a bunch of people sticking needles into themselves? That conversation is super-repetitive.

We never saw Lars and Liva and their beautiful daughters again. Or Owl, Dad's best friend for years who lived in London, or another close friend for years, Jon, the African doctor who had stories about lions and elephants and stitched up my lip on the kitchen table at Waimauku.

Even Nils and Baz were fun to be around, before everything went bad.

When we were living together in Bali at the Whitebox house, Baz used to take Tobey and me out on his motorbike for night-time adventures. During the day there would be the Chris de Burgh wars, but at night the three of us were on his motorbike, helmet-less and hair blowing free. We'd burn down the roads and finish up at some remote lookout somewhere. Sometimes he'd take us for crème caramels at a fancy hotel. I've no idea why he bothered with two scrawny kids, I was twelve, Tobey almost nine: how good could our company have been? But he never made us feel like stupid kids. He treated us like people.

I don't know how old Baz was, he was kind of ageless. Super skinny: all wiry and athletic. A bit like Nic Cage playing a skeleton. He wasn't into fashion exactly, more of a timeless seventies ambience: double denim, tight t-shirts and mirrored aviators. His hair was white-blond, but this had happened prematurely, probably when he was around five. He didn't seem *old*, old. Somewhere between twenty-seven and sixty.

We always liked Baz and were sorry he left the way he did. He and Dad argued; the argument got physical. Tobey and I were out the back, dancing around or doing something stupid, and didn't understand what was going on. We didn't see him go or what state he was in when he left, but Mum said she'd washed a lot of dark blood off the walls. I don't know what Baz's skills were like, but Dad was a mean fighter.

And maybe Baz was a bad guy, but he was pretty cool to us. So many people came and went during those years, it's hard to remember everyone, but there are a couple of people who stood out, and Baz is one of them. I was very sad to hear he'd been thrown out a window.

1984

School, again

Of all the things I was crap at, school was top of the list. As far as I could tell, the trick to being normal was to blend in, seamlessly as possible. Octopus-style. This was the constant goal, and the reliably dismal failure. Each time I promised myself that *this* school would be The One. But something always cropped up and I'd be revealed. Sometimes all it took was for the teacher to introduce me to the class.

'We have a new student. Her name is Saylor and she's come from Delhi. Now, does anyone know where Delhi is?'

In a time when normal family holidays rarely went further afield than a summer caravan park down the coast, Delhi may as well have been Tralfamadore.

I'd be standing at the blackboard, blazing red face, handling things badly. Yes, they had chairs in India. And schools. No, they didn't have Rice Krispies. Yes, they did worship cows, but it's not like they thought cows were gods, well not *exactly*.

In the very early days when Mum made my lunches, they hadn't helped. Back in the seventies most mums didn't send their kids to school with sprouted lentil sandwiches. Mine was way ahead of the curve.

One time I opened the brown paper bag to discover lunch was an ex-jam jar of stewed apple, raisins and long strands of grated coconut. Not quite what I was expecting, but fine. Except I couldn't open the glass jar. One of the boys saw me struggling and had a go. He couldn't get it open either, so the jar got passed around. Each kid having a go was peering inside at the increasingly blended apple and coconut gratings and yelling out their guesses of what it could be.

'Those weird white things, are they… maggots?'

'Ohmygod, do they actually eat maggots in India?'

'Ew, she's got maggots for lunch!'

A couple of kids started gagging.

Finally, it got to the burly PE teacher, who was able to wrench the lid off. As he passed the jar back to me, he held it up to the light, examining my lunch with the kind of fascination you would view a particularly lively worm farm.

'Are there bugs in this lunch?'

'No sir, no bugs.'

Maggot Girl kind of stuck.

Generally, I wasn't too sad when we moved away a couple of months later.

But now it was 1984. I was thirteen and Teenage School would be different. I was feeling pretty good about it.

Mum and I drove into the city to get some 'school-appropriate' clothes for me to wear before my uniform arrived. Neither of us had the faintest clue what school-appropriate actually meant, so we went to the chain of shops that *Dolly* magazine said had the 'coolest streetwear trends' available.

This being the eighties, I was keen on neons. Mum liked the rockstar black lace. We compromised, meeting in the middle with some outfits that were straight out of *Dolly*'s fashion pages. Also a set of fluorescent lime and orange stretch belts and some fingerless lace gloves.

It was pretty exciting. Mum and I were bonding massively. She was delighted I was finally showing an interest in fashion. I was thrilled I'd be blending inconspicuously with the other Australian teenage girls.

On this giddy roll, we careened into the hairdressers next door for a trim. We hadn't cut my hair since Amsterdam and it was long again. As I settled into the chair, getting caped up, Mum and the hairdresser spontaneously decided a spiral perm would go superbly with my new clothes. *When Doves Cry* was blasting through the salon so I couldn't really hear what was being said, but they both looked super happy as they lifted and pointed to sections of my hair.

I rocked up at the suburban school gates the next morning looking like the Bangles' try-hard kid sister. The school uniform everyone else was wearing was a discreet knee-length navy tunic. My hot-pink lace midriff top and aggressively shoulder-padded tiger-print blazer did not exactly blend in. This being years before Julia Roberts' *Pretty Woman*, or Whitney Houston's massive hairpiece wanted to dance with somebody, the poodle-esque mess of ringlets on my head was seen as an unfortunate birth defect.

That afternoon I jogged back from Teenage School to ask Mum about my uniform.

'Oh, don't worry about *that*. Haven't even ordered it yet. You'll have plenty of time to enjoy your new clothes.'

When Mum went down to the school supplies shop later that week, she was told that this being practically end of term, my uniform would have to be ordered in specially.

Three long, loudly-dressed weeks later, the uniform finally arrived. I couldn't wait to wear it. The next morning I was at the bus stop in time for the early, early bus. The school gates were still locked when I got there. After about ten minutes, someone shuffled over, glanced at me sadly, then swung them open.

A school handout the week before had mentioned something called Mufti Day. I hadn't the foggiest what a Mufti was. But I did know asking questions that everyone else knew the answers to was *not* how you fitted in. I'd decided to worry about Muftis later, then forgotten all about them.

I sat on the school steps, watching the teachers come through the gates in unusually casual clothes. Then other, shorter, younger-looking teachers milled past in brightly coloured clumps. I started to get a dark, sinking feeling as I realised the short teachers weren't teachers.

Gradually the playground filled with jeans and tops and miniskirts. When the bell rang, I was the only kid in the entire school in uniform, surrounded in a sea of colour and denim. Even some flashes of neon and lace.

It turned out Mufti Day was code for Wear-Your-Own-Clothes Day.

Unbelievable. But, also, believably typical.

Another difficulty at school was sport. Balls kind of scared me. I could see everyone else found them delightful, but the whole idea of something flying aggressively towards my head was unsettling. Maybe you needed to get used to them at an early age. Balls just weren't a thing in my family. At home, if something was ricocheting through the air towards you, you ducked.

Worse, any time that a ball was near you, it meant everyone was looking at you. Various PE teachers had tried to get me involved. Besides not getting conked on the back of the head, my key objective was to do whatever I had to do as quickly as possible. Attract minimal attention. Melt back into the field. Avoid anxiety vomiting.

At one school, we'd done softball. You only had to do three swings. Somehow I manage to make contact with the ball hard enough that the rest of the class didn't need to pass out in horror. Things like high jumps and gym were OK, if you overlooked all the times I'd flopped over, spraining an ankle or wrist. Running was simple enough, unless it was relay racing with a team to let down.

At this school, the girls could choose either tennis or hockey. Mum had enjoyed tennis at her school, and felt it had the best outfits on offer.

Another lavish investment was needed: Light-blue and silver matching skirt and top. Socks with light-blue bobbles and silver-piped trainers. Light-blue hair grips and elastics. Not only did I have the full kit. I rocked up with my very own tube of balls and a brand-new, tightly-strung, light-blue-and-silver Dunlop racket. I had everything needed to play a great game of tennis. Apart from any ability whatsoever.

There was one court and a line of us waiting to serve. Everyone else was wearing mismatched old t-shirts and shorts. There was a loose set of doubles going on. Each time someone missed the ball, they left the court and went to the back of the line.

I nervously joined the line. The coach was yelling out things about love and deuce, but the jist of it seemed similar to softball, you swung your bat/racket and hit the ball. The players having most success were those who lunged dramatically at the ball. The other key move was to lean forward, knees bent, legs wide, while swapping the racket from one hand to another. That bit looked doable.

It was meant to be a seamless game with the exchange of players never slowing the flow of the ball.

I shuffled forward. Heart thumping in my chest. One more girl ahead of me.

Then I was next in line.

Then it was my turn. I felt a bit queasy.

'Next girl,' came the call. Waving my racket around I scurried into place.

The coach frowned, motioning a halt to the action. 'Wait, wait! You left- or right-handed?'

'Right?'

'You sure?'

I nodded. I wasn't.

'Serve!' screeched the coach.

The ball looped across the net. It was closer to the other girl on my side. I didn't want to crowd her, so I just leaned forward, swapping my racket from hand to hand. Next two balls I let her get too: she seemed to be enjoying herself and I didn't want to push in. She was lunging all over the place like she really knew what she was doing. I edged to the back of the court to give her extra room.

Feedback came from the coach: 'Hey new girl. This isn't dodgeball. You need to actually hit that little green ball!'

The ball looped over the net. Unmistakably towards me. All eyes now pointed at me: the other players, the line of girls waiting, the coach, the assistant coach, half a dozen parents in the carpark.

I hopped up on the spot and ran towards the ball like my partner had been doing. Somehow my racket got caught between my legs. I tripped, pitching the tightly-strung Dunlop high into the air, and skidding the last few yards to the ball on my right knee.

The ball bounced brightly past me. As I wilted onto the court, clutching my knee.

When I stood up, there was blood dribbling down my leg straight into my pristine, blue-bobbled socks and a red, knee-shaped skid mark across the court. Luckily, I wasn't asked back to Tennis Club.

★

When I was fourteen, I went to live with Nanny and Aunt Erin again. Mum and Dad were over the suburbs and moving back to Bali. Nanny was living in Sydney now. I don't think I was in trouble. This was pitched as a great opportunity for me to go to school properly. Every day, all week long.

I don't know how detailed the talks were before I was involved, but within the fortnight my family had left the country and I'd moved into a 1920s block on the harbourfront with my grandmother and aunt. Dad would pay my share of the rent and bills, plus an unspecified amount for my care and expenses.

I hugged my family tightly goodbye, and we all stood and looked at each other on the kerb. Me bound for the eastern suburbs of Sydney, them for the airport, then Indonesia.

'Take care of the kids,' I said to Tobey.

She nodded seriously.

'Be nice to them.'

She rolled her eyes, 'Ergh. Don't get all mushy.'

My heart felt heavy and lumpy to see them go without me. But nothing ever felt particularly stable or permanent, so probably I didn't take the year Mum and Dad said they'd be gone too seriously.

Similar to how it had been on Norfolk Island, it was pretty harmonious living at Point Piper. The flat was small, but cute. Nanny was strict, but fair. Erin and I were both studying. Me to be a kid, her to be an osteopath. Life was good. Except for maths.

Usually when we rocked up to the enrolment office of a new school, there'd be questions about records from previous schools. Mum would breeze over this with exotic tales of lost luggage and inconvenient fires at storage warehouses. Even if we had kept any report cards, the dates on them would have just raised more questions about the long gaps in schooling. Also sometimes our surname was different.

Generally, I'd just do a few entrance tests and that would be that.

There were several schools near Nanny. She liked the sound of the elective one that was getting terrific academic results. Before they left for Bali, Mum had taken me to the school board offices to be assessed. It was all pretty breezy stuff, I remember going into a little room, sitting there by myself and being given different exam sheets. I ticked away at the boxes, wrote a few bits and was out a couple of hours later.

Everything was fine until we got the results back. I'd got into the competitive school, which was nice, but their whole learning system was structured into six tiers of aptitude, from A to E. They were a bit manic about their academic standing and this tier system was very serious.

No one could understand how I could be all tier As, and then get a dumb-ass D in maths.

Personally, I was used to being rubbish at maths, but at this school it was a real issue. If you were in tier A for English, you weren't just expected to be in tier A across all the other subjects, your aptitude letter was who you were here. All your classes were As. All your friends were As.

Stupid maths. After Grannie May had taught me how to read, I'd been able to fudge my way through schoolwork fine. That side of things wasn't the problem, not since those first days at St Cluny.

But then, when I was about twelve, I started a school and there was maths. Not arithmetic or times-tables (which, quite frankly, were grim enough), but slippery, meaningless maths. It wasn't just about catching up. I didn't even understand what I had to learn. The other kids around me were all nodding their heads and cracking on, happily measuring out their isosceles triangles.

It was like walking into a room where everyone was upside down, speaking a different language, with a feather up their butt, pretending this was normal. Except it *was* normal and I was the one with the feather up my butt. Normally, we'd just move away before any teacher started asking too many questions and things got out of hand. But that wasn't going to happen here.

The first few weeks at the elective school, I sat at the back of D class. Smiling like a banana, trying to look normal. Sweating deeply around the armpits. This was meant to be dummies maths, but I still didn't understand a squiggle of it. I'd tell myself it was just an hour a day. A swampy, awful hour of being revoltingly dense. But just an hour.

I wasn't the only one suffering in D. There was a general atmosphere of shame in the room. Everyone – from the teacher up front, to the three kids in the back row with me – seemed humiliated to be here. Just a class away from the dreaded Es: mouth-breathers so backward, they didn't wear watches because they couldn't even tell the time.

The teacher yelled at us like we were hard of hearing. He had a really loud voice anyway. He'd peer down at you from behind super-thick glasses, his tiny black eyes pinpricked with abject disappointment. Anytime we had hand-ins, he would pass back our marked papers very sadly.

One afternoon he asked me to stay back to tell me that I was doing badly, *even for this class*.

'Are you not even trying? You're holding back the whole class.'

I'd never asked a question and we hadn't had any tests yet, so I didn't understand quite how I was holding back the class, but I was fully prepared to agree.

'Sorry sir.'

He sent me home with a note saying I needed private tutoring. Poor, horrified Nanny Starling booked emergency coaching the next day. After school I caught a bus to a dark office where a small patient man with a thick accent tried to explain a logarithm. I got it for a minute, then it slipped out of grasp again. I tried and tried, but all I did was waste everyone's time and money. Deep down, I knew it was never going to make sense to me. The maths part of my skull just hadn't formed properly.

One morning the hammer fell. 'Starling, pack up your things and come to the front please.'

'I'm sorry to tell you Starling, we've been forced to move you to 9E,' he boomed at me and the rest of the class when I got to his desk.

Everyone stared. Someone snickered.

In a fog of shame, I walked along the hallway to 9E and knocked on the door. There was quite a bit of chatter and noise coming from inside.

'Enter.'

The teacher was leaning on the class-side of his desk, legs crossed to the floor, casual as could be. I shuffled in, barely raising my eyes. 'I've come from 9D sir.'

'Yes, yes. Hello! Welcome. There's a spot for you there Saylor.'

I looked over, instead of neatly seated in tight rows, everyone in E was lounging over their desks or balancing haphazardly on the back of their chairs. The *whole class* was casual as could be.

These kids looked normal. None of them were visibly drooling. They had watches. Some of them even looked cool. There was a vague *The Breakfast Club* kind of vibe.

Class 9E turned out to be superb. I still couldn't do the maths, but it wasn't the end of the world. There were hand-outs and an official outline, but no one worried too much. Being shit at trig didn't define these kids. The teacher never shamed us. No one was going to kill themselves over maths here. Not when we had calculators.

1985

Cedar Creek

Point Piper was over. I was back living with my family in Bali.

The house Mum and Dad had rented came with a monkey guard dog. She had her own miniature house on a post near the front gate and wore a thin chain attached around her waist.

Having a monkey as a guard dog was pretty common and you could see why. They're crazy territorial and absolutely flip out any time someone comes near their land. Shrieking and leaping at the end of their chain like they're going to tear you apart. Monkeys put the fear of God into even the most intrepid dogs.

Years earlier we'd been travelling through countryside just outside Mysore, southern India, and needed to make an urgent stop. We were sat in the car, waiting for Tobey to finish peeing behind a banyan tree when we heard a scream. We looked back to see six-year-old Tobey, knickers not quite up, dress tucked in, running for her life from a horde of furious monkeys. We yanked Tobey into the backseat and hit the accelerator. The monkeys still leaping after us, waving their fists.

Our house monkey wanted war too. Being chained to a mini-house on a pole probably hadn't helped her mood, but she belonged to the property and we weren't allowed to set her free. Tobey and I tried to make friends with her instead. For weeks we tried to bribe her affections with different types of bananas and increasingly exotic fruits. She threw them back in our faces. Literally: she had a strong arm and an excellent aim. Each time we'd retreat, smeared in bits of banana and papaya seeds.

At first, we thought she just wasn't familiar with us. But she was consistent in her welcome – hysterical screeching, teeth barred in violent menace, rushing at us like we were deadly pencuries – until we moved out.

Only Dad could safely approach the span of her chain. She'd happily hop onto his shoulder and let him pet her, stroking her head, until she'd close her eyes, entirely relaxed. Like a real little suck up.

If we tried to get involved, she'd smell us creeping closer and bare her teeth murderously over Dad's shoulder. The landlord explained that she just didn't like other females. Nice.

In traditional Balinese compound style, our house was actually three self-contained houses within a tall wall. There was a main building, where Mum and Dad, Tobey, Griff and Lola lived. Next to that, like the monkey, I had my own mini-house.

Mine had a bedroom, lounge and bathroom. The bedroom had a raised sleeping platform, then some steps leading to a tiny inside garden that was actually the shower. There was a tiled spot to stand and shower in, and the rest of the room was plants. Its ceiling was just bars, so you could lie in bed and look up at the coconut trees and stars. It was magical. Having hot showers in the rain was dreamy.

There were frogs and lizards living in the plants in my bedroom shower, but I was careful not to splash them with soap and shampoo foam. One morning, I spotted a flash of slithering green. I rushed to lift back the leaves and see what it was. A little green grass snake. Entirely harmless, unless you were a frog or insect.

In addition to the open roof, there were several drainage gaps at the bottom of the wall, so the snake could easily have made her escape, but she chose to stay.

Anytime I found any dead bugs, I'd bring them back for my little shower buddy. I'd leave them on the same rock and they were always gone when I'd check back later. She was pretty cute. The frog population thinned out a bit which wasn't ideal, but hopefully they'd just hopped out the gaps. If they hadn't the sense to do that, my shower was now a mini circle of life, I told myself in a David Attenborough voice.

The third house, towards the back of the compound, was Katuk and Made's. They were a recently married couple who, like the monkey, came with the house. They hated us too.

Officially Katuk did the cooking and housekeeping and Made was the gardener-driver. Theirs had been an arranged marriage, but not well arranged. By the sounds of things, they'd despised each other on sight. Feelings which, in time, had only deepened. When we moved in, their loathing of each other had escalated to the point where it took up most of their day. Apart from how shit foreigners were, they agreed on nothing.

It would definitely have been nicer to live in our home by ourselves, but since they were there first and their wages were drawn from our rent, it seemed rude to ask them to leave.

So they stayed, a comically dark cloud down the back of the compound. Katuk cooked a couple of half-hearted meals when we first moved in, but then stopped all together. She told us she didn't like to clean. Fair enough. Mostly she sat on the veranda of her house looking peeved and doing her nails. She would disappear for weeks at a time to visit her family. The village she was from was only a couple of hours away, but Made needed to drive her. Which involved him visiting his own family in a neighbouring village from hers, and staying over a few days.

It was nice having a break from hearing them shrieking at each other. But since they needed the minivan we were renting with the house to get to their villages, we'd be without transport.

When Katuk and Made were home, having a driver meant that we kids could do most of the errands. The good thing about Made was that even in the best of times – ie: when Dad, the Man of the House, was in the van – he was a fast driver. When it was just us kids, Made tore down the narrow Balinese laneways like they were German autobahns, taking corners like a racing car driver. On proper tarred roads he'd put his foot down hard enough to get the gauge all the way through the red and shuddering off the edge of the speedometer. The whole minivan would shake as we hurtled along.

It was pretty fun. Tobey and I would do most of our errands at night. We'd only be going to the supermarket half an hour away. But with all the windows open and the warm night wind whipping our hair, we burned down that dark dual carriageway as if we were on the highway to hell.

To best capture the mood, we started leaning all the way out the windows. There were no seatbelts in the back, so it didn't feel like much of a stretch from there to start sitting in the van's windows: our backsides on the sill, facing each other across the roof of the van. So much fun. So much extra wind. Made scorching along at maximum speed, completely undeterred.

After a while I started standing on the windowsill, balancing there like some kind of van surfer. I didn't think much about it. It just seemed like innocent fun. But each time I had to go a bit further, stay out a bit longer. The rush of wind so pure and intoxicating. When you're stepping out on the windowsill of a speeding minivan, coconut trees and fields flashing past in a blur, you don't really think about anything else. I'd find myself looking forward to it all day. Any time there was drama at home, I'd be thinking about all that sweet, sweet rushing wind.

Finally, I graduated to climbing up and sitting on the roof of the van. You can't even open your eyes properly in the airstream on the roof of a van on a highway. There's nothing to hold on to and nothing in your head but roaring wind. Inside Made would be gloriously not giving a hoot. He didn't even bother looking back.

I only stopped doing it when Tobey started wanting to climb out too.

It made me shudder to think about what would have happened if she'd climbed out and Made had slammed the brakes or had to turn suddenly. Or even if a bug had splattered into her eyes.

But also, I missed it terribly and didn't regret a second of it. Apart from, yet again, setting the worst possible example an older sister could set, it was one of the most fun things I'd ever done. There's nothing like the rush of putting yourself in harm's way. Just to see if you dare; to see if you're lucky enough. It feels really zingy.

Made and Katuk were with us for a few months. Until one night we heard Katuk screaming. Really screaming. We all dashed from our houses to theirs. Seeing us, Made ran off.

Katuk said he was threatening to kill her. We told her to hide in my room, while we went to talk to him.

We found Made in the laneway outside our gates. Dad, Tobey, me and Griffy. Dad started calling out to him, trying to calm him down. Made looked so over-the-top enraged I almost giggled. But as we got closer, he pulled out a knife from the back of his trousers. A proper nine-inch blade. We all stood there, gobsmacked, as he stabbed the air, aiming at each of us in turn. Even little Griffy.

Who threatens a four-year-old?

Even he could see he'd lost all ground. For a full minute nobody seemed to know what should happen next. We all just stared at each other. Then Dad told Made to leave and never come back. Made glared at us, his eyes red and mad, and ran off down the lane. We never saw him again.

Katuk packed up her bags and left that night too. I found out the next morning that while we'd been out in the laneway trying to reason with her husband, she'd been nicking anything that looked of value from my room. She'd taken all my jewellery: even yanked the diamanté stars off my favourite pair of socks. Maybe she thought we were just spoiled foreigners who deserved it, and maybe we were, but I loved those little red starry socks.

★

Besides the shower with the little grass snake, the other ace my mini-house had up its sleeve was that it was bang up against the compound wall.

Boys were starting to seem interesting. Maybe not as interesting as the girls at school had thought they were, but I was starting to catch on. One in particular had caught my eye. Ric worked at the music shop down the road. The shop was a hangout for locals and tourists. Everyone sat on the steps out front, listening to music, talking about music and flicking silky eyes at each other.

I was a bit cagey about the flirting situation, but when Ric suggested it might be fun if I snuck out and came dancing with him, I couldn't disagree.

There was a rickety old bamboo ladder at the back of the compound. Around midnight, I leaned it against the wall next to my mini-house and climbed up. The ladder was light enough that I could pull it up to the top of the wall and use it to get down the other side.

Ric was waiting on his motorbike in the laneway outside. We hid the ladder in some bushes and sped off to the 21 Club. The coolest nightclub in Sanur. Or maybe the only nightclub in Sanur.

Probably I could have just strolled out through our front gates. They opened with a loud screech of metal, and the rattle of wheels rolling along the paving stones was deafening. Plus of course, the dread guard monkey. But in the main house Mum and Dad were shooting up around the clock. They would have been pretty out of it by then. I'm not sure they would have stopped me anyway. Maybe it was just more fun to pretend to go to bed, then tiptoe out into the night.

When we got to the club, there was a queue of taxis dropping people off, and a long line at the door. Spotlights circled the coconut trees like a Hollywood premiere, and a low throb of music hummed out from beyond the big double doors that everyone was keen to get through.

Ric took my hand and led me up the stairs and straight past the queue. In addition to his job at the music shop, it turned out Ric worked at 21 Club Fridays and Saturdays as a dancer. The bouncers were happy to see him and there were no questions about my ID or cover charge. Which was ideal, because I had neither.

Through a second set of doors, the music hit us. There were mirror balls throwing light, a crowd on the dancefloor. A massive DJ stage. People everywhere drinking and laughing. Ric was right, we had a lot of fun.

The club was a friendly place. A mix of tourists you saw once, maybe twice, before their holidays were over and they flew back to their homelands, and the locals who you saw most weeks. Every night was like a Saturday and after 11pm, it was always packed.

Being Ric's friend and the only white girl who kept coming back, it didn't take long to get to know the staff and regulars. The bartenders would give us free drinks, but I was happy drinking water. I just wanted to dance and listen to the music. Sometimes Ric would pull me up with him on the podium and I started to feel like part of the place too. It was really nice. Things at home weren't great, but no one talked about their real lives here or asked awkward questions. The music was too loud for anything except dancing and laughing.

Ric would drop me home around dawn and I'd sleep until 10.30am. For a while, we did this three or four nights a week.

At the 21 Club, everything was centred around the DJ stage. The stage itself was mirrored and raised, and the two most popular DJs were treated like rockstars. Wandi was there to play the music. He'd barely acknowledge the whoops and applause, spending his set frowning down at the desk, one oversized earphone clamped to his head as he mixed in tracks.

The other guy was more interesting to watch. He'd be dancing along behind the turntables. He'd sing a line into his microphone before the singer in the song. Or he'd get everyone waving their arms to the music like we were at a gig. Somehow, he made all of this seem cool. Maybe because it was the eighties. After his sets he'd always be talking closely to some pretty tourist. Ace wasn't his real name, but no one, including his mother apparently, could remember calling him anything else.

Things were getting a bit strained between Ric and I. There were frustrations, mainly over whether our relationship should involve more than a goodnight kiss in the back lane (his view) or be limited to dancing and discussing the music we liked (my view). He was older, so it would have seemed pretty childish to him.

Then, one afternoon I was at the music shop and Ric pulled up with an extremely attractive Japanese tourist on the back of his bike. The fact that they were both wearing embossed towels from the five-star hotel she was staying at made it clear he hadn't just given her a lift.

A few weeks later, I bumped into one of 21's bartenders down on the beach. He wanted to know where I'd been and promised me a lift if I ever felt like coming back to see my other friends.

Going back into the club, I felt sheepish. I knew Ric would be there. Twirling about on the podium, all tall and handsome with his superb body-popping moves.

As I walked in, the music changed. Cutting abruptly from the middle of one track to the opening bars of my favourite song. I looked up at the DJ stage and Ace smiled.

That night he came over and spoke to me during his break. He was as likeable in person as he was up on the stage. He told me he'd heard I'd broken up with Ric. It wasn't sad news, he said; Ric wasn't good enough. I was amazed one of the DJs had noticed me, let alone kept track of my teen romancing.

Then he asked if I'd go out with *him*.

'What, like a date?'

He nodded.

'What, like here?'

He looked horrified at the very thought, 'Not here. Somewhere else. During the day.'

Two days later. Just after lunch, he came to the house. He knocked on the front gate and asked to meet Dad to see if it was OK for me to go out.

We went to a matinee session at a cinema in town, then dinner and he drove me home. And that was that, I was a smitten kitten. Maybe not as much as a normal girl. But I could definitely see what all the fuss was about.

Everywhere we went people would wave and say hi to Ace. Balinese are beautifully warm, friendly people and his job at the club was high-profile, so I didn't really think about it. It wasn't until our fourth or fifth date that I realised the man I was seeing was famous. And not just famous. A local-boy-done-good national treasure. As a kid he'd had his own TV show that had run every Saturday night for years.

We were caught in traffic at a major intersection in town. The lights had changed, but the traffic wasn't moving and people had started looking around out their car windows. It was a burning hot day, most of the engines were still running. People hitting their horns.

We were on his motorbike, so out in the open. Someone yelled Ace's full name. Then another person whooped, and suddenly people were jumping out of their cars and coming towards us. Suddenly we were being mobbed. People touching us, wanting to shake his hand, pat him on the back, say hello.

Ace was gracious and polite, always happy to sign their bits of paper and cigarette packets, but being crowded in like that felt like being trapped. I knew the attention had nothing to do with me, but eating in a restaurant, looking up and seeing every pair of eyes pointed at us was never going to feel comfortable. Ace was wonderful, his fame wasn't.

★

Poppa had bought an old cattle farm somewhere in the wild, unpopulated hinterlands of Queensland, Australia. His reasons for the purchase were never fully understood. Dad said it fulfilled some nebulous function for his accountant. Outside of a few blurry photographs, Poppa had never seen Cedar Creek, and had little intention to do so – it was in the outback! He'd got the land cheap and it was only after the paperwork went through that he realised the farmhouse on it was still standing.

For a year or two, the property sat there. The long-abandoned house still standing and gathering more dust and cobwebs.

Then Poppa got a call from Dad.

From Bali we'd flown back to Sydney and run into the ground.

Unless you're some kind of rockstar millionaire with plenty of minions and money at your disposal, being addicted to something like heroin can be a shitty, Catch-22 sort of scenario. Without minions to do the waiting around for you, just getting the heroin is a full-time job. But, heroin's expensive. Without piles of spare cash, you'll need an *actual* fulltime job to pay for it.

Also, because of the way heroin operates in the body's nervous system, you'll need to keep upping the dose to get a decent high. Everyone's always chasing their first time, but the more you spend on your habit, the hungrier it gets. Every day becomes a sweaty, achy scramble for money for heroin.

Which is a roundabout way of saying that all the money was gone. We were staying in a fleabag hotel down a back lane in Kings Cross. Back then Kings Cross was where you came to do seedy things. Along the main drag, there'd be touts out front the strip clubs. They'd follow you for a bit, walking alongside you, putting their arm around you. They'd be telling prospective punters that the girls inside were young and hot, practically virgins. To any girls they'd talk about what great money you could make inside. These guys worked on commission, so they'd be really pushy. Getting down the road felt like an obstacle course.

There were prostitutes working the streets too. They'd be there plying their trade from 10 or 11 in the morning all through the day and deep into the night. Just in their bras and knickers and fishnet stockings whatever the weather. Tobey and I felt sorry for them. You could tell most of them were junkies: selling their bodies to buy drugs seemed an awful life, and under their heavy makeup some of the girls looked very young, not much older than us.

It was high summer when we were there. There was a garbage strike on, and the laneway was piled with three weeks' of the kind of rubbish that nightmares are made of. There was no air-con in our room, but the smell coming from the piles of rubbish was so bad, we couldn't bear to open the windows for more than a few minutes.

The stink of rot and decay sweated through the walls into everything at the hotel. The whole place was stained: the carpet and the bedspreads, the noisy little hotel kettle and the two chipped cups and saucers. Everything you touched was sticky. Our glamorous days felt about one thousand percent behind us.

Glossy brown cockroaches scuttled over everything. We'd look through the bars down onto the lane and see relay races of rats. As the strike went on, the rats got fatter and bolder. They'd be fighting and eating out in the open, not even bothering to dart away when they saw you coming. The stink got worse.

The hotel had been the cheapest one Mum could find, and even then we couldn't afford it. We'd overstayed, and didn't have enough money to pay the bill and leave. Not that we had anywhere to go. Whenever we went out, we'd have to creep past the manager at the front door, timing it so he'd be on the phone.

Mum and Dad had prioritised heroin above other bills for a while. Now they'd started to choose it over food. And nappies. Pride, self-respect. Dignity. Basically everything else was less important. Their whole existence was about scoring enough just to get through the day.

Tobey and I would be scrambling around too: looking under the bed and down the back of the couch for change. Going through all the pockets and bags for enough coins to get some food. There were more than a few days when there wasn't enough change. We'd nick sachets of Nescafé instant coffee and sugar out of the maid's trolley and snack on those.

It was a grim, sticky time. We were all going crazy: holed up in a rotten, sinking ship. On Christmas Day we sat in the car all day waiting for Mum and Dad to score. Just looking out the windows. No presents for Lola or Griffy. No nice food. We each got a dripping ice-cream cone to eat in the car and went back to the hotel room.

Dad had called in all the favours he could. No one was taking his calls any more. Mum and Dad hadn't anything left to hock. All the family heirlooms had gone. Anything with any remote value. The guys down the pawnbrokers weren't antique experts. They just dealt with street resale value. Gold artefacts worth thousands were exchanged for a $50 hit. Mum and Dad had hocked Grannie May's wedding rings, their own wedding rings.

And now there was no money. Nowhere to live. No 231. We'd heard that it had been demolished. The house, the great hall,

Poppa's glass slipper study. The gardens, the grapefruit and plum trees, my poor little macadamia, all of it bulldozed by contractors. 231 didn't even exist anymore. No one would lend us more money.

So Dad was on the phone promising his father he was going to clean up his act. He was going to give up all the drugs. If only Poppa could help him out, this one last time. We could see him in the phone-box, leaning hard on the glass, his mouth was saying, 'This is the *last* time Dad, I swear. We're done with all this bullshit.'

Down the other end of the line, Poppa must have been thinking, that old song. But all the same, he wired us money for petrol and food and a map. He told Dad the address and said we could stay there for free as long as we needed. If we cleaned up the place, and quit the drugs, he'd wire more money.

So we got in the car and drove. Out of Kings Cross, across the harbour bridge, through the suburbs and north. All through the night and the next day. Mum and Dad up front and the four of us kids in the backseat. Hundreds and hundreds of miles, up and across Australia. We drove and drove.

Finally, we arrived at a one-street Queensland town.

We got a box of stuff at the general store – food, matches, candles, cleaning products. Dad got a few packs of Coopers strong ale. There was a dusty little goodwill shop: we picked out the cleanest-looking sheets and blankets and a few pots and plates.

We had no idea what to expect at the house, but we knew it was isolated: the dirt road that led to it wasn't even on the map. The address was a vague set of directions that involved turning left at a tree. None of us were expecting mail, but if any came, we could pick it up from a post-box in town.

About half an hour out of town, Dad turned off onto a dirt road. Mum pulled the directions out of the glovebox and we followed the dirt road down into a steep valley.

We drove for another forty or so minutes without seeing anything. Probably we were all thinking the same thing: There couldn't be anywhere for hundreds of miles to buy heroin. Mum and Dad were already getting shaky. The gear they were holding was enough to get us there, maybe one more not-nearly-enough fix in the night, but then it would be gone and they'd start the drying out process. We could feel the tension in the car. It felt like an execution was coming.

The music was off. No one was talking, not even Lola and Griff, all of us silently watching out the windows at the empty landscape bumping past us. The axe was hanging over all of us. We knew the next few weeks would be bad. How bad I didn't know for sure. Each time Mum and Dad had tried to come off heroin had been worse than the last. I knew there'd be screaming and vomiting and pain. The dread in my stomach was like a stone.

The deeper we travelled into the valley, the narrower it became. Steep, flinty mountains closing in on the flatlands, rising up on both sides around us.

It was a drought year. The landscape was withered, beaten-down. There was nothing we could see that wasn't a shade of brown or dried-out yellow. Everything was either dead or slumped into the process of getting around to it.

The dirt road petered out. Now we were just driving over dusty field. And there, up ahead, at the very end of the valley, was the farmhouse.

Dad pulled up out front and we looked at our new home.

In the dying light, the cottage looked shrunken and dilapidated, sunk in on itself. Paint was peeling off in long strips. The steps out front looked like wonky teeth. One of the steps was missing.

As we clamoured out of the car, each of us yelped as our feet squelched into something soft. Even Dad.

The ground was covered in dead cane toads. Thousands of them. Like a carpet of dead bodies. It wasn't easy to find clear gaps to put our feet down.

'What is it Martin? What's killed them?' said Mum.

'I don't fucking know. It looks like they've been microwaved.'

We stood there gaping in horror. The whole scene was so far from any reasonable reference, it was hard to understand what we were looking at.

Cane toads aren't great looking at the best of times. Mottled brown and warty; bigger than an angry man's fist. It looked like their stomachs had burst out of their bodies. They were all lying on their backs, with their internal organs exploded up and out across the grass.

We found a reservoir of dark water around the side of the house. It was about 20ft wide but too murky to see its depth. It could have been 6ft or bottomless, either way it was clogged solid with bodies. The edges of the reservoir were crusted with the dead. Five or six toads deep there, as if the water had suddenly turned to boiling acid and they were clamouring over each other to escape. The bodies radiated out from the house and pond. None had made it more than 30ft before exploding.

It was like a horror film.

We never found out what had killed the toads or how there happened to be so many thousands of them. It was just one of the mysteries of Cedar Creek.

A long, narrow valley in the middle of nowhere, in every sense Cedar Creek felt like the end of the line. I never saw a cedar tree. The creek had long since dried up. The only neighbours were a small fibro shack a few miles back up the valley. God knows what those people were doing. They never made contact. A couple of times we saw them out front of their house as we drove past. We waved hello, but they just turned their heads away.

The first days were bad. Mum and Dad were coming down. What was going on in their bodies seemed like what had happened to the bodies I was raking up outside. The crying and sweating and shaking looked as painful as what had twisted and blown apart the toads. There was nothing we could do, bring them water, try and get them to eat: nothing helped. The first week was a clenched blur, cleaning inside, raking outside.

All through the night they cried and shook. Somehow, we got through it, just like we always got through things. As a family we got through each afternoon, then the night, the next day. Until enough days had passed and Mum and Dad were out of bed and eating again. Walking around and getting dressed.

I watched them sitting in the sun on the steps outside one morning, drinking tea and smoking. They were talking and making promises to each other like two people who had just survived a war.

Mum and Dad would have intended to quit. They always did. But on their first trip back into town, they went to the pub, started talking to some bikers who had some connections. Someone knew someone. Blah, blah… a local supply was found.

Within the fortnight Mum and Dad were making plans to leave. First it was just day trips into town to score. Then there were plots and schemes to get money further afield. The details were vague, but on one of these trips, Dad was driving back up from Sydney and got arrested. Our old friend from Palm Beach, Craig with the red-rimmed bunny eyes, came to collect Mum. He and Mum and baby Lola had to return to Sydney to see about raising bail and getting Dad out of jail.

And then it was just Tobey, Griff and me at the old farmhouse. Mum would come back to check on us every couple of weeks. She'd drop off some food, stay the night and be gone again.

It was pretty isolated. Sometimes the phone line worked, most often it didn't. There was no electricity.

A rusty old generator in the concrete shed powered the lights. It ran on gas, and because our gas was in short supply, we could only run the generator at night. The rule was only after sunset, only after it got dark. And deep in the valley, with no streetlights or neighbours for miles, it got as dark as anywhere.

In a time before, when there was still green grass and a creek running here, Cedar Creek had been a fully operating cattle farm. The generator was kept in the shed where the cows had been killed (processed, is what they called it).

With the sun setting behind the mountains, I'd walk down in the dusk. There'd be fading light outside, but in the shed it would already be pitch black.

The shed was massive. Bigger than the house. Once you were fully inside, it was too dark to see if your own hand was being held up in front of you. It was so dark, you could see shapes forming in the darkness.

Inside the shed, there was a long corridor and sectioned-off concrete cubicles. There were no windows and one narrow doorway. It was always cold. No matter how warm the evening outside, you could feel the temperature drop as soon as you stepped through the door.

Someone, at some point, had spray-painted indecipherable graffiti across one of the walls.

Tobey didn't want to go into the shed, not even during the day. She said it was creepy. With us being stuck here and so isolated, I didn't want to admit I was spooked too. I brushed it off as a pesky daily chore, but as the sun began to dip, I'd be dreading going down there.

The generator was in the far corner. To get it started, you had to simultaneously hold the choke and pull up the throttle. Like a lawn mower. You needed both hands to do it, so you would have to put your flashlight down.

With the torch on the dirty cement beside you – its small yellow cone of light pointing up to the ceiling – you'd have to crouch down and lean right over the generator. Feeling with your hands around the back of it. Your heart beating like a hammer. Hoping the motor would catch, and really, *really* hoping nothing was watching from the other corner.

Sometimes, it would take five or six goes before the old motor caught. And each time you had to wait a beat for it to steady itself, before you could yank the throttle out again.

It took every bit of nerve I had to stay put. It never got better. Maybe it got worse.

Sometimes I could swear I'd felt something coming up behind me. The hairs on the back of my neck on stalks. My imagination screaming with what *that* thing might look like. I'd whip around but all I could see behind me was inky darkness.

As soon as the engine caught, I'd grab the torch and bolt, sprinting back up the hill to the farmhouse.

I wasn't usually this easily spooked. Being alone at night with the ghost in Tanilba House hadn't fazed me. But there was something odd about Cedar Creek. You could understand why Poppa had been able to buy it so cheap.

During the day there wasn't much to do. It was just the tall yellow grass, the weird dark reservoir next to the house (possibly the only body of water Tobey and I never tried to swim) and the dried-up creekbed.

Ordinarily we would have been off exploring all day: trekking up the mountain ridge. But we'd been warned a pack of wild boar were living up there. Word in town was that the Cedar Creek pigs had nearly eaten a man after a hunting trip had gone bad a few years back. The pigs had gored and chewed his foot to the shin. Apparently, it was only because he'd been out with friends who all had shotguns that he'd been able to come back at all.

Whatever truth there was to this story, I wasn't keen on taking too many chances. I'd read somewhere that wild boar were the fifth-most intelligent animal. Before dolphins, but possibly ahead of us, and far more dangerous than a bear with their razor-sharp tusks, razor-sharp minds and constantly bad moods. I'd also seen *Razorback* (low-budget horror film set in the Australian outback where an oversized killer pig eats everyone).

The three of us still went for hikes, but it wasn't very relaxing. I knew pigs could run faster than us. The tall grass could easily conceal a sneaky, stalking killer pig. There weren't a lot of trees to scramble up, and we did not have shotguns.

Tobey caught me pocketing a knife before we left the house one afternoon, 'What you going to do with that?'

'It's for the pigs.' This in my big-sister, I-know-best voice.

'What, so you're going to *stab* them?' she laughed.

It did seem unlikely. As it turned out, no contact was made. We often saw tracks and droppings, but we made sure that we were always out of the long grass by early sunset, and the killer pigs left us in peace.

★

Most of the time we had no idea where our parents were. No one had mobile phones yet, so we couldn't ring them to check if they were alright. Our landline buzzed empty static half the time, so we didn't know if they were trying to call us either.

We didn't know if Dad was still in jail. If Mum and Lola were safe. As far as we knew, they were somewhere between here and Sydney in NSW. But that didn't narrow it down much. This was an area of around a million square miles. You could fit seven United Kingdoms or five Japans into Queensland alone, and we were here somewhere in the dry dusty middle of it.

What were they doing? Where were they sleeping. Did Lola have her special rusk biscuits that she went mental without? Were gangs of prison men beating up Dad? Was Craig driving safely? A lot could go wrong. You tried not to dwell on it, but there were plenty of very bad scenarios playing through my mind.

Who was Mum buying heroin off? Just on that side of things a lot could go wrong. When we were living in Tanilba Bay, before the hitmen and drug squad, Mum and Dad shot heroin that had been laced with boric acid. It's hard to believe there's anyone out there who would mix odourless, white crystals commonly used to kill rats and insects into something that people inject directly into their veins. But apparently, it's not uncommon.

Mum and Dad realised almost immediately. They spent a horrible night. The poison roaring through their veins. They were shaking and sweating, twisting in pain. Throwing up. Diarrhoea. Their bodies desperately trying to expel the poison. I couldn't call anyone, and I honestly didn't know if they were going to be OK. There was no google page I could check. All I could do was bring them water and hope we'd get through this.

Then, as the sun came up, gloopy, bloodied pus started oozing through Mum's skin. All over her face and some of her neck. Thick and yellow and bloodied raw.

It was literally one of the worse things I'd ever seen. I don't know if there is medical precedent for this, if any sort of research exists, but it was like the poison was pushing itself out of her skin. And then there wasn't skin anymore. Her whole face was an open wound of blood and pus. Which probably sounds awful to read, it looked far, far worse. And then it hardened, like a massive scab. She looked like a monster. Nowhere else on her body, just her face and neck, and not at all on Dad. Mum had shot a bigger load before they realised it was bad gear. He had also vomited a lot more.

Someone dropped off a new batch of heroin around breakfast-time. Mum and Dad slammed that straight into their arms and were up and running again. But for a few days, it was hard to look at Mum. Her face was just two big sad red eyes in a crackling scab. Poor Mum, she must have wondered if it would ever come off.

When it did come off, her skin was amazing. Totally clear and smooth. Like a toddler's. Absolutely glowing. Everyone was joking that it was the best beauty treatment possible. But I don't think anyone, *anyone* would have signed up for that. It felt like a close shave. Another time where we'd almost lost a precious Starling.

Mum and Dad had also got heroin that made them sick when we were living with the monkey guard dog in Bali. Within seconds they were twisting and writhing in pain, totally incapacitated. Apparently, the only cure for bad heroin, is better heroin. I had to go get some more. It was night-time, so the shady doctor's would be closed. But I could catch a taxi to the Harley's Angels clubhouse in Denpasar. They weren't expecting me, but Dad said to ask for Dewa, the leader. He'd know what to do.

I was wearing white shorts and a lace midriff top from being at the beach. For reasons that I can only describe as me being dumber than a bag of rocks, I ran out the door without getting changed. So I was still in this outfit when the taxi dropped me off in front of two long rows of motorbikes.

It was a dark part of town I'd never been to before. The taxi-driver was meant to wait for me while I went in. He insisted I pay him first. Finally, we agreed I'd pay him half now and half when I got back. He didn't even wait for me to get inside before he'd hit the gas.

I tried to pretend I knew what I was doing as I stalked past the bikers outside, but I felt about as self-conscious as a weedy fifteen-year-old girl dressed for the beach should rightly feel.

Inside it was like a scene from a movie. All men and all black leather. Pool tables, drinking. Plenty of face and neck tattoos. No women. Everyone seemed pretty surprised to see me.

Someone led me to Dewa and he just looked at me and laughed. Crazy white girl. But he was great. He knew a guy here who had some gear on him. Not only did they sell it to me, Dewa and some of his men drove me home on their bikes. They didn't like the idea of me walking around by myself in this part of town. Certainly not in the middle of the night.

Riding helmet-less on the back of the leading bike in a bunch of roaring Harleys was superb, and Mum and Dad were fine in the end, so this was all a happy story. But it proved, yet again, that you couldn't trust the cockroach of drugs not to make everything very unpredictable.

Wherever they were, it would have been very good to know that Mum and Lola and Dad were safe.

★

One afternoon I was lying on my bed, re-reading a much-thumbed *Dolly* magazine, bored out of my skull as usual, when the need to open my cupboard door came urgently to mind. It felt like an odd thought, especially because there weren't any cupboards in my room.

I looked up. Cut into the wall, just below the ceiling, above my bed I realised was a small hidden door. We hadn't noticed it before, because it had been painted over with thick layers of paint.

I couldn't see why anyone would build a cupboard that high. You wouldn't be able to get anything in or out of it without a ladder. The house was unusually utilitarian for something built so long ago though: there wasn't a decorative frill anywhere, so the cupboard must have served some purpose.

I dragged my bed out of the way and went to get the ladder from under the house. Standing on the second-to-last rung, I chipped through the layers of different shades of white paint with a butter knife until I could prise open the door.

The cupboard was empty. It was a small space, built just under the roofline. Like a crawl hole. Maybe big enough to hold a person if they were sitting curled up around themselves. I climbed up and sat in the cupboard myself to see if this was the case. It was. But it wouldn't be very comfortable: like sitting in a crate.

Then I saw the markings on the inside of the cupboard door. Lines of tiny symbols, like a code or language that had been painstakingly scratched deep into the wood. It must have taken hours and hours, maybe days. Who would bother? Why?

As I ran my finger over the symbols, a shiver passed through me. A feeling of dread. What if someone *had* been here. Locked in. Someone who couldn't read and write but had wanted to say something, to leave some mark of their being here. Something to show they had existed.

I felt cold.

I jumped down the ladder and sealed the cupboard back up. The door fit back neatly, firmly into the wall. Almost entirely camouflaged again.

That night I had nightmares. I woke up the next morning sweating and feeling weird. The cupboard door was wide open. I made sure to close it up properly this time, banging it shut with the broom handle.

When I walked back into my room a few hours later, the cupboard was open again. I jammed it shut and taped over the door's seams with some thick black electrical tape that I'd found, just to be certain.

The next morning the electrical tape had peeled back. But only where it was over the door. There was tape across the neighbouring wall that was still firmly in place.

The door was wide open.

I got a hammer and hammered in a nail through the wooden door to shut it fast. For good.

The next morning the nail had come out.

It was just lying on the floor, bent in the middle from where I'd hammered it badly. Above my head, the door was wide open.

At this point I was properly freaking out. This wasn't something that had any reasonable explanation. I couldn't think of anything to tell myself to make this OK. All morning I sweated in panic about how I was going to fix this.

That afternoon I got the ladder out from under the house again and climbed back into the cupboard.

I sat there. Heart pounding in my ears, I ran my finger over the lines of symbols carved into the wood.

I half-expected something hideous to happen: all the doors in the farmhouse to slam shut or the light bulbs to blow. But nothing happened. It was very quiet and still, I could hear Tobey and Griffy chatting out front. I could hear the wind blowing through the tall grass outside the bedroom window.

I thought about how scary it must have been to be locked up here so far from any other people. So far from help. I felt so sorry about whatever terrible thing had happened here. I knew it must have been terrible and probably had happened to someone small: someone young and vulnerable.

Locked in this tiny, stifling space. In the dark and all the way out here, down the end of this long valley. They would have felt so very alone. I wished I could have helped them somehow, I wished *someone* had helped them. But I didn't know what we could do for them now.

After that I hammered and hammered, half a bag of nails into the door until it looked like a pin cushion. The door stayed shut.

On another hot, dry and boring day I was standing in the kitchen, doing the dishes, when I looked out the window to see a faint haze of smoke down the road. Blocking our exit out of the valley.

There are a lot of things that can kill you in the Australian outback, but bush fires are feared more than pretty much anything else. The speed and intensity of a firestorm can take hundreds of lives. They can roar out of nowhere, giving you little time to run. Everyone knows that the smell of smoke is a warning you can't ignore.

We had no car, no working phone line. I tried to remember when it had last rained. I couldn't remember when it had *ever* rained here in Cedar Creek.

Tobey and I wet all the blankets. I grabbed our passports, some snacks and whatever odds and ends I could throw together into a bag. Basically, the photo albums and a hairbrush. We didn't have any drinking bottles so we filled the buckets and all the pots with water.

By this time, we could see the fire. It was coming over the ridge towards us. It was feeding on the tall grass, and moving fast. There were no trees in its path, so the flames weren't high, but it was coming right for the farmhouse. The tall grass grew right up to the walls of the house and there was nothing to stop it.

My plan was to go down to the creek and all of us hide under the wet blankets. I'd seen a TV special where a family had survived because they'd hidden under wet blankets. It wasn't an amazing plan, but I knew we couldn't shelter in the house. Besides being directly in the line of the fire, the house was decades-parched weatherboard: it would go up like kindling. We did not want to get trapped in the cowshed.

The creek was entirely dried up, but I figured the rocks surrounding it wouldn't burn. From there we could follow the riverbed either down and out of the valley, or up the mountain. Whichever seemed safer depending on the direction of the fire.

At this point I was pretty proud of my plan, I imagined recounting it in a TV special of my own, a brave yet humble expression plastered across my face as I described how I'd saved my siblings.

We ran backwards and forwards ferrying the water and blankets. All the while the fire was getting closer. With Tobey and Griffy safely under the wet blankets, I went back and splashed down the side of the house closest to the fire. I didn't think it would do much good, but it was worth a try. The fire was just a few yards away now. Roaring through the grass. The air was black with smoke.

Choking and coughing I ran back to the riverbed. Where we all crouched on the stones, waiting to see what would happen next. It seemed pretty clear the house would go up. We waited as the smoke billowed and darkened. We could hear the crackling of the flames.

We took turns to sip the water from a mug we dipped in a bucket as we watched. I assured Tobey and Griff we'd be fine. I didn't want to scare them, but as the flames got closer, I started to picture us being found weeks later: roasted like three little pigs in charcoaled blankets. Sitting in the riverbed, I had the opportunity to take in how narrow it actually was. How effective could a few wet blankets really be against a bushfire? What kind of idiot plan had I got us into?

I also had time to think bitterly about all the things I'd left inside. The rest of the food. Our clothes and books. My stack of *Dolly*s.

We huddled closer together. All wet under the dripping blankets. Coughing a bit.

And then the fire went out.

Poof. Just like that. Suddenly there were no flames at all, the smoke just casually drifting away.

It was super anticlimactic.

We crept back to take a closer look. The ground in front of the farmhouse was scorched black, deep into the dirt. We kicked at the clumps of charcoaled dirt and grass. There was no reason I could see for the fire to have stopped. No one had mowed for years; around the back and side of the house the grass was waist high. Dry as old paper. But the fire had just petered out, right in front of the house.

Inside, everything stank of smoke. Over the next week, we washed everything we could. The towels and sheets. All our clothes, but we couldn't get the smell out of the mattresses.

We lugged back the wet blankets. Emptied all the buckets and pots and unpacked the hastily packed backpack. It was kind of embarrassing. I felt like a right banana for overreacting.

That night we had to sleep in a few layers of smoky clothes and towels because all our blankets were still wet. Tobey and Griff giving me dirty looks from under their piles of clothes.

Years later, long after all the Starlings had left, we heard the farmhouse *had* burnt down. Good riddance I thought when I heard it had finally gone. I thought of those lines of symbols carved inside that cupboard and I hoped that whatever had been tied to the house would be free.

There was something not right about that place. You could feel it under your skin. When we were living there, I'd tell myself it was all in my imagination. Some days I'd be saying it to myself dozens of times.

The men who set fire to the farmhouse had taken tins of petrol with them. They said it took a lot longer and a lot more gas to get it burning than they expected. But burn it had, once it caught, right down to its charcoal stays.

★

After the fire, I started to worry about what would happen if something really went wrong. More wrong than a grass fire. No phone, no car, in the middle of nowhere. What if Griff cut himself? We didn't even have bandages or aspirin. What if one of us got sick? Bitten by a venomous snake or spider?

When Mum and Dad came back, they were celebrating. Dad was out and there was more money. Now we had plenty of gas and could run the generator all the time. They had friends with them who they'd met on the road.

Suddenly the farmhouse was full of people and music playing during the day. There were two cars out front and plenty of food in the cupboards. Everyone was happy.

Except me.

'How long are we going to stay here?' I wanted to know, spoiling the fun.

'Not long. Just till we get organised. It's not a bad place though, is it? No neighbours to worry about.'

'You can't leave us here alone anymore.'

'No, no. That's over. We're back now.'

'But what about when we run out of money?'

They just looked at me. There was plenty of money right now, why was I always so negative?

Watching them drinking and shooting through their gear, I felt about eighty-seven. The old nag no one wanted to be around. I stalked out of the kitchen, past everybody cheersing their beers and laughing.

I lay on my bed, my mind a sulky teenage/boring grandma carousel of all the bad things. I thought about what the man with the business card at the airport had told me about how I'd leave home as soon as I could. I'd been thinking about those words a lot. But what about Tobey and Griff and Lola?

I could see Mum and Dad weren't going to change. Not any time soon. Once the money ran out there would be more schemes. They wouldn't leave Tobey and Griff alone, but with me at the house, they would leave us here again and again. You couldn't stop them. They couldn't stop themselves. Mum and Dad weren't going to change unless they were forced to. Circumstances would need to change before they did.

The night blew in, dusty and tattered. It was selfish, selfish, selfish, but I had to get out of this farmhouse. I looked up at the secret cupboard door, pin-cushioned with nails. I was going mental here.

I told myself that maybe being selfish was the best thing I could do for my brother and sisters. I don't know if it was. Probably it wasn't, but what else could I do? Staying here wasn't much help. At least if I got a job somewhere I could send them back money.

And there was another thought. A thought that was thrilling: wild as wind on a highway. A thought that had been roaring at me; collecting weight somewhere in the back of my mind for a while.

Maybe I didn't have to be in my childhood anymore. I could be something else. I could make different mistakes: my own ones. Maybe it was time my real life started.

★

My family dropped me off at the bus station. They were heading into town to stock up on supplies. I'd be catching a series of buses, threading my way into Brisbane, then down to Sydney.

I told myself it was just like when I'd lived with Nanny Starling at Point Piper. It didn't mean anything. It wasn't any kind of goodbye. Not to Tobey and Griffy and fierce little angel-face Lola. I just needed to get away for a bit. A break from living Mum and Dad's life.

We all hugged each other tightly and then my family got back in the car. Little Griff's face and hands waving out the back window as they drove off.

I sat on the bench looking down the empty road.

In the shoulder bag next to me was everything I owned.

It had all happened so fast. I'd told Mum and Dad I needed to go, and here I was, less than two days later, actually going. In a few minutes I'd be gone.

I was fifteen and more alone than I could wrap my head around. My heart felt so heavy, I could barely swallow.

But I had $20 in my pocket, and an invitation to stay with a friend from school for a week or two.

Maybe that was all you needed to start a life. Sometimes you just had to throw it all at the sky.

Thank you

Childhood is the adventure we've all taken. It might be that place we all keep coming back to. So this wasn't a book I ever thought I'd write. But it kept pestering me, tapping on my shoulder, tiptoeing into other things I was doing. It wanted to be told. And once I started, the words flew. Dancing out onto the page, like a right little extrovert. Reminding me things. Telling me who I was. Writing is great like that. So is childhood. And maybe the trick is to remember as warmly as our hearts can stretch. So here we are, I've written it and you've read it. Life is unexpected and so cool.
Thank you for hanging out with me.

And if you're a kid reading this, hang in there. You're doing great. Pretty soon you'll get to make your own mistakes, which is another adventure altogether.

Oh and if you can, try not to eat the octopuses.

★

To dear Elaine Gowran, whose friendship is greater than upsetting manuscripts. Thanks for your expertise and compassion. And sharp eyes.

To my friends who have been there, supporting me from the beginning of this book. Chel, Jacq, Charley, Anna, James, Susie, Speth, Rich, Tracey, Gill – I know how lucky I am to have you in my life. *Very lucky.*

And to my family who have been there from the *very* beginning. Thanks for being cool about me writing this story. I love you. Always. Five to the sky cowboys.

Milton Keynes UK
Ingram Content Group UK Ltd.
UKHW010725080823
426520UK00004B/333

9 781739 633653